MIRROR, MIRROR

I felt good enough to try to get back up when I heard something big, something flying overhead. I looked, but there was nothing. I scanned the sky for a moment, but the sound had gone. But when I looked back down at the beach, somebody was looking at me. Or, rather, something was.

I let out a scream and even as it was echoing away to silence, I was backing up, feeling the ground around me for any sort of weapon.

"No, wait! I'm not going to hurt you!" the thing said.

I stopped, but I wasn't about to immediately trust anything with a huge, hairy body and black bat wings.

"I know my body looks odd," the thing said, "but look at my face. Not my body, but my face. See if you don't recognize me."

I frowned and stared at the creature. It did have a human face, and not an unfamiliar one, either. I gasped.

It was with a sick certainty that I realized that this horrible creature was me . . .

By Jack L. Chalker
Published by Ballantine Books

THE
MARCH HARE
NETWORK

BOOK TWO

OF

THE WONDERLAND GAMBIT

JACK L. CHALKER

A DEL REY® BOOK
BALLANTINE BOOKS • NEW YORK

A Del Rey® Book
Published by Ballantine Books

Copyright © 1996 by Jack L. Chalker

All rights reserved
under International and Pan-American Copyright Conventions.
Published in the United States by Ballantine Books,
a division of Random House, Inc., New York,
and simultaneously in Canada
by Random House of Canada Limited, Toronto.

http://www.randomhouse.com

Library of Congress Catalog Card Number: 96-96297

ISBN: 0-345-38691-4

Manufactured in the United States of America

First Edition: May 1996

10 9 8 7 6 5 4 3 2 1

For the late James H. Schmitz,
an author you should know,
for some of the non-Dick inspiration here

A NOTE FROM THE AUTHOR

This is the second of three books which will make up the saga known as *The Wonderland Gambit*. The epic began with *The Cybernetic Walrus* (Del Rey, 1995), which is, or should be, still available in all good, well-run, competent bookstores. If it isn't in yours, suggest that this is a sign of a troubled future in a crowded book market and tell them why you're going to a better bookstore.

I had promised those who read my remarks and introduction in *Walrus* that this volume would be the one where we go over the cliff. Not *quite* so, although this book, like *Walrus*, stands somewhat alone and throws what I think are several unexpected curves. Please remember that the motto for the entire series is "Everything you think you know is wrong."

You *will* get a lot more information in this book and widen your circle of friends as well as your understanding of how reality works, and we'll meet some rather interesting folks as allies who were inexplicable last time and then travel to some other miniuniverses.

But next time, the real fun begins, and maybe then we can try to offend almost everybody . . .

Thank you all for still reading and still thinking. You are a shrinking elite, and we need you desperately.

Jack L. Chalker,
Uniontown, MD
April 4, 1995

I

THE ART OF INCARNATING

Being reborn wasn't at all like the way I'd pictured it.

Okay, okay, it was almost *literally* how people would picture it, but that's not quite what I mean.

One minute I'd been in Angel's body, sliding, being pulled by Wilma Starblanket into a void that looked like nothing so much as a TV set on an empty channel, my last look a terrifying glimpse of a virtual control room infested by gigantic spiders; then I was into the static field and, well, curiously liberated.

I had no sense of body at all, no sense of any kind of physical presence. All around me, stretching out, up and down, side by side, as far as I could view—"see" is not quite the right word—were webs of varicolored light, lines, and crosshatches forming beautiful, intricate patterns along which beads of light, like teardrops on a spiderweb, oozed down and around, this way and that, as if they had sentience, as if they were somehow guiding themselves or being guided to an unknown and unknowable destination.

And yet I had a feeling of curious detachment, not devoid of emotion as such but sapped of those emotions caused by physical body chemistry and left with only those, such as wonder, that exist in the higher functions.

It was—*beautiful*. Beautiful and yet somehow comfortable even as I realized that I was riding along one of those colored strands just like all the others and that I, in this state, probably looked no different from the other droplets of shimmering liquid light.

I knew the place. It was comforting and familiar. I had been there before, not once but many times. I didn't feel any sense of danger or apprehension, thanks partly to that familiarity. Bad things couldn't happen to you in there, not in this state. To be otherwise would be the equivalent of waking up in heaven and having an angel blow you away with an Uzi.

There was a small sense of disappointment that I was being directed rather than moving under my own control; it wasn't much, but it meant certainly that whatever new world I was heading toward would come out of the mind of someone else, someone who'd gotten there first. The fact that the process seemed so automated meant that a routine runtime module had kicked in; that in turn meant that whoever had been first had entered due to death rather than transferring alive as I had done. Therefore, whatever reality would be formed would be of the subconscious—always dangerous and not easily kept in check. We all carried such enormous baggage . . .

Ahead, in the direction we were moving, I could see the throbbing mass of energy that was our destination, the point of entry into the new program, the new virtual universe.

The main difference between me and most of those who would follow (and a few who had come before, or it wouldn't be there) was control. When you died, your link to the net would be the only part of you left; you'd travel, frozen, deactivated, along this same route to be born again as usual, to go through a life in real time. You'd be someone else, somewhere else, free not to take all the twists and turns and make or unmake all the choices that had created the prior you. Just in case the creator of the template universe was dull and unimaginative, you were assured some differences off the bat by being reborn as the opposite sex, assuming that was a factor in the new universe. There would be other changes, too, and because your new life would be dominant, what you knew and who you were in the past would be mostly gone or otherwise suppressed.

I had killed a couple of people in the last hour of my prior existence; those who were of "us" would be ahead in that frozen state and would reach the template ahead of me. Strong linkages, strong relationships, would bind us together to a degree; it would be unlikely that, say, we would be born into different cultures in widely separated locales. In the end, most of us had been bound at least somewhat together, even Angel and me and Walt Slidecker.

But I hadn't died, and neither had Wilma. We'd managed to draw so much net energy, we'd actually broken down segments of the world that we *thought* was ours and had passed beyond it, although not easily. That gave us an added measure not only of this experience riding the beams but also of control once we reached the new template.

I couldn't control who or what I'd be; that was in the hands of whoever had gotten to the next world first and provided the raw material for that template. I could, however, control where and when I entered, and from that point on there would be inside my head two people—the one who had been born and raised there and the old "me," complete with all those important memories and past skills.

Even the dead had a certain sense of identity that would shape them to a degree, but for those of us who could make the transition *this* way, past identities tended to be more solid. You tended to retain more of yourself than did those who didn't recall. This very sense of old identity made it likely that you'd retain your sex and most of your talents and proclivities. That meant that Wilma would very likely remain not only a woman but a Native American woman if such people existed ahead. It also meant that when they came over, Al Stark would still be the same menacing son of a bitch he'd been all along and Les Cohn would still be a man, a doctor, probably Jewish, and, as always, an enigma.

Me, I wasn't so sure about. I still expected to get into computers, sure; I didn't know how to do much else. Still, there were worlds without computers, about which I had only tiny snippets of memory I'd earlier dismissed as fantasies, dreams, or psychological ghosts in my head. I knew that there were universes where I didn't really have a profession, and even though they were no clearer or more defined now than they had been before, they were certainly clear and recallable in a limited, simplistic way. They showed me mostly as a sidekick, spouse, or nonentity. Without access to computers, I was strictly a supporting player.

In fact, I had no internal evidence that I'd *ever* been anything but a secondary player, at least until this last time. That was probably why Stark hadn't bothered to bottle me up and put me through his brainwashing machine as he'd done with most of the others.

Would I have done it last time? Even if Matthew Brand's crazy *Alice in Wonderland* creations hadn't been pushing and protecting me at the same time? And even then, what had I done without being pushed? Angel had been the wielder of power, and Wilma had provided my courage and direction. Even then, we'd gone in not to blow up the operation but to save Angel, and we'd failed miserably. We'd actually managed to draw so much power from that project, we'd begun poking holes in the master template, ignoring physical laws in a way that violated every fiber in my engineering soul even as I did them, only to screw up and wind up saved at the last moment by a man who could be an even worse enemy than Alan Stark.

And thanks to that incompetent version of the Gunfight at the Yakima Corral and letting others do the hard stuff, I'd wound up wearing Angel's body.

So what would I become in the new template? A guy, like a Cory Maddox in my last life, or a girl, like Stark had said I was two lives before, a life I didn't remember except in those scenes? Did that explain Cynthia Matalon, who was never quite sure who or what she was?

The problem was that in this state I had academic knowledge but no emotional sense of who or what would be best for me. Hell, in the one life I could remember and review, I'd gone through more than half a life, well into my forties, and what had I done? I'd gotten in on the ground floor when talent still counted most, and so I had never really gone beyond a mediocre BS degree. When others around me became famous millionaires, I missed all the opportunities and usually sold out for a song. That was why, when I'd come up with the one creation that really meant something, the wireless neural net connection, I'd had the rug pulled out from under me. Even Brand hadn't considered me important enough to recruit for his first big independent think tank project.

If Stark hadn't become aware of my invention and decided it was useful, I still wouldn't have known any of it. I'd have grown old and died, and so what? Until I met Riki, I'd never had a real sense of communion with others, let alone emotional commitment, but even that had been less than grand. It had never been easy for me to score, and I was always hesitant, awkward, the few times I did. I was never much with the ladies even though I wanted to be, and when Riki came along, she was ten times more experienced than I'd been and very much in charge in that department.

Still, it had been something of a benefit being a guy. I comfortably went places no woman would without even thinking about it; there was a subtle tension or pressure on Riki that I'd never felt. Even something simple, such as walking alone into a strange bar, was something I'd do but she probably would not. And I'd never had to deal with that postpuberty female plumbing. I wasn't positive that one had any advantages over the other, but it did seem that in a society like that last one, being male was a definite plus.

I decided finally that it didn't matter in the end so long as I was in a world and culture where I could do what I loved best. My primary goals would be to find Wilma and any others who might be handy, avoid Stark's clutches, and learn as much as I could about this bizarre situation where nothing was truly real, nothing was what it seemed. If I could access the kind of power and control Stark had managed in the final stages of his operation last time, but without him and his henchmen, I might have a crack at solving this mystery.

Who, or what, were we? Were we real or the products of someone else's imagination? Was God a programmer? Were we in some vast computer, trapped, without the knowledge or the means to get out? Who and what was "real," and how would we know it when we saw it?

In point of fact, was even this transition state real, or was it some kind of bizarre set of signals in my brain, my *real* brain, wherever that was and whoever I really was? Like that out-of-body experience and moving toward a light that folks report when they die or *think* they die?

Well, *this* was the afterlife, and I suddenly found myself . . . moving toward a bright light. Yeah, that was *exactly* what was happening. So was I dying or about to be born again?

If the latter, they'd forgotten to give me the instruction manual or I'd lost it a long time ago.

I tried to slow down, maybe stop, and figure this all out, but whatever this place was didn't hear me or follow instructions. I wasn't ready yet, I tried to tell it, wasn't prepared to start a whole new life until I'd at least had a chance to reflect on the old one. But I kept going until I was right in the line, right on the beam or channel, heading straight for that light. All at once I was blinded, surrounded, engulfed by the brightest energy sensation I had ever known.

And then it was dark and strange. Well, not completely dark, and there were sounds around me, weird sounds, some pleasant, most unpleasant or a little scary, with one regular kind of *thump*, *ka-thump*, *ka-thump* that seemed to be all around me, almost a part of me.

The strangest thing was that with just that feeling of warmth and floating and those weird sounds I nonetheless discovered that I had a measure of control. I could slow it down, make things work in slow motion, down to what seemed to be a dead stop, using the overwhelming *ka-thumps* as my benchmark. In a sense I had control of time, from freeze frame right past real time, zooming faster and faster, so fast that the noises seemed to vanish into a wave of pink noise . . .

And then, speeded up tremendously, I moved, down, out, into brightness and cold and all that, and I realized that I was being born.

It was a strange, not quite out-of-body sensation. I wasn't exactly inside or attached to the body, yet I was connected to it inextricably and forever. Cory Maddox was still Cory Maddox, a sometimes fascinated, sometimes repelled observer from a different parallel existence that may or may not exist—and may or may not have ever existed except in someone's mind. Still, I was a real person, and I was thinking as clearly as I'd been inside that transfer state or whatever it was. I remembered my old self, my old life, my old talents and skills, likes and dislikes, ups and downs, experiences and emotions, just as I always had.

But I was also getting fresh input from this new personality, this new person who had been born with me physically attached. It didn't take Einstein to figure out that this new person was also me, or would be me, yet was unaware of me at this point and was having a normal babyhood. Since information was being processed through that baby's brain and then to me, I still didn't have a great deal of information, but there was a way to get it. I could speed up the passage of time to a blur and beyond, just like hitting fast-forward on a tape recorder, then slow it down and even stop it to examine what was going on.

What I couldn't do was rewind. *That* made wholesale fast-forwarding of this life a little risky and mandated doing it only in small doses.

I was male, something that might work to my advantage if all the others went through the same way I had. It was said that you retained your sex if you came through still alive and alternated if you died; both Les Cohn and Al Stark had seen me last in Angel's body and might well assume that I'd come out female here.

In point of fact, it was almost disappointing how few differences there were between this life and the last one. Cynthia Matalon had come from a world where the South had won the Civil War; my own mental flashbacks had shown strange worlds and stranger existences in my past, only glimmers of which remained in my subconscious.

There were *some* differences, but not the kind that would disturb anybody who was expecting more, and some of those differences were of the sort the kid wouldn't appreciate but I would. Mom, for example, was still Mom, but she'd gotten better genes or something this time—she was some looker, something no kid would ever think about Mom. Dad was a bit darker complected, still no muscle man but in pretty good shape. In fact, if it hadn't been for the complexions and the differences in hair and eye color, I almost might not be able to say that they were different at all, since what kid really remembers his parents when they were young and in top shape? No matter what, they always have that twenty or more years on you, don't they?

Me, well—I don't know. I was always the geek, not the jock, but *this* me was in pretty fair shape and liked the outdoors somewhat. I also had Dad's jet black hair and very dark brown eyes, and I was a pretty good-looking kid.

Just as I couldn't hit rewind, so, too, I knew that I had only to will it and I would merge with that kid completely and somewhat inseparably. *That* I didn't want to do, at least not yet. Somewhere, eventually, everybody else would be entering at his relative age to me, those who weren't here already, and if I entered too young, I'd have school and all the rest to contend with. Plus, as the two parts of me merged, I might become a slightly different person. I *definitely* didn't want to repeat grade school even if I could do great in it this time. College was a different matter and one that was very tempting. College had been a happy time in my old life and had had both the opportunities and mobility of being older and the more fun aspects of youth. It was a tempting idea, anyway.

I idly wondered what would happen if I fast-forwarded all the way through, but the answer to that was obvious in a logical sense. Sooner or later I would encounter some of the others; Stark and Cohn would certainly be looking for me, and maybe others as well. If the programming knowledge and skills carried over from my old self weren't there to be used, then from their point of view I'd have very little value; they'd just blow me away somehow, and I wouldn't remember this life in the next template.

No, I *had* to sync myself with this new identity and do it before they found me. The college-age option was looking better and better. They, after all, would have the same problem I had about when to merge with my new life. Les was maybe five years older than I was, certainly not ten, and I was pretty sure he'd still want to be an MD, and that takes time. Stark was about my age, give or take a couple of years; it was not enough of a difference to put him in a position of power while I was still in college, certainly.

I'd never been too great on politics, so I couldn't say what big or little things were different in this world; it didn't *seem* all that different, anyway, except for slight variations in fashion, fads, some look and feel in architecture and manners. Things seemed a little calmer, a little more repressed and conservative. Still, I had a solid middle-class upbringing in a medium-sized community—unlike my old memories, Dad *had* taken the district sales job, and I grew up in and around Coos Bay, Oregon, not a bad place at all.

My grades were pretty mediocre, and I was more of a jock than I had been before, but clearly I wasn't going to be handed a scholarship to Stanford in computer science or mathematics. That meant either a local college or, at best, Oregon State, where I *did* manage to get a minor but useful football scholarship, at least for my freshman year, with the possibility of a bigger one if I worked out.

I was ready to slow down the passage of time now, insert myself into this new and different life, and proceed from there. What guy in his forties who'd never been athletic or particularly good-looking wouldn't have relished the idea of repeating college, starting at age nineteen, much better looking and more athletic?

In hindsight, I should have seen it coming and known better, but I didn't. It was one of those great traps of this new incarnation thing, one that simply had never crossed my mind. Because I let it slide a little while going through those freshman basics college courses that bored me before and now, getting in some football, it just blindsided me.

Rather, a three-hundred-pound gorilla named Ralph Kindred blindsided me on the field. It wasn't even in a game, but in intramural scrimmaging, and I would never be sure whether he had intended to put me out or just rough me up a little. It seems his girlfriend, whom I hardly knew or noticed, had developed one of those irrational crushes on me from a distance, as I found out later. But he came in, hit me like a ton of bricks, and I was lying there, out cold. When I came to, I was being hauled off the field on a stretcher, and the team doctor and university medics were looking at me as if I were dead. I was having trouble seeing out of my left eye, it was true, but I wasn't feeling *real* pain. I wasn't feeling much at all . . .

The primary injury was to my spine; it slowly became clear that I had no feeling to speak of from maybe a little below my midchest. There was also something wrong in my left arm; I had feeling, but it just didn't move correctly when I tried. My neck, right shoulder, and right arm and hand, well, they were fine.

Other than that, Mrs. Lincoln, how was the play?

Now I didn't want to be joined at all, but I felt this irresistible pull that told me that I was nearing the limit and that if I didn't make a decision, I'd have it made for me. I managed to fight it off or at least keep it back for a little more than a year, which at least spared me a lot of anguish in the hospital and endless physiotherapy, but then the pull became overwhelming. I felt myself going closer and closer together, becoming more and more integrated with the physical personality . . .

I awoke to an all too real quiet and for the first time experienced this new self in more than an observer's capacity. It was a very *strange* feeling, lying there in that bed, staring up at a dark ceiling. My head on the pillow was normal enough, as was my right arm, and even my left arm *seemed* okay, although I knew it wasn't. In addition to the permanent spinal cord damage, somebody else had gotten me on the left side of the head with cleats, and that had given me some sort of brain or nerve damage as well. I had no real vision in the left eye and only limited control of my left arm and hand; if I didn't wear an eye patch on the bad eye or keep it closed, it was tough to see. The extra hit had caused some of the palsied effect in my left arm and hand. I tried it and discovered that even when I moved very, very slowly, it was prone to spasms or jerks.

A few inches below the armpits the body sort of faded

out. I could use my right hand and feel it, but otherwise it just wasn't there. It wasn't a question of movement or jerkiness or anything—it simply faded out. That part of the old me found it eerily fascinating and unnerving at the same time; the new, physical me was by that time somewhat used to it.

The weird part was, the essential functions were working down there. Food was being processed, the heart was pumping, the lungs were operating normally. I just had no feeling of it and no way to initiate voluntary muscle action.

Wearing a damned industrial-strength diaper was the most embarrassing part. Particularly since I could tell it was soiled only by the smell and needed somebody else to change it.

I wasn't going to be any ladies' man, after all. At least not unless I found somebody very strange.

It occurred to me that I was a sitting duck for Stark or his cronies if they found me. What was I going to do? Hold them off with only one good arm?

Not that it really mattered. In fact, the only hope I might have in *this* life, I knew, was if Stark *did* find me, crazy as that sounded. An energy field strong enough to break down the program that was what I'd believed was reality had been achieved at the old Brand project before I had had to get out. Inside that field, drawing on that kind of energy, we'd managed to do an incredible number of almost magical things. I could repair myself in such an environment. Somehow I *knew* I could.

And that was when the irony struck me about this new existence, this alternative to living. How Stark had maneuvered me into hell I had no idea, but that was where he'd put me. Put me, the one person left with some knowledge of the system and at least an educated crack at the riddle of the Brand Boxes, in a situation where I'd be entirely under his control.

My past life was already beginning to seem like a dream existence. Only my knowledge of a technology that I couldn't know anything about and the details in my memories of that life kept me believing that it had really happened.

My name was Andrew Cornell Maddox, but I'd *been* Cornell Andrew Maddox in my past life. Not a big difference. They called me Cory Maddox then; growing up, it had been the only defense against being called Nellie without fighting over it. Now I was Andy to the family. Not much of a switch, but it was a radical difference in self-definition, and I pushed Drew to the outside world. Drew Maddox. Sounded stuffy, but what the hell. Andrew sounded like some poor little rich kid, and Andy Maddox sounded like a guy who got off on tractor pulls in Mayberry.

Not that it made any difference. Not now.

Well, at least OSU had a major accident and liability insurance policy, and my dad was an even better insurance agent now than in my previous life and had access to all the money I might need. What I wound up with was a trust fund for bug-eyed bucks that basically would cover my care and medical costs for life, however long that lasted. Mom wouldn't hear of putting me in institutional care, even if it was at one of the fancy places for the unlucky rich, and I'd eventually wound up, after a year and a half of therapy, back in my own room, in my own house, with a day nurse and sessions with physiotherapists three times a week at a rehab clinic in town. If somebody picked me up, dressed me, and strapped me in the wheelchair, I could operate it within the limits of its electric motor. Of course, I couldn't go out without being accompanied, and Mom was always paranoid when I was out at all.

I spent a lot of time in the room watching TV. No problem with the remote, but the television in this life was a bit more sedate and laid back and much more limited than the zillions of cable channels I'd once been used to. The programs had about as much violence as you'd expect but not a hell of a lot of sex or even swearing. It *was* a very different place in subtle ways, almost as if the fifties had never ended and half a century or more later everybody was still pretending it was *Leave It to Beaver* time. Lots of variety shows, clean comics, old-style sitcoms, and detective stories and westerns where people died but never bled much. Women weren't exactly forced into the kitchen—there were women doctors and lawyers and even cops represented, although not in the numbers my old self remembered—but the guys mostly wore suits and the women, even the girls, seemed to all wear dresses or skirts. I tried to think back and couldn't remember Mom in anything other than a skirt, although in my past life I hardly remember her ever wearing much except jeans.

It finally struck me that the fifties wasn't the real model here; maybe it was more like the thirties. Both were decades I didn't remember but only saw reflected in movies, but in the thirties movies the women were tough, and in the serials they punched out the bad guys and hopped on trains and Dale Evans could shoot as well as Roy Rogers, but they all wore skirts.

It was very odd in spite of my having an entire parallel memory of growing up in this very environment. Not enough to think this was a really bizarre and alien universe but a constant reminder that it wasn't the one I knew.

I wasn't even sure which I preferred. In Coos Bay it wasn't all that unusual in warm weather for the kids to play by themselves and for some neighborhoods not to lock their doors, and drug problems other than alcohol were pretty much confined to junkies, of which there were few. People complained about the crime problem, but it was safer than kindergarten compared with the Seattle I'd lived in, and Seattle had been among the better places in that world to live.

Technology, too, wasn't quite up to snuff. What I'd previously had in my laptop in computing power still required a couple of rooms to replicate in this world, but they were headed in the right direction. I began asking for books on computers and computing languages, gagging when I discovered how much FORTRAN was still around. Then I began looking at Assembler and the beginnings of what might develop into a Pascal on one side and the start of a Basic on the other and marveled at how they had not yet invented the wheel, so to speak.

I could write programs on a level they could hardly believe. The trouble was, the technology was at least twenty years behind that of my previous world. I began to wish I'd paid more attention to history; clearly something hadn't given these folks the jump start we'd had.

Possibly it was because it was a less competitive world. Apparently the atom bomb hadn't worked right or something, and the Allies had been forced to invade Japan in a real nasty battle that took two years and killed millions of Japanese and maybe half a million Americans. Before that the Germans and Japanese had managed to collapse Russia, which was in a miserable state. The conquerors hadn't really been able to replace the old regime—it was too vast a territory, and they were unprepared for controlling it—and that had pretty well done them in. They'd kept the valuable parts, and the rest had disintegrated into a hundred third world nations. It was *Germany* we finally defeated using the atom bomb. A lot of that country just, well, didn't really exist, including Berlin, and large sections of Poland and Russia weren't very livable, either.

I'd have figured that what with the war lasting so much longer, they'd have even better computers, but apparently the fighting had lasted long enough that it pretty much bankrupted the winners, too, and we were decades recovering. It showed how different just a few things could make a whole new existence.

And it made reality in Coos Bay a lot more familiar than I expected it might.

Frankly, I think I could have coped with a home computer, a modem, and a good, solid connection to the Internet or even one of the commercial services. The trouble was, while the transistor had been invented and all that, the technology here was out of my version of the early seventies at best, with some of it more like the sixties and everything, from fashions to values, more like the fifties. It wasn't the best world to be bedridden in, even if a lot of medical knowledge wasn't all that different. Wars still tended to improve that discipline.

After a while it got so bad that I was yearning for a good smutty *Geraldo* and hoping that maybe Al Stark would show up at the door or maybe Les Cohn, whose full role in this whole business I still wasn't sure of.

What I couldn't figure out was the whole business with the Brand Boxes and the transition between worlds. Wilma and I had pretty much *fought* our way through world to world, outwitting some very nasty spider-type creatures just to get over. I couldn't see Al and his gang mussing up their clothes by coming through that way.

The other thing about mostly lying around and going through what books you could get folks to bring you from the library was that you spent a lot of time just thinking, withdrawn, going over and over things whether you wanted to or not.

Matthew Brand was at the heart of all this. I'd never met him and knew him only by his reputation in the one previous life I remembered. I probably couldn't recognize him in person if I bumped into him, having only seen some photos, yet something about him continued to bug me. He hadn't vanished into this new life. He hadn't gone through all this machinery. He'd created in those modules, the Brand Boxes, the ultimate virtual-reality systems, and in the course of perfecting the Boxes, he'd vanished into one.

Now, wait a minute.

If the Brand Boxes were, as Stark and the others maintained, an invention in my old universe, then what about Brand? Did that old universe keep existing until we were all out? Were there hundreds, thousands, millions of universes still existing because one or more of us had gotten stuck there?

Did Stark and Les and all the others who hopped from universe to universe fight their way through each time stark naked, or did they walk through without getting a hair out of place? If so, how?

It was an exciting thought. Suppose Brand *hadn't* invented the Boxes as part of some government project back in the old existence. Suppose he'd already had them.

But did that make sense? You couldn't just touch your head to one of them and enter their virtual realities; they were plugged into a larger computer, and you had to be prepped in a special module, almost like a coffin, with liquids and waste management and intravenous feeding, as well as cybernetic contacts.

Then there was the vision of Walt Slidecker and his funny little aliens unloading stuff from one of the virtual-reality tunnels . . .

Unloading what? And where did those little creatures come from?

Deep down I knew we'd all been fooled somehow, fooled by those few who had known back then what was going on. What had Stark claimed? Nine lifetimes? More? Hard to remember the details.

And Brand—was he those various Alice in Wonderland visions that kept popping up? He was at least partially responsible for them, of that I was sure. In at least one case, under certain drugs, we'd managed to reach him in a point of massive energy between the universes. Meet, converse, and even use that power.

It was not likely that I'd find any such drugs here—unless it wasn't the drugs at all.

That thought excited me, gave me some hope. What if you could access some of this power without outside aids? I mean, what had called the tunnel into existence back at the complex? How had Walt and Cynthia known where their tunnel with their little creatures would appear, and how come it appeared in such a nice out-of-the-way place? Should I spend this existence learning meditation, some kind of transcendental Buddhist system that would allow me to reach beyond this false but nonetheless entrapping reality?

Somehow Stark hadn't seemed to be the meditating type or the drug-using type, either. Still, there had to be something, some linkage, some way to trigger at least access. If it was a matter of will, I could find it.

Hell, I had nowhere else to go and nothing else to do.

For a very long time I got no results at all, and I began to wonder just what I could do. I kept thinking of Wilma, who at least believed she'd reached the American Indian version of the Buddhist "that behind all that" and jumped into trees in the shaman's underworld. I never really believed it, but I'd seen an underworld that was at least as strange, so perhaps she wasn't kidding. I mean, didn't people have visions all the time? Didn't some folks claim to see things others could not, travel to astral planes, whatever they were, see auras or spirits?

What was insanity, anyway? In my past life I'd had a psychology teacher who'd addressed that question and claimed that sanity was relative. You walk into a room and a person is standing there staring up at the ceiling. You look and see nothing and ask what it's all about, and he tells you, "I'm staring at that six-foot purple rabbit hanging by its ears from the light, of course!" You start edging for the door and the phone to call the men in white coats, when all of a sudden a bunch of other folks come in. They all stop, stare, and exclaim about that purple rabbit hanging by its ears from the light fixture. It turns out that everybody *but* you sees the thing. So who's crazy?

The Harvey argument is only a variation of this. Elwood P. Dowd claimed his best drinking buddy was a six-foot rabbit named Harvey. Nobody else—except a psychiatrist eventually—could see the thing, but it was definitely real as it turned out.

Did that help me here? Was anything I could see, hear, smell, touch, or taste *real*? Or was this all an illusion, coming from some vast, impossible computer fed by somebody's invented reality? Didn't the Christian Scientists believe that? That everything we thought was real was actually illusion? I always thought they were kind of nuts, but then again, did you ever see how many *old* people were in Christian Science reading rooms? A lot.

That was what made the Brand Boxes even more bizarre. I mean, boxes that contained whole worldlets existing *inside* virtual universes? The reflection in the reflection of the mirror?

Well, I worked at it. I tried all sorts of concentration exercises, chants, and mantras. Nothing really worked. Eventually the frustration began to get to me. I sniped at my parents, I sniped at the rent-a-nurses, I got angry at the television, I stopped trying to sort things out or even leave my room. Nothing seemed worth it. Even time and the passing of the seasons seemed irrelevant.

The longer this went on, the more Cory Maddox's life seemed but a dream, a fantasy of the crippled and bedridden wreck I was. That was the worst of it. I began to doubt who I was, who I had been, and the more I doubted, the less real it became to me.

Ultimately Dad had a heart attack, and I became an impossible burden for Mom when she also had to care for him. I began to notice just how *old* they'd gotten and in particular the look in my mother's face, the kind of hollow, shopworn look of someone who's had about all she can stand.

"I just can't do it, Andrew," she said to me one morning, already looking so weary that she might drop at any moment.

"Honey, I can't even handle your father and this house any-more, and I really do wonder if we did you any favors keeping you locked away like this."

I had grown so self-pitying, so hopeless, and yet so comfort-able in my cocoon that I almost made a cutting comment that would have hurt her forever, but something inside me caught it just in the nick of time. Instead I said "I understand," even though that wasn't how I felt. I just couldn't bring pain to her, not even as low as I'd sunk. "I suppose I can do nothing any-where at all."

With nothing but early retirement and disability checks coming in for Dad, nothing at all in the way of income from Mom, and limits on what could be spent toward my care, it was ultimately decided that Dad would be best off living near his heart specialist up north in Portland, and Mom and he moved into a much more manageable two-bedroom apartment there.

The insurance company went nuts trying to figure out just what to do with me, though. A nursing home wasn't the best bet—they were full of ninety-year-old folks with Alzheimer's, and even for the ones with active minds and limited bodies all the activities were geared toward old folks.

There were some group homes for paraplegics and quadri-plegics, but they were mostly run by religious groups, and we'd never been the churchgoing sort. I'd been baptized in the Episcopal Church and we'd attended on very rare occasions—Christmas and Easter—over the years, but it wasn't a big deal, and neither were the Episcopalians in Coos Bay or Portland. At least they didn't run any nursing facilities. But the Adven-tists ran one in Coos Bay, the Mormons ran one outside Port-land, and the Roman Catholics had one in Vancouver, Washington, just across the Columbia from Portland. Given a choice of who I'd rather be trapped with, I picked the Catholics; I bought their doctrine no more than I did that of the others, but Episcopal theology was close enough to Catholicism so at least I knew what the heck was going on. The Catholics weren't averse to a little bit of vice, and the location of their facility was close enough that my parents could still visit regularly.

In Cory Maddox's world there'd been some kind of reform movement, with masses in English and nuns wearing street clothes, but not in Drew Maddox's world. Here nuns still wore long black robes and tall white hats, and mass was always in Latin. Still, I'd been right about a few things. There was some nonsacramental wine for dinner and a wee drop of whiskey now and again, and even if they tried to convert me, they were always pretty reasonable human beings. The nuns seemed more otherworldly than the priests; the middle-aged father who was in charge of my ward— actually a complex that was sort of half hospital wing and half apartment—was a pipe-smoking, bourbon-loving Canadian named Pierre Lebeck who insisted on being called Father Pete, since he just couldn't abide being called Père Pierre. I got the idea he was a psychologist of some sort and we were his practice, but if that was true, he was *very* low key about it.

"Come! You should get out a little and see at least your minuscule universe!" he would chide, pulling on a pipe that as often as not wasn't even lit. I don't think he actually *ever* lit it except in the lounge and outside, but it was always in his mouth, and, with his long, lean looks and French proboscis he looked a lot like Sherlock Holmes in priestly garb.

"Go away!" I would always insist. "I'm paying for this room, and I'd like to be left alone!"

"Uh uh. I am like the social director on a cruise ship you've paid thousands to sail on so you could do nothing but relax who insists you go all out for volleyball, aerobics, and morning jogs. It's my whole life's mission to make people like you miserable."

This went on for a while, but he was too likable to fight for long, and besides, he did the one thing Mom and Dad would *never* have thought of: he bribed me. I was allowed none of the excellent confections they turned out, no dessert at all, except in the lounge, and if I deigned to appear there, I could also have access, within medical limits, to the small bar.

He also, quite deliberately I think, got me smoking, something which the doctors disapproved of in spades and which I wouldn't have considered on my own. "Cory" had smoked cigarettes way back when, in an existence I hardly believed in or thought about anymore, but even he had quit for his health years before he had "crossed over." Father Pete didn't try cigarettes; one couldn't smoke in the rooms anyway, for very good reasons, only in the lounge or dining areas or outside. No, he got me interested in cigars—big, fat cigars that absolutely required either a space of my own or forced me outside onto the patio.

Like the occasional whiskey or mixed drink, it was a vice which I could truly enjoy but one which forced me to move and circulate. I certainly understood the motives and saw the same thing played on some of the other patients there. It didn't matter because it was a pleasure in a life that had presented far too few pleasures since that day on the football field.

I wondered if the nurses, all nuns, really carped about this outside of our hearing, but I suspected that they'd been selected because they knew who their patients were and what their jobs were and would be more tolerant than most.

So it happened that I started buzzing for assistance to get dressed and into my electric wheelchair every day—and went on out to the lounge and often out onto the patio for a cigar, where I got to remember the feel of wind and take in fresh air, cigar or not.

I had to admit that I'd just about lost all belief in Cory Maddox. I'd even dropped Drew pretty much, although I still preferred Andrew to Andy. I was really beginning to doubt that all that had gone before had been anything more than some sort of wish-fulfilling fantasy.

And then, one day, as I sat there smoking my cigar, two nuns walked by and caught my attention. There wasn't any way to explain it, but I simply *knew* that I'd seen that pair before. Almost exactly that way, although they weren't nuns. Not then.

The faces, the voices . . .

At that moment Father Pete was coming up the path, and he passed right by them, nodding and smiling, then turned to come into the quad and spotted me. He stopped and came over as I hoped he would.

"Hello, Andrew. Nice to have a day with a bit of sun for a change, isn't it?"

I nodded, but my mind wasn't on the weather. "Father, you know those two nuns you just passed?"

He turned and looked toward their receding black forms in the distance. "You mean them specifically? Yes, a bit. Not well."

"Just humor me for a minute. What are their names?"

He thought a moment. "One's Sister Mary Alice, quite a smart lady. She's got a doctorate in clinical psychology, would you believe? The other is a teacher and librarian. Sister Rita, I believe. They haven't been here all that long. Why? Do you know them?"

I shook my head. "No, I doubt it. They just reminded me of a couple I knew once." I was lying, of course. I knew with this confirmation that I hadn't been crazy to begin with, and an awful lot of my despair faded.

Sister Mary Alice. Doctor Alice McKee, I presume? And your companion, Rita Alvarez . . .

Very much as they were, very much still together, too, and as women.

Then they knew!

The question was, Did they know me? The old Cory hadn't

been from Coos Bay and hadn't been crippled, either. I also looked different, not only from the physical problems but also because I'd kept a full beard and rather long hair for this short-haired age; also, like a lot of people who just lay around a lot, I was fat.

I was, however, still named Maddox, and that made me vulnerable to either of them, since either one would certainly have access to the hardly classified personnel and patient files here.

Was that what they were here for? Why else would we, those two and me, converge on this one spot in this most unlikely of settings?

At least, if things kept to the same level of consistency, I wasn't likely to be assigned to Dr. Les Cohn—not here. McKee and Alvarez were two good Catholic names, anyway.

It was unlikely to be sheer coincidence, but I suddenly remembered that someone had once said something about there being synchronicity between the lives. The closer you were to somebody in the past life, the closer you'd be in the next. So far that hadn't held true—otherwise I'd certainly have run into Ricki and Wilma by now. Maybe, though, it took time. When had Cory met Ricki? Well into adulthood, that was for sure. And Wilma—that was even later. Maybe this was sort of relative.

Something bound most of us together, life after life, both because we could know and because we were the group. It didn't make any sense, but it was nonetheless true. I'd lived twice in Washington State now, not once so far as I knew in Sri Lanka or Burundi or France or Mongolia. That could well change the same way our names and some of our physical features changed, but not dramatically, not all at once, at least as far as I could see.

The point was, those two were here, as they'd been nearby when Wilma and I had managed to cross over. Whether they knew I was here or not, they were surely here for some purpose, since unlike me, they had some choice of movement and some freedom of action. How had they gotten to this plane? Had they made a run for it below giant spiders, or was it a lot easier if you knew what you were doing? And what were they up to?

Most of all, what the *hell* could I do about it even if I found out?

II

THE MARCH HARE
INTERVENES

"Remember the sisters you thought you recognized the other day?" Father Pete asked casually as we sat in the lounge waiting for the baseball game to come on TV.

I stiffened a bit. I'd seen Alice McKee once more walking from one point to another outside, Alvarez not at all, and I wasn't sure I wanted to see either of them. I certainly did not want them to become aware of me if they weren't already. "Yes?"

"I had a pleasant dinner with the mother superior and several guests, including those two, just last night," the priest told me. "Sister Mary Alice is here on retreat, while Sister Rita is using the convent up the hill as a base while she's taking some librarian-type courses in Portland. Seems that they're going to go to some standardized computerized method of cataloging books tied into the Library of Congress or somesuch and she's got to have a refresher course. Most interesting, both of them. They apparently knew each other before either took her vows. I wasn't able to find out how or when, though."

I could tell you, Father, but you wouldn't believe me. "Well, I believe at least one of them is in fact who I thought she was, but I'd rather she not know I'm here. My experience with her in the past was very unpleasant. I'm afraid that's why I reacted so strongly to seeing them."

"Indeed? I wouldn't have thought that either would have crossed your path before. They said they were new to the area."

"It—well, it's not worth going into. I just would rather our paths not cross. You didn't mention me, did you?"

"Actually, no, considering that you didn't think either was the correct person before. Well, they won't be around much longer. Sister Mary Alice is taking on a two-year slot in the education department at Stanford—it appears they have quite a program there on comparative religions and have rotating chairs, and she's been accepted. Sister Rita was talking of going for her doctorate in library science, but where I'm not certain. It would be unlikely to be Stanford, I suspect. Not with church budgets being so tight. Most likely Catholic University or Notre Dame if she's good."

Oh, she's good, all right, I thought sourly. But somehow I didn't see those two splitting up at this point. If McKee was heading to Stanford, then Alvarez, I felt certain, would be at least in the neighborhood. Still, I'd been around this place long enough to recognize the subtle differences in the penguin uniforms and colors; they weren't in the same order, which would separate them in any event.

"Have you ever given a thought to going back to school, Andrew?" Father Pete asked me, not for the first time. I'd wondered where this was going, and now I knew. "You're a smart young man, and even if you have a broken body, you have a fine mind. What's that genius fellow over in England? Can't hardly move but a finger, yet he's supposed to be figurin' the whole nature of the universe."

"I know who you mean. But he's also an atheist bent on proving God isn't necessary. I'm surprised you'd push *him* as a role model."

Father Pete shrugged. "There's some folks who just don't get it. Never did. Others, like Ben Franklin and Albert Einstein, come back to faith late in life. You know what? I bet the fellow's not spent a ten-millionth of one percent of the time thinking on and researching *real* religious questions than he has figurin' how to explain the big bang. I read one of his books. Dances around what he'd rather not face and rigs up a whole alternative time so his calculations come out and sets up a scenario where his math's all right but isn't any more believable and has far less evidence of reality than God has for Himself. No, he'll die not having what he most wants, the explanation for all that is, the unified theory or whatever they call it, because he can't be bothered with what others who were also smart came up with to explain it. That's creation, my lad! For every wrongheaded interpretation and every abuse of power and intellect in His name, it doesn't get around the fact that God is the answer. No, it doesn't."

I gave him a half smile. "You never have any doubts? What if one day you woke up and discovered that everything you think you know is wrong? Not just about religion; I mean *everything*. That the whole universe was just some kind of computer program that could be turned on and off, and you with it?"

He seemed surprised at the response but chuckled. "Now, suppose you were right. Would it change anything?"

"Huh?"

"There is a great sacred mystery to it all, Andrew. That's what, I suspect, attracts me most of all. If there's a God, then what are we, what is all this, everything, but expressions of His thoughts, His will, His—well, imagination, as it were? I believe He is my creator, but in a pragmatic sense He's also my boss. If you want to think of him as the chief programmer and us as computer simulations, well, why not? We can't really *know* on His level, so we use constructs so that our minds can grasp what is there enough to act upon its existence. I have no problems with people who want to think of it that way, only with people who reject out of hand or because of their traditions or what they or their Aunt Louise *thinks* is religion. The

Church gives me a system for dealing with it, but I can't pretend to truly understand it. I *do* believe that if clever people spent as much time studying the evidence rather than simply the traditions and their own background on religion as they do with any other field of study, they'd come up with results that would at least disturb them."

I gave up. "You may be right, Father. You may be right."

I hadn't bothered with the idea of going back to school for several reasons. For one thing, in spite of the fact that I knew intellectually that this was merely some sort of gigantic Brand Box existence, it was reality as far as I was concerned, and my parents were still alive here even though they had died in my past life. Seeing them resurrected, interacting with them—it was tough to break with them, particularly since I wasn't at all sure that I'd ever see Dad again if I went anywhere.

And, of course, what would I study? I was still way ahead of some folks in the computer field, both hardware and software, although things were getting better even if they were developing along slightly different lines. Here computing remained centered in California, Digital Research made the deal with IBM and became dominant, and nobody ever even heard of Redmond, Washington. The battle was between IBM/DRI and Apple, although in one respect history was going down the same path.

Two weeks later, when I picked up the latest *Time* magazine, though, I began to have second thoughts about my lack of ambition. It was the usual review of technology and trends that they did once a year or so, and one of the articles in particular caught my eye. Or, rather, a photograph caught my eye and held it in a vise.

"Virtual Reality Emerges from DOD Shield," the headline said. Under it was a picture of a large brick building and the caption "Supersecret experiments to teach fighter pilots went on here unsuspected for years."

It was the first use of the term "virtual reality" I'd seen in this universe, and the story was about a massive research project that had been developed by scientists with Defense Department money to create an environment where pilot trainees for the new superjets could get a nearly perfect simulation of flying. Not just the usual flight simulator but much more. They'd used it for experiments in weightless environments, too, and other such training and had, it seemed, taken it all the way to convincing ground simulations.

I recognized some of the equipment. The giant, gyroscope-like device for moving in all directions seemed a bit oddly designed but familiar enough. Full-blown suits, helmets with virtual vision and sound—all of it looked amazingly familiar. Oh, the *look* was different, more in line with this universe's oddball concept of style, but it was clear just what it was and what they were doing with it.

Who "they" were became apparent from the photo of the lab directors and pioneers in this research.

"Doctor Lee Henreid and wife, Robyn, also a PhD, in front of once secret and still restricted lab at Stanford University . . ."

Rob looked a little more homely as a woman but recognizable for sure. I wondered which way Lee really did swing, frankly. He'd changed hardly at all, still a good-looking blond hunk. I bet that a lot of the folks around there wondered why he wound up marrying somebody who looked like that.

Lee knew—and Rob didn't. That was one easy way to tell, at least.

I also knew that the publication of the story meant two things. First, they now had something better than the VR in the pictures and the article, something so much better that they no longer felt it was worth keeping under wraps. Second, they were broadcasting for those who *knew* to come to them and also perhaps to tweak the subconscious of those who didn't really know but might have some kind of magnetic draw to such a project, anyway, for reasons they might not understand.

Alice McKee was headed to Stanford. And after meeting Rita Alvarez here, I was convinced that somehow Sister Rita was heading there as well and just needed to consult on how best to do it. Father Pete was right: the Church would never pay for a Franciscan nun to go to Stanford, not when it had its own highly ranked universities in the field of library science.

I wondered just how much they really *were* nuns. I mean, I knew who I'd been and what was really going on, as much as any of us did, and I still was more comfortable and felt more Andrew than Cory. No matter when they'd inserted themselves here, they had a lifetime of memories, of reasons for going into the Church, of religious training, all that. Could Rita just walk away from it psychologically? It was an interesting question.

Stanford would be a budget buster for me, too. I could go back to OSU, of course, and there were a number of smaller colleges I probably could get to accept me if I could somehow deal with my own physical limitations without their having to rebuild their campuses, but Stanford?

If I wanted to go there, I'd either have to win the Publishers' Sweepstakes or . . .

Or deliberately expose myself and see if they came for me.

I could do that here, of course, but I wasn't ready for it yet. Maybe not ever, considering that I would most likely be consigning myself to Les or Al Stark and a bit of not so subtle reprogramming in a Brand Box followed by death.

Wait a minute. Did they have Brand Boxes here? How could they?

But if they didn't, then where in *this* universe was Matthew Brand?

Still, I had a choice between something and nothing at all. The plain fact was, sitting in a wheelchair, unable even to change my underwear by myself, in a nursing home for younger permanent dependents, I either made some kind of move or I was as good as dead, anyway.

I got some pens and paper and drawing tools and over the next couple of weeks had at it. Father Pete was so delighted to see me take an interest in anything, he got me pretty much what I wanted within reason and admitted that he not only didn't understand exactly what I was doing but didn't understand how I knew it, either. Even so, it was something that was involving me in a future, and he was all for it; from my standpoint it was a risk, but I felt I had to do *something*. And when I was done, I cleaned it up and put it in excellent shape and wrote a cover letter explaining my physical situation but suggesting that there was more if they were interested. I had Father Pete drop it in the mail.

Then I had to hope that the recipient didn't toss it, didn't laugh at it, and at least understood what a neural network might be.

Summer went on, and fall approached, and I heard nothing more from anyone. I was beginning to think that as usual, they'd left old Miscellaneous Maddox to rot, when, one day in early October while sitting on my bed in my room reading a novel, I was suddenly aware of someone stepping into the room. He wasn't anyone I'd ever seen before—I was certain of that—nor was he any sort of priest. He was middle-aged, with gray medium-length hair and a matching short, full gray beard and mustache, wearing a tweed suit and a rather plain matching tie.

"Yes?"

He looked apprehensive, nervous, although it was hard to see what sort of danger he might be in from somebody like me. "Mister, ah, Maddox?"

"Yes?" I repeated.

"I—I am Doctor Harold Kaminsky." He fumbled uncertainly, opening a briefcase, rummaging through it, then removing a folder and handing it to me. "Did you—did you send this?"

I opened the folder and saw that it contained not the originals but photocopied versions of the letter, paper, and diagram I'd sent back in June. "Yes, this is mine."

"Wh—where did you *get* such concepts? I *have* to know!

This—this is—um . . . Do you know how far in advance this is of what we were working on?"

I began to smile. "I had an idea that some of the things would be new to anybody in that field, yes. At least I kind of *hoped* so."

"An—anybody in 'that field,' Mister Maddox? There *is* no such thing as 'that field,' at least not yet. I—I have to admit that we had you checked out. There is—isn't—there's *nothing* in your background to show that you have any sort of background or interest in this!"

"That's true," I admitted. "When you are flat on your back for years, though, Doctor, and you've seen every episode of *Leave It to Beaver* 127 times and you've read every book and magazine available three times, you try to expand your interests. I found neurophysics fascinating, maybe because I was hoping to find some way around my, well, condition. When you have little to do but think and find something interesting and go over all the literature you can find on it, you sometimes start coming up with things. You checked the math, I assume? And ran the three lab proofs I suggested?"

"Of course! Of course!" He hesitated. "Well, one out of three. The other two require a level of computer sophistication that would take us into the government realm to attempt, if there. But if you came up with this, why did you send it to *us*? You could have sent it *anywhere*!"

"Well, not exactly. I had to send it somewhere where I was sure somebody would be able to understand it and might not dismiss it as a joke. I also know about the medical research done at Stanford, which is closer than Rochester or Baltimore, not to mention in a nicer climate, and I saw the *Time* article on the former government projects and thought maybe there would be computers there capable of handling some of this."

He nodded. "I—I think there are. They are still a world apart from us, those people over in the Schumaker Building. They might as well be on the other side of the country for all the interaction we have." He didn't sound very pleased by that, but I was.

"So what do you do at Stanford, Doctor?"

"Medical research. I—I thought I made that clear. We are working on a brand-new field, one we call cybernetics. The problem, of course, is in miniaturization. You—your creation here doesn't involve that, but it shows that if we can solve that problem, we might be able to use this concept to interface the human nervous system with our machines."

That was somewhat disappointing. I could no more show you how to create millions of transistors on chips small enough to do the job than I could build a Brand Box. When I was working on the long-range broadcast network in the old world, I got what I needed the old-fashioned way: I picked up the phone and ordered the parts I couldn't make myself.

I couldn't help pushing the man a little. "Doctor, all this is well and good, but why are you here? I've got most of those concepts filed and ready for patent submission, so they're covered, but there was no sense reinventing the wheel."

He got the idea. "Just what do you want, Mister Maddox?"

"I want to be able to be there with access to what's already known and working on ways of improving and refining and expanding this concept until maybe I can restore at least movement to the parts of my body that need it. I don't have a lot of higher education in the formal sense, but if that isn't a good thesis, I don't know what might be. I want in, Doctor. I think the real question is not what I want but what you are prepared to offer."

Kaminsky scratched his beard in a nervous fashion and thought a moment. "Well—we—we certainly can offer you a full scholarship. All expenses, even for your special needs. We—we have a resident hospital there for our volunteers."

This was almost comical. He was offering me a four-year scholarship in exchange for contributing to their research, being a guinea pig, and—oh, yes—turning over some ideas potentially worth millions.

"I assume that's a scholarship to the graduate level in engineering or computer science," I responded coolly. "I have no intention of wasting my time with English Lit 101 and Art Appreciation 1 or even Physics 100. If I can do *that*, I think I'm up in the graduate league."

He looked shocked. "You—you mean you want to go straight to the *doctorate* level from a *high school* education?"

"I think I've proved that I can handle the work, and that's the major criterion," I responded. "Of course, I'd do the thesis, you'd do the book, and we'd share the patents." I paused for a moment to let that sink in, then added, "But then again, I can always contact others. The climate may be poorer at Johns Hopkins, but I'm sure somebody there will find this of great interest."

That got him. Like most professors, he understood academic blackmail very well.

"Look—I—I can't, don't, have the authority, but I will put it to those who do. Please do nothing until I can put it through."

Hooked and being reeled in. "How long should I wait, Doctor? I've got a lot more here now . . ."

He almost salivated. "M—more? I, uh, give me a few weeks, please! Until Christmas, perhaps. You couldn't enter until the next term, anyway."

I shook my head. "I'm not going to rot here another year if anything goes wrong on your end, Doc. No, if anything *did* cause a hang-up, I could be too late to go anywhere else until next September, and I don't want that. You must understand that this body isn't in good shape. No body that doesn't move on its own can help but fall slowly apart, no matter how much daily physiotherapy and machine exercise you get. I don't know how long I've got, but it's probably not a very long time, and it could be over at any point. I don't have time to wait any longer, you see." I looked over at the wall calendar. "It's October 9 now. I'll give you until November 15. That's enough time. After that I contact Hopkins and maybe others as well, and you wind up in a bidding war."

"But—but that's just a *month*!"

"You and your staff are smart enough to realize the potential of what's there," I noted. "You must also realize that it's not going to help you without a few additions that aren't all that obvious. I've solved the problem, Doctor. The only thing we're waiting for is manufacturing to catch up with us, and it's developing rather rapidly, as you know, in just the directions we need. Maybe even the government—"

"No, no! I—I'll see what I can do. I promise. I'll be back with you by November 15, one way or the other, I promise! Do nothing rash!"

I got a real charge out of the encounter and a sense of being in control of something in my life for the first time since the accident. It was only when it grew quite late and there were no sounds around except those of the climate control ducting and some of the worse-off patients down the hall that I began to worry a bit.

I'd started something rolling, all right. I'd had my enemies land in my backyard, and I'd proceeded to tweak them in theirs.

Now what?

No matter what else could be said for things, the fact is that I had my head and one arm, and that wasn't a whole hell of a lot to duck for cover with if I had to. Not that it wasn't already too late for that to mean much. No matter what came of this, I was committed.

The package was small and neatly wrapped, addressed in a firm hand with no return address visible.

"Andrew C. Maddox," it read in the kind of handwriting I don't think people have had since the nineteenth century. There followed the address and room number. The postmark wasn't much in and of itself, but it certainly was jarring.

The package had been mailed from Yakima, Washington, a day or two after I'd had my Stanford visit. Although nobody in *this* incarnation seemed to have much to do with Yakima, the link with my past life and all that I'd learned could hardly be ignored and made it unlikely that the postmark was coincidental. There were still a lot of folks, friends and foes, I hadn't seen or kept track of here.

I carefully opened the package, only slightly tearing the brown paper, and pulled out a small gold-covered box of the sort that fancy chocolate companies might use. With a fingernail I broke the four pieces of tape holding down the lid and opened it.

A little logo on a card on top of the inner lining paper read "Zyzzx Cookie Factory."

Substitute "Software" for "Cookie" and you had the name of Matthew Brand's improbable venture in the previous universe. But how could this be from Brand? He was trapped in a Brand Box in the past universe, wasn't he?

Or was he? Whose word did I have for it, and what the hell did a Brand Box do, anyway?

Almost as if I feared it might blow up in my hand, I put it down, removed the card, and peeled back the paper.

Inside it all was a chocolate brownie.

I carefully reached in and removed it with some difficulty from the form-fitting packing, only to have the card fall off the tray and onto my chest facedown.

There was writing on the back of it in the same incredibly precise hand that had addressed the package.

It said, "Eat Me."

I have to be the only human being in all creation who would get goose bumps from a brownie and a message like that, I thought, still feeling the hair on my scalp tingle a bit.

I didn't do what it said, not then. Clearly there was something in the brownie, something probably a lot more potent than some of the other brownies that were around here, even the spiked ones. I didn't want any kind of medical alert if I went comatose or something. I would wait.

The trouble was, it made time almost stand still to do so,

and it also gave me a lot of time to brood. Who the hell could have sent it? Was it a trick? Maybe, but not from the Stanford crowd, surely. They knew by now just where I was and that I was a crippled sitting duck. Why bother? Brand? Even if he were somehow able to interact, it would surely be as he had done it in the past, via access to that electronic never-never land outside perceived existence. Hookah-smoking caterpillars and waistcoated walruses didn't bake brownies, let alone walk into post offices and mail them. Stark hadn't let Ricki live in prior existences, so with her in his hands the last time, it wasn't likely he got full of magnanimity or something, so she would be as ignorant as Rob. The Stanford crew wouldn't bother with Yakima, nor would the two "sisters" who'd both headed away from here to the south or wherever by now.

It could be Wilma. This kind of stunt would be very much up her alley, although I never remembered her having fancy handwriting. I wanted much to see and talk with her again, that was for sure. Still, would this be the way she'd do it if she found out where I was? And how could she?

If not Wilma, though, that left only one other, the man with his own independently controlled rabbit holes and help from some pretty weird-looking critters.

Not that I could see what Walt Slidecker would want with me now.

Still, who else *could* it be from?

It was past midnight before I dared to find out.

Now, lying there in the dark, I fumbled in my drawer and for a moment panicked at not being able to find the box. All sorts of things, including the thought that some eager beaver had just cleaned things up and thrown it out while I'd been at dinner or that I'd dropped it under the bed or whatever, came to me until my fingers suddenly touched it.

I brought out the box, using my erratic left arm as a stop, opened it, reached in, and removed the brownie.

Well, I thought, *here goes!* I bit into it and found it very sweet and extremely chocolaty with absolutely no aftertaste or undertaste. It was, in fact, a really superb brownie.

Oh, brother! Don't tell me that in this world Matt Brand became a cookie king! I thought sourly. "Abandon hope, all ye who enter here" might well be the message.

I finished it, washed it down with a little water, then lay back, feeling wide awake and not the least bit chemically augmented. I could hear the ticking of a master clock in the lounge. It seemed to drone on and on with nothing else happening while I was wide awake and aware of every annoying sound in the place and every snore in the compound.

One of the nurses made her rounds, and I heard her go by even though my door was shut. That was Sister Frances. I knew that because she had the habit of humming Broadway show tunes off key when she walked.

At one point another nurse making the rounds opened the door quietly and looked in, checking. There was always the understood license to do this a few times during the night, a balance between privacy and medical necessity. I wasn't sure which one of the nurses it was, but the figure was hardly unusual.

I was now in complete despair. Somebody had deliberately twitted me with a good brownie and nothing more. Why? To what purpose? A message?

It seemed like another hour or more before the door quietly opened again and a shape that was definitely *not* familiar entered and closed it with a *click*. The night-light showed the form, but I really wanted to turn on at least one of the lights.

"No, leave them off," the visitor said in a reedy, nasal man's voice that had the accent of an English dockworker. "It's better that way, and it won't attract attention."

He—*it*—stood there near the door, almost six feet high, the big ears going up another foot and a half almost to the ceiling. The eyes were huge and black on a sea of white, and the two front teeth protruded and looked dangerous even if squared off.

He was a six-foot light brown hare wearing a checkered

coat, baggy trousers, and an oversized, out of proportion head that looked more cartoon than real.

"Sorry to be a bit late, mate," the March Hare apologized. "This ain't as bloomin' easy as it looks."

I tried to see if it was some kind of costume. It looked rock solid, as real as the nurses, and it had actually opened and closed the door to enter. If it *was* some kind of costume, though, it was damned near perfect.

"You sent me the package with the brownie?"

"Well, let's just say I work for the bloke wot done it and let it go at that, huh?" The big nose twitched, and the whiskers shimmered. It was odd that I could see such detail in the near darkness, I thought, and then realized that in fact some things were not at all normal.

The March Hare looked me over. "Got yerself into a pretty pickle if I *do* say so," he commented. "One good arm, is it? That'll teach you next time to give a little margin!"

"If I could remember the past times, I wouldn't have made the mistake *this* time," I pointed out.

"Yeah, well, we all live and learn, don't we? Now you also done and just about *announced* that you were here, that you're damn near helpless, and for them to come'n get you, too. *That* wasn't exactly all that bright."

"I had to make something happen."

"You could commit suicide, you know. *That* is 'something happenin' ' too, ain't it?" He sighed. "Well, okay, it's done. They're in no hurry—they already got your wireless neural net connector last time. Stark ain't got much use for you. He's Alf Starkey here, by the way, and he's a navy commander attached to the National Security Agency this time. Like before, he's working with one Lester Eugene Cohen, MD, who's on the staff of the Stanford Medical Center and holds a reserve commission in the marines. I assume you saw the happy couple who direct the current project in the magazine."

"Yes."

"Okay, here's question number one. If you could get sprung

and had some unrestricted access to the power matrix as you had for a short while in the last go-round, what could you do with it?"

"What? What do you mean, 'do with it'? I was flying blind the last time and managed to swap bodies and do a lot of super stuff until I got whacked over the head with a table leg or something."

The March Hare thought for a moment. "All right, let's get some of the rules straight and then we'll see where we can go from here. It should be pretty damn clear that I can't take 'em on alone, face to face. They have access to the power grid and most of the Brand Boxes, as you call 'em."

"The Brand Boxes! But weren't they left behind? I mean, how could the Brand Boxes be here? In *this* world? The technology isn't here to build them!"

The March Hare sighed. "Look, the Boxes are the one real thing you can count on. They exist, period. No matter whether you're in the caveman era or the Arabian Nights or anything else, the Brand Boxes are *always* present. Now, don't start asking me things I don't know the answer to, like *why* they're always present, but they are. The only time you aren't in a universe with a Brand Box is when you're *in* a Brand Box."

"You—you really don't know? I mean, I thought you—"

"No, I'm not Matthew Brand. And I ain't too sure *he* knows what the hell they are, either. He just discovered 'em and studied 'em and figured out how to use 'em. He—you—everybody. All the tight little group. All of you are caught in this crazy self-contained system. None of you really knows who or what or where you are, and I think that includes Matthew Brand. He's just smarter than the rest of you, that's all. Smarter in *some* ways. Couldn't fight his way out of a paper bag, and he's real easy to sucker, I tell you. The usual smart nerd."

This was news. This made the unknowable mess even worse. "Then if Brand's not your boss, who is? Walt?"

"Don't get too nosy, now. Besides, I'm crazy, see?" He crossed his eyes for effect. "So you're right now getting shit from somebody who's not mad as a March Hare, he *is* the bloody March Hare! Right?"

"Um, yeah, I think."

"Don't think! Listen! See, this whole thing's got *rules*, and unless you know the rules, knowin' the rest don't matter. Like, think of it as one big bloody endless game."

I had thought of that. "I don't like the game if it is one."

The hare sniffed. "So you don't *like* the game? So what? So you don't like your life or the universe or whatever? So what? It is anyway, right? I mean, arise and walk if you don't like bein' in that bloody stinkin' bed!"

I sank back and nodded. "Point surrendered. Go on."

"Okay, then, here it is, as much as you need to know. The object of this here game, see, is to find God and kill 'im."

"What?"

"Just wot I says. Find God and kill 'im. Could be man or woman, old or young, but it's one o' the same old crew. Until you find who came up with this bloody mess of a world, you can't get out of it except by dyin', see? Nobody can. You find the one what come up with all this, and you pop 'im off, and *then* you can move on to the *next* creation. That's what good old Al did the last time. Went nuts goin' through one after the other tryin' to figure out which one was God. Of course, even God don't always know he or she's God, so that makes it a little harder. But if you can't figure 'im out by other means, the last way to do it is with the Brand Boxes. You can sort of disconnect God if he or she's in a bloody Brand Box, see?"

That last bit hit me like a ton of bricks. "Wait a minute! Are you saying that's why they put us all through that last time? Not because we were really needed on the project but because they were trying to see if any of us were the ones who came up with that universe?" The one comfort I'd had all along was that somehow they'd needed me for that wireless interface to the Boxes from the pods, that I had created some essential technology for them. This said they couldn't have cared less.

"Pretty much. Don't do a lot for the bloomin' ego, does it?

Of course, Starkey's got more ambition than that. So's his so-called friend the doctor. They figure that sooner or later they're gonna be able to come through first conscious, hale, hearty, and with their own plan. Got it all set up in their own little Brand Boxes, they does. 'Course, they ain't got the same idea of just wot paradise is, and they know it. So do their cronies, each of whom's got their own luverly idea of heaven. Starkey, though, he's the one to watch, 'cause he's driven by more than just some crackpot vision. He really believes, deep down, that he's got some kind of divine mission to keep you all in check and in tow. He'll brainwash you, lead you around by your nose, do anything he has to to make sure he's got everybody under control. He comes close now and then, but he never had you all and it drives him bananas, it does."

"And Walt? What about him and those whatever they ares?"

"Walt's workin' his own bloody game. It ain't too certain where his friends come from. They was first in one of the old universes, and everybody thought they was just part of the show, you know, and then *boom!* They shows up with a mind of their own where they couldn't be. Walt made some deal with 'em that got him out from under old Al, but only he knows wot. Now you know the nutty bolts of it, at least until somebody pops you off and you wake up ignorant again, which is pretty bloody likely considerin' your current state, wouldn't you say?"

I thought for a moment. "You—I *assume* it was you—got me out of a sticky situation in the last universe. I became somebody else entirely. You mean that can't be done again?"

"A reprogram? Yeah, probably, but wot's the use of it? Wot did you do with the *last* opportunity? Tell you wot I can do, though. I'll give you a crack at an exit. You can't leave this universe alive, at least not now, not until we find out what incredibly boring mind thought this one up. But you made it, so you can't stay here and you can't go down to

California. They'd stick you in a Brand Box and forget about you."

"How can they do the Brand Boxes?" I challenged him. "Even if they have the Boxes, the support equipment, power system, everything else needed to use them properly isn't anywhere close to the technology here yet."

The March Hare was unfazed. "Oh, they have it, all right. It all comes through. They don't come in on the run like they made you come. They come through almost like they was *drivin'* or even *flyin'* it. Right comfortable, they are. *You* came on through the rabbit hole; *they* rode here through the bloomin' Channel tunnel! You wasn't supposed to make it through alive, Cory, my boy! You only made it 'cause you come through with Wilma and she's a survivor with guts and some experience in this stuff, whether she knew it or not. You and Rick, you're pushovers. Al's conditioned most of the guts out of both of you in the Boxes over the ages. You surprised him by comin' back at all to the old place last time, but you were gettin' your guts from the raw energy that place finally was able to put out, and our help is lettin' you tap it." He paused as if hearing something I could not sense.

"Me time's nearly gone," he continued in a low, rushed tone. "You got choices, Cory, I'll give you that much. You forced yourself into this game from the weakest possible position, but now you got to *play*. I'm gonna deal you into an alternative, but that's all. Whether you go meekly into their hands down south or lie here and wait for 'em to come for you is your own choice. Them's easy; the third one's mine."

"Which is?"

"Lie back and shut your eyes, lad, and I'll send you on a little trip to Wonderland for an answer. Yes, that's it, just relax, eyes closed, and wait. It'll come to you . . ."

I did as he instructed, or tried to, and there was only the sound of my own breathing and the ventilation. It did occur to me that I'd never heard that huge rabbit nose of his or any sounds of a large creature breathing, but that was to be expected. I just hadn't expected a hologram to bother with opening and closing a door, that's all.

I was suddenly afraid that he'd left, and I opened my eyes and got a sharp *"I said close 'em!"*

I did, and then I heard him moving as if he were a real physical entity, approaching my bedside. I could almost feel his presence and got very tempted to open my eyes again but didn't.

Then, suddenly, I knew that I was alone. There'd been no sound of him leaving, no opening and closing of the door on the way out, but whatever sense of presence I'd felt was gone.

I was about to open my eyes and do a reality check, when suddenly the entire room dropped away from me and I was either floating or falling. I didn't keep my eyes shut now; I opened them—and almost wished I hadn't.

I was heading headfirst down a long, rough-walled tunnel, roughly oval in shape and dimly illuminated from behind. It resembled for all the world the inside of a massive hollow tree, only I was going headfirst down that tunnel and feeling the drop and the wind on my face, and I wasn't in full control of the descent.

I wasn't alone in this rapid and scary flight, either. My passage disturbed all sorts of small creatures, many batlike but others unlike anything I'd seen this side of gargoyles, from their apparent slumber on the walls. They would shriek and take off in panicked flight in all directions, yellow and red and orange eyes flashing in the semidarkness.

The sensation was not unlike that of a roller coaster, and it was nearly impossible to relax and enjoy the ride even though something intellectually whispered to me that somehow, for all the speed and all the little creatures and the rest, I was coming very close to one wall and then another but never actually hitting them. It *was* a sort of guided descent, only I wasn't consciously doing the guiding.

How long this went on I couldn't say; subjectively it seemed like hours. Finally, though, I broke free and clear into a vast cavern or something very much like one. Above was a great dome of a dark blue color, but it was layered from the horizons to the top like the sky an hour before sunrise. Below was a vast body of water over which I flew, skimming the surface, disturbing the relative calm. I came down until I could actually feel spray on my face, then suddenly soared upward perhaps fifteen or twenty feet in the air. Ahead of and below me I could see a vessel, a great boat of ancient design made of intricately carved wood with a single mast in the center for a sail that was not raised. Instead, the boat was being rowed by oarsmen, strange, humanoid creatures wearing garb like some ancient Egyptian god-things, with long, muscular black arms leading to rough, taloned hands and with faces that were more doglike than human. The long snouts and big eyes and small pointed ears produced not a cute or cuddly but rather a menacing tone. These were not lapdogs, but humanoid cousins to the wolf.

The oarsmen—there must have been forty to a side—did not look up at me or in any way acknowledge my presence, if in fact they knew I was there at all, and the drummer in the front kept his canine gaze on the rowers and beat out the slow, steady cadence. The helmsman, though, cocked his head to one side, as if sensing something odd, and then looked up and most certainly saw me. His jaws opened, revealing rows of sharp white teeth, and there was a saliva dribble from one side of his mouth. Keeping his right hand on the tiller, he raised his left and pointed a gnarled finger at me; from the end of it shot a glow of green energy of a form I'd seen before.

I could not avoid it; it struck me, enveloped me, and seemed to burn. For the first time in a very long time I *felt* not just at the shoulders and above but completely, over the whole of my body.

Momentum, though, took me away from the ship and its

eerie and threatening occupants, and soon they were lost from view. I felt odd, tingling all over, but I wasn't completely aware of anything that had changed. Then, slowly, I was aware that I *could* feel a complete body and that I had a measure of control. Carefully, I tried a bit of experimenting, shifting my weight slightly to one side and then to the other, and saw that I traveled in those directions. It was almost like driving a car; a little went a long way in controlling my actions.

I slowed a bit and went down as I saw a reflection in the water below. Quickly checking and not seeing any obvious obstacles ahead, I took myself once more to just a couple of yards from the surface and looked.

It was my own face that I saw staring back at me, the same one I'd had before, but it sat atop a dark, metallic purple body, a monstrous body, one with a serpentine tail and great bat's wings that were keeping me aloft.

I cried out, as much in shock as in terror at the vision, and for just a moment lost control, but I managed to get myself back into controlled flight before going headlong into the still waters.

A shore was approaching now, and I allowed myself to head for it, although the landscape was so bizarre, it might as well have been on a distant planet. A forest, a vast thicket with huge trees rising from it toward the "sky" and beyond, lay all around. I grew a bit nervous flying such a dangerous winding path after a while and turned, rose a bit, and landed as carefully as I could on a thick branch of one of the master growths. The branch was a few yards across and perhaps half a mile long— plenty of room.

Talons in my feet bent down and gripped the wood, making my perch as solid as if I'd grown from it. It was time to stop, time to look around and take stock of this bizarre place.

My form would have seemed freakish in any other setting, but it seemed to fit in perfectly around here. This was a world of eternal twilight, of strange creatures not merely of another evolution but of a *lot* of other evolutionary paths flitting about in the air and running over the ground and up, down, and all around the trees. The textures and shapes had an unreal quality about them, as if drawn by a master three-dimensional artist. Everything was as real as anything else to me, yet all seemed at the same time permeated with a sense of unreality.

It was in some ways the antithesis of the realities I could remember, either of them. They were not real, yet they seemed totally so, while this place could not be real yet was.

And I and all the plants and animals around me weren't the only ones here. The dog-faced characters on the ship surely weren't the only ones of their kind, forever sailing like some ancient Flying Dutchman, nor were even *they* the sole lords of this world.

What I had first taken for some kind of animal going along the forest floor, occasionally showing itself in breaks in the trees or climbing over obstacles, now was a clearly humanoid shape. The skin was strange, light blue in color, and from the back the creature appeared human but was covered with various lines or stripes or—tattoos?

I took off again and followed the blue man below, certain that he didn't know I existed or couldn't do much about it. He certainly was headed someplace definite, and that was what I really wanted to find out, and without any irritating green ray baths springing from fingertips, whatever that had done to me.

Why had I been sent here, and how could I return? Worse, did I *want* to return to a bedridden existence after I had this level of freedom, no matter how fierce and gruesome I might appear? What had the March Hare, whoever he really was, had in mind in sending me to this place?

And was it a real place in any sense at all, or did it just exist in the March Hare's imagination or mine?

Would that fellow below me know? I looked ahead and saw a clearing right on the beach, maybe a mile ahead. There was a campfire of some sort in the clearing, and around it sat a dozen or more—people? humanoids?—of varying colors, all pastels, like the pastel blue man below. I realized that this was where he almost had to be headed, and so I forgot him and headed for the group.

It suddenly occurred to me that the way I looked, I wasn't the sort of creature who would be exactly welcomed with open arms and believed about my good intentions. Although these creatures could pose a danger to me, ignorant as I was of this whole region, I was much more likely to panic the hell out of them. I sure would scare *me* in other circumstances.

With that in mind, I flew a bit inland from them, between the big trees, and approached from the other side so I wouldn't be surprised by the blue man. I came down a good hundred yards up the beach and in the thicket, even though it made for tough going overland. I wanted to approach them without their seeing me, if at all possible, and see just what they were and whether I could communicate with them instead of panic them.

As I approached to get a good look at them without exposing or entangling myself, I could hear that they were not silently contemplating the fire but were sitting around it chanting in some eerie, guttural, yet melodic tongue.

They did in fact appear human except for their coloration and were of average size and girth. There were eleven there at the moment, six women and five men—Blueboy would make an even dozen when he arrived. No two were of the same color, and all were adorned with the painted designs I had taken as tattoos. The designs were of many colors and included circles, lines, and very elaborate but precise patterns. All were naked.

I couldn't help wondering if the skin colors, too, were applied and the hair was dyed, with the rest applied first as kind of a base coat for the designs. It was hard to tell, as there were no uncovered areas or unevenly covered areas that would make it obvious, but it had that look about it.

The people themselves had a less uniform look beyond their

coloration and adornments. They seemed to be a racial mix, from very Oriental to African, European, Australoid and Polynesian, all the peoples of the earth in just these few.

The air was hot and moist; I couldn't imagine why they had a fire, for they appeared to be cooking nothing but simply staring into the flame and chanting. Every once in a while, though, the flame would coalesce into, well, almost a *shape*, ghostly and with hollow eyes, that would twist around and inspect the circle before collapsing back into the fire.

I remained still, watching but doing nothing from my place of concealment. After a time Blueboy arrived and took his place in the circle. None of them bothered to look around or otherwise acknowledge his arrival. However, his place was clearly prepared for him with the men and women alternating around the fire, and he settled in and immediately took up the chant as if he'd been there all along.

The fire suddenly roared, and once more the Shape was visible, going through the same motions, checking, it seemed, everyone there.

Teacher's taking attendance, I thought, not knowing why that came to me, but it did seem to fit.

The chanting rose in intensity and loudness, and the Shape seemed to become more real, more solid; the eyes were no longer two holes but had in them a burning life with clearly delineated bright yellow pupils.

Suddenly it was no longer a fire but a real shape, a dragon-like creature that radiated power, its skin pulsing as if the fire still burned just below its surface.

The chanters suddenly stopped and fell forward, prostrating themselves before the great neck and mean-looking head of the fire dragon. Its yellow eyes flashed, and I could see the corners of its mouth turn upward in a kind of grotesque, monstrous smile.

Suddenly it stopped, turned straight toward where I lay hidden, and roared, fire belching from its throat.

There was something about its power and attitude that struck fear into me. I gave an involuntary cry as I realized that it knew I was there and wasn't thrilled about the idea.

Suddenly the humans were on their feet and rushing toward me, crying manically and looking hostile as all hell. I turned and tried to fly off, but it was as if I didn't have the wings at all. Something was preventing me from becoming airborne, and without those wings I would have to fight or run.

I tried running.

They came after me, screaming like banshees. The only thing that saved me, I guess, was the fact that folks who are stark naked and painted up don't usually have anything to shoot or throw.

I wasn't exactly speedy, though; this body was not built for long periods of running on the ground. It had an awkward center of gravity, and the wings stuck out inconveniently.

I turned in toward the forest growth, knowing that they could navigate the paths in there better than I could but that my claws could hold on to wood a lot more firmly than bare feet could.

First I had to get up there, though. Where I'd thought it would be an easy climb became more sheer and restrictive to somebody my shape. I twisted, turned, dodged, and suddenly came up against a stone wall. Turning, frantic, I saw them coming and watched as they fanned out to hem me in, my head looking to and fro for someplace to run.

Now that they had me, though, they seemed less sure of themselves, closing in very slowly and cautiously. Their flesh wouldn't provide much protection against my claws.

"All right!" I yelled at them, my voice sounding hoarse and labored. "Just stay back! I mean you no harm, but if you come, I will have no choice but to hurt as many of you as possible!"

I wasn't sure if any of them could understand my speech, but they did seem a bit startled and stopped for a moment. Then, though, they came slowly forward once more. Suddenly, one of them, a silverish young woman with designs in red and blue, barked an order in a strange tongue and they stopped again.

She frowned, looking me over as if I were some bizarre specimen—which I guess I was—and then shook her head slowly from side to side.

"Cory?" she said as much as asked. "Is that *you*? What in hell are *you* doing down *here*? And where did you get those *wings*?"

III

OLD WINE AND NEW

It was so startlingly out of place and moment that I couldn't believe I had actually heard it.

"W-what?"

"Jeez, Cory!" the woman exclaimed, a bit disgusted. "Snap out of it! It's me, Wilma. Remember? We arrived together."

My mouth fell open. Finally I managed, "Wil-wilma?"

"Take it easy; get your wits together," she told me. "I'll call off the folks here." She turned and said a lot of stuff in that strange guttural language. I swear most of them looked disappointed, but one by one they turned and went back the way they'd come, probably to the fire circle.

"Wilma—what? What are *you* doing here? And like *that*?"

"I asked you first. Never mind. This is where I came before, even in the old life. It's the netherworld, where the shamans of the earth gather. I guess that's why you were sent this way by whoever it was you said. They wanted you to link up with me. Now—your turn!"

I managed to ease up a bit, although I was shaking a little. "I—I blew it, that's all. Waited too long to put myself into the world, and my new self got himself a broken back and partly severed spinal cord, that's what. I've been stuck ever since as basically a neck and an arm and a half."

First slowly, then probably too quickly and too disjointedly, I poured out the whole situation, the details, everything up to and including the Stanford University compound and the Stanford Medical Center approach, all the way up to my visit from the March Hare. She let me run on, aware, I guess, that she was the first really friendly person who could understand what was going on and still not be a threat I'd known since coming here.

Finally I ran down, and she said, "Well, that's tougher than me, I guess, although I'm not any great shakes. I didn't have much book-learning education back then, and I don't have any more here. I got a thinner body, which is kinda nice, although I know it won't last, and a little different name and tribal group, but it's not all *that* different. The big difference here is, 'cause I had more experience in the old life, I got more knowledge and power than the big men who thought they was in tune with the spirit world here, and they're scared of me a little bit. Overall it don't bother me none, but I'm just as trapped as I ever was. I come down here not only to gain some knowledge and power but also to get away from them up there a little."

"Wilma, tell me. Is this place different than you remember? Or is it the same?"

She thought a moment. "Pretty much the same, I guess. They even remembered and recognized me."

"Huh? There are people here?"

"Something like that. Not exactly people. You ain't exactly people yourself at the moment. Close enough. But I didn't mean people in any sense. I meant the spirits. You saw one. They're real, and they're here, and they have great power. They can give and draw energy to and from all things, since all things have their own distinctive energy patterns. I can't explain it much more'n that."

That fascinated me. "But they're the same? And they *remembered* you? They *recognized* you?"

She nodded. "Sure. They don't see like we do. They only see that pattern inside. The same pattern that's in the trees, even the rocks, in the waters, and in the air. The elemental patterns."

I thought I was on to something. If this place was the same from universe to universe, then we had to be somewhere fixed, someplace around which other things changed.

"Wilma, how big *is* this place?"

"As big as the whole inside of the world," she responded.

I sighed. "Wilma, the world isn't hollow. Even the illusion of the world isn't hollow."

"Maybe it is. How can we know for sure?" she retorted. "After all, this place has turned out to be more real than Yakima was."

"Point taken," I conceded.

"Don't worry, though. This place ain't on the same plane as the other world. This is the spirit world. It's like the region we come through to get from Yakima to here. It connects all things and all people and all places."

That was a fascinating concept. "You mean you can go other places from here without going through the intervening space?"

"Near as I understand you, no. Not like that. What I *can* do is talk with them, walk with them, act with them, like in the circle back there. No matter where I leave, I'm gonna wind up where I come in 'cause my body's not really here. It's in a trance *there*. But there are folks here from India, from China, Japan, the Himalayas, central Africa, even *France*! We all come here and talk shop and swap what we know and get together to learn and interact and pray to the gods together. Then we go home and wake up, and we got a little more than when we put ourselves under, that's all. If we do it right, then the spirits will guide us and grant us a little more power and skill. If we don't, maybe we lose some."

I was disappointed. "You mean I'm going to wake up in the same old place in bed, just like before?"

"Yeah, that's almost certain. Sorry, Cory. I'd love to be able to bring you out where I am, but it ain't the way the system works."

My hopes dashed, I said nothing for a while. Finally I decided to change the subject. "Has anybody from Al's old group come close to you? Or maybe Walt?"

She seemed to be thinking over her answer. Finally she said, "Well, no to both in the sense of folks like you and me who know that *this* place is more real than the so-called real world. But I did come across one or two of the dead and reborn."

"You did! Where? Yakima?"

"Nope. I don't get to Yakima this go-round. We got a Native American Cultural Institute in Seattle—ain't that a great title? I been there a few times as a native guide, more or less. The medicine men get to get rid of me for a while, I get to go to the big city, and, you know, pretty Injun maiden sits around fake campfire and tells the yokels whose grandparents stole the land and penned us up how important we were so we can supplement tribal funds and maybe buy a few necessities with our share. I seen a couple of folks who I *knew* had to be new versions of old folks, but not the sort that would know me."

"Who, exactly?"

"Wouldn't do to say right now. It wouldn't be right."

"*Who*, Wilma? Tell me."

"Well, we had this get-together with folks who do other native Disneylands a few months back, and I saw a real familiar face out of context. Young Japanese-Hawaiian girl in a *real* sexy and revealing outfit, particularly for this supermoral time. Long black hair, big brown eyes. Danielle Tanaka she said her name was."

"Well I'll be damned! So it *is* true! I saw the picture of Rob, but I wasn't impressed with the sex change there."

"Oh, she's all woman, all right. I can't say how much of a total change there was, 'cause if you think, I never actually knew the old Dan Tanaka. The only reason I made the connection other than the name was 'cause we was so linked up in that last bit of business, I sort of saw you talk to him and then blow him away."

I nodded. "Figures. And that means you might even bump into a whole lot of folks who were at the company, both incarnates and reincarnates, and never recognize them, too."

"Well, I thought of that, but I ain't been too worried over it. My name's totally different this time, my tribe's different and moved a bit, and I'm a *lot* better lookin' and a little younger. They'd only know me by that little bit of business and Stark's descriptions, so I never felt in danger."

"Don't underestimate him or any of them," I warned her. "Remember, we're supposed to have been through this many, many times, and you're one of us. So somebody like Al, who has, I guess, ten lifetimes worth of memories and knowledge and experience, has probably seen you before in this kind of circumstance."

"I was never worried," she assured me. "Not unless I have to actually go against them like last time. I didn't know what the hell I was doin', and I didn't know nothin' 'bout facin' down them bastards."

"Like I did? It was all by ear. And now—well, it looks like in my case it was all for nothing, too. Frankly, I'd just as soon stay here, even like this, alone and outside the sun, than go back and wait for them to come for me or finish me off. I can't do *anything!*"

She thought that over, then asked me, "What would you do if you *could* do whatever you wanted? That is, if you were like you used to be?"

Having that question turned back on me was unexpected. What *would* I do? This incarnation business threw everything into a cocked hat. Career, marriage, kids, ambition of any sort—what the hell difference did any of it make? What *would* I be doing if I could get around normally?

Would I be playing the game? Probably not. Not find the god, or at least the template maker, who might not even know that he or she *was* the maker of the world. I mean, suppose I did and supposed I killed that one and got to the next level first? Then I'd have the same cadre of folks who managed to slip out of it gunning for me; one would eventually get me, and then there we'd go all over again, right? I never did like to play games I couldn't win or lose. I'd never been a big one for computer games even when I was helping program them, because the best ones you could never really beat and the ones you could, you got tired of after a couple of weeks.

Hell, that was the problem with *this* and with all the violence and nastiness of Al Stark and Les Cohn or whoever they were this time around.

You couldn't even lose.

"This isn't a long-term existence I look forward to," I told her honestly. "I mean, even healthy and all. It's all like variations on an endless present piggybacking on somebody's imagination—or, in the case of the one we got now, lack of it. You can't stay out of it, though. They'll come after us eventually unless they get real lucky, in which case we'll be left to live our lives and die and wake up and not remember anything and be at their mercy again."

"I've thought about the same things," she admitted. "There is a great deal of pressure on me to marry, to have married by now, and have kids. I have to admit I kind of like that idea, but how can I? You want your kids to have a future, not be canceled out. You want your husband to amount to something, to be in some ways a creator, even if only of ideas and visions. I can't pretend on that level. Not on that level. But what can we *do*?"

I sighed. "If I had the guts, and some way to figure things out, and a lab that might be able to make sense of things, I'd like to steal a Brand Box," I told her. "I'd like to find out how it works. How it retains and activates its programming even across these existences. Where it came from and exactly what it does. Where is all this information accessed from? I'm with you—I don't want to prolong this, I want *out*. Otherwise, let me live my reincarnated lives in places and forms that the others, the crazy ones, can't find so at least I can live from moment to moment, life to life. Deep down, though, I want to *solve* this."

She nodded. "Do you think you could, though?"

"No. Not alone, anyway. And yet somehow I think that I'm being pushed into that. Whoever or whatever Walt and his weird crew of Martians represent is one faction; the Wonderland characters are another, whoever or whatever they are. And Brand—where the hell *is* he if he's not the Wonderland creations? Did he find a way out? Is he still trapped in one of the Boxes? Is he playing outside the rules of the rest of us?" I sighed. "*That's* what I'd be doing. Maybe I'd flop, but so what? I want to turn the tables. I'm sick of being a victim of everybody else's factions. I want *answers*, damn it!"

She smiled and winked at me. "Go back to your home. Give me the name of the place and whatever details you can give me about finding it. I will find it. You stay there and stay alive, and I will see what I can do about the rest."

I felt no great surge of hope, but still I asked, "Do you really think you can do anything?"

She grinned. "I have more power than you might suspect. And I can get here without monster bunnies banishing me to this place!"

"Wait! What if—?" I began, but she shook her head and waved off further questions.

"I don't know what we can do. Just stay where you are and in one piece and we'll see what we can do together. Promise me!"

"I—I'll do whatever I can, considering my limits."

She spit and looked angry. "Don't run and don't hide in your problems no matter how bad they are! You draw rabbits because that is the basis of your courage. See if you can draw *lions* instead, like the old Cory Maddox did!"

Her arm went up and made a pass, and before I could say or do anything else I felt a push. All the light in the inner world went out, and I was falling down another rabbit hole.

I woke up in my own bed in the sanatorium in Vancouver with a painful cry from deep in my throat. I was drenched in sweat, but it was daylight, and for a rare change the sun was streaming in my window.

The trouble with these sorts of things, I'd learned the last time, was that you were never sure they really happened until you had some follow-up. Did I *really* get visited by the March Hare, or was that wish fulfillment? Did I *really* go into some sort of netherworld and find Wilma, or was that more of the same?

That was another big problem with this stuff. You could never be certain of the reality of *anything*.

A day went by with nothing happening, then two, then three. I was just about to give up on the whole thing. But while I was outside smoking a cigar and watching the dramatic clouds go by after a storm one afternoon, I got a visit from somebody I didn't want to see at all.

"Hello, Maddox," said Sister Mary Alice.

Close up, Alice McKee looked older and tougher than I'd remembered her, although she had been a fairly tough cookie from the start.

"I wondered if your being here was an accident," I responded. "I guess not. I thought you'd left, though."

"I had. I'm going back and forth now until I wind up some last-minute work in this area. I don't really start at Stanford until the spring semester."

"You make a good nun," I commented sourly.

"And you make an excellent quadriplegic," she retorted with a nasty smile. "I find being a sister quite satisfying as well as convenient. It's almost natural, although I admit I wouldn't have thought of it myself. Curious, really. In all the lives I can remember my parents pushed me to the religious life. In none of the old ones did it take. In this one it did. And in the last one and this I wound up with the same degree, same specialty, same field, doing much the same thing. I am not pleased with the extreme conservatism of the Church in this instance, which not only wouldn't consider women priests but still says the Latin mass, but I can work around it."

I couldn't quite get a handle on her. Was she taunting me, or was she really being sincere? She clearly had an ulterior motive in seeking me out after ignoring me for so long, though. I decided to let her set the pace. I'd had a lot of practice here having intellectual fun with Father Pete and a few of the other guys in the quad. There were, understandably, a few folks around with whom you didn't take this kind of tack if you valued your life and health, but this wasn't one of those cases.

"Funny," I told her. "In both the lives I can remember I had much the same sort of feeling toward the Catholic Church that you do. I didn't think the Pope was anything beyond the administrative head of a large church, I thought women could be fine as clergy, that sort of thing. I probably have the same ideas on birth control, abortion, and the like as you. But you know, they always called me a Protestant."

She sniffed. "You will never understand."

"I understand perfectly. Every founder of a major Protestant movement started as a Roman Catholic. Luther, Calvin, Henry the Eighth—you name 'em. But *you*—you are the strangest of them all. You *know* this isn't real. That even the Church, this retreat, the Bibles, and the rest over here aren't real. The closest thing to a religion that we know of in our existence is probably Hinduism, although without the castes.

Maybe Buddhism, with its Hindu-style reincarnation and our own ignorance of and search for the that which is behind all that."

"You know better," she responded. "You know that this *must* be a reflection of a reality somewhere. That these universes begin with the original premise of the first in, but that all the details are then filled in by copying from an original. I think even *you* have figured that out by now, Maddox."

I nodded. "But I don't know if it's a current or past reality or one just outside, with us trapped in some gigantic Brand Box reflected over and over again in the mirror, or if it's much more complicated than that. Still, I'll grant your point, and religion *is* faith at its heart. It's just that I don't see a lot of faith in the people you run with, and ye are judged by the company ye keeps. You're a brilliant woman, McKee. Why are you with those power-mad megalomaniacs?"

"You've only had limited exposure in your active memory," she replied. "I've been around a lot longer. A *lot* longer. Five lives worth of memories so far, some *very* different from this and the last world. I'm not the kind that can accept oblivion every cycle, Maddox, and I'm also not one to let everything be in the hands of powerful forces when I have no powerful friends of my own—like your current position. You've only seen the window dressing, Maddox. You haven't seen the machine. They run it, they control it, although they don't know what the heck it is or how it does what it does. Brand—now, *he* was different. *He* seemed to actually understand some of it, to be getting close to how it worked, to being able to not merely tap and drive but change the way things worked. When he suddenly woke up and realized he was just delivering what the others needed to people he detested, he figured a way out. I have no idea how he did it, but it's beyond me to duplicate it, so I have to go a different route, just like the rest. They're in control because they have the keys to the car, so to speak. Until I can get those keys or a duplicate set, I'm a passenger. It's the only smart way to be, Maddox."

I had figured it was like that. Still, I said, "And you don't think your 'drivers' don't know that?"

"Sure. But it's the 50 million monkeys syndrome, Maddox."

"Huh?"

"Given an infinite amount of time, an infinite amount of lives, I'm going to be there when he forgets and leaves the keys in the other coat. Sooner or later it's bound to happen."

I was struck by how casual and open she was about all this. I didn't remember her ever being anything but stiff and cold with me and most other people. "Are you saying I'm playing ball for the wrong team?" I asked. "Heck, I don't even remember being invited to play."

She looked at me almost sweetly and smiled. "You weren't. And I'm not sure how much you will be playing this time, either. Frankly, you've never been much of a factor in all this. I think that's why they were so surprised last time when you roared up and complicated everything. We underestimated Slidecker, it appears."

"Huh? I never knew Walt was involved until *after* I got dragged down there. And I sure tried to avoid Cynthia Matalon. She scared me. Still does, I think, no matter what she became in this life."

"Oh, she's still dear little Cindy," Alice McKee told me. "And if anything, scarier yet. This gentle fifties kind of world isn't prepared for somebody like her, I think."

I frowned. "Hold it. She was your prisoner, just like Angel. You mean she switched from Walt to you? Or Al didn't kill her?"

Alice Mckee frowned. "No, she was—liberated. By Slidecker, we suspect. He took advantage of your disruption and killings to get inside when all attention was focused on you and your companion in the back. He retrieved Matalon, and we're not sure what else he might have taken. There was quite a mess in the labs."

It was odd; my "new" life had taken on such prominence that the time spent living it, even growing up in it, had seemed very real and perceptible, while my old life had faded almost to fantasy status. Then, in just a matter of a few months, the old reality had come back to the fore but had still seemed as if it had happened to somebody else, stimulated by the sight of the two nuns who hadn't been in the past life and then by a photo and article in *Time*. Now, with the March Hare's appearance and my visit to the underworld, wherever it was, I was sitting here, as much the *old* Cory Maddox as the new, if not more so. And that brought up a lot of questions, some just for curiosity, some a lot more pressing. I wanted to do this slowly, though, while McKee remained in a chatty mood.

"Tell me something. If you're really a nun and not just using it, how can you justify this? Getting in bed with Al, even on a strictly political level, seems, well, like hopping on board with Judas Iscariot."

"To you, perhaps. Not to me. He and his group seek the truth, and that's all the Church truly asks. They seek a secular truth, and their methods may not be your methods, but they are nonetheless valid."

I nodded sourly. "Yeah, like the Spanish Inquisition. That's your mind-set, Sister, and why I can't go along. It's the logic that says 'Okay, torture 'em. If they don't convert and die, then they'll be welcomed as martyrs in heaven if we were wrong about them, or they'll go to hell as they deserved if we weren't.' The old witch-ducking test. If she drowns, she wasn't a witch."

To my surprise, it really pissed her off. "And who made you the arbiter of right and wrong, Maddox?" she spit. "You spout the good and noble line, but you believe in nothing. Five lives I've lived that I can remember. *Five!*

And in none of them have *you* actually done anything positive for *anybody*. Not one! In most cases you were a shrinking violet, keeping out of it, always hiding behind somebody. You'd get some nerve and maybe act once or twice, but only when others had already gone to their doom and there was no other choice. And then—what? You got yourself killed trying to talk your 'reason' to others, or there was this last time, when all you managed to do was blow up half the station and make a run for it—after running away for a couple of *years*, taking yourself completely out of things. Some builder!"

"Just because I am wrong doesn't mean you are right," I retorted. "I guess what you are and where you are really *are* right. True believers always think that they have the answers, and everybody who doesn't agree with them a hundred percent is their enemy. I don't believe in absolutes."

"Just cop-outs," she said acidly. "A rationale for having no convictions at all."

"Pragmatists keep the world turning. When the true believers take over, people get hurt, even killed."

She sighed. "We could go on and on like this, but to what end? *You* have all the time in this world, but *I* do not."

Here it comes, I thought, tensing.

"My people believe that you should not be off in the medical center," she told me flatly. "They were perfectly content to leave you here, but they don't like the idea of you involving a lot of smart people with connections outside our little family in all this. On the other hand, partially thanks to you, our supply of experienced programmer types to help run things is drastically reduced in this plane. We don't *need* you, understand—if we did, we would have invited you down before this—but we could *use* you now that things are changing for you."

"And if I'm not suitably enthusiastic?"

She chuckled. "You're not that stupid. What are you gonna do? Run like last time? Tough to do on one arm and a battery charge, and even if others came and helped you, what sort of existence would you have? You need a full-time nursemaid and support setup to take care of you, and you know it. Romantic ideas of being on the run, spying on us, and perhaps hitting us where it hurts aren't very practical for a head and an arm. We can't just leave you as before—you'd wind up in someone else's arms for sure, perhaps someone inconvenient to us and with knowledge we'd rather not spread. That means you either come with us, and with the proper enthusiasm and work ethic, or one evening you'll get a visitor, perhaps after you are asleep, and in the morning the bed check nurse will find that you've expired during the night of what they will say is 'natural causes.' It takes a bullet wound or a hatchet chop to get an autopsy in a place like this."

The truth hurt, but there it was. "And this is my invitation, huh? The trouble is, all that was almost a lifetime ago. I managed to come up with the old neural connector design because it's something I put so much time into in the past that I could draw it again in my sleep, equations and all. But the routine of actually creating—hell, when I did it, I realized I didn't fully understand it anymore myself."

She sighed and shook her head like a frustrated schoolteacher. "Cory, Cory! You don't get it, do you? You don't need to remember like that. One session with your Brand Box and it will all come back in spades. Why, I've been able to output my own doctoral thesis from two lives ago twice now to printers just by using my Box."

I began to realize that there was a *lot* more I had to learn about this whole operation. "Die now or die later" wasn't actually a wonderful choice, but in a circumstance like this "later" seemed the better choice. Who was I killing by making that decision?

"You know you've got yourself a programmer," I told her, resigned.

She smiled sweetly. "Of course we do. That's why it's already all been arranged. We—the both of us, along with some hired help—leave tomorrow."

Frankly, I didn't know throughout the rest of the day and into the evening whether I was depressed or excited. It was depressing to be so firmly in the hands of my enemies, even if I had called them down upon myself, but it was also *movement*. After all this time, after what to me was a lifetime spent ignorant of all this or crippled in a room or wheelchair with occasional outings and lots of doctors and therapists, I was finally going back into the belly of the whale. In some ways I was a player again, however limited.

The problem was, how the hell did I tell Wilma? She might well be on her way right now to Portland to spring me or confer with me in real time or do *something*, and here I was being carted off to Stanford. She would of course figure it out, particularly now that she knew about the installation there, but knowing that I was inside and getting in and out safely was something else. This wasn't some shaman underworld, and there were probably few trees in there to pop in and out of.

I wondered if she might not have been tempted to act very quickly. She'd said she was based in Seattle, and Seattle was only a few hours drive to the north. If all she was going to do was talk to me, she could phone or be here by midafternoon. The fact that she wasn't there by dinnertime made it clear she had some kind of plan or had run into some sort of opposition. I wished I knew which.

The truth was, I really wanted to get my hands, so to speak, on the controls of the computer and the Brand Boxes without being some sort of third-party invitee. There was so much I needed to know that could only be done hands-on, and Alice McKee had only increased the riddle with her talk of Brand Box memory from life to life, the moving of the whole complex between planes, and all the rest.

I also would have loved to have a real list of how many

people there were who were part of our group and not "VR" people like almost all the world. Somewhere between twenty-six and thirty-six, or so it was implied, but how could we know for sure? And what did it mean that Walt had his Brand Box? Did each of us have an individual Box there? How many Boxes were there, and were there ones for us and ones with programmed realities, or were the two types one and the same? I had to know.

I began to be terribly worried that somehow Wilma would rescue me.

"So you are leaving us today, eh?" Father Pete said with genuine regret in his voice.

I nodded. "Stanford. At least there I can use the one thing I have left: my brain."

"What of your parents? They are elderly and live across the river, do they not?"

That was a big emotional pang inside me, but it was one I had to accept. We'd talked about it on the phone the previous night, but Dad wasn't in shape even for a trip over to see me off and Mom couldn't leave him alone, so that was that. They were taken aback by the suddenness of all this but not unhappy that perhaps I could make something of myself. I knew intellectually that they were virtual constructs of my parents, possibly from my own memories and now running on their own as part of this vast program, but damn it, they were real enough to me, and it was very tough. Even tougher when you had a distant but still distinct memory going back a whole lifetime of attending a certain funeral for somebody you loved yet were reconciled to never seeing again who now was there once more.

"They're happy for me. I've been mostly a burden to them, and they're not in the best of health, as you know, Father," I told him.

"And yet you do not seem to me to be overjoyed at this move. I thought that might be it."

"No, that's not it. Sorry, Father, but I don't think I could explain it to you or anybody. Still, I'd like you to do me a favor if you will."

"Yes?"

"I have some friendships from a number of quarters and one that just recently was renewed after a long time not hearing from one another. If anybody comes by and asks for me, will you be certain to tell them where I am? Tell them that I went down to Stanford with Sister Mary Alice and that I'm under the care of the Henreids? Will you promise me that you'll do that?"

He nodded. "Still, if you don't really want to go, if something is pushing you—"

"No, I want to go. I just don't want to be cut off from everybody else, you or old friends or whatnot. The more people who know where I am and who I'm with, the better."

He frowned and looked thoughtfully at me. "You sound almost as if you expect to be held prisoner or something."

"No, not that, but you must have read the *Time* piece about this place. It's government, security, you name it. They'll have employees looking out for me, but they won't work for me and won't be giving tons of information away. I just want to make sure, dependent as I am, that people aren't brushed off. Okay?"

He nodded and smiled. "Okay, I promise. I'm confident that Sister Mary Alice will keep a good watch over you as well."

You bet she will, Father, I thought sourly. *At least until they can get their flunkies all around me.*

Father Pete and a couple of custodial types helped me pack, and it was discouraging to see how little I had that was actually mine. My whole life, it seemed, at least *this* life, could fit into two medium-size suitcases.

I made the rounds and said good-bye to the patients I'd known to some degree and to the night staff as well. It was odd, but I'd been closer to the staff than to the others; I just seemed to have more in common with them. Most of the guys in the dorm were either bitter or pretty much resigned and without hope of any kind. I could understand them, but that didn't make for great personal friendships.

Around six in the evening, a van pulled up outside and the sliding door opened to reveal a wheelchair lift. Sister Mary Alice was there, along with a driver and an attendant, both in medical whites but without any insignia or other identifying things that might have said what they were or where they were from. The attendant opened the back doors and put my bags in, then came over toward me. As he did, I got a good look at his face and let out an involuntary gasp. This was going to be a lot harder than I had thought.

"Hi," he said in the most genuinely friendly tone he had. "I'm Erik Viskovski—spelled W-r-z-kowski, but don't bother to remember it 'cause nobody else can. Rick's good enough for me. I've been hired to be your flunky, you might say. You name it, I'm the one who'll get it if you can't." He frowned. "What's the matter? You look like you've seen a ghost or somethin'."

"Um, ah, that's all right. I just, well, you remind me very much of somebody I knew once, long ago. Just about the same face."

"Yeah? What was his name? Maybe it's some relative of mine."

"Not likely," I responded, thinking fast. "Besides, the one I knew is dead now. Still, the reason you gave me the turn wasn't the resemblance so much as the fact that my old friend was a woman."

"Yeah? That's funny. Guess I'll have to grow a beard or somethin', huh?"

"No, no, that's all right. A lot of people have those kinds of faces, and it's no big deal. Still, it gave me a brief turn." I paused, trying to change the subject. "You're coming with us?"

"All the way and maybe beyond," he responded. "Tell you the truth, I'm in the navy. Pharmacist's mate on the destroyer

Huey P. Long out of Bremerton. We just finished the eleventh month of a six-month tour in the Red Sea, and I was due a shore assignment. You're it. Must be somebody important to rate like this, I figure. If you're not, pretend that you are, anyway."

"*Al's in naval intelligence . . .*"

Clever boy, Commander Albert Starkey. *You son of a bitch . . .*

It was startling how alike in mannerisms, way of speaking, all those little things Rick was to Riki, aka Angel. I knew what they'd said about the reincarnates changing sex and I had come close to that myself, and I remembered Wilma's comment on Danielle Tanaka, but to actually *see* it, and in somebody you knew so well . . . Hell, I'd lived with, slept with, fallen in love with Riki; clearly there was more to this than half an octave lower in the voice and a five o'clock shadow. There was enough of her in him to make it down-right *eerie*.

The driver, too, had a somewhat familiar face, although he did not arouse the same sort of reaction in me that Rick had. I'd shot Jamie Cholder to death with the same action that I'd used shooting Dan Tanaka. "James" was a lot heavier and a bit older and meaner-looking than Jamie had been. I might not have fully noticed the close resemblance if I had not been prepped for it but instead had encountered him in isolation.

Still, it was kind of nice to see somebody you'd blown away walking around again, male or not. It kind of lifted a bit of guilt from deep inside that I hadn't realized was there until now.

Alice McKee smiled, her face framed by the habit of her or-der, and knew exactly what I was thinking.

"Fascinating, isn't it?" she asked sweetly.

"Yeah. I assume this was for my benefit, too."

"Why else? Besides, you know the policy on gathering in the clan. It will take some work to figure out whose game *this* rather pale plane came out of."

"Well, it's not *my* kind of life," I told her, kind of walking around the subject as Rick closed the doors and clamped down my wheelchair and Jim started the van.

"Oh, we *know* that," she assured me. "Nor mine."

Father Pete stuck his head in the window. "Good-bye and good luck!" he called to me. "May God be with you both!"

Sorry, Father, I thought sourly. *God can be with her or with me, but I sincerely doubt if He can be with both of us.* But aloud I called, "Good-bye, Father Pete! Maybe we'll talk on the phone or at least write!"

"By all means let's keep in touch!" he returned, and backed away. Jim Cholder put the van in gear, and we started down the access road toward the highway.

If Al was gathering the clan again, Wilma might well be in danger. That might have been why she had not contacted me within the day and a half since we'd talked and why she was still keeping out of sight. If she couldn't track me to where I was going, though, she should have turned in her Indian heritage.

Of much more concern to me was the presence of Rick. It was a reminder, I suppose, but it was also going to be hard as hell. Besides, how could he ever figure out or understand why it was a problem?

We headed west, then turned south and crossed the Columbia and went through Portland. It was already quite dark, yet there was something both familiar and upsetting about looking out and seeing lots of cars filled with people going to and from all the various mundane places people visit all the time. We passed some shopping centers, bright stores, and brighter restaurants, and it was a reminder of how much of normal life I had been cheated out of and a reminder that the world was going on with its business even if I wasn't there.

"You didn't get out much, I guess," Rick commented.

"No, and it was deliberate," I told him. "It's kind of like coming from the funeral of your family and seeing that the whole world's going about its normal business oblivious to your tragedy and uncaring about the loss. You don't want to think about life just going on like before when you're stuck out of it like I am. You like to pretend that the world is what you can see and those you can talk to and that all this is like some TV show or movie. Not real, not part of the world that revolves around you. You know it's there, sure, but you don't want to think about it much. It hurts."

"Well, there's no reason why you couldn't go out once in a while once we're settled in down south," he noted, not grasping the point. "We'll be close to Frisco, after all."

"*You* enjoy San Francisco," I told him. "I doubt if I'll even go out on the campus much. You've got no idea what it's like to be a freak around a bunch of healthy college kids with raging hormones and a sense of indestructibility. No, you got a pretty boring assignment with me. I'd request a transfer."

"I'm sure we'll get along just fine," he assured me.

We exited a few miles south of the city, and I suddenly had no idea where we were. "What's this?"

"It's a two-day drive down there," Sister Mary Alice noted. "Why waste that time when we can get the government to give us a bit more speed, even if not much more comfort?"

"Can the government transport a nun?" I responded a bit flippantly. "I mean, what about separation of church and state?"

"Oh, I think we'll be able to look the other way on that one," Rick responded just as lightly.

Where we were going turned out to be not a military base but a small civil airfield. We drove out past the small administrative building and Civil Air Patrol headquarters and onto a rough Tarmac, pulling up next to a plane that looked a lot like a DC-3 from the days of World War II. The tail was down on a tiny rear wheel, the nose was turned up, two large wheels were chocked under the wings, and there were two propellers, one on each side.

"This thing's an antique anywhere," I noted. "We're not gonna fly in *this*, are we?"

"Sure. Why not?" McKee responded. "It's actually a left-over from an old reserve unit that kept it so that the officers could fly junkets, pretty much. It's got reasonable room, can get us to San Jose Airport in two, maybe three hours, and it's something that can be used off the books, as it were. We just have to return it."

"Who's flying it? Anybody I know?"

"Not that I can think of," she responded. "At least nobody told me if they are. Just a few reservists who want to chalk up some extra flight time and temporary duty."

It was almost a relief to see that that was true. As far as I could tell, I'd never seen any of those guys before, nor were they particularly interested in us except for the fact that I was crippled and needed extra attention. Rick was maybe five-ten and looked in good shape physically, but he would have trouble lifting me. Not so Jim Cholder, who, with Rick clearing the way and a little balancing help from the loadmaster on the plane, got me into a bulkhead seat and belted in comfortably. The air crew didn't seem unduly surprised to see a nun among the party, though, so I figured they'd been tipped off about Sister Mary Alice.

Rick took the aisle seat next to me; Cholder took the opposite window seat, but mostly because he was going to try to nod off and wanted the plane wall for extra head support. Sister Mary Alice sat in the aisle seat just behind us. "Comfy?" she asked.

"You'd think dear Al could have gotten a fancier plane," I grumbled.

"Oh, he probably could, but this is very convenient and is more or less off the books. Cheer up. I'd prefer better myself, but at least it isn't outfitted for a few dozen men to sit against the walls in their parachutes before jumping out."

She had a point.

We sat there for a few minutes while the pilot and copilot went through their checklist and the loadmaster stood just outside on the top step of the entry door smoking a last cigar. I had managed to be buckled in and still be at a slight angle, my back against both the wall and part of the seat, so I could turn my head and see a fair amount of the plane.

Two bells sounded, and then the engines started one by one, giving out less than reassuring puffs of smoke and sounding like they were missing half the time before finally catching and getting in sync. The loadmaster extinguished his cigar, came in, and pulled the rope which pulled the stair up into the plane and at the same time closed the door, which he then latched. He took a seat in the back, and we slowly taxied onto the runway.

It was already after eight at night, and there wasn't a heck of a lot of traffic in and out of Portland at that point and none out of this field, so it didn't take long before we were rushing down the runway and then lifting slowly into the air. It was a noisy plane and a noisy, bumpy ride, but I remembered hearing once that this family of airplanes was about the safest that ever flew.

In my old life I'd been in airplanes many times, and in my hallucination or whatever it was I'd had wings, but in *this* life, and with my most omnipresent memories, it was a novelty. I looked over at Rick, who was sort of leaning back, eyes shut, apparently trying to relax for a little while.

"Rick, can you turn me a bit so I can look out the window?" I asked him, feeling guilty about disturbing him.

He opened his eyes and nodded. "Sure." Clicking off his belt, he leaned over and pretty much turned me so that my back was flat against the seat.

"Thanks," I told him.

"Any time. That's what the job is," he responded, then settled back in his seat once more.

The turn so I could see out the window was pretty much a wasted effort, too, at least right now. Low clouds, which were to be expected in the Northwest, after all, seemed to blot out everything below, and there was only a sliver of a moon through wispy clouds above.

Everybody seemed to be catching a nap or some kind of rest. I couldn't twist enough to check on McKee, but I got the distinct impression that she was lightly snoring behind me. Cholder was awake, staring out the window on his side at nothing in particular, but seemed relaxed. For the first time I noticed that he was wearing a sidearm. Interesting uniform for an ambulance driver.

Rick was out as well. I was beginning to have the distinct impression that the two navy men had been pulled away at very short notice and had already had a long day with more to come.

Looking back at the sleeping Rick, I was again struck by how nearly identical the face was. He was clean-shaven, with nothing in the way of facial hair and just a military-style crew cut; there was little to differentiate the two. How astounded he would be, though, to peer inside my head and see the yang to his yin, the female Riki.

Looking at him like this, sleeping so peacefully and so innocently, I had one of those strange fantasy flashbacks I'd been prone to in both this life and the last, almost like an impossible memory without context.

Rick was there, looking much as he did now, but in jeans and a sweatshirt, his eyes an eerie but attractive dull green color instead of the brown he now had. It wasn't the last time; in this vision, he was the husband and I was the smaller, shorter wife with short curly brown hair and blue eyes. We were giggling, laughing, trading mock insults as young newlyweds often did, and we were painting a room, a room in our new house . . .

Just like that it was gone, faded into a simple fragmentary scene like a particularly vivid dream.

The last time, I'd been the big-shot programmer and she'd been the artist, but the feelings had often been the same. Wilma had been my friend, but Riki had always been my mate, my lover, at least more times than not.

Not this time. Apart from the fact that we were two guys,

which some folks didn't have problems with and others did, there wasn't anything of me worth mentioning below the shoulders.

Well, I'd try hard as hell not to make *this* kind of mistake again if I had the chance to remember it, even if I had to relive my whole damned childhood in real time. It didn't make a lot of difference, anyway; once you inserted yourself, you had all the memories just as if you'd lived them.

Things got a little choppy while I was just sitting there thinking, and a small pamphlet was jarred out from the overhead ledge and dropped down into my lap. I thought it was odd that it would make such a convenient drop, and I picked it up with my good hand and looked at it. Nothing printed on the front, two small staples holding it together. Odd. I opened it and discovered that there was only a typeset poem inside. I wondered what the heck the reserves would have in a poem, and I started to read it:

> *How doth the little crocodile*
>   *Improve his shining tail,*
> *And pours the waters of the Nile*
>   *On every golden scale!*
>
> *How cheerfully he seems to grin,*
>   *How neatly spreads his claws,*
> *And welcomes little fishies in*
>   *With gently smiling jaws!*

Something suddenly struck the airplane with great force. It wasn't enough to spin it out of control, but it was nonetheless like a giant hand not hitting but slapping the top. It was a good argument for keeping your seat belt fastened; my body and those of the others so rudely awakened strained to be free and float violently to the ceiling.

"Holy shit! What the hell was that?" I heard the pilot say.

Now everybody in the back was awake and panicked and

trying to talk all at once. Outside, there was still nothing but darkness.

The blow came again, no stronger but no weaker, in almost the same place, causing the plane to bounce around the sky like mad. I wondered how much altitude we had and how far from the mountains we might be.

"It's like something's hitting us on the roof!" Rick said nervously, looking up as yet a third *thump* was felt, this time knocking the lights out momentarily.

I heard McKee saying the rosary over and over behind me and couldn't help thinking that maybe the nun bit wasn't all an act. Unlike the others, she and I knew that even a plane crash wouldn't be the end, but who wanted to go that way? Pain was still pain, and a reincarnation without prior memory wouldn't be much different from real death for all practical purposes. It was crazy, but even as I was, with everything happening now, I didn't want to go out.

The pilot turned off all lights, apparently as convinced as we were that something fairly large, if unimaginable, was actually attacking the plane.

"Mayday! Mayday! Hello, Eugene. Hello, Eugene. Severe turbulence encountered; am attempting to make an emergency landing at civil field north of your city. Please put me on scope. I—"

Thump! Bang!

There were now the sounds of an aircraft in trouble and the sensation of a not altogether controlled fall. It was totally dark, black as pitch inside and out, and I don't think I was ever more scared in my life than this, even back in the old labs and inside that tunnel between realities. Everybody was either yelling or praying. I could hear air rushing in, and my ears popped painfully.

And then there was sudden, total, complete silence, as if everything in the world was standing perfectly still.

I suddenly opened my eyes and gave out a cry that froze half-uttered.

I was in an unfamiliar bed, in an unfamiliar room, and I

wasn't very familiar with myself. I wasn't crippled in the least because I wasn't in my own familiar body. I was somebody else, but I had no idea who or whether this was another reality or something totally new.

Whatever it was, it wasn't something in the rules that had been explained to me.

I could remember back two lives, as programmer and as paraplegic, but nothing about this one at all. It didn't take any thought, though, to realize that I was definitely not a small child and that, impossibly, I was suddenly a girl.

IV

TURNING INTO ALICE

For over forty years I'd lived and grown up in a world I thought I knew, one that was hardly perfect but at least had definite rules and made me relatively comfortable.

Then that world had been yanked from me and replaced first with an insane fun house look and feel that said "anything goes" and in which nothing was certain. In that world both Ricki and I had become two entirely different people and then had combined with Wilma to produce a tremendously powerful unit we couldn't fully comprehend. That had ended when we'd been shoved down a bizarre connecting tube past even stranger creations and into a whole second life, but I had been convinced that I knew the new rules, at least as far as I could. If you died, you lost conscious memory of having lived before and were reborn as a member of the opposite sex in a universe that came partly from a computer and partly from somebody else's head but looked real. If you made it out alive, you remained the same sex and retained your memories.

I'd gone down in that plane, no question about it. So how come I remembered everything up to that point but nothing of this new world in which I was most certainly an adult? Did Wonderland, after all, have no underlying logic?

It had been unnerving in the past to face others who'd remembered me as a woman while I had no such memory or repressed identity and was a naturally heterosexual man. I'd used Angel's body briefly, but that had been more as a tool than as an identity. I'd never felt female in that body or any other that I could remember, save some fantasylike snippets of dreams, or particularly wanted to. Now, suddenly, here I was, with *none* of the preparation growing up female gives you, let alone the exhaustive memories I'd had in my second life. I didn't have the foggiest idea what the hell was going on in this crazy existence.

I got up and sat on the side of the bed. Well, I sure wasn't Miss Body Beautiful, at least not in the model sense, unless the artist was somebody like Rubens. Most women I had known would have said I was fat, but my own perspective was not theirs and the proper word was "chubby." The breasts were a fair size, though, big enough so that while I clearly slept by choice in the buff, I nonetheless slept with a bra on.

My observations continued. The place was a small studio apartment, one fair-sized room but nicely arranged. The bed was queen-size, but there didn't seem to be anybody else's stuff around, at least not obviously.

I was also short, not disproportionately or unusually so, but short. The step stool with the handle was needed to get things out of the cabinets and other, higher places. Maybe five-two, tops. Looking around with nothing specific in mind, I couldn't help thinking that nothing in the place seemed new or recently maintained or painted. It was a cheap place in a poor neighborhood but apparently not a horribly dangerous one. There was a dead bolt on the door and a chain as well, but not the whole plethora of defensive locks I'd seen all too often.

The john was more a water closet in the literal sense: toilet, basic shower, no tub, and little else. An old weathered vanity just outside it was clearly the toilet, sink, and makeup area. The back of the door did have what I was looking for, a full-length mirror of sorts, although it was dirty and cracked. Still, it would do.

The young woman I saw looking back at me from there was, almost surprisingly, not at all a surprise. It was almost as if I'd known pretty much what would be looking back at me before I'd actually looked, if that made any sense at all. Chubby, kind of blocky in a way, with a wide but cheery face and high cheekbones, a dark olive complexion that seemed Mediterranean, big brown eyes, and naturally curly shoulder-length dark brown hair. In her late teens or early twenties, certainly no more than that. What stood out in the mirror but didn't so much on self-examination were clear stretch marks in the abdomen, marks not made by weight or dieting, although they were hardly disfiguring or intrusive. The overall appearance was of someone casual yet independent. I didn't have a hell of a lot of body hair, but what was there I clearly hadn't been troubled to shave off. This was somebody who thought she was kind of cute just the way she was and didn't give a damn what others thought.

But who the hell was she, and why was she so familiar?

Hell, the place had hot and cold running water and a rattle-trap refrigerator and an old rusting electric range, so it wasn't the kind of culture that used spears and wrappings. I was more than half-surprised there wasn't at least an aged black and white TV around. What I did find was an old cord radio the size of a dictionary and weighing almost as much and a phonograph and a few well-worn vinyl records. The lack of CDs didn't surprise me; they hadn't been a mass-market phenomenon in the last world, either. The records themselves weren't much of a clue; they were basically pop/rock singers I'd have bought in either of my previous incarnations, which proved only that wrong rules or not, I was at least partly in the right place.

Figuring out why the rules I'd so recently learned were be-

ing violated—assuming, of course, that I hadn't just been lied
to—wasn't a high priority. Finding out who the hell I was and
some details about my new self were paramount. Even with
peeling paint and junk store furnishings, the fact that I was living on my own was encouraging. It meant I could avoid some
of the more intimate questions for a while.

I hunted up a teapot and put some water on to boil. The re-
mains of an old Melita-type coffee maker were there, with
some strong-smelling coffee, and I needed something to get
me wide awake and clearheaded right now. While the water
boiled, I checked out the clothes.

Not much of a wardrobe, really. Two pairs of clearly
secondhand jeans with small holes in different locales, a bunch
of T-shirts that looked like the kind given away by everybody
who gave away T-shirts, a couple of bras that had seen better
days, some stained panties, and a pair of old, worn tennis
sneakers. There was also a red jacket that was of equal age and
wear, not heavy but kind of medium-light, with the logo of the
Raiders on the back. Hmmm . . . The Oakland Raiders at that.
Had they moved in this incarnation?

On the peeling dresser I spied what was most valuable—a
ratty old leather purse. I opened it as if seizing on a cache of
gold bullion and dumped out the contents: eight bucks in ones,
a fair amount of coins, the key to what was probably my one
and only door, and several cards and papers. No car keys, so
that dashed that hope. No checkbook, either, which was worrisome. And a nasty-looking sharp pointed knife that was something of a sobering reminder that this was, unfortunately, a
modern world.

One card was an official California State Assistance Card,
something I'd never seen or heard of before, but it had a lousy
driver's license type of picture of me on it and some basics.
Name: Korinna Kassemi Ajani.

The name went through me like a small electric shock not
because of the obviousness of the first and middle names but
because it was so right. Kassemi was my mother's maiden

name. Where the Ajani had come from was yet to be explained, but it wasn't parental. Unless, of course—well, I might well have a different dad. That was somehow a bit unnerving, although I couldn't say why.

The woman in the mirror was definitely me as I was on the flip side of things, the Cori or Kori whom Al and McKee and the others had known. That was why she was so familiar. Sometimes, in past lives, in past existences, that had been my normal, expected reflection, give or take some height, or weight, or a bit here or there.

Height: 5'3". Weight: 168. Heavier than I thought. Damn. And who tells the truth to somebody making out a card like this? Birthdate 6-17-80. Yeah, but what year was it now? I rummaged through some of the other papers and came up with a consistent date of 02. That made me twenty-one or twenty-two, depending. That was okay with me. Old enough to sign contracts and drink a beer.

A couple of other papers gave what little extras I was going to get. The state welfare application was basically a workfare kind of thing in which I was classified as making enough to support myself in subsidized rent-controlled housing with food coupons. My educational level was listed as 8, which I took to mean I was a dropout at the minimal dropout age or, equally possible, had had a pregnancy. And where was the baby if I had had it? No indication. Well, it was something I couldn't help being curious about, particularly considering the stretch marks, but it wasn't something I really had to know now. Adopted, with others, dead, aborted—maybe it was better I *didn't* know.

Basically, though, everything said I was supporting myself, which was why I could have a place of my own. Everything also said I didn't earn enough to do much more than what I saw.

The county public assistance form said I was working as a waitress at Alice's Diner on San Pablo near University.

Huh? How was that? Alice's? Hmmmm . . . Probably just

somebody who got beat on "Alice's Restaurant," but who could know for sure? It might be nice if I knew where it was, where it was in relation to where *I* was, and when I worked there. The fact that most of the papers and cards were recent and new seemed to imply that I'd just started this existence. That would help me blend in and avoid some embarrassment.

The coffee was cool enough, and I almost gulped it down as I turned on the radio, discovering that I had to wait a couple of minutes for the *tubes* to warm up, of all things, and pulled on some clothes. I hoped the diner provided a uniform or wanted casual dress.

The station playing in the background was a San Francisco station, which meant I hadn't moved far from where I'd—crashed? Hard to tell where I was in the Bay Area, but it was a start.

There was a mimeographed sheet with the stuff that was folded up, and when I took a look at it, I went back to the card with my photo on it and turned it over. Mag stripe. Fascinating.

The implication of all this was that I'd just gotten all this new stuff the previous day, apparently spending all day getting it, although I'd had this place for a week or two. That was handy because the neighbors and I wouldn't be expected to know each other on a first-name basis and also because I had the information on the system right here. It was damned clever, too.

That card acted as my food stamps through a reader, would permit me to use mass transit with some limitations, and even was my MediCal free clinic card and prescription card. The whole thing was designed to prevent somebody from having much cash around that could go for drugs, booze, or whatever. Your paycheck would be sent to the county office, which would pay the rent and other fixed expenses, and then you could pick up what was left. That wasn't going to be very much, it was clear.

Of course, that didn't keep you from finding other means of

making money, but if you were obvious or aboveboard about it, the odds were that you'd lose benefits. And they could turn 'em off simply by canceling your card.

Okay, so that gave me the basics but didn't tell me how I had wound up in this sort of situation or why I seemed to be riding this edge between basic work and welfare. No obvious kids, no needle tracks, so why was I in this position? It didn't make a lot of sense, but what the hell. *Nothing* had made much sense since the first time I'd heard Cynthia Matalon's rendition of "Everything You Think You Know Is Wrong."

I figured I might as well adjust for the time being to this situation, at least until I could find out the new rules and maybe regain some control of my life.

The news came on the radio, but I barely paid attention until something caught my ear and then froze me in place.

"Rescue crews have located the place where an air force reserve C-47 aircraft went down in bad weather late last night in the mountains just northeast of Eureka. The plane, an antique kept for training purposes, was carrying civilian passengers on their way to Stanford for government work. Bad weather has prevented any helicopters from getting to the spot as yet, and there are no roads except forest service access back in there, but spotters state that there are definitely survivors and that the aircraft, although badly damaged, managed to make a belly landing in an area of clear-cut forest and remain intact. More information later on this breaking story . . ."

What the hell? It *couldn't* be! It just *couldn't* be! Could it? Could this still be the same world, the same reality, I'd been in before? Was I somehow now both here and in that plane wreck? I wanted to grab the radio and wring its electronic neck for more information, but it was impossible.

Was Drew Maddux inside that plane? Had I somehow managed to alter my position without knowing how I had done it? Was I dead or alive up there, and what did the other one know or remember?

Or, worse, could I be both of us at the same time?

This was getting weirder and weirder. Like I didn't already have enough to worry about in *either* situation!

I fixed a sandwich and tried to figure out what to do next. I wanted to just sit there until I got all the details on that crash, but how long would it be, how quickly would it be old news, and what good would it do me to know it two hours early, anyway? I sighed and drummed my fingers on the small table at which I was eating.

There wasn't any use sitting around, I decided at last. I didn't have much cash—even with the change it was probably no more than ten or eleven bucks—but at least I could begin to get some grounding here.

I stuffed what little there was back into the purse, leaving only the papers on the dresser. Then I took a look in the mirror and gave my face a little water and my hair a little brushing. I took a deep breath, slid back the dead bolt, undid the chain, and opened the door.

It was a pleasant day, not hot but certainly not requiring a jacket. I stepped out onto an outside concrete balcony that was kind of like a hall because of a thick iron grate that went along the entire outside of the balcony area. It wasn't a tall building—I was on the second of maybe six floors—but it had the stench and look of poverty. Still, there was some pride here, too. Yes, there was graffiti in English, Spanish, and maybe a couple of other tongues as well, but there wasn't a lot of trash. The tubed lighting, held inside a somewhat protected set of steel clamps, looked whole and seemed like it might actually light up at night. From the looks of the few people about, including a couple of very young kids running and screaming up and down the balcony, this was low-income subsidized housing, *not* a project. That helped. If folks were paying rent here and could be thrown out for misconduct and sent to really mean projects, they might well keep the place up.

Not that I was fooling myself that it was safe either for a

young woman alone or even for older men. You would still have a percentage of losers here, and you'd still need to watch out, particularly after dark, for predators.

It was strange how insecure and exposed I suddenly felt, even out in the sunshine and fresh air. *Young woman alone.* The curse, and defense, was paranoia. I wasn't exactly a karate expert.

The open pay phones on a stalk at the bottom of the stairs appeared whole, but there wasn't a phone book to be seen, and that was what I needed. There was a convenience store a couple of blocks down that I'd spotted from the balcony, so I headed there, hoping that they would have one intact. When I reached it, I saw that it was kind of a parody of a chain store, but it accepted the CAID card, which I knew now was the welfare card I had, and also had a big sign in the window saying CHECKS CASHED!

I went in and saw the pay phone with no books, and so I went to the counter. The clerk was an Asian woman, possibly Korean, with a fairly thick accent, but she got the idea.

"Excuse me," I said, uncharacteristically shyly for me. It was the first time I'd spoken, and my reaction to hearing my own voice was *Jeez! I sound like a male munchkin!* In truth, I probably sounded better than that, but it was one of those voices. Sharp, nasal, kind of a low soprano on helium, but very easy to understand for all that. "Do you have a phone book I can look at?"

"Phone book. Yes. Which you want?"

"Do you have a Yellow Pages?"

"Yes, yes." She reached under the counter and handed me a surprisingly thick book. "Oakland—Alameda County" it read. That figured. I thanked her, took it over to the coffee counter, and looked up "Restaurants." There was no Alice's Diner listed. I took it back, surprised at how heavy it seemed, and thanked her.

"You wouldn't happen to have any others around, would you?" I asked her.

"No, sorry. This is it."

I sighed and wondered what the hell I should do. I was already feeling not only paranoid but very put upon; almost everybody except the lady behind the counter and the little kids on the balcony seemed a lot bigger than I was.

I walked out, trying to get some self-control and telling myself, *"Think! Think!"*

Just around the corner was a taxi sitting at the curb, the driver a young black man smoking a cigarette and reading the paper. Getting up some nerve, I approached the cab and leaned down. "Excuse me, but do you know where an Alice's Diner on San Pablo might be?"

He looked over, frowned, looked thoughtful, and then said, "Not in this area. That sounds more like Berkeley than Oakland. I could take you through the city and up to Berkeley on San Pablo, though."

I shook my head. "No, sorry, I don't think I have the money for it. Thanks anyway."

I turned and started to walk away, but he called me back. "Miss? You might try the number fourteen bus. It goes all the way to El Cerrito for a buck."

Now, *that* was an idea, and within this area, with the card I had, I wouldn't even be out the dollar. I couldn't imagine that I'd have a job paying the basics that would require me to cross the bay or something like that.

It was in fact in Berkeley, up near the university, as the crossroad suggested, and while it was a fairly new place, it was built to look like and feel like a classic diner. I went in and saw from the clock on the wall that it was a little after one in the afternoon.

The manager, a big, beefy guy who looked like he should have had a cigar stub in his mouth, came over. "Well, hello! You're kinda early, ain'tcha? You ain't due till four o'clock."

I shrugged and pretended to know what I was doing. "Sorry. I just got bored and didn't have much else to do, so I figured I might as well come up here. I'm still getting used to this, remember."

He shrugged. "Suit yourself. I don't need you early, though."

I saw that the three waitresses in the place all wore uniforms with skirts and stock designs, kind of fifties kitsch, but I figured they'd have one for me when I came back.

The more I saw the place, both from the bus and while walking around, the more it felt like the same world, the conservative and boring one I'd become used to in a sense. I wasn't the only woman wearing jeans, but there weren't a lot of us; skirts or godawful-looking pedal pushers out of some ancient *I Love Lucy* episode seemed standard.

Walking around the neighborhood, I saw a lot of mostly clean-cut young college types who looked out of place with this university's reputation in the first world I'd known, and more of them were male than female by far.

There was a TV and appliance shop nearby, but it was unlikely they'd have any news until after I needed to be at work. Still, I blew another two precious dollars at a soda fountain— yeah, they still had 'em there—on a Coke and some ice cream while waiting for the radio behind the counter to hit the news.

It was, at least, the lead story.

"Two dead, one injured, three safe in air crash north of Eureka," the radio reported. The pilot, the loadmaster, and somebody who sounded a lot like Rick were reported to have only minor cuts and bruises. The other navy man, who had to be Cholder, had several broken bones, and another male passenger appeared to be paralyzed but alive. The copilot and a female passenger not yet identified pending notification of next of kin were said to be dead.

It wasn't the report I had expected. I figured that the paralyzed man was, well, *me* and that they just hadn't realized that he'd been paralyzed all along. The copilot—well, that could mean that something had come through the cockpit window in the crash, or if he was dead and Cholder was hurt, maybe the worst damage was on the left side of the plane and that was where he'd been riding. But the lone female—there was only one—Alice McKee—and she'd been behind Rick and me, hadn't she?

This was weird, too. She got zapped, I got suddenly transmuted to somebody else a hundred or more miles south, and nothing at all added up.

The only way Sister Mary Alice could have been killed, and not Rick and me, in that plane would be if . . .

If somebody had been out all along to kill McKee. Somebody for whom Rick and Cholder and me were all irrelevant.

Somebody who had a lot more control and a lot more abilities here than he should.

There was another dimension, too, one inside me. It was eerie to hear that I was supposedly still alive someplace else, but there was a tremendous sense of relief and emotional longing at the news that Rick was in good shape. It was the same way the male Cory Maddox would have felt toward Riki, or Angel, but not quite the same. I couldn't explain it, but I sure wanted to get in contact with him, too, and in more ways than one. Not that he'd know me from Adam or, rather, Eve.

Trouble was, though, that Stanford might be just south across the bay, but it might as well be another world away for all I had.

So, with no other choices, I started work at Alice's Diner, complete with one of those belted dress uniforms. It wasn't brain surgery; the menu was basic but full, the customers were typical of a university area, and while there was a lot of sass and at least three attempts to pick me up, the fact was, at the end of the shift, at midnight, I didn't feel overworked. I also had about twenty-five bucks in tips strictly off the books.

The more I did it, the more the little tricks for increasing my tips became obvious, particularly with the older guys, and the more confident I became and the more comfortable I was as a young woman, as Kori. In fact, it seemed all too natural to me, as if it weren't new at all.

It was after midnight when I got out of there, though, and

that brought the same fear I'd had before on the streets, only doubled. Even in this neighborhood, which was a pretty safe one, things took on an almost sinister, threatening tone, a sort of setting where Cory would not have had the slightest thought of anything remotely dangerous. Going back to the apartment—after midnight—*that* was even scarier, at least without an escort.

So of course I wound up using the tips on a cab, shelling out fifteen bucks to be driven back home, although the guy was nice enough to sit and watch until I was safely inside.

I wasn't going to increase my wardrobe or spending money much *this* way.

About the only other expense of the evening, though, was picking up a local paper. They had fairly detailed information on the crash, but what was most unnerving was the fact that at one point they quoted *me*! Or, rather, they quoted Drew.

But—*I'd* been Drew. If I was now Kori, then who the hell was *he*?

I could believe almost anything about anything at that point, but I simply couldn't accept the idea that I could be two different people at the same time. Maybe I could, but somehow it was a concept even that subconscious region where all the forgotten lives still existed in tiny fragments of truth and fiction, personality and skills, could not accept.

Maybe whoever or whatever had caused that crash had wanted more than just to kill McKee. Maybe McKee was just a throw-in, a goodie on the side.

Somehow I had been lifted, and whatever made me "real" had changed. Kori felt too comfortable, like an old and familiar suit that had been well broken in. I'd *been* Korinna, I'd *liked* being Korinna, and I was beginning to adjust to being her again. But she didn't *quite* fit here. She was more comfortable with the older universe, Cory's universe or a close cousin. Kori had no past here. She was created instantly, fully formed and set up for limited maintenance. I wasn't a Maddox or Maddux because I couldn't be. Maybe a distant cousin on my mother's side, if that. Even Drew had been born into this world, as Cori had been born and raised in his. I'd been *inserted*.

Why?

In a sense that was easier to answer than "Who?"

Somebody with the power to do it or the devices, control, whatever, desperately needed a way to get into the government research center run by the Henreids at Stanford. Somebody who wouldn't be likely to get past Al and Rob and Lee and Les and that crew. Somebody who probably thought he couldn't fool McKee for long, either, which might have been why she was knocked off.

And now they, or one of their own, more likely, pretending to be me, was on the inside. Not exactly trusted or free, but that would be too much for anybody to hope for, wouldn't it? Those people over there weren't dumb, and they knew the system. But they knew mild-mannered Cory or Drew and knew he couldn't walk and had only one arm and couldn't wipe his ass properly.

"Cory, Cory! You don't get it, do you? You don't need to re-member like that. One session with your Brand Box and it will all come back in spades. Why, I've been able to output my own doctoral thesis from two lives ago twice now to printers just by using my Box."

And what did it mean that Walt had his Brand Box? Did each of us have an individual Box there . . . ?

That was who I was. I was somebody else recorded on a Brand Box. A Brand Box that *wasn't* in the hands of the Stanford bunch.

Had Walt Slidecker taken more than one Brand Box when he had snuck in there? He seemed the logical choice for this. He was the only opposition, the only one with any others on his side, the only one who would know what was going on, and the only one *I* knew who could open his own rabbit hole.

Was Walt the March Hare? Or the one behind him, anyway?

Had I been in the way the *last* time, as Cory? Had I surprised him by coming back when I was supposed to have been scared away for good?

It was an interesting idea. Last time I'd crossed up his attack and maybe revealed it; this time I'd be of precious little help to him except as a blind for getting somebody in. Why not just kill me once he had me over here, though?

Was there still some connection to Drew? Would Drew die if I did?

Then why leave me with any memories of what was really going on? Unless . . .

Unless my knowledge might still be needed as a backup.

And why so close? I could just as easily have woken up in New York City or Halifax or Ireland.

I wasn't any more of a player now than Riki and I had been players when we'd met the Caterpillar, nor was it likely that I would be for some time. Still, I was here, and I could be a player.

I could also be more easily watched and steered away from trouble if I was slightly too far away to do any mischief but close enough to always be under surveillance of some sort.

Jeez, that made me more paranoid than I had been before! I suddenly felt like that wiretapper in that old Gene Hackman movie who gets so paranoid, he rips up his whole house because he is convinced everybody else is spying on him. No use in doing that, though. Even if I found it, they'd just put in a better one that was harder to find.

Over the next few weeks things tended to go easier, and my sense of strangeness vanished. By going with the flow I became more and more Kori Ajani. It wasn't that my two past selves vanished but rather that they became less of an issue in my thoughts and dreams. It was almost as if a huge weight had been lifted from me and a ponderous costume had been discarded. I just felt a whole lot happier.

I started looking at guys in a sexual way without feeling self-conscious, too, and playing up to them when I needed to. After a week or so I never had to worry about taxis. Somebody would always run me home, even if he had to make a special trip just for me. The extra bucks saved weren't piled up, though, but got turned into a nicer and wider wardrobe, some cheap but decent-looking earrings, the same level of drugstore perfume and cologne, that kind of thing. I didn't need a beauty school or the like, either; the fact was, it came to me as if I'd grown up with it.

Cory had never liked dancing, and Drew—well, he'd have killed for the leg power to do it—but for some reason I knew a *lot* of dances and just *loved* it. Of course, I had only Sunday and Monday off, but that was enough time to look forward to things. And any cute guy I found the slightest bit interesting who could take one or both of the nights and take me to some clubs, well, that was fine with me, particularly some of the neat spots in San Francisco and up in Marin.

Most of the proffered drugs scared me, but I admit I wouldn't turn it down when guys bought me drinks and I'd do a little pot now and then as long as it wasn't laced with something else and didn't cost me anything. And, yeah, I found it pretty hard to keep control when the mood hit, and I guess I did it with a dozen guys everywhere from vans to the backseats of old Chevies to apartments, theirs and mine, and not just on weekends.

As I got into this lifestyle, my character went through other changes that I barely noticed. I no longer read unless I had to and took decreasing notice of what was going on in the world. I picked up a cheap used TV and got hooked on midday soap operas. I was dumbing down somewhat; unable to be ignorant, I was nonetheless talking like a white trash girl from a low-class background who'd dropped out of the eighth grade or been kicked out.

Again, I didn't really forget. If anything, it was because I still *knew* that I let myself go. I wasn't going to get hooked on anything or let somebody control me more than they had already, but otherwise almost anything went because I knew that deep down, in the end, it didn't matter.

In the back of my mind I had a vague plan for when it felt as if things were going wrong, some way I might be able to get in contact with *somebody* for a rabbit hole exit when necessary. It was an ill-formed plan with few specifics and little relation to reality, though.

From the tips and from letting other people buy me things and becoming a real expert at thrift shops and secondhand places, I did manage to have some mad money, though, and occasionally there'd be a Sunday or Monday when nobody was available or I was tired or had my period or something but didn't want to stay locked up and was well enough to move. At those times I would take a bus up to the BART stop at Jack London Square and then take the subway across the bay and its creepy fault to San Francisco where I would do some shopping without much buying, dressing well and trying on clothes and other stuff at Saks and Neiman Marcus.

It was during one of those times, coming out of Macy's and walking down to Market across from the Marriott there, that I saw him walk by.

Deep down that had always been in the back of my mind, and most of the guys I went out with, or at least went all the way with, had had something—looks, mannerisms, likes and dislikes, that kind of thing—that reminded me of him. Now, though, without even thinking about the possibility, on a sunny Monday afternoon, Richard "Rick" Wilisczik, in navy whites with a chief's stripe, walked by me as I stood there.

He looked—well, *great*. Probably a lot better than *I* did, I reflected, although coming off a shopping afternoon, I looked about as good as I ever did. The clothes were used, but they looked pretty good on me—at least as good as anything did—and I had makeup and medium pumps on because salesclerks looked at that sort of thing before deciding whether you were worthy of their attention. As I said, I had gotten to be an expert at secondhand shopping.

I followed him, not particularly trying to hide but trying to act nonchalant while catching up to him, maybe figuring out a way to catch his attention when I did. I admit I had no plan. I was working strictly on uncontrollable emotions I couldn't explain to myself, and I didn't care if anybody else saw me or anybody might be following me or him. The only worry I had was that somebody that good-looking wouldn't give chubby little me a second glance. Looking the best I could look wasn't exactly the same as saying I was anything to look at.

Rick went into an art supply store, which wasn't at all surprising. Man or woman, spouse or partner, Rick had always been an artist, and the talent seemed to flow through.

Figuring that he might be parked in one of the municipal lots in the direction he'd come from, I sort of stopped and waited for him to come back out again.

He finally did come out with some large bags under his arms, but he turned in the wrong direction and continued walking down Market. Finally he turned up a side street and then down an alleyway, which wasn't the world's best place for somebody like me to stay inconspicuous. The alley did have some businesses on it, though, and one was a medical supply house. There was another guy in white—not, I noted, Cholder—behind the wheel of a gray government van parked in front of it, and Rick tossed his art stuff in and said something to the driver. Then he and the driver went into the medical supply house.

My heart sank, because I knew he wasn't going to come back my way and there was no way that wasn't obvious for me to go into that supply house. It began to look like maybe I was up the creek on this one, but then I had a bright idea and walked a bit farther. The alley was one-way; the truck had to pass to get out, and nobody was going to pass that truck.

I heard 'em load something and peered around to see them putting a bunch of boxes in the back of the van. Then Rick closed up while the driver hopped in, and Rick then made it around and climbed in the passenger side as I figured he would. They sat there for a moment, apparently going over a checklist. Then the driver nodded and put the truck in gear.

I timed it as closely as I could, praying a little that I didn't time it *too* closely—I'd spent too much of one life laid up in a bed rotting as it was—and stepped out in front of the van as if I were walking forward. The driver slammed on the brake, and I was genuinely startled when I saw how close it was and fell, not too badly, onto the pavement.

Doors opened on both sides, and the two guys were on me in a moment with apologies and helping me up and all that.

"I'm all right, honest," I assured them. "Just shook up is all." I looked at both of 'em and tried not to show a preference for Rick, giving each a come-on smile. "Guess I just wanted to get fussed over by two cute navy guys, huh?"

"You sure you're all right?" the driver asked, really concerned. "We could take you to a hospital for a checkup."

"Nah. That's okay. I think maybe I skinned my knee through here, but it ain't no big deal." I gave 'em both a wicked, playful smile. "I won't scream whiplash or somethin' if you guys buy me a drink or dinner sometime, okay?"

"Now *that's* a deal," Rick said approvingly, and the driver gave him a kind of nasty "don't horn in on my luck" look and said, "Hey, *I* was the driver!"

"Nah! I want it from the both of ya!" I told them, very sure of myself and feeling great that the ploy had worked so well. "Wanna go now, or are you two still on duty or somethin'?"

"As a matter of fact we are," Rick commented, disappointed. "Are you from the city here?"

"Nope, I'm from over in Oakland, but I work at Alice's Diner on San Pablo near University in Berkeley. Four to midnight, Tuesday to Saturday. That fit in with either or both of you? I'm—Rina. Rina Ajani."

"Larry Santee," the driver responded with a soft, nice smile.

"And this here's Rick. He's a Polack, and nobody can say his last name, even him."

"Vilacheck," Rick responded, looking mock offended. "W-I-L-I-S-C-Z-I-K. You just say it like it's spelled, that's all."

Well, I didn't have a phone in the apartment, but I gave 'em Marlene's number downstairs. I normally didn't like it since she and Beth, her roomie, were call girls, but they were set up there through a pimp, so I figured they might just pass the two guys on to me. These guys wouldn't pay for what they could get for nothin', or so I hoped.

Well, I got a number for them, too, just in case, and then finally they had to split. I watched 'em get back into the van and drive off, hardly feelin' the real skin-up I had.

Several things had happened. I'd made contact with Rick, the *real* Rick, and the other guy, Larry, seemed pretty nice, too, particularly compared with what I'd been sleeping with of late.

Second, I was somewhat back in the game, even if I somehow, deep down, didn't give a damn about it at this point. At least I'd had the presence of mind to give them the not-fake name of Rina instead of Kori, which wouldn't have meant anything much to Rick, I guess, but might to his bosses.

But also, I was still dumbing down somewhat. I could feel it when I talked to them. Back on my own I could at least think things through, but when I was talking to them, I suddenly felt and acted like, well, *me*. Not Cory, not Drew, *me*, Korinna, low-class, ignorant, and loose. Was that the way whoever it was had set me up? I wondered. The closer I got to that damned project, the more hormones and the less brains I'd have? Well, if that was the case, it didn't matter to me. Not now.

The fact is, deep down, I *actually didn't* care. This time it wasn't my problem, and there wasn't a thing I could do about any of that stuff, anyway.

Well, of course, I spent a lot of the next week like a schoolgirl with a crush, and not keeping my mind on much else and not even caring much about whether I screwed up. I kept expecting one or the other of them to come into the diner any moment, and when they didn't, I always kept checking with Marlene and Beth about phone calls and such. But they swore to me that no Ricks or Larrys had called—at least not navy ones for me—and I started to get a little scared that maybe they weren't gonna follow up.

I tried calling the number they had given me after a few days, but one time it didn't ring and the other time it was an electronic voice message system that kinda scared me for some reason.

Finally, when I was at my wit's end on Saturday, I was called to the phone at the diner. Since I didn't have any idea who knew to call me there, I was puzzled and figured maybe the apartment had been broken into or something, but it was Rick.

"Hi. This is one of the sailors who almost knocked you down last Sunday."

"Yeah, I know! Hi, yourself!"

"Look, I'm sorry for not gettin' to you earlier, but it's been real busy here and they had us goin' this way and that. How late do you work tonight?"

"Pretty late. Till midnight. But I'm a late type myself."

"Well, I like to be when I can. Look, Larry's gonna have some duty tomorrow, but I don't. Can I just pick you up at the diner and we'll find a late dinner or something?"

"I know some okay places," I assured him. "Come on by. I got some club clothes here, so it ain't no big deal. Um, you know where this place is?"

"No, but I'll find it. See you later, doll."

I felt a shiver run through me. "Okay, hon, see you then."

There was no question that my feelings, my emotions about Rick, were totally out of control, but I didn't want to control them.

I had zero expectations that he would call by that point, and I always figured I'd be dealing with the two of them, not just him, but I had packed just in case, using my biggest bag. The mesh-type panty hose and spiked heels and real mini-type miniskirt I picked up from the sources Marlene and Beth used, but that and a too-tight pullover were what I'd brought. Didn't take up a lot of room or weigh much in the bag. Not that I was gonna put them on under anything other than these circumstances, with the guy I wanted already there. Not unless I wanted to change jobs, anyway.

I couldn't help but wonder over the next few hours, when work really *crawled* and everybody seemed unendurable, just how long, how many lives Rick and I had been romantically involved, maybe as Cory and Riki, or Kori or Rina and Rick, or maybe less orthodox combinations. It had to have been almost from the start, though, to last through all this.

Even as Josh and Angel we couldn't be parted and were so close that we'd woven our identities together like you'd sew two pieces of fabric into one.

I was also pretty much convinced that no matter how good a macho guy I made and no matter what a hell of a woman Rick made, it was in this current configuration that we'd started or fallen into or been placed into this series of Alice in Wonderland lives very long ago.

This was confirmed when he showed up just before midnight, looking incredibly handsome and sexy and in casual dress. There was nothing military about him except the haircut and some of the bearing.

I knew a lot of women who hated it when strangers gave 'em the eye or worse, but when I came out of the ladies' room about a quarter after twelve and took Rick's arm, I liked every whistle and catcall from the rest of the diner. I liked the look on Rick's face the best.

We wound up at a small club in San Francisco, good food and nice and dark and romantic but not too much action for late Saturday. It didn't matter. I couldn't tell you what we ate or what we said, but we wound up parked at the turnout just north of the Golden Gate Bridge, looking back at a mostly fog-shrouded San Francisco, ignoring the chill, dancing to his portable radio. That led to a cheap but decent motel just off the main drag where U.S. 101 and California 1 split and a night all the better for getting very little sleep.

Very little, but some. Lying there in the early morning dawn, my head on his chest, I had dreams that made no particular sense then but that proved more understandable later on, when some of my more practical wits were required.

The conversations, for one thing. Two men, vaguely familiar voices but impossible to say why they seemed familiar, discussing, well, me. No faces, just shadows in the dark, but radio could sometimes tell you as much as or more than television . . .

"Rina Ajani. Not a lot on her, just what's in the Cal files. Full first name is Korinna—yeah, that gave me a start, too. If we didn't have Cory Maddux live and kicking, I'd swear this was the flip side."

"No big deal. Maybe that's the attraction. She made only the usual expected impression on Santee, but there was a clear and immediate measurable attraction on the part of Wilisczik. Made me think that her rough similarities to Corrine might have been the trigger. Figures. I mean, lots of people look like other people."

"Yeah. That's why everybody winds up marrying the wrong people! Guess you're right on the rebound stuff, but if Maddux wasn't alive and kickin' . . ."

But Maddux was, and so was I. No matter what limitations the March Hare had, he'd sure managed to pull a few tricks even these types had never seen before. Flying saucer creatures back in the first plane, now splitting me in two in this one. Creepy, but you had to admire it.

It also meant that I was safe, at least for the moment. Even Al wouldn't figure out this one, and the closer I got to any of 'em, the less Cory, Drew, Corrine, or whoever I became mentally and the more just Kori or Rini.

Sunday was an even better version of late Saturday. We slept late, checked out in the nick of time, got breakfast at a pancake house nearby where they looked at me like I was turning a long-term trick but didn't refuse to serve us, and we kind of made a short tour of scenic places with few people around and a lot of creative opportunities for one on one.

"It's too bad we can't keep this up a while," Rick said with genuine regret that evening.

"*I* could," I assured him. "And I'm off tomorrow, too."

He nodded. "But *I'm* not, and I'm still in the military, so it's not like I can take a day off now and then. Besides, I'm a male nurse with a patient who needs almost constant care."

There was just enough of the old me left to be both fascinated and frightened by that idea, knowing who it was. "So who took care of him today?"

"Oh, there's no twenty-four-hour duty except on ships in wars. I go twelve on, twelve off with him, and another guy does the same. Not Larry—he's basically a pool driver. It's not as bad as all that, since every other day he's sleeping for six to nine hours. Not much chance to build up a lot of energy when you got one good and one bum arm and that's it. I feel sorry for the poor guy, but he's workin' hard for 'em. Every five days they give us one off, which happened to be today for me. I'll be back on midnight tonight to noon tomorrow, and the next day off I have is Saturday. Of course, Larry will be off—"

I cut him off. "Screw Larry! Or, rather, I *don't* want to screw Larry! I think I'm in *love*, baby!"

He wasn't sure if he was in love or just highly infatuated at the moment, I knew, but clearly he didn't want this to end. I kind of felt he didn't want to share anymore, either.

He sighed. "I don't know what to do. I guess I should get a few days to try and see what's what, anyway. I'm not sure my heart could *take* two or three weeks of this, anyway! Hey! Don't give me that look! I was just kiddin'! Or maybe, if I wasn't, what a way to go, huh?"

I smiled and blew him a kiss. "Well, you can run me home, I guess, if you want. We better start now if you got to be back almost to San Jose before midnight, change clothes and shower, and all that."

The truth was, we didn't say much going back to my place in that plainclothes motor pool Chevy, but I knew that we both felt the same way toward each other and that somehow we'd find a way to work it out.

He was not impressed by my neighborhood and my early California apartment, like maybe last renovated by the Spanish around 1680. Still, he didn't want to let go of me, at least not then, and that was no guess.

"They've had me rooming with a guy in these little apartments just off campus," he told me, thinking. "If you want, there's a Sleep Cheap Motel just down from there. You want to grab some toiletries and a change and maybe stay there tonight? You can sleep off the weekend, I'll have some chance to do it on this watch, and then I'll pick you up for brunch and a nice evening out if we don't fall over, and I'll get you back home Tuesday in time to go to work. How's that sound?"

It sounded *real* good to me. Real good.

It was only when we were on our way, past South San Francisco, south toward Redwood City, Palo Alto, and Stanford, that it struck me that within a matter of a couple of hours Rick would have spent time with, had conversations with, and even slept in the same room with the same person in two totally different roles.

I wasn't sure if I wanted to meet Drew. I wasn't sure I had the nerve.

V

THE DOMESTICATION
OF ALICE

"Damn it!" Rick said as we pulled up to the diner Tuesday afternoon, ending what had been one heck of a weekend. "There's just got to be some way around this mess! I don't want to have to wait six more days before we can get together again!"

I nodded. "Yeah, I know. This has been the best two days I think I can *ever* remember havin', but I'm gonna go nuts startin' now. I can't just quit 'cause that's a condition of my rent and medical and all, and it's the only way I got to get some money. Navy petty officers don't make enough to keep their girlfriends in apartments, right? And you're in a dorm."

He sat there drumming his fingers in a very familiar way on the steering wheel, looking ahead, then at me. "You're right," he admitted. "The only way we can make this go is to get married."

"*What?!*"

He sighed. "Yeah, I know, I know. It's just two days, and we don't really know each other at all, but I know a couple of guys I grew up with had long courtships and live-in times and whatnot, and they're separated or divorced. Got another friend who got married on the spur of the moment, and ten years later they're still goin', with some nice kids and a decent life. You never can tell, no matter how much you prepare." Another sigh. "I dunno. Ever since that plane crash I been kinda seeing things different. I walked this time, but two people died and another's banged up, maybe scarred ugly. I been thinking that any of them coulda been me. Maybe it don't matter if you plan or not. You take chances, and sometimes it works." He looked me straight in the eye. "We can't just move in together. I don't have the place or the allowances for it, and you'd have nothing. So marry me. We'll get family pay and money for a place, and you'll be covered by military insurance. It won't be easy; the money's not that good. But thousands of people manage it. Oh, shit! I'm just no good at this!"

"Okay," I said softly.

He started. "Huh? Okay what?"

"Okay, I'll marry you."

"You mean it?"

"I'm gettin' the best of the deal, I think. You're young, handsome, great in bed, and smart, too. You're gettin' a dumpy little fat broad who couldn't even add up a dinner check without an addin' machine."

"I think you're better than that," he responded. "At least I thought I saw something more, a lot more, in you."

"When?" I asked him, figuring he'd say six months or something.

"I'll put in for leave and official notification," he told me. "As soon as they say okay, we'll go up to Tahoe or Reno and just do it."

"What 'bout your family?" I asked him.

"Not much family left. Nobody I'm close to, anyway. You?"

"I'm an orphan. Why else would I be livin' this way? I got nobody."

And that was the way it turned, so fast that I could hardly believe it.

The gang at the diner was really happy for me, or seemed to

be. I was told I had the job as long as I needed it, and they even chipped in and got me a little gold bracelet with the restaurant's name and some bells and birds and stuff on it as a present.

Rick was in contact with me every day. We kinda arranged for him to take a collect call from me at two every afternoon, which was after he was off and before I went on. Alvin Stabisky, the six-foot, three-hundred-pound very male owner who was "Alice" to the diner, gave me off Saturday even though he could be shorthanded that day. Rick took me out for a fancy Italian dinner right off Fisherman's Wharf and then gave me this *gorgeous* engagement ring that I knew he couldn't possibly afford while tipped-off waiters came over and played romantic Italian violin stuff at the table.

The full approval from the navy came in not long afterward, and in less than a month we'd gotten the okay and even had a unit in a pretty nice navy block at the Naval Experimental Laboratories at Moffet Field Naval Air Station near Mountain View that I'd never heard of before. The air station was a pretty big place, with an airport and lots of buildings, hangars, and the like, and also blocks of duplexes and town-house-type dwellings for the enlisted personnel there. It was almost a miniature suburb in gray, and it was under a twenty-minute drive to Stanford. Rick bought a surplus navy car maybe ten years old and looking and smelling it. It wasn't much, but it cost only a couple of hundred bucks and got you where you were going, at least if you remembered to keep the windows open a bit. Still, it passed California emissions for some reason, so we got it.

And right around the end of October, before the snow started to fly in the Sierra, we managed to make our way to Reno and the Romance of Elvis Wedding Chapel—no kidding, they even had continuous Presley tunes playing in the background—and we actually did it.

The navy and, I suspect, the institute (as everybody, including Rick, seemed to call it) wasn't too generous about the honeymoon time, since it meant they had to bring in somebody else to do Rick's job, but they gave us seven days and we made the most of them.

By the time we got back to the Bay Area, any remnants of either of my old selves and the knowledge they might betray seemed so deeply buried that I wasn't aware of their being there. Hell, I was a programmer who had trouble with complicated arithmetic like checkbook balancing and long division and adding up a bunch of figures to see what the total cost was. I'd been the person who twice had invented or at least sketched out and designed head-mounted and full-body wireless direct networks to neural nets; now I not only couldn't have told you what a neural net was, I couldn't have spelled it. Rick tried to teach me how to drive, a skill I'd possessed in a past life, and I didn't have the nerve or coordination or whatever to do it. I did manage a bicycle very well, though, and I liked using it, even for longer trips. It kept me in reasonable condition, got me fresh air, and moved me farther than I would have cared to walk.

I also had a card that had my photo on it and said I was in fact an official navy wife, name of Rina Ajani Wilisczik, already getting used to letting people call me Mrs. Wilisiznick and leaving it at that. I also had gotten my hair cut shorter and tried dying it blond, but what came out was kind of a rusty reddish brown that I accepted.

Things went pretty well for quite a while. I easily made friends on the base, small as it was, although I was a little self-conscious at being probably the worst educated of the wives and one of the few who didn't work outside the home. I'd done that, and I suppose that if I could have found something where they'd actually hire somebody like me that also had suitable hours and transportation, I'd have taken it. But I didn't miss the diner nearly as much as I thought I would, and finding any job that would match Rick's hours and days off would be a pain.

That meant, as we had expected, that things were *really*

tight, but to me it didn't matter. Some of the local base personnel, with Rick's approval, tried to get me into a GED program
for a high school degree, but while I looked at it, it kind of
bored me, and it was hard to see what good it would do to pass
a test and paste the certificate in a scrapbook or something. The
truth was, I had very little ambition or interest beyond what I
now had, and much to the disgust of some of the independent
career-type women around, I was totally content to have a life
that centered on my husband.

Rick was taking a few courses at Stanford as part of the
arrangement he had and apparently with the encouragement of
the institute, which meant Al and the Henreids. He'd switch off
with another guy during certain periods on his shift and take
some medical courses; he had only a few more to get a full RN
degree, I discovered, and then he'd mark time until the navy
hitch was near its end in a year and see if they'd spring for
medical school to keep him.

His art talent, though, made me almost cry that he couldn't
make *that* pay. He'd been doing a lot of drawing in anatomy
and physiology, and he'd done some really great nudes of
me as well. He had a knack of making flat stuff look three-
dimensional against really neat backgrounds. Me, I got interested in making my own clothes and some for him, too, and
I also took a couple of no-credit adult classes given at the
county high schools in jewelry making and ceramics that were
really neat.

One time Rick insisted that I come to work with him. I'd
been resisting it since the start and had no desire to get near the
place, even though I no longer had a conscious idea of why it
scared me so much. Still, he was insistent. "I want to show you
off!" he told me. "Besides, we're having some bigwigs in, and
it's kind of a reception."

"I don't have nothin' to wear!" I protested. "Besides, all
them smart folks with their doctor degrees and all—and me
talkin' 'bout cookies and sewing patterns 'n' tryin' to not say
'shit' or 'fuck.' I just feel out of place in that kinda group."

"I haven't seen *anybody* or any group you couldn't charm the socks off of," he responded. "Just come along—for me. Just this once. I promise we won't be there a long time."

In the end there was no way out of it, so I resigned myself and gritted my teeth. As we drove toward the freeway, though, I began to feel panic, like we were driving to our doom or something, or at least our less than pleasant destiny.

The building itself, off to one side of the campus and barely connected to the university by anything obvious, looked innocent enough. One of those very modern block-long four-story classroom-type buildings that were styled in a fake Spanish motif, with a parking lot on one side and in back a one-story rectangular block, looking like solid cement which had been painted over with a kind of abstract Mexican mural that showed some real talent and creativity. Looking at the classroom building gave me cold chills, but the sight of that huge "block" almost made me want to throw up.

We walked around and went into the classroom building by the main entrance, which faced away from the rest of the campus but looked at nothing in particular. You just had to walk a ways around and halfway down the building to get to it, which was kind of weird. Wide-open spaces with tall lights around, though—you sure couldn't go in and out without *somebody* seeing you.

Rick needed a special card inserted in a slot just to get the outer door to open; that got you to an inner one that had no obvious way to push or pull open but did have a small speaker box and a flat plate with the slightly recessed outline of a hand next to it. It also had a light that glowed red.

Rick put his hand on the plate and said slowly and clearly, "Wilisczik, Richard Angelo, 214-443-14300, chief petty officer six, permanent staff, and companion, wife, Rina Ajani Wilisczik."

There was a moment's pause and then a buzz, and the door slid back, revealing a pretty normal-looking hall.

"Rick, I feel like the walls're closin' in on me already! This shit feels like a fuckin' *jail*!" I whispered, clenching his hand tight.

"Just relax," he responded as soothingly as possible. "It's a lot of crap, that's all. Just don't go where the guards are in front or the doors won't open, and it's just like any other office job from this point."

A woman sitting behind a reception desk looked up at us. For some reason she seemed vaguely familiar to me, but I couldn't place her.

She smiled when she saw Rick. Most women did, of course. "Ah! Chief Wilisczik!" she greeted him, pronouncing the name correctly as "Vilacheck."

He smiled back. "Rina, this is Betty Harker-Simonson, our chief receptionist and guide to everybody here. Nobody could find or do anything without her. Betty, this is my wife, Rina."

"So *you're* Rina! We've been *so* curious to meet you and see who could have snared our Rick!"

"Hello," I managed. "Pleased to meet you."

"They're mostly in the Kindall Room," the receptionist told us. "You know the way, Rick. You can leave your coats in the cloakroom just over there."

I had on a long red sparkling dress I'd made myself from a pattern and some cloth from a fabric store, with a waist belt, bracelets, a matching thin gold-plated chain necklace, and big red and gold crescent earrings. I even had crimson-painted nails, even if they were the press-on type. I never could stop biting my nails. With the red pumps, a blush, and lipstick, it was the fanciest outfit I had. Rick had at least pretended to be bowled over by it.

There was a gathering of mostly professional-looking people inside, but for some reason those rather ordinary types gave me such a turn that I could feel my heart pounding. I couldn't shake the feeling that I somehow already knew all these people and that none of them were all that nice.

There was a really conservative husband and wife introduced as Michelle and Bernard Alden. The names didn't sound familiar and there was something wrong about them that I couldn't finger, but they still had that "I should know you" quality.

"Religious nuts," Rick warned me in a low whisper long before we were in range for them to hear or notice us particularly. "Just don't bring up God or public prayer or stuff like that."

"That type is in a science place like *this*?"

"She's a programmer, sure enough. And he's a state politician."

There were others there who gave me the same sort of feeling: Dr. Herbert Koeder, a paleontologist by trade, whatever that was; Dr. Solomon Prine, deputy computer supervisor; Dr. Ben Sloan and his wife, Dorothy, the only two African-Americans in the room—they were introduced like a series of people out of old and not very pleasant dreams, the kind you didn't want to remember when you woke up.

Larry Santee was there as well, along with a stunning young exotic-looking Oriental beauty with big lips and waist-length black hair, dressed in a tight Hawaiian-style dress with a flower in her hair. It was weird—I had more of a feeling of familiarity with the girl than with Larry, even though I'd at least seen him before.

"Hi, kids!" he greeted us warmly.

Larry, at least, I didn't feel uncomfortable talking to. "I'm sorry I stood you up," I told him a bit playfully. "Seems I got a little involved, and before I knew it, I was tied up and hauled off."

He laughed. "Yeah, I can imagine, you devil," he responded in kind, looking at Rick. "Still, I think it was all for the best. Folks, meet the most beautiful new grad student at Stanford, and smart, too. Danielle, this is Rick and Rina. Don't worry about their last name. You couldn't remember it, anyway; it's all consonants."

Danielle looked very shy and very sexy at one and the same time. Oriental conservatism be damned; anybody who dressed like that around *these* parts was advertising. Still, I said, "Pleased to meet you, Miss—um . . . ?"

"Dannie is just fine," she told me in a western American accent that said she probably hadn't been near Japan except on a tour in spite of the looks and almond eyes. "Larry says you have problems with your last name. I have problems with folks spelling 'Tanaka,' for some reason, although you'd think it would be easy."

I felt another stab of recognition I couldn't place, but it was Rick who jumped in and saved me from having to say much more. "That's what I tell people about my own name. W-i-l-i-s-c-z-i-k. Vilacheck. Just like it's spelled."

Dannie thought that was the *funniest* thing, and I wanted to move on quickly. My sense of discomfort at being in the midst of these people was almost universal, but my sense of jealousy was more specific.

Lee and Robyn Henreid had that same sense of familiarity and threat, but they also made such an odd couple that Rick and I seemed physically matched. Lee was a tall man with long, genuinely strawberry blond hair—most guys with that type of hair were losing it by his age—and steely blue eyes who looked like he should be modeling romance covers; Robyn was small and plain with a putty nose and spinster hair and no fashion sense at all. She looked like she belonged as the third banana in a situation comedy.

They also had oddball projections as personalities, or so it seemed, and not just to me but to Rick and others, as I confirmed later. They were both PhDs. Lee had a soft but deep voice that had a bit of a lisp to it, and he moved kind of like a hairdresser, while Robyn had a firm low soprano that was loud enough and crystal-clear enough that it seemed to be almost the voice of a sales or presentation expert, somebody who would be at the front of the room giving a clear lecture to an audience that would not notice when the amp and microphone cut out.

Standing over by the bar were two men having a casual con-versation, and I didn't like either of them on sight. One was a tall, rather handsome man in a naval officer's whites and the braid and epaulets of a full commander; the other was a bald-ing man with a big nose and little blue-gray eyes and a kind of bucktooth grin in a black suit and conservative striped tie. In spite of my starting to pull the other way, Rick was determined to go over toward them, and I had little choice but to follow.

"Honey," Rick said pleasantly, oblivious to my near terror as we stood before these two men, a terror I myself couldn't explain, "I want you to meet my bosses. Commander Starkey is our liaison with Washington and in effect runs this place and is my superior officer, and Dr. Cohen here is my immediate boss and the one pushing me toward medicine as a full career."

"Delighted," Cohen responded, and Starkey said "Charmed" and bowed slightly. I felt like both their eyes were boring straight into me.

Rick got me a drink—a whiskey and soda—and I almost in-haled it. While he continued to make small talk with the com-mander and the doctor, I polished it off and got another. I had needed a drink bad, and when the first had no immediate effect, I ordered a double and drank a second one.

By the time Rick finished, or *could* finish, considering they were his bosses, I was beginning to feel no pain at all and was nursing a third drink and second double.

"Well," he said, not noticing, I guess, "that's all the impor-tant people. The rest are from the university and Washington, and I know them about as well as they know you, which is not at all."

I took a step, suddenly felt a bit dizzy, and latched on to him for support. "Whoa!" I managed.

He looked at me and frowned. "You all right?"

"I—I think maybe I'm a l'il bit drunk, love."

He rolled his eyes, got me firmly in hand, and started for the door slowly but steadily, nodding to folks as he went. Both he and I had the thought that I was getting drunker and less steady by the minute and might not make the door. By the time we did, I was happy, uncaring, dizzy, and not quite aware of what planet I was on. Rick guided me down some hall and off to one side, out of view of the reception area but on the same floor. It wasn't a room, more like a lounge area in the middle of the building, but it had some nice chairs and couches, and I managed to settle down into one of the latter. I felt a *lot* better, a *lot* steadier when I did so.

Then, suddenly, I seemed to fall right through the couch.

I was falling, falling down the hole, twisting, winding, yet not hitting the sides . . .

Something told me I'd been here before.

This time there was no dramatic flyover, no grand transformation. This time I hit the hot sands, and it stung.

I cried out, rolled over on my back, and spit out some of the sand that had gotten into my mouth. Then I just stretched out and lay there, the sand feeling very warm but not intolerably hot. My eyes were closed as I tried to keep the universe from spinning around so fast.

I heard somebody, or *something*, running toward me and managed to open my eyes and raise my head a little. What I saw was another of those somewhat familiar figures, that of a woman, stark naked but with her body all painted up, running straight for me. I tried to at least sit up, but I couldn't. Not yet. All I could do was groan and wait for the woman to reach me.

She knelt down beside me and then started what for all practical purposes was a routine physical examination. Finally she finished, with me just continuing to groan and unable to function, and stood back up, looking down at me. "Stay here. Do you understand me?"

I managed a nod.

"Okay, then. Stay here. I'll be back in a couple of minutes with something to help your head."

I sank back, and I'm not sure how long it was before she returned. Certainly minutes, maybe half an hour. I didn't feel much better, and I mostly wanted to just keep my eyes shut and remain as I was. It wasn't a hundred percent comfortable, but any other position would have been worse.

I felt a strong arm helping me raise my back a bit, and the woman offered me a gourd with something liquid in it. "Drink this. It'll make the aches and dizziness go away."

That sounded good enough for me; I drank in the first mouthful of the stuff, then choked and tried to spit it out. That shit was *foul*! She was intent, though, and forced it down. Almost as soon as it was all gone inside me I began to sit up on my own and see perfectly well, only I was coughing and spitting and letting loose with a string of curses.

"That fuckin' cure's worse'n the goddamn *disease*!" I protested.

"Yeah, well, you're up on your rear end now, anyway," the woman noted.

I was coming out of it, and even though the awful taste remained, I was remarkably awake, aware, and clear-headed. I knew precisely where I was and who she was.

"Wilma?"

Her head shot up, and the expression was suspicious, not concerned as before. "How do you know that name?"

"Wilma, it's *me*! Cory! Don't you recognize me?"

"You ain't no Cory *I* ever knew. You got the wrong plumbing."

For a moment I was startled by this. Then, suddenly, I realized that falling back into this netherworld when I'd passed out had instantly restored not just the old two but all three personalities and existences to perspective, although physically and perhaps primarily I was still Rina.

"Wilma—you remember when we all kind of merged together and I took control of Angel's body and came through with you? This is kind of like that. I'm Cory Maddox and Drew Maddux, and I'm also Korinna."

"Yeah? And how do I know that? You don't look like nobody *I* ever saw."

"I probably *do*, but you don't remember it." I managed to sit up and stretch. "What *is* this sand, anyway? It's *hot*."

"Gold dust, mostly. Don't change the subject. You can't be Cory 'cause he's still alive and kicking in the hands of the institute. I *know*. I've actually seen him and talked to folks who talked to him. *You* I never saw."

As carefully as possible I explained what had happened as much as I could, not really understanding it myself.

I don't think Wilma bought most of it, but she was willing to at least accept that I wasn't a threat inside her domain. "So why are you back here?" she asked at last.

I shook my head. "Beats me. At least I'm human this time, for whatever that's worth. Somehow—I don't know how— somehow I think the complete 'me' is bein' stored down here someplace, somehow. When I'm here, I'm whole. When I'm up there, I'm just one mostly. Almost like, well . . ."

"What?"

"She'll be all right in a while," Les Cohen assured Rick. *"Just too much booze too fast."*

"Then maybe I should just take her home."

"Nonsense! Why risk bouncing her around and all that? Besides, you're on duty tonight, aren't you? So where's she better off? Home, out cold and alone, or here, where you can check on her?"

Rick sighed. *"Yeah, I guess you're right."*

"Go on back for the facilities tour and relax. I'll make sure she's comfortable and station a nurse outside the clinic. If she wakes up, which I doubt before tomorrow sometime the way she looks now, I'll call you. Okay?"

"They've got my body up there!"

Wilma must have thought she was facing a madwoman. "What in *hell* are you talkin' about? You're right here!"

"But I'm also *there*. Two different reality planes and some interconnection between the two. *That's* how it's done! Somebody's got an active switch on me somehow."

"Well, you sit here and babble, lady. Me, I'm goin' back."

"No! Wait! We need to connect somehow—on *that* plane!"

Wilma was dubious. "Yeah? Why? Even if I buy what you're selling, you said you didn't remember much of anything when you're there."

"Maybe, but I didn't know much when we first met, either. Besides, I met somebody at the party tonight you already know. Sexy Danielle Tanaka."

That got her interest a bit. "Yeah? Where? At the institute?"

"Yes, right along with all the others from the old project in new and old roles. Old Dannie's gone from bein' a lover of *Playboy* fantasies to *bein'* a *Playboy* fantasy but havin' just 'bout the same fun. The last time we met here, you said she was doing cultural stuff and in Seattle learning the ropes. I don't think she was at all, Wilma. I think somebody located you and she was sent to check on you."

"But she wouldn't remember being Dan Tanaka! You blew his brains out!"

I sighed. "Well, thanks for finally accepting who I am. Yeah, I blew his brains out, but I got the strong idea here that some precious chosen few can be restored. I'm not sure Danielle *does* remember or *is* one of the elect—Rick sure as hell doesn't—but she's sure in with 'em, anyway."

"Quickly now! You make sure Wilisczik stays out of here! Mack, just the basic networked head mount will do. I don't want to do anything full unless there's more there than meets the eye, but as long as she's kind of dropped into our lap, let's take advantage of the situation!"

"Why do you keep freezing up like that?" Wilma asked me.

"I—I'm *listening*. In some way I'm overhearing some of what's going on back around my real body. I passed out drunk, they must have taken me to Les's infirmary just like before, and now I'm being hooked into the net there. They can't do a full Brand Box thing with me there, not with a head mount, but they might be able to do some interrogation and a little programming or whatever. I don't know what he's up to, but that's why whatever is lookin' out for me dropped me down here. For protection."

It was kind of like removing the core memories all the way down and shifting them over to a different storage area, one to which the interrogators didn't have access. All their devices would read what they had but could not get over to me as I lurked in the next virtual "room," as it were.

Unless they knew that I had done this, was capable of this, and knew just where to look or somehow traced this link I had, they would find a rather boring and not terribly bright girl with no connection to computers or anything else.

"Classic stuff," Les muttered, sounding as if he still had something of a moral compass in spite of it all. *"Mean childhood, abusive home, runaway at age thirteen, on the streets and into drugs for a few years, knocked up and pregnant, got help from a Catholic agency, kid adopted out, she runs from them, winds up on welfare, then this stuff with Rick. Not dumb, not a genius, but functionally illiterate and fairly ignorant. Clearly Rick's reacting to the physical resemblance on the subconscious level; she's grabbed on to him as a life preserver. Nothing sinister here."*

"Well, Jeez, thanks a *lot*, Les," I muttered. "He's decided I'm just an ordinary ignoramus dame," I explained to Wilma.

"Don't *try* to listen, particularly while the body's still hooked up to whatever that gadget is," she cautioned me. "You have a link. They just didn't see it."

"Listen to the expert!" I retorted a little snidely. I knew damned well that Wilma didn't have the slightest idea how any of this worked, at least not in any recent life. She got here by popping into hollow trees . . .

"She's going to be out for a while," Les commented, apparently doing a basic look-over. *"I don't know how much she drank in a short time, but it must have been a whale of a punch. Give me terminal access, leave the connection on, and I'll put everything away in a little while."*

"What're you gonna do?" someone unfamiliar, maybe this "Mack," asked.

"A little insurance and reinforcement, that's all. Can't exactly do a reprogram, not without getting her into a life-support module, prepped, and all the rest, and what's the use of that? Don't worry. I know what I'm doing. And I'll do some reinforcing on Rick, too. As long as we have this situation, we might as well take advantage of it."

I frowned. "He's pulling a Les again," I commented. "You know, you really want to *like* the guy, and then he's just so offhandedly on the wrong side."

"Like what? What's he trying to pull?"

"I dunno. Probably just making sure I stay dumb and devoted. As he said, he can't do much without me completely in one of the Boxes, but I bet they had practice. The thing is, I don't know who or what I'm gonna be able to do or remember once I wake up there. That makes this time doubly important."

Wilma sat down in the golden sand and thought for a moment. "Not much to do if you won't even remember me when you get back."

"I'll remember. I just won't have a lot of specifics, and the closer I get to the bad guys, the worse my memory and smarts get, apparently for my own protection. But I knew the bunch of 'em were bad when I saw 'em, and I knew Rick was just the same as I always felt he was. Figure I'm probably gonna be safer now after this than at any time in the past. They had us in Brand Boxes once, and we still screwed 'em up—remember?"

"Well, be careful. Give me your address and how to get there off the freeway. I'll link it up and work it out if you look pretty much as you do now. I have to watch it, too, you know. If they had Tanaka on me, then they know my name and face."

"That's *right*! You be *very* careful, Wilma! I don't want 'em gettin' you this time!"

She nodded and repeated the information a few times so that she could remember it. "Now, I've got to go. I'd say get some rest here. Don't explore. This place can be more dangerous than you know if you don't have a guide and protector. There's citrus and tropical-type fruits all over, and nothing right in here can hurt you. If it smells okay, eat it. Just relax and let it take you back. I'll figure out something and be in touch."

"Okay. I—I wish you could stay. I really do. You're the wild card in this for me, Wilma. I don't think I coulda done what we once did without you."

"Yeah, well, it beats bein' a squaw on the kind of reservations *we* got."

She seemed to recede into the forest and was gone. I could feel her presence vanish shortly after my view of her did, but it hadn't been the same. Oh, that was the same Wilma, all right, and she finally *did* accept who I was, but something was different somehow. I didn't know what exactly, but maybe I was the one who'd changed a lot. I sure wasn't the man, or woman, I used to be . . .

I wasn't hungry, but I did find some of the fresh fruits growing from vines wrapped around or up against the big roots, and they *were* good to smell and taste. They made me kind of dopey, though, sort of like being a little drunk here and a lot drunk there but just relaxed and spaced out no matter what.

I settled down in the cooler brush just off the golden sands and dozed.

The wheelchair made its familiar low whine as it was steered by the joystick mounted on the right arm. I knew pretty much where it was and thus just who and what my point of view was as well.

I was back in Drew's paralyzed body, looking over at the master console in the lab. Nobody was on; it was late at night, Rick was still with the VIPs, and for a brief moment, having slipped my handler of opportunity, I was completely alone at the console.

Or, rather, he was alone. Even though I had the most time and mileage in that body, the fact was, I was just a passenger.

Going right up to the main keyboard, the lone active hand

tapped out a series of access codes. The central monitor flipped on, and I could see a picture. It was me, Rina, out in the infirmary, with security code information and life signs in small white ever-changing numbers all around the outside of the picture. They'd put a head mount on me, one of a design I'd never seen before but clearly just that, and a few taps on the keyboard brought a close-up showing the unit number on the side. This apparently was also the access code. I wondered what I was supposed to be seeing if my eyes were open, but there was no clue as to that.

"Well, you passed muster, darlin'," I heard Drew's voice mutter slowly under his breath, talking to himself, I realized, although it initially gave me a start when it seemed he might be talking to me. "But I'm too close to let you muck it up when they turn the power on again. So live happy . . ."

I wasn't too thrilled at this. *Great—not only Les is playing games; so is whoever's running Drew.* Well, at least this second guy had earned it. I knew what it was like to live that way all too well.

"Drew" tapped in more codes, and this time he got readouts far too complex and fast-scrolling for me to follow, although they seemed well within his own abilities. It wasn't any sort of superman stuff; it was instead a demonstration of just how I'd been fooling myself that they might need me to help program this sucker. This was way beyond anything I had ever fooled with. I was rusty as hell, but I sure remembered enough to know how much of this I didn't understand.

Drew's hand went out, and he flipped a switch and depressed a lock bar, turning on a red light on the console. "Lock on subject."

"Locked on," the computer responded.

"Bring up total program on subject into memory."

"Reading. Done."

"Alter as follows. Subroutines enabled as keyed. Acknowledge by sequence number." He reached to the keyboard and did a capable one-hand typing exercise that showed he'd done *a lot of this. Number and letter sequences, some running dozens of number and letter combinations, showed up on the screen, none of which made any sense to me, nor would they without looking at the underlying code—if then.*

"Running. Acknowledge forty, thirty-nine, thirty-eight . . ."

The computer kept counting down as "I" slept on the monitor and watched on the console. Finally the computer said, "Done."

"Erase record of procedures from master and security files. Override condition Calypso Pete Evans Sutherland."

"Code acknowledged. Erasing. Acknowledged. Confirmed. Done. Reset. Ready."

The screen went off. Drew punched the bar for voice commands off and then put something else up on the screen. I could follow what he was doing now and knew that his security override had allowed it. He was running a set of routines in which he had little interest but which would show up if anyone tried to find out what he was doing here. Al almost certainly also had audio and video bugs, but I assumed "Drew" knew how to disable them.

Les came in and seemed surprised but not disturbed to see Drew there.

"Oh, hello, Drew. Working late?"

"Trying to crack that damned code again."

Les chuckled. "Drew, you're going to have to be patient. We've got a fair amount of time to spend here yet getting things back even close to where we were last time when you screwed everything up, and the technology here is just getting to the point where we might be able to hope to get some of the additional hardware made. You be good and you'll ride through with us and walk out of here. Cause more trouble and you'll wake up as somebody you don't even know."

Things began to fade out in my mind as Les fiddled with the console and started to bring up the same image Drew had just looked at.

"Who's that?" he asked, as if he didn't know.

"Rick's wife. Resembles your normal feminine side, actually, except that you were taller and thinner the last couple of times out. Had a sad life here, actually."

"So what are you gonna do to her?" Drew asked.

"Make her life a little happier, that's all."

"You always act like all the others are real," Drew noted. "Why do you care?"

"I dunno. I'm a doctor, and my name's Cohen, not Mengele, which means a lot to me. Besides, who's to say that they're not real? That they don't live normal lives even if they didn't exactly evolve? Until I know for sure, I'll treat everybody as normal. I just treat a few as being abnormal, including you and me."

I fell into a soft, deep sleep as the voices seemed to recede farther and farther from me.

It was after noon the next day when I woke up in the infirmary with a lot of confusion and a headache. Les wasn't there, but Rick and a nurse were.

I had a couple of crazy dreams I could barely remember, but they were fading faster than my head was pounding. I seized on Rick's concerned face. "Where—where am I?"

"In the hospital at the institute," he told me. "You drank a little too much and passed out. Remember?"

I groaned. "Oh! That's what happened! I—honey, help me up! Can we go home now?"

He laughed, caught me, and got me unsteadily to my feet. "Yeah, I think it's time we left. You've been out the whole night!"

"Oh, my!" I felt embarrassed, and even worse, I might have embarrassed Rick in front of his bosses. I said as much, almost breaking down in tears as I did so.

"Hey! Relax! It's cool! Besides, nobody else saw it except the doctor. Come on. I'll help you. One step at a time. I got the car in the ambulance bay just outside the back door here. Not much farther . . ."

The fact was, I *hadn't* remembered where I was or why I was there or anything else. Once I got into the car, I didn't reflect on it or anything else in the past again. It wasn't amnesia. I mean, if somebody asked me how I had met Rick, I'd tell 'em the official version—the accident one—and if anybody asked where I last worked, I would tell 'em Alice's in Berkeley. But once the need to remember was over, I simply filed it and never thought of it again until it was needed. I was also uninterested in the future as such. Oh, I don't mean I wouldn't plan a week's meals or not look forward to a night out or even a vacation, but anything not really directly affecting my life and routine seemed unimportant. My whole life revolved around Rick, and I had no other interests. In truth, I had an unstated and unreflected-on yet constant low opinion of myself; other women could be the leaders and movers and shakers and more power to 'em, but I didn't want any more than I had and felt I was doing the best I could.

After a while we joined a local Catholic church and got remarried in it. My chief instructor was a devoted nun who spent a lot of time with me, and we became fast friends. I never could get the hang of driving, and she had a license but no car, so sometimes we'd drop Rick off for work and she'd help me with shopping and things like that. I just adored Sister Rita.

I had been so embarrassed by the drinking business that I swore to the Blessed Virgin what I'd already promised Rick and more: that I would never again take a drink with alcohol in it, that I'd never take drugs, you name it. Everything I promised Rick I wouldn't do, but he could change that. A promise to the Holy Mother of God was absolute and forever. From that point I not only laid off drinking but stopped smoking in any form and even gave up things like caffeine and red meat, although I'd fix them for others.

Also from that point I no longer seemed to have any reaction toward Rick's coworkers or bosses. I didn't like or not like them. They mostly intimidated me and made me realize how dumb I was, and I interacted with them only when Rick made

me, and then I mostly kept quiet. He never talked about what
he did there, and I never felt any curiosity about what that
place was. It was just where Rick worked. I *did* get involved
with some Catholic service wives through the Church, but
even then I never felt totally comfortable, since most of them
had far more education than I did.

The next May Rick graduated from Stanford with his BS in
nursing and became a full-fledged RN. He was at the top of his
class and got a job offer from the university medical center. It
would be something of a step to leave the navy rather than stay
in, but I didn't want him switched out to sea duty, which would
be a sure thing if he reupped. This would keep us in the area,
together, and mean more money and opportunities in the long
run. Rick never hesitated in deciding to leave the service and
take the job; by that point we both knew I was pregnant.

Rick was due to leave the navy and the institute in August,
so we decided to take a little vacation honeymoon like we hadn't
had before he started his job, using the accumulated back
leave. In the meantime, the university staff office found us
a nice two-bedroom apartment not far off campus that
was within our budget—a house was out of the question in
that area—and I looked forward to furnishing it and setting
things up.

We went to Hawaii and did the usual tourist things, a lot rec-
ommended by Dannie Tanaka, who would have her PhD in
biophysics of all things in February and seemed to be dating
every guy she met. I took an instant serious dislike to her. She
was everything I wasn't—gorgeous, brilliant, capable of almost anything—but still, I had no desire to trade places with
her. I only wished I had what she had.

I guess I also might have had more than a touch of unreasoning jealousy. She was doing research work that was half at the
medical center and half at the institute, and she came into contact with Rick all the time once we settled in. I had never
cheated on Rick and never would, but as I got more and more

huge, it seemed he was spending as much time working in her areas as he was spending at home with me.

Some of it was my condition. I loved the idea of being a mother but hated being pregnant. Couldn't sleep right, didn't feel sexy at all, and felt fat and ugly; in the last two months it looked and started to feel as if I had a large fruit growing in my tummy.

Coming back from the hospital once, we spotted a police car, lights flashing, pulling into the Schumaker Building, the institute where Rick used to work. It was nighttime and they turned off the lights fairly quickly, but we eased on by and could see a couple of the security agents who worked there taking this woman out of the back of the police car as the cop got signatures and looked on. She looked kind of familiar, some-how—didn't everybody?—but in that light the only thing you could see was that she wasn't too happy about going in there and was dark, kind of Oriental-looking, but with a bigger build than, say, Danielle Tanaka.

"Why would they have somebody in handcuffs delivered *there*?" I wondered aloud, even though I was the one who never wondered. It was so bizarre that I couldn't help it, al-though by tomorrow it would be a footnote in my mind.

"I'm not sure," Rick replied. "They're doing a lot of work on both physical and mental behavior in there, I know. Who knows who she is? There's enough law there, though, at all levels, that it's not something we have to worry about. Proba-bly a volunteer for an experiment from one of the prisons near here, that's all."

"Yeah, that's right," I responded. "You was carin' for that crippled guy, right? Wonder if they found a way to help *him*."

"I can answer that. They didn't," he said sadly if matter-of-factly. "He was a nice guy, but there were limits. He died be-fore I left."

I felt a kind of shock go through me, a weird kind of feeling I'd never had before, but I couldn't explain it. For a moment I felt as if I were going to pass out, and Rick, noticing, asked, "You okay? Want me to pull over?"

I shook my head, and things seemed to clear up. "Huh? What?"

"You looked like you were getting sick."

"I'm okay. Just hold me close for a little bit, Ricky. Kiss me and tell me you love me."

He did pull over, undid our seat belts, and for just a little while in the dark it felt like being a teenager again, only with my belly there was only so much we could do. It was enough. At the end of a few minutes I couldn't remember what had scared me.

Angel was born near the end of March, almost on time. She was a pretty baby, and you could already see she'd be a pretty child as well. Labor was short, the delivery was uncomplicated, and I think it took me all of two weeks to want more.

Sister Rita was all over Angel as well and introduced me to somebody new, a full-blooded Indian woman named Sasucha, "Sassy" for short. She had a build more like mine, but she was taller and definitely stronger and had a classical Indian face and long black hair. She was a refugee, I was told by Sister Rita, hiding out away from her people, among whom she'd been wed to a man who'd become an alcoholic and batterer when she was only fifteen years old.

It was like we'd known each other forever right from the start in spite of the two different races. Sassy even pointed to my high cheekbones and suggested that I might have some native blood in me. She didn't have much more education than I did, so I didn't feel inferior. Also, she couldn't have kids, or so she believed, and there was no way she was goin' back, so she loved baby-sitting and playing with kids and helping out the women who had them. She mopped floors and did windows and the like to make some money but was mostly living off Catholic Charities.

Rick liked her as much as I did, which helped a lot, and while she was exotic-looking in a sense, she wasn't a beauty queen like Danielle who could raise hackles of jealousy.

It did seem like I had little breathing room, though. I always thought that if you were nursing and didn't have periods yet, you couldn't get knocked up again. Guess what.

I was on my bike to go down to the small convent next to the Church, which was just off Page Mill Road about three miles from the quad where we had our apartment off Route 82. I rode a lot when I could, even though the traffic got to me sometimes, and in this case I definitely wanted to tell Sister Rita the news in person even though we had our own phone now. It was kind of a nice day, with warm temperatures and little wind and a lot of sun, and the sun, while playing hide-and-seek with fluffy clouds, was a bit warm. I had Angel in a papoose-style backpack, well strapped in on my back. She liked riding and tended to be very quiet and make unintelligible comments now and then on the passing scene but did no crying.

I was used to going in there, and most of the staff and nuns knew me. I never disturbed them when they were at work or at prayer, but today, in the afternoon, they were away or gardening or something like that, and I expected Sister Rita to be around someplace, maybe catching up on her reading. She wasn't in the convent area, though, and one of the other permanent sisters said she thought Sister Rita was in the small office of the preschool they ran there. It being Saturday, there wasn't much activity on the preschool level, but it was one of Rita's pride and joys.

I went down the hall and could hear her speaking to somebody, possibly on the phone, since I couldn't hear any other voice; it was clearly a dialogue.

I stopped outside, not wanting to disturb her. I could wait, so I sat on a bench and decided it was as good a time as any to see if Angel was hungry.

". . . Definitely Matalon," Rita was saying, her words mostly passing into one of my ears and out the other. But when you are sitting there close enough to hear with no way to move, you, well, *listen*.

"I don't know how many meetings they've had, damn it! A *lot* from the looks of it. I tell you, it's the last round backward. This time we got Maddox out of the way without doing anything, but if they pulled Rick's box . . ."

I was suddenly *very* interested, but only out of curiosity. I had no idea what she was talking about, and certainly there were lots of people other than my Rick with that name. Still . . .

"Yeah, yeah, I know we got the wife and kid, but deep down, what's the difference if they're spooks? And we know she's a spook 'cause she's got the kid. Yeah, I know, but you're due to power up to fifty percent within the week, right? If he *knows*, if he's had his Box read back from the last session, then he knows how to interface with the power grid and knows what kinds of mistakes his group made last time. No. We *can't* nail him! Shit, we nail him and we don't know who or *what's* out there. You remember those Boojum creeps! And *something* tore off the roof of the plane right above Allie and plucked her out and crushed her. Don't forget that! No! Yeah . . . Yeah, okay. If he can't divorce spooks in his head, then he's still dead meat. That's the way to go. Time for some Q and A here, I agree."

Angel took that time to take in a little too much milk and start coughing. There wasn't anything I could do about it, anyway.

I began to wonder if I really *shouldn't* move. This wasn't any Sister Rita *I* knew; this was like somebody else entirely, somebody colder than ice, somebody who sure as hell sounded like a danger to me and mine.

Sister Rita's head peered out into the hall and spotted Angel and me. I saw her face show real concern, indicating that she realized I'd overheard, and then watched the concern turn into something of a threatening smile.

She was still on the phone. "Hold on! God works in mysterious ways," she continued as I tried to figure out what to do next. It wasn't like I could run far, not with just a bike and with a baby to look after.

"Why don't you drop over right now?" Sister Rita asked the person on the other end of the call. "Mrs. Wilisczik and her cute little daughter are here right this minute for a visit."

VI

REALITY AS A DECK
OF CARDS

The trouble was, I didn't know what to do. In fact, looking back on it, there wasn't much I coulda done no matter what. I had Angel in my arms and only a bicycle for a getaway, and Sister Rita was in pretty damned good physical shape. She could also be tough and mean and nasty—I'd seen hints of that in her dealings with everybody from the types who you always want to blow off to salesmen who didn't move fast enough to suit her.

She hung up the phone with an "Okay. Soon," and came out into the hall at a pretty fast walk. She seemed almost surprised to see me still sittin' there and burpin' the baby but kind of pleased as well.

"Rina! I'm *so* sorry about all that! I hope you didn't think we were talking about *you* or anything!" she said, suddenly all sweet sugar again.

"I kinda figgered you was," I admitted. "All this time—we *trusted* you. We thought you was a good person, a real nun."

"Oh, I'm a nun, honey," she responded, sounding fairly relaxed. "I'm also a bit more than that, and being a nun doesn't automatically scrub you clean. Sort of like there are priests who have affairs, priests who have other priests as lovers, child molesters, you name it. Don't worry—I don't molest children. In fact, I'm seeking God just like everyone else around here. I just happen to have some inside information they don't."

I stared at her with a look that said I didn't understand a word she was sayin' right then. All I could manage was "Huh?"

She sighed. "Never mind. Where's your husband?"

"What? He's at the hospital, ain't he? I mean, he's at work."

"No, he's not."

"But he was there this mornin'! He brought me home!"

She nodded. "Yes, that's true, but he didn't return. He called in, in fact, with car trouble, but he never called you at your apartment."

"How do you know if he did or didn't?" I got suddenly more worried about him than about myself. "He coulda had an accident!"

"He didn't. We have your phone tapped. In fact, somebody's gonna get it for this, 'cause he was supposed to be under observation at all times."

I frowned. "Who's this 'we'? Who gave you any okays to listen in on our calls? You can't *do* that!"

"You can do *anything* if you don't get caught," she responded. She tapped her foot and looked a little heavenward, one of her habits when she was thinking. "Don't worry about it, dear. We've had your head through all sorts of tests, and you just don't have the smarts for this. Look, all we're trying to do is the best for everybody. Nobody's trying to hurt anybody or do anything funny or crazy or whatever. We want to talk to Rick, that's all. A couple of people you know will be here in a few minutes. All they want to do is question you. I swear to God, Rina, you can even call your apartment and, if Rick isn't there, leave a message about where you'll be. Is that fair?"

I didn't follow that at all. "I just think I should go home," I told her. But I knew she wasn't gonna let me go, and there was no way I was gonna do nothin' that might cause her to hurt Angel.

"You know that's not possible, my dear," Sister Rita responded with a threatening undertone to her sweet smile.

I was terrified, as much for Angel as for myself, and I got a clear idea that Rick was in trouble, too. Trouble was, both fear and a lack of a clear way out kept me frozen, sitting there on the bench. I knew I *oughta* move, *oughta* do something to defend me and mine, but I just *couldn't*, even though that scene of the strange woman being wrestled into the institute popped into my mind with frightenin' clearness. Maybe I was slow, but no way was I *that* slow.

"Who *are* you people?" I almost wailed. "What gives you the right to do this shit?"

"You wouldn't understand," she responded, sounding patronizing but also probably correct. "Just keep these things in your limited mind if you can. First, we don't want to make a mess, we don't want to hurt anyone, but we will. Deep down, none of us would be very disturbed if we had to make you and the kid disappear. Second, you have nothing we want. You are strictly bait. If you do exactly as you are told, nothing bad will happen to you because we don't care about *that*, either. Third, you have no fight in you. You can't do anything to hurt anybody, and you know it and we know it. So just let things happen. Don't try to understand it."

It wasn't just that I knew I didn't understand *nothin'* anymore and that my happy world had been turned on its head in the space of a few minutes; I also knew that she was right 'bout me not bein' much of a threat. Oh, I'd been able to play the worldly girl, all bluff and bluster, when I waited tables, but even that seemed a lifetime away. I didn't have enough toughness in me to squash a bug anymore. Not since . . .

Not since I had passed out that first night at the institute long ago.

I decided not to let on that I'd figured that out. They had me down as a low-grade moron when I was more ignorant than stupid in a lot of ways.

I took the nun at her word that Angel and I weren't the real cause of all this. They wanted Rick for some reason, and for some reason Rick had disappeared. That meant that he knew who they were even if I didn't and that he'd gotten wind of them and had to split without having a chance to tell me. I was certain he wouldn't desert us, and that made me feel good until I realized that this was also what Sister Rita believed.

Bait, she said. We were bait.

I heard a car pull up in the lot outside, out of our view, and knew it was whoever Rita had called. She heard it, too, and looked a little tense, like she wasn't all that sure it wasn't somebody she didn't want to see. She had her head in a noose one way or the other, and the nice life she'd been living was over. I didn't know what it was, but I had a sense that she didn't like any of this, either, that she might have been happier if things had just kept going along.

There were footsteps and some conversation, then Sister Rita relaxed when she saw Commander Starkey and Danielle Tanaka come into view. I wasn't at all pleased to see either of them.

I looked up at Sister Rita and said, "God will never forgive you for this."

She nodded and replied almost wistfully, "You're probably right. But just as you love Rick, I, too, had a love, and the people who killed her are people Rick has chosen over us. I don't have a choice of sides here."

"But you're a *nun*! A bride of Christ!"

She shrugged and said rather sadly, "Yes, but I'm afraid I'm a bigamist."

The commander walked in, wearing casual navy khaki and looking very official and clean-cut but all business. He was the one I was most afraid of, and I didn't like him being there one bit.

He nodded at Sister Rita. "Our sweet little Indian maiden tried to duck out on a pretty fancy Harley when she saw us coming," Starkey told her. "It was hell to catch her. Surprise,

surprise. Seems our good doctor's work on her didn't take very well, and *she* had the full Brand Box treatment."

"Are you sure about *her*?" Sister Rita asked, suddenly looking less confident and nodding toward me.

"Oh, sure. She's a spook, remember. Not the same thing. No, Cohen thinks that Slidecker or whoever it is has a spare couple of Brand Boxes and took a complete backup of the woman before exposing her here. We did the job, then they replaced the original. What a waste of time and effort, eh?" He sighed and turned to me.

"I really, sincerely apologize for all this. It's none of your doing, and I hoped you would never become involved, and that's the truth. I'm going to have to ask you to come with us now, but I can virtually promise you that we'll be able to release you and your baby later on. Please, this is important. We're not evil, Mrs. Wilisczik. We're just doing our jobs in a situation that's complicated for all of us."

I didn't have much choice, not with Angel there in my arms. I got up, and Starkey looked back at Sister Rita. "I think you should come along as well. I don't want any of us exposed until this plays itself out."

Sister Rita didn't look thrilled. I could almost sense that she was as scared of Commander Starkey as I was, but she didn't protest. Danielle Tanaka mostly stood there watching us and said nothing. I wondered if she had a purpose for being there or just happened to be in Starkey's company when things broke. It was rumored that she'd moved in with him; it was the local scandal.

We walked out, and I saw that Starkey had brought one of the vans. There was somebody inside, and when the side door slid back, it proved to be one of the security men and Sassy, of all people! The Indian woman looked mad as hell, but she was outweighed by her guard by maybe two hundred pounds, and it wasn't likely she could get far if she made a break for it. They did seem pretty confident: no handcuffs, no guns, nothing like that.

They put me in the backseat next to Sassy and, with the fit tight, put the thin Danielle Tanaka in on the only side where you could get out. Commander Starkey took the middle seat and sat kind of sideways so he could watch us and trip anybody trying for the door. Sister Rita sat in the front passenger seat while the guard started things up and backed out of the space. I heard a series of *thunks* as the automatic door lock kicked in.

"As I say, just relax, ladies. It's strictly business here. Don't make it personal."

"I can't figure you out, Starkey," Sassy commented. "Where do you get off in all this? Power? Seems like you just keep doing the same thing over and over. For what? So you can have fun terrifying people and imprisoning them in little hellhole universes?"

Starkey didn't seem to take it badly at all. "Duty, my dear. Something you'll never understand. It's my *job*. Things have gotten into an ugly enough mess now, with at least one powerful faction against us, but it's not something we can't handle."

"Like you handled Cory 'n' me last round, right?"

He shrugged. "I had the power; you had a backdoor out and made it. So what did it get you? He's dead—natural causes, in fact—and I have a pretty detailed sim of him in a Box, so that's that. You—well, where'd it get you but here? Soon I'll have Rick and the rest, too. Maybe even dear old Walt. I should have had him last time, but there was a diversion, if you'll recall. The nervy bastard actually crawled in and stole stuff while we were having our little showdown! Not this time. This time we'll be ready for him."

She stared at him and shook her head in wonder and disgust. "What do you mean 'we'? Your duty to *who* or to *what*? You don't even know. You're as much a programmed automaton as any of the ones you brainwash. You don't even know whose orders you're following."

"Does anybody? The priests say follow God and the Pope, or Buddha and the true path, or the Prophet to one of the heavens. Scientists say we're the prisoners of heredity and hormones, steered by environment. Free will's a myth. Even the little lady here. I mean, if we'd left her alone, she'd have run her whole course and it wouldn't have made a damned bit of difference. I never did know for sure if the rest of the country, let alone the universe, was actually there unless one of us was or whether it was provided as necessary—it's like the sound of one hand clapping in the forest. Rina here might not even have *existed* without my intervention. Think of that!"

"What did you have to do with her?" Sassy asked him, curious now. I couldn't really follow it, but when they start talking about you, you listen real, real close.

"We *invented* her, of course! Rick has proved—troublesome—in the past. He's got the talent always and the guts some of the time. This time I think he's got the full lot. But he's a reincarnate. He doesn't remember any past lives, and he doesn't remember us except in tiny snippets in his dreams. With Walt and dear Cynthia out there I didn't need any more talented enemies, and consider what they and you managed with Rick and Cory last time out. So we gave him a reason to stick around. We ran into the girl by accident while going through a records search for somebody else entirely. Those of us who remembered were struck by how closely she resembled Cory in the female phase. We knew it wasn't her, and after all, we had Cory here, didn't we? But the physical resemblance was so uncanny, we knew it would attract Rick irresistibly. So we took the spook, wiped her memories, and gave her *just enough* of Korinna's personality and habits and traits and a real instant attraction to Rick. Then we wound her up, set her up, and eventually arranged for the two to cross paths without either realizing they were set up. Worked pretty well, too, until today."

What was he talking about? What was a "spook"? I didn't like being called names, 'specially when I didn't know what they meant. Even so, I knew he was trying to say that he had made me up. "I'm not a TV character," I told him. "I'm *me*!"

He smiled. "Think about growing up. I don't mean the information—names and dates and the like. I mean for you to *remember*. Scenes of going to school. When you got your first period. Your first sex with a boy. When you learned anything at all. Think hard. I'll bet you can't come up with any solid, vivid memories of any time before you woke up in that Oakland apartment."

"I don't want to." But, the truth was, he was right. I didn't have those memories. I didn't even know what was missing or even that anything was until he said it, though.

"You can't because it didn't exist. You *did* think you were Cory for a while, deep down. That's because we got a lot of the personality from a Cory recording we had. When you passed out, though, we took the time to completely eliminate Cory from your memories and background and give you the more passive and less intellectual traits you have now. I *did*, however, figure that your having the child would really hold Rick down. You see, that's one big difference between the spooks created by the program and us. We can't have kids. Not *real* ones. That would drive us nuts."

Angel was sucking away on her pacifier and seemed dead asleep. "This ain't no doll baby, mister, no matter what you say."

"No, not to you. Let me just admit that your baby is as real as you are."

"And all of us and any of *this*," Sassy put in. "But not all of us have immortal souls, do we, Sister Rita?"

"Shut up!" the nun snapped.

Outside, we were getting close to the turnoff for the institute. Funny, all around us there was traffic going here and there, a normal day for most folks. I looked out the window and saw a motorcycle pulling around and heard the roar of the engine as it passed. You couldn't really tell, what with the all-leather outfit, helmet with visor down, and all that, but I could have sworn that it was a woman on that thing. Big sucker, too. One of the Harley monsters.

Sister Rita looked over just as the chopper passed, and the bike's rider looked briefly at us before going straight ahead again. Sister Rita kind of jumped, almost as if she'd somehow made eye contact with the rider through that dark visor. Commander Starkey turned and looked out to see what had caused the reaction. He turned back and relaxed, smiling at the still nervous Sister Rita.

"Don't worry," he told her. "There's thousands of 'em out here. And if it *is* her, so what? I almost wish it *were* her. That would mean they're setting up to hit us when we unload, and that would make things very easy in this case. This world has some potential! If we can move through it undisturbed, maybe we can actually make some progress and not have to do things like this or look over our own shoulders for a while."

"It is a dull, drifting world," Sister Rita commented, almost absently looking out at the traffic. The motorcyclist who'd started all this was way ahead and nowhere to be seen. "Either it will fall off into an abyss or it will continue gray and dull forever. From *my* point of view, we might as well leave it."

"What are you people?" I asked, genuinely upset and confused. "Martians or something?"

They ignored me, and I had the funny feeling that they really didn't give a damn about anybody except maybe themselves.

"I think you just need a vacation," the commander commented.

She stared at him. "I'm a *nun*! This isn't just a uniform like the one you have on! It's part of who and what I am. I wouldn't stop becoming one even if I *did* take it off, either!"

He sighed and shrugged. "I don't know how you can still believe in that stuff or accept it any more than as a convenience. You've certainly broken at least one of those vows."

"And I continue to do penance for it and wonder if somehow it is partially my fault that she's dead! *You* don't know the truth! Perhaps all this is merely hell, infinite and forever, and you are actually serving the devil himself!"

"I will admit that's not the first time that has been postulated, and it certainly isn't the other place. Ah! Here we are! We're going in the ambulance entrance this time, since it's daylight. You, Indian—no funny moves, no heroics. If you do, I assure you that you will never walk again in *this* life and I shall have a wonderful little Box for you in particular. Now, everybody relax and let's walk inside and do as we're told, okay?"

What could I do?

I got the impression that Sassy was more than ready to make a fight of it but knew the odds would be against her if there wasn't a diversion. I tried to think of something *I* could do, but it was wide open anyway and bright sunshine, and nobody was around to speak of 'cept institute people. Where could she go?

They were real pros, I'll say *that*, too. Got us out of there and inside the building so fast, I almost didn't realize we were all in, then closed the doors on us. We went by the security post inside and then through a second and nastier set of doors, and when they closed behind us, it really felt like we were in some kind of jail cell.

Doctor Cohen was there to meet us, dressed in his usual medical whites. He smiled like there was nothin' wrong and came over to me. "Well, looks like a very nice little girl," he commented. "Quiet, too. I've had a crib sent over, so if you want, we can let her try to sleep here in the infirmary, with nurses all around. You're breast-feeding?"

I nodded, not sure if I wanted to let go of Angel and not sure I had a choice.

"All right, then. When she's hungry, we'll put the two of you together. In the meantime, she's much better off here."

They really had set up a nice, quiet little corner nursery nook in one of the two emergency room stalls, complete with a little mobile and lots of stuff to look at and just enough light. I didn't want to let go, but she looked so peaceful and content, I couldn't not do it. There was also somethin' 'bout the doctor, somethin' I couldn't really put down to anything more'n a gut feeling, but I just *knew* he wouldn't let Angel come to harm.

Still, them havin' Angel and all, it definitely was better for
keepin' me obedient and quiet than if they'd thrown me in a
cell with leg irons.

We kept on goin' back in the place, out of the infirmary,
down some office corridors, then through a back hall and down
into some kind of basement, I guess. You didn't see many
basements in northern California—nice way to get buried in a
quake, for one thing.

This wasn't just a basement, though. It was a kinda, well, *tunnel*, and there were guards and passes and shit every this way
and that. Finally we was in a *big* underground room with lots
of dials, switches, and TV-type screens with everything from
words and numbers to some people's faces on 'em, all meanin'
nothin' to me. The couple with faces on 'em showed folks in
some kind of sleep and fixed up to all sorts of tubes and shit.

They split Sassy off from me then, and the commander and
the doc and others went off with her someplace. Me, I now had
just Danielle and Sister Rita with me, but it was enough. They
finally got me down some more stairs and into a small room
with a couch, a small table, an office-type chair, and nothin'
much else in it.

"Take off all your clothes and give them to me," Danielle
Tanaka ordered.

"What!?"

"You heard me. *Do it!* Do it or I'll have some of the strong-
arm types come in and do it for you, and then we'll see if and
when you see your baby. Now—*take 'em off!"*

I did, wondering what kind of perverts these people were.
Now, standing there bare-ass naked, with not even shoes on, I
watched as Tanaka handed the bundle to Sister Rita, who left
with 'em.

"Now what?" I asked her.

She looked me over. "No, that's fine. Your clothes are going
quite a ways from here, and I can tell you right now there is
nothing in the way of bedspreads or other useful stuff any-

where near. The only way *out* is the way we came in, so you know the number of people, cameras, and checks you have to pass. You think about it."

I did and figured out the method pretty quick for a dumb broad. They didn't need to watch me all the time or worry 'bout me escapin' or nothin' like that 'cause I was like this. Even if I somehow got past everybody, where would I be? In the main buildin' or outside stark naked. Yeah, sure.

"What now?"

"Now you'll sit and relax. We'll feed you if you need to be fed here, and we'll bring the brat to you if she needs those big tits of yours. Otherwise you stay here, do what you're told, and wait."

Well, okay, so I wasn't so totally scared that I just rolled up into a ball in the corner and waited. Sure, I peered outside the door and looked at the ends of the hall. There weren't any big male guards that I could see, but the TV cameras had been put there to be seen, not to be hidden, and could and almost surely would bring them big men the moment I stepped outside, not to mention give 'em their jollies on TV.

The room itself might have more stuff, only hidden, but it wasn't worth lookin' for. There was a big cooler in the corner that turned out to have cold water in it, only they forgot cups for it. There was also a place where it looked like they'd had doughnuts or somethin' that morning—none still there, but lots of crumbs and shit.

They actually *did* bring Angel down. Hard to say how often; I got real bored and went to sleep on the couch for some of the time, and there weren't any windows or clocks, and they took my watch. Angel had a clean diaper, which at least showed somebody was lookin' in and really carin' for her and not just leavin' her there, and she didn't eat no more than she usually did, so that took one load off my mind. They let her stay a while, too, although eventually they took her back. I think I coulda stood it better if they'd left her in the room.

There was a small bathroom with a door on one side of the room. Not much, no shower or anything like that, but a toilet, a sink, soap, and one of them hand dryers that never really dries your hands. Every once in a while a woman I didn't know would bring in some food. It was mostly fast-food stuff, or it looked and tasted that way, anyways, but it was fillin'. They didn't know I didn't touch coffee or tea or caffeine, but they learned quickly to bring me juices and milk and stuff like that.

It was funny, though. With nobody to talk to most of the time, no clocks, no day or night, no TV or radio or things like that, I began to just lie there most times between visits by Angel or meals and just, well, *listen*.

For all the basement stuff, I wasn't exactly in the middle of nowhere so far as the institute was concerned. People went up and down the hall all the time, usually talkin', most probably not knowin' I was even there, goin' here and there and maybe even home to dinner. I dreamed of goin' home, of wakin' up and findin' out this was all some kind of bad dream, but it wasn't.

It was funny, though. In the times when there was *no* sound, nothin' at all, just some far-off whirring of the air-conditioning or heating or whatever it was that never seemed to change, just lyin' there, starin' at a blank wall, propped up against the far corner on the couch, head down and kinda restin' on my knees, just sittin' and starin' and not thinkin' of *nothin'* at all, I—I started to *see* things. Not normal things and not the things in crazy movies, either. Weird stuff. Wavy lines. Colors. Electrical lines in long patterns, energy flowin' like paint along a bunch of strings . . .

At first it startled me more'n scared me, and I jumped and everything was back to normal. After a while I learned that you just sat there and stared and didn't think of anything, kinda like hypnotism or something. Just stared and went blank, and sooner or later it always came . . .

After a while it was clear that there was more than just the patterns and the flows and the colors. It was almost like, well, lookin' at somebody's *drawing* of something. You know, like the way they draw up a house. Blueprints. Yeah, that's it. Blueprints but not blue. Drawn by colors of energy on the thin air—at least I guessed it was.

Things were even, well ... *labeled*. Like real thin but in perfect printed block letters. When I realized what it was and kinda pulled back to see the whole thing, it said *"WALL."*

It was kind of tough to keep it in, though, 'cause every time I saw this, I'd start to wonder 'bout it and think 'bout it and everything would come back to normal. Took a while to get used to it, to see what I could see without bein' deep into it and then thinkin' later. After that I got so I could look past the *"WALL"* and see *"WC,"* whatever that meant. It was kinda floatin' there just above the outline of the toilet with the little words *"TOILET"* block printed, which was across from the *"SINK"* of course.

I was beginnin' to get real good at this. Kinda like Superman. X-ray vision was kinda neat.

The far wall did much the same. It was an *"I-WALL,"* which may mean anything but I took it to be "inside," then *"CORRIDOR"* and another *"I-WALL."*

After a while an occasional person would walk by goin' one way or another up and down *"CORRIDOR."* While they, too, popped me outa it for the first few times, when I figured they wasn't comin' in and couldn't feel me lookin', it didn't bother me anymore.

Even their clothes had labels, but when I tried to find out what was under 'em, I wound up with one of them outlined skeletons that was real gross 'cause it was still walkin'.

I tried to figure out what was goin' on and finally decided that either I was goin' nuts from this, which was possible, or I was seein' something *real*.

Or maybe it was sayin' that everything I saw when I was "normal" was fake. Everything. Lookin' down at my own knees and feet and seein' only skeleton and right through that made me real nervous. It was as if all this, *everything*, was just some kind of *drawing* or something. An animated cartoon in three dimensions.

Did *they* know that? The folks who was keepin' me here? If they did, why did they act like they didn't? Maybe they were too smart, I thought. Maybe they couldn't blank themselves out enough to see this.

Then I made a mistake. I looked down below *"RUG,"* below *"FLOOR,"* and I saw the next level down even though I heard 'em say more'n once there *wasn't* a next level down. It was there, though, all burnin' bright like some tremendous controlled fire, blue-white with reds here and there; inside this *big* chamber that went as far as my new sense could see, there was *something*. Something was down there. Maybe more than one something. I couldn't tell nothin' 'bout them, nothin' 'bout who or what they might be, but I suddenly felt that at least one of 'em got some kind of feelin' of bein' stared at and turned and then saw *me*. It started toward me, and I got real scared and pulled back and shook myself out of it.

When I was lookin' again at a normal room and hearin' normal sounds and seein' normal things, I still sat there, sweaty, half expectin' some giant hot monster hand to come through the floor and grab me and drag me down. It didn't happen, though.

From that point on I didn't try to see through the floor anymore. In fact, it was a while before I could bring myself to do anything more at all, but it was *so* damned dull . . .

There was no word from nobody about *nothin'*. They'd taken Angel back again to the nursery or wherever they was keepin' her, and I was left again with not much to do and nothin' much to think about. I'd even stopped feelin' embarrassed or afraid. I was just plain *bored*.

Maybe I couldn't go *down*, but how far could I see or go in the other directions? I relaxed and tried to concentrate on Angel, the closest thing to me in all ways that I knew as well as myself. It didn't take long with that one idea, that one emotional image, in my head to blend it with the blueprint shit. It started slow, with me just lookin' at the wall and then through it and then up the corridor. Then I suddenly found myself takin' off like a rocket, goin' this way and that down this corridor and that and up this stair and that and then across to this place and straight up— *Well, I'll be damned! They got an elevator up to the clinic!* I wondered kinda idly why they hadn't brought me in that way, but maybe I wasn't supposed to know that.

I actually beat Angel back to her crib. She was all cooin' and like that, and I didn't really care for it all that much 'cause I thought she was gettin' much too friendly with the enemy. Still and all, it was no big deal, and everything, even her tiny little self, was just them three-dimensional blueprints of color and flow.

I don't know when it was that I realized that I was sort of outside my body. Not really, I guess, but I might as well have been. I mean, I was lookin' *down* on Angel's tiny skeleton form wrigglin' in the outline labeled *"CRIB,"* and I seemed to be able to go other places without comin' all the way back, so I started to do it.

I actually took a look out of a window on the clinic level and saw that even outside it was all blueprints and signs and shit. Jesus! Wasn't *nothin'* really real?

I decided in a kind of offhanded way to see if I could find my way back the way they'd taken me down. I wasn't really thinkin' no deep thoughts or any of that. I was, well, playin' a game, flyin' down a badly animated cartoon that still seemed to show what shoulda been there. I didn't question it, even though I'd never done it before. I mean, for all I knew this was some kinda ESP or somethin', or maybe they were doin' this to me; maybe this was what they were doin' at the institute. How would I ever know? And I sure would never figure it out. That left, well, doin' what was fun and seein' what I could get away with.

Even what I could see by this point was gettin' far too complicated for me to figure out. I mean, there was *zillions* of patterns and I dunno how many colors and signs and labels and all, and it was gettin' real confusin'. The only thing sure was that all this power was flowing *out* of the subbasement where I didn't want to look and just a little bit of it was headin' the other way. Whatever they were—gods, aliens, machines—this, all of it, even *me*, was their show.

I was pretty sure that nobody but me could see this, but I also got the idea that the people who ran this place *knew* at least part of what was here. That's what all this was about—*that* much I could figure out. Two sides both knew that this was some kinda crazy different way to look at the world, maybe a different way to *run* the world, and both sides wanted it.

I reached the control room we'd come through before. I could recognize it 'cause so many of the power lines and patterns came together there and 'cause there really *was* outlines of TVs and chairs and controls and all that. People was harder to figure 'cause they were animated skeletons, but I finally got a clue as to who was a guy and who was a girl by the way they was built low down and the fact that the girls seemed smaller on average and walked different. Who was who was harder. They didn't have names on 'em; they had long letter and number labels that kinda floated inside 'em. I could read 'em, but what the fuck did *"AZQ-77622323-4IW78"* mean? I mean, it took enough work for whoever had done all this just to fit them damned labels inside!

It was a lot weirder to look at the TV screens, 'cause I could almost make out real faces there. Not that they weren't all unconscious and strapped in and with all sorts of shit on their heads and in their bodies, but something in the way the pictures were shown by the TVs there wouldn't take on the blueprint. I saw 'em instead as almost like real TV pictures, but made up of lots of blurry dots. I could also see that different controls on the big control center board were sendin' out shit to them and that some streams of the energy that made all the outlines, in real fast strips that looked real up close like zillions of dots and spaces, ran wherever the folks in the TVs were.

My head or eyes or whatever you want to call it that was seein' all this even though I was still down in that room went through one of those strings of dots and spaces, and for just a second I got the weirdest picture in my head of a big castle and a lot of naked pretty girls around. I went through another, and for just a few seconds there was the sound and feel, even the smell, of a huge crowd cheering as somebody was whippin' somebody up on a big platform. I didn't want to try and stay within the trails, since I felt that they had more power than me and pushed me along the floor toward big throbbing lines goin' down. I didn't want to get trapped.

Still, what *were* those? Fake worlds? Was *that* it? They made up these fake worlds and then drugged folks and somehow sent 'em 3-D movies with smell and feel and everything so they was sure they was livin' in them worlds and not here?

Like me? Like us?

I mighta been dumb, ignorant, anything else, but I began to figure I knew somethin' they weren't so sure of. They was here, puttin' people in these movie worlds or whatever they was, so's you couldn't just go *see* the movie, you *starred* in it, just like it was all real. And while they was doin' that, all of *them* was in one, too!

I realized that my ignorance and Angel were probably the only two reasons they hadn't locked me away in one of their weird shows. Even if only the doc and a couple of others believed that Angel was real at all, and me, too, the fact was that enough people were just not ready to kill a baby who *might* be real. Me, maybe, but not the kid, and they hadn't had much time to figure out how to do both.

"But not all of us have immortal souls, do they, Sister Rita?"

Now, that was funny, too, 'cause if I could do *this*, then I sure as hell oughta be able to see a difference between me and Angel and anybody else, like the ones who thought they had souls and the ones who didn't, right? So where was it? The skeletons and the very thin outlines around them were different colors and taller and shorter and like that, but there was no orange glow inside or even a blinking red light. If any of 'em had souls, they didn't show up, and there was no label for it, neither.

But maybe—maybe the ID tags were the souls. Not everybody had *them*. Not everybody in the control room even, let alone Angel and her nurse.

Did I? I suddenly wanted to know.

I continued on, back the way I'd come in, and finally couldn't figure how to get down 'cept by the elevator way back in the clinic. Didn't matter, though. I didn't want to go all the way down, but goin' through one floor shouldn't be a problem.

It wasn't, yet it was. The active dots and spaces and lines from the control room went along wires, I guess, or somethin' like wires; they had to go somehow, just like phone lines, and that was between the floors. It meant that I passed through a whole bunch of them, givin' me a whole lot of scenes at once.

One of 'em reached out for me and came right through the floor after me. Not one of the heavy lines goin' *down* but the thin little lines goin' *up*.

I felt something, someone, touch my mind.

I heard a man's voice say, not out loud but almost like he was inside my mind, *"Don't fight! Relax and give me control! I'll let you go very quickly, but we need to talk!"*

I was scared and started to pull away and fight him. Hell, I didn't know what I was doin' *then*; to let somebody else have control of my mind that I maybe didn't even *know* was like, well, kinda mental *rape* or something. I didn't know what this was, after all.

I moved away fast and went on toward what I hoped was my sleepin' body in the room just as fast as I could. I was *scared*. Scareder than I was of the sons of bitches who had snatched me. They were only nuts; this was, I dunno, almost like sacrilege.

I saw my body, flowed toward it, got into it, felt it flesh

out again, felt myself breathing and the flow of the air-conditioning on my skin. For just a moment I felt safe.

Then I sensed it, coming for me like a fireball, and realized for just a second that the SOB had *followed* me! There wasn't anyplace to run and no time to run even if there was, but I tried to fight it off. It *burned* . . .

When I came to, I was still naked and lyin' flat on a pretty cold table made of some kind of smooth plastic. In fact, everything around looked like it was made of the same stuff, only with different-colored lights inside and maybe some colored dye to give it a different look. It was kind of spooky but also cold and unfeelin'. I was being held down on the table, faceup, my arms, legs, and waist held by straps that looked like they were poured of the same stuff. The thing was, though, I wasn't goin' *nowhere.*

I looked around and found I still had that burnin' headache, but even that paled before the shadow I saw against one of those smooth walls. Whoever or whatever it was, I sure was helpless.

"Whatever" proved to be more the word as the *thing* came into view. Now it looked like a man, sort of, but it was made of the same stuff as the walls and tables and all the rest and had a kind of inside blue light. The thing was, there was no face, or at least features. The face looked like a real face, but it had only indentations for eyes, a nose with no holes, kind of statue-like lips, and Mister Potato Head ears. Still, it moved real smooth, smoother than human beings moved, and I knew it could see, hear, and was in some other way alive. At least I didn't have to worry 'bout one thing: there wasn't nothin' between its legs. Still, it kinda looked and moved more like a man than a woman.

So did his voice, even though it was flat, kinda without any real feelin'. With each word the body glowed a little bluer, flashin' to the beat sorta, only centered in the chest.

"I am sorry to have had to bring you here," the thing told me. "It would have been easier if you had not fought and ran."

"So who are *you*?" I came back.

"I have no identity. Nothing here has identity. It is all the same here. It is a life without time, without pain, without pleasure, love, or hate, without wants or needs or desires. It is designed that way. It is another construct, an unreality that is nonetheless real, smaller, and more limited than your own and a subset of it."

I didn't follow all those big terms, but I got the idea. "You mean this ain't real, neither."

"It is real for me. I was placed here so that over time all that I was in past lives would become meaningless to me. I would remember data but not feeling. To an extent this has happened. I cannot even academically relate to who and what I was. Terms have no meaning; memories of irrational behavior make no sense. I sense that much of what I speak about you do not understand, and that is all right. Imagine the other way. Imagine that you knew the definition of, but did not truly understand, love, hate, friendship, sadness, humor, any of that. You knew the words, you could call up pictures of the actions, but you could not comprehend them."

I did kinda understand what it was sayin', and in more'n one way I felt sorry for it. But fact was, *it* had *me* tied down. I didn't do nothin' to it.

"Okay, so you're stuck just like me. Why me? Why here? And what next?" I asked it.

"You are here because I was given access to something and asked to provide it if a certain set of circumstances came about, including this opportunity."

"You mean you were ordered to do somethin' to *me* if you got the chance?"

"I am not a robot. A request was made and accepted because those who have run this place for a very long time are doing a poor job and are not in any way solving problems that require solutions. They are clearly the wrong people to be in charge. It is therefore logical for me to aid those who wish to wrest control from the current administration."

"Um, yeah, sure, Mister Spock, it's all logical and all that. But what does any of this got to do with *me*? What can *I* do?"

"You are incomplete. A part of you was taken away from your mind and stored. At the moment there is no way to get to that specific storage medium, but there is a backup that will do. You are linked to the backup but are not in a position to access it. I can provide that access."

"What—what d' ya mean, I'm 'incomplete'? You mean part of me is missin'? *They* said that. They said that they made me into somebody who would love Rick and Rick would fall for, that they done it for their own use."

"That is correct," the thing told me. "However, they do not know that others also had opportunities here. You will see. You will figure it out when you arrive at the backup location. There you can be restored and made whole. Just remember, do not be afraid of anything with a hint of familiarity there. Control your fear. That alone will help you greatly."

I was more afraid of what Frankenstein was gonna do than of anything else right now. "So what happens *this* time?"

"All reality is programming. We cannot know the real; we are trapped in an endless series of simulations, all of us, and some, like myself, in simulations within simulations. I am going to use a little of the technology available here to stimulate your brain in a way that only certain substances could. This will cause the reaction to take place starting here, at which point you will be let go and immediately spring back into your body, asleep in the room. That in turn will produce the desired result. You may experience some dizziness or discomfort."

"Like I'm not now? I can't even follow this. What—"

I didn't get any further. Instead, cold glasslike hands touched my head, and there was a sense of massage, and then the lights went out. I don't mean I got knocked out; it was more like a whole series of crackles and lightning and explosions in my head took place that caused even the plastic place to look kinda eerie and blueprintlike. Things snapped in and out and up and down, and for a second I swore I could see a real guy where the thing was, a guy I mighta seen before someplace. But then things began happenin' much too fast to follow.

I got suddenly higher'n a kite, dizzy but happy, and the whole damned universe seemed to be swirlin' around. There was noise like mad and all sorts of jabberin' like a big crowd in a stadium all talkin' at once. Then, for one brief moment, I was back in the room, back on the couch in my own body, and I opened my eyes, looked around, and started to say something aloud just to hear my own voice. Then I suddenly was falling through darkness with no parachute and no brakes!

I screamed, and there was a sudden feeling of warm, almost hot mush under me. I opened my eyes and found myself on a beach in some weird place.

That sand was *hot*! I got up, feelin' that I was still in my body and just someplace else, and looked around. Giant trees, bigger'n any I ever saw before, bigger than redwoods, bigger than sequoias, just *huge*, came right up to the beach, their roots like frozen big, fat worms twisted this way and that. The water was smooth as glass and looked almost black, reflectin' what was more like a colorful ceiling way, way higher above me than any sky.

It was hot and lonely and scary, and worst of all, I had to take a piss somethin' awful.

I didn't trust water I couldn't at least see a little into, and I wasn't so sure 'bout them trees, so I squatted. The sand didn't wet like normal sand or litter box stuff; it was kinda odd, almost like it was gold dust or somethin'.

I was just getting back up and wishin' I had some toilet paper when I heard something, something *big*, soundin' like it was, well, *flyin'*. I looked up real fast but didn't see anythin'. When I'd looked all over, though, I realized I didn't hear it no more and looked back down.

Somebody was lookin' at me. Or, rather, some *thing* was.

I give out a scream, and even as it echoed, I started backin' up while lookin' for a rock or big stick or somethin' to use as a weapon against it.

"No, no! Wait! I'm not going to hurt you!" the thing said.

I stopped, but I wasn't trustin' nobody with a black hairy body and bat wings. "Seems like everybody and every creature is hell-bent on tellin' me that they don't mean to hurt me, just fling me 'round from crazy place to crazy place," I muttered aloud.

"I know the body looks—well, *weird*, kind of devilish, but it's something somebody designed to help me. Look at my face! Not my body, my face. See if you don't recognize me."

I stopped, frowned, and stared at the thing. It did have a human face and not an unfamiliar one, either. I gasped. "You're the guy Rick was lookin' after while he was finishin' school! Or you got his head, anyways!"

The thing looked pleased. "Well, this is a start. Yes, I'm that person. Cory Maddux. In here, instead of me being looked after by somebody like Rick and in an electric wheelchair and dependent on others, I can use this body. It's not *my* body, and it's kind of a nightmare body designed by whoever put this crazy place together, but it's one I can use. I've been stuck here since Wilma—Sassy to you, I think—separated us."

"Sep—separated us?"

He nodded. "I was flying south to the institute with Rick and others when something hit the airplane and forced it down. I don't know even now who did it, why, or how, but whoever it was has a lot more power over reality, *that* reality, than I do. They wanted to get their man into the institute, to the computers, to the records. They took my consciousness, what was truly *me*, and, apparently knowing that Al and Les and company were setting you up as their little puppet, pulled a fast one by putting all that is really me inside you, too. But when you— we—drank too much booze at the reception and passed out and wound up in the hands of Doc Cohen in his own clinic and labs inside the institute, there was no way to hide the fact that the guy they thought was Cory wasn't and that you—we—were.

We got to here, where Wilma was able to separate the two of us before Les got to us. Since then you've been on your own and I've been trapped here."

I frowned. I didn't follow this guy any more'n I followed the character with the blue plastic face, but I got the basic idea. "You're sayin' that you and me are the *same*? I hate to break it to you, buddy, but—"

"My mother's maiden name was Nora Kassemi," he said. "What was *your* mother's name?"

"I—" He had me. But I wasn't no relation to *him*, or at least I couldn't believe I was.

"Can you see her face?" he asked me kinda gently. "Can you hear her voice? Can you remember growing up?"

I frowned. I didn't like these kinda questions at all.

"No," I replied.

"We're two sides of the same person," he tried to explain. "We don't seem to be at all alike, but we are. I have the lives, the memories, the understanding, and the education you lack. You have the life, the emotional highs and lows, the human personality traits nerds like me never seem to develop. Male or female, it doesn't matter. We're *one*, and we're split and we shouldn't be. Look at my eyes, my face, and *know* it's true."

I didn't want to look. I didn't want it to be true, but I knew it was.

"What—so what *is* all this?" I almost wailed.

He sighed. "Beats the hell out of me, babe. But I think that everything right now is riding on us. We need to be whole again. I was hoping Wilma would be here to handle this, but I don't think she's coming."

"Wilma? Sassy, you mean. They got her. She's in the institute."

He didn't like that. "All the more reason to do this. What about the guy pretending to be me?"

"Maddux? They say he's dead."

He nodded. "Figures. Are they powering up the place yet?"

"I dunno. I dunno what that means. They got me and my baby inside the institute, though. We're prisoners, too."

"Your *what*? Holy . . . Oh, boy!" he sighed. "Baby . . ." For a little while I didn't think he was gonna go ahead with whatever he had planned, but he finally recovered.

"Look, we've got to do this," he told me. "If not for ourselves, then for the others. What about Rick?"

"Free. Escaped someplace. I'm the bait. Me and Angel."

"Angel . . . The baby's name? Hmph . . . Okay, okay, let's do it. Do you have the guts? Do you want to know what's going on enough to trust me? To maybe beat those people at their own game?"

"Well, I'd sure like to get outa there," I admitted. I had a thought. "You—you say you're a part of *me*, really? That we're sorta the two sides of one person?"

"Something like that."

"Then—you got the number? I don't have a number."

He looked suddenly puzzled. "I—I don't understand."

"When I look through 'em, some folks got numbers floatin' inside, and some don't. They said some of us don't got souls and some do. I figured that the number had to be God's serial number for the ones that do."

He seemed almost speechless at this idea. Finally he said, "I'll see what you see and know what you know if this comes off. Are you willing to try it?"

"What's gonna happen? To me, I mean."

"Nothing. Nothing at all. You and I will become one person. We will become whole. Nothing is lost. We gain. Both of us."

"What do we do?"

"Take my hand. It's my normal, human hand. Okay, now take the other one. It shakes a little, but just hold on. Good girl! Now, just look at my eyes, and I'll look at yours, and make your mind as much of a blank as possible. Just relax . . ."

He wasn't a great looker, but he did have nice, pretty eyes, and they weren't hard to look at. He also felt normal, although of course I didn't have to touch that body. I just relaxed, lookin' at him and, let's face it, pretendin' that it was Rick's face I was lookin' into, Rick's eyes . . .

I woke up suddenly and looked around. It was just like Rina had left it, just like always, and the body felt a little stiff from being in one position so long on the couch but otherwise okay.

I felt odd. I had all of Cory I in me, and Cory II up to the crash, and Kori up to the party and the second encounter on the shaman world's beach, and Rina's entire life with Rick up to, well, *now*. I had all those memories, all those feelings, and as I'd promised her, nothing was missing, nothing was lost that I knew of.

Somebody had gone to a lot of trouble to set this all up. I only wish that in all the stuff they'd done they had left something telling me what the hell I was supposed to do now.

VII

THE SUTHERLAND ENIGMA

Being whole again in a woman's body wasn't the same this time as it had been in the last incarnation. After all, we focused inside Riki as Angel's body then—interesting that the daughter was named the same—to maximize the power I alone knew how to drive. Not this time. In that case the body was mostly a tool; now it was the only body I had, and it was set up with the same physiology, the same hormones and enzymes, and some of the same organization as before.

I was now setting what seemed to be a record: three incarnations, two sex changes, and only two lives! I mean, sure, what I'd told Rina had been kind of a line—that nothing would be lost—but I'm not sure I really believed that. But I was here, now, with all of two male Cory lives and the accumulated knowledge and skills they had, but I was also *her*, the wife and mother, with many of those uncertainties and hang-ups. Physiology had a lot to do with who you were and how you felt and acted even between two different men or two different women; I was more Rina than Cory even with more of an education and greater skills. I guess the easiest way was to think of myself as

Korinna, as *Kori* once again, only this time very much inside the belly of the whale.

And I still didn't know what the hell I was supposed to do or even what I *could* do.

Rina at least wasn't the shrinking coward she thought she was; she'd grabbed on to rather than run from that curious "blueprint" phenomenon, and she'd used it to go many places and do many things. She'd even finally had the guts to merge with me. Now I had to use her guts and whatever I had of my own, along with my far greater experience, to work out a plan.

The institute types had talked of a power-up, but there was no sign of it yet. I had no idea what the power-up was supposed to do or why it was so vital to them, but I knew what happened when they did it and knew that the power couldn't be confined to their own use. I could certainly make use of that power myself, possibly with a lot more control than the last time, but I was still no match for Al's experience, to think of the key problem but not the only one. I suspect that Lee was no slouch at it, either, and Les was still too much of a question mark.

I needed what they already had, frankly. I needed somebody on *my* side with experience, somebody who could be my instructor. There wasn't anybody in the institute who would fill that bill without being one of the enemy—or was there?

Who were those people locked away in the pods, their minds interconnected to Brand Boxes? It seemed to me that if it was assumed that the monitors showed everybody locked away whom they had on a leash and that there were no more than eight life-support modules below, then there were only eight people locked away. Wilma was certainly one of them, but who were the others?

I realized, of course, that they had to be enemies of Al, which made them friends of mine, at least insofar as this business went. People of the opposition possibly, even probably, people I didn't know and hadn't even met in any of the continuous incarnations I *could* remember. Locked away in little

Brand Box universes created by Al's gang, as sex slaves, as that bizarre clone of Klaatu's robot with the soul of a pod person who'd rerouted Rina to my consciousness—or vice versa. There were real people inside those life-support modules, but they were people who neither perceived nor were perceived beyond that by this one.

That made them all at least potential allies if, somehow, I could get to them.

I wondered about Rina's scary encounter with the creatures "below" the room. Could that be where the Brand Boxes were? Well, I *was* Rina, damn it, and it sure didn't seem like that even with my extra Cory knowledge. What she—*I*—had felt under there was more powerful and more menacing somehow than any mere Brand Box–trapped mortal.

Even here, it seemed, the devil was down below our feet.

Even after going through all this so far, it was still not possible for a human consciousness to really accept the idea that *nothing* beyond thought was truly real to us. All of this—the smells, sights, and sounds and the detail to the nth degree—was being generated somehow, somewhere, as a virtual-reality statement by a computer and computer *program* that had that much capacity, that much power, that much of everything. Only under certain circumstances could even we, who knew better, look under the covers, peer down beneath the surface.

It was far too advanced and complex for us to really comprehend when we *were* able to do it.

We weren't Edisons, none of us. We were folks who knew how to play records occasionally once the machinery was there and a few of the controls were explained to us. Matthew Brand was supposed to be the Edison, but even he couldn't have built and designed all this. This was beyond any human mind—it was computers building computers building programs that made programs that maybe could approach this stuff.

Brand's claim to genius was that he was, by reputation anyway, the one person among us who might be able to at least understand how the system worked and why.

Was even Al looking to become a god by finally mastering all this, or did even he just want to figure out the location of the "off" switch?

I sat up straight. Yeah, that was a real question, wasn't it? Just what the hell did they think they were doing here with this? What had Al spent nine, now maybe ten lifetimes trying to do? What was this "half-power" business?

As mysterious as the situation in which we were stuck was the more localized question: *Just what the hell are all these people doing?*

I sat there in my prison room trying to figure out all sorts of things. If all this was illusion, if nothing was real, then anything was possible, wasn't it? You could turn yourself into a March Hare or switch from male to female or whatever was needed.

But try as I might, I hadn't been able to put as much as a ripple on the surface of the water in a paper cup by mere concentration. Things *hurt*, and yeah, things felt good, too. Things were consistently cold or hot; the flavors and smells seemed countless. I was getting a slight sinus drip from being in the buff in this place for so long with all that circulated and filtered air.

It was all *real*, damn it! Not just the personalities and emotions but *everything*. Or if it wasn't, then none of us had any way to tell the difference or change the outcome in any way other than the usual conventional methods all people interacted with.

I hadn't even been able to repeat what my "physical" half, Rina, had managed with the grand tour of the electrical circuits. I couldn't help but wonder if that access hadn't been somehow arranged by the folks who seemed to be pushing me this way and that but also protecting me. Maybe not, though. Maybe I just couldn't do it because my Cory half intellectualized things too much.

What it left me was dead bored. There was nothing in the room to read, and even if there had been, I didn't dare show much interest in it because Rina wasn't at all interested, or maybe even capable, of using it very well; it would have been a dead giveaway. Likewise, I couldn't write or draw, even if I'd had a pencil and paper, or do much of anything. There were only so many showers you could take, so many ways you could redo your hair with a simple comb and brush set. By the end of the first cycle as my whole self I already knew every damned board in the paneling and every piece of lint in the rug. I was dead bored.

Those folks down the hall and below, imprisoned or voluntarily experiencing the various flavors of Brand Boxes down there—were they, too, really somewhere else? Simultaneously inside a small Brand Box and also within and wholly contained by a much larger Brand Box, this complex? And maybe beyond that? An illusion in which you could have an illusion of having an illusion . . . ?

Jesus! How easy it was for this crap to bend your mind into giant superpretzels!

And if all this was some kind of superprogram, where did all the little shit come from? It's one thing to make up trivia for the front pages, but not fillers and some of those personals. What kind of program could be written to contain such details? How huge must it be? Why wouldn't there be one hell of a lot more bugs than were evident? Where was its data source, and how enormous a storage and processing unit must you have to keep it all running constantly at this level?

If we were all people somehow trapped in such a program or in a machine with such a program, then what was Angel? Was my own baby daughter just another string of numbers? And whether she was or not, what made her different from me or the others here? What would happen if she were taken through a rabbit hole or rode it through down here to the next universe that the system and somebody's subconscious might dream up? Would she just vanish? That was a horrible thought but also the most logical possibility.

In fact, what would happen to any of the—what had they called 'em?—spooks? Ghosts, phantoms, spooks. *Unreal people.* How easy it must be by now for ones like Al to think of folks that way. Walt, too, I expected, and maybe many others on both sides.

Not Les—not yet. That gave me some hope that there was at least one of them with a moral compass left, however limited that compass might be. I had a sneaking suspicion, though, that even Les's compass had more than the usual directions on it.

The other, more immediate question was why I was being left here, effectively dumped in a small meeting room with a blanket and little else and left to rot. If Angel and I were both incentives to trap Rick, the trap had certainly failed by now— and we'd both have been far better as lures out in the open, I'd think, where the temptation to try to contact me would have been enormous. Nor do I think they spent any time getting their jollies watching me in the nude through their little ceiling surveillance camera. With the obvious exception of Tanaka, who, male or female, had devoted part of his/her life making up for an incredibly repressed childhood, there wasn't much evidence that anybody was all that interested, anyway, particularly in the likes of me, when there were so many better-looking broads around.

It was almost as if I were being kept out of the way by the cheapest methods available in terms of resources and manpower. I was a nuisance, certainly no threat, and was being kept around, it seemed, mostly just in case they had to produce me and prove that I was still alive and sort of kicking as a part of some anticipated bargain.

Or insurance. If Rick actually was with Walt or the March Hare, would the safety of his wife and kid cause him to back off? Back off *what*?

The worst part was, I was so stir-crazy, I'd have happily done something risky, even crazy, but they had that angle covered with Angel. Crazy escapes with a baby in your arms weren't exactly bright, and without the baby they had me cold.

And then they started their half-power test.

*   *   *

By the time things began to happen, I was so mentally dulled, I doubt if I was even much aware of them. Still, it was clear that more people than usual were present and that there was a lot of traffic up and down the hall to various parts of the complex. Lights flickered, not only dimming but occasionally becoming brighter. Some of the older fluorescents quit, darkening the room a bit.

I was so much on the edge that I found the light show entertaining. Even *that* was more than nothing at all. I did begin to wonder what would happen if all the lights eventually failed. I was sure there was some kind of emergency lighting in the halls and such, but it would be dark as pitch in here. *Just what I need,* I thought glumly.

Shortly thereafter the lights did go out, and I found myself in the darkest dark I could ever remember. It was scary and claustrophobic in the extreme, and worse, after a couple of minutes it seemed clear that nobody had given me a second thought when it happened.

It was scary and disorienting. Even when all the lights go out at home, there's a moment of blackness as the power fails and then a very slow adjustment to where you can see the dimmest objects. There's always a light source somewhere, from the windows, from the moon coming in, *something*. Not here. This was like a deep cave, and this room had been picked because nobody ever needed it. If there'd been any emergency lighting here, it wasn't working now.

I felt myself giving way to irrational fears, fears that I'd never had as either Cory but that Rina knew all too well. Worse, rather than impelling me to act, to rectify the situation or defend myself against some imaginary creepy crawlies, it just made me cower there for a while on the couch, staring into nothingness, literally paralyzed, praying that somebody would come in.

Nobody did, and after a while I summoned up what courage

I had and eased off the couch. There was one thing, at least—
I knew every little bit of the place by heart. Even so, I needed
to feel, to bump into things, to orient and guide myself. Just
so, the chair, the small table, yes, now across should be
the door . . .

I can't tell you how long it took me to get up the nerve to
look out or where that came from, but I finally did and saw,
well, not much. The corridor was almost as black as the room
except for a fading set of reflective tapes along the floor. Different colors—red, green, yellow, blue—probably guiding
somebody who knew which was which to different places.

I turned not left but right, toward the Brand Boxes and the
life-support modules. If anybody was around, it would
be down there, and escape really wasn't on my mind, just
company.

I did feel a twinge of self-humiliation at that realization,
though. I never was the brave one, not really—not even in that
business two lifetimes ago in this very complex. Rick was the
guts, essentially, or at least the force; I was usually along for
the ride. Still, with Angel upstairs and no place to run anyway,
what choice did I have?

At least the glowing tape was still easy to see, and after I got
to the corner, there were little lights shining down every
twenty feet or so, making little pools of light along the corridors. Unfortunately, they also washed out the tape and made it
easy for somebody to see me. I was torn, I had to admit. On the
one hand, I wanted to find people, but on the other, after all this
time, I wasn't sure I wanted people to find me.

The left looked more promising; it seemed to have more
emergency lights and also had the green and red stripes which I
took to be primary. I just started to move down there, trying to
keep out of the little light circles as much as possible, when
there was a whine and the whole place seemed to vibrate for a
minute or so, like it was an airplane warming up for takeoff or
something. When it did that, I felt a sudden surge of, well,
power, well-being, you name it, flow through me, wash over

me like a series of waves. At the same time, less excitingly, several of the emergency lights went *pop* and burned out.

I continued on, remembering where I'd felt that same eerie sense of tingling power before, in the final times when I'd approached the complex in Yakima so long ago. It gave me a sense of near invulnerability, although it sure shouldn't have, and reinforced my confidence and will, at least in the short term.

I was going down still; that I could tell. Not via stairs but rather by a sloping floor that seemed to carry me down a little bit at a time. Suddenly I heard voices ahead and stopped for a moment, filled with fear, until I realized that whoever it was certainly wasn't talking to or about me. Taking some deep breaths, I kept on, hugging the far wall, avoiding as much as possible the few remaining emergency light stations. I was beyond any planning now; I wanted to see what the hell was going on.

The corridor gave a sudden last twist and then opened into a chamber that had a familiar look. In some ways it resembled the huge control center above, but this was no remote station but the real thing. There, along the far wall, I could see the life-support modules, some very definitely occupied, and ahead, almost in the center of the room, looking out on a vast number of screens and displays, kind of like the bridge of the starship *Enterprise*, they sat and watched.

They were all there, at least all the ones associated with Al and this installation. There was Larry Santee, Danielle Tanaka, the Aldens, the Sloans, Dr. Koeder, Betty Harker-Simonson, the Henreids, Les Cohen—the whole rogue's gallery, including a couple of folks I wasn't sure I'd ever seen before.

And of course there was dear old Al in his navy officer's khakis, sitting in a chair to the side of the main chair on the control console. I couldn't see in the semidarkness of the control room who was in the chair, but it didn't take long for that familiar voice to betray itself.

"I have interlock," Rita Alvarez reported. "They've really

got a lousy primitive electrical system here, though. I think we've already blown every bulb and maybe the air conditioner and who knows what else above."

"Forget it," Al told her, lighting a cigarette, the smoke billowing up through the reflection off the lights on the command console. Several of the others seemed disapproving and a couple coughed, but nobody complained. Al ran the show, and they all knew as I did that he was nobody to play with.

I kind of wondered where all the power in here was coming from for all this stuff if they'd shorted out the complex. Certainly not from the electric company.

"You all felt the surge and may have had momentary visualization when we ramped up power," the security chief continued for the multitude. "We're all networked into the basic energy matrix, so when we bring more of it directly on-line here, the same power that surges through the command and control center will course through us to the same degree. Interestingly, the transfer pulse rate is a nearly constant forty cycles per second, which happens to be the same frequency used by the limbic system of the human brain. Many of us, including Matt Brand, believed that in some sense this was because the data source for the universes was being passed in some continuous I/O connection between our own brains and that of the source. The source, of course, could operate at any frequency it wished or required and probably does work at a different rate internally, but any real variation in the connection between that source and ourselves would disrupt and maybe fry our own limbic systems, so forty it is. The classic Brand Box is forty at all levels, but it's probable that the vast difference between the primary source and our own selves is part of the reason for the surge in power we feel when a connection is made."

"In effect," Les Cohen put in, "the regulator is not perfect; it's simply good enough."

"Seems to me that if it can create the whole damn' *world*, it's pretty close," Danielle commented.

"But is any of this *real*?" Robyn asked. "That's what we've been asking ourselves since it became clear that you weren't all totally insane."

"No guarantees on the insanity," Al came back, getting a chuckle. *If they only knew,* I thought. "On the other hand, we first have to ask what 'reality' is in the first place. The brain is essentially a sealed unit. It gets all its input from biological sensors that translate sight, smell, touch, you name it, to the brain via electrochemical impulses. These are mostly reliable but not always so. Everybody has some false memories they are absolutely certain are real, and by the same token not everybody gets all the information out there, if anybody does. Color blindness, real blindness, deafness at certain frequencies or at all frequencies, even false touch and smell. We can fool the brain, and by suggestion or drugs or a combination of the two we can even create false memory or alter perceptions. How 'real' is the reality we're getting now? How much is false, or illusion, or simply interpolated data? We don't know. It's our *shared* perceptions that give us the definition of reality beyond ourselves. We all agree that this blinking light here is yellow. We might see it as slightly different yellows, but it's yellow to us all. I'm Al, she's Rita, he's Les. We all confirm this to each other. But as we all know now, that isn't totally reliable, either."

"The whole damned world's an illusion, but a consistent one we agree on," Les continued. "That brings us to the source of that illusion, the common point that connects our real brains, wherever they lie, and the program providing this complexity one to the other. The Brand Box is a model of this. Total immersion with medical monitoring in the modules gives the 'real' body what it needs, but beyond that the head mount and sensory connectors to the brain and spinal column give our relatively modest computers there complete control over your own input-output. From that point the program recorded in the Brand Box becomes the *only* connector between your brain and whatever is beyond it. It draws its information in turn not only from the program we put in but from the larger master program of which it is a part and about which we know little. That was Brand's big contribution. He figured out how to tap into the larger virtual reality we think of as the real world and use it as background fill for whatever primary pattern we choose. We don't have to supply all the details; the wider, larger program does that."

"I've been totally paranoid ever since you told me about this stuff," Robyn commented. "I mean, damn it, what *is* real? How can we be certain that even here, in this room, we aren't inside an illusion?"

"Indeed," Dr. Koeder chimed in. "I've spent a rather long life in a nearly total pursuit of certain specific types of ancient dinosaurs. Paleontology has been my total devotion. Now, suddenly, I'm told not only that it is likely that my life's work is an elaborate fraud but that my *current* life is as well!"

"Your precious dinos couldn't have existed, anyway," Michelle Alden commented sourly. "Nothing real can predate God's creation."

Koeder looked at her as one might look at a particularly large and nasty cockroach.

"It's almost certain that the common elements of reality, even much of the history and probably all of the natural sciences, are consistent," Les told them. "That's why it's so real and so detailed. It's simply relaying what actually exists or existed. We don't have to argue creationism here; it's certain that we're all in a created universe anyway but that the prime universe might be somewhat different. From the records here we've been trying for a very long time to find that reality prime, but with no real success. For one thing, we aren't consistent across universes—we've all lived many times as many different people, but we don't remember them beyond our fantasies and dreams. We can keep up memory for a while, even a long while, many lifetimes, but eventually we'll lose. We might not lose to another or to anything deliberate, but the odds are that one of these days you're gonna step off a curb and be hit by a truck or get a cramp while swimming and go under or whatever. In some cases you just might not be located by whoever has control of this center in time. This place, which exists across the universes—not the whole thing but *this particular place here*—has multiple purposes. Finding the truth, what is real, is paramount, but we also need to collect you all and record your lives on the Brand Boxes assigned to you. That's the only way we can be *certain* that no matter what happens, your life experiences won't be totally wasted."

So *that* was it! And that was why they had been so anxious way back when to get both Rick—as Riki—and me—as Cory—into Brand Boxes then. They'd not only given us a ride in a very real virtual-reality system, they'd also taken the time to record our "life experiences" just in case. I wondered how many of these people had already had the Brand Box experience, how many had perhaps not only given at the office but also gotten back some of what they'd lost from the older recordings. An accumulation of data, experience, intuition, and sweat, too—that really was too valuable to be lost.

But lost to whom? Not to them, certainly. Once they were recorded, they became in a sense expendable, although with periodic updates they might contribute more. Whoever had control of this place didn't have just the place itself and all the devices and Brand Box technology, they also had the accumulated wisdom and experience of dozens, maybe hundreds or even more than that, of lives for every single person here.

And that also meant that back then, if Walt used us as a diversion and got in here and stole a couple of Brand Boxes—he couldn't get more; they were made to be portable but they were heavy and awkward—he had that experience for those people now instead of Al.

Although, knowing Al as I now did, I was pretty damned sure he was a good enough computer man to keep backups.

But hold it! If Walt stole Brand Boxes, that implied that he had a way to use them to both record and play back. That meant another control room somewhere. A backup control center? Somebody else's? What?

Here was Al's happy crew, but who, or what, was connected to the March Hare Network?

It wasn't as if I could raise my hand and ask my own questions at this cozy event. Hell, I was keeping back in the darkness of the hallway, just watching and learning.

"Why us, Commander Starkey?" Larry Santee asked from over in a far corner.

"Huh? What do you mean?"

"Why *us*? I mean, what's our common denominator? Why are *we* the chosen people who pass from world to world like some folks would from room to room while the rest are, well, I guess part of the program. I'm no computer programmer or controller or even operator. I guess I could manage to push buttons on simple stuff, but this isn't what I do, and deep down it doesn't seem like I ever did. You're a national security agent, the one gentleman here's a dinosaur-bone hunter, and we got an English teacher, a bureaucrat, one doctor and a nurse or two, a homemaker, a politician, a preacher, even a nun. Pardon me, sir, but it don't make sense. A few in this group fit, but most of us don't. There are some big brains here, but I'm just an average guy and I know it. So are some of the others. *Why us?* How'd we all get lumped together in this—this— *trap*?"

Several others nodded and mumbled in agreement.

"Good question," Al admitted. "I wish I had a good answer, but I don't. We're generally consistent from one world to the next, even if we might be a different sex or have a slightly different background or set of skills. We've not only had the familiar, we've had some pretty odd existences as well. There was one that was essentially Bronze Age technology, with this complex buried deep under a stone religious shrine and eventually discovered and made operational by the couple of us who remembered. Lots of belief in magic but not much development of paleontology, or biology, or physics and mathematics, let alone computers. Still, the differentiation, the levels, were still present. If you can figure out how we're connected in any logical manner, in some way more like one another and unlike the rest of humanity, you let us know. Nobody, mind or computer, has figured it yet." He turned and looked at the board. "Ah! I think the circuits have figured out an isolation path. Let's try this again, shall we."

Al reached over and turned Rita around in the big high-backed command chair. For the first time I could see that she was naked and that her entire head and face were covered by some kind of elaborate helmet while her body was basically "dressed" in probes and sensors so thick that her naked-ness seemed almost not to exist. She was *really* wired into the system.

"I've done a self-check this time and run the full diagnostics," Rita assured him. "We'll manage to do it right this time."

Al nodded. "I know you will. Okay, everybody. HMDs on, please."

I saw everybody reach down and pick up a small, light head-mounted display unit that covered the eyes and went back as flaps to the ears. I wished I could have one, too. Then maybe I could figure out what the hell this was all about.

In front of Al and Rita, on the big control board, a whole string of little yellow lights were popping on one after the other in seemingly random fashion until eventually they formed a rectangular pattern.

"Stand by!" she warned loudly. Then, "Supply on; link established."

I felt the vibration begin again and a very, very slight version of that sensation of tingling, pleasurable power.

"Five percent!" she called out as lights began to show elsewhere on the console and dials and digital readouts began counting upward. "Ten percent! Everybody with me? Just *think* your answer. It takes some getting used to. Here we go—the point at which we burned out the house last time. Fifteen percent. Got it! Great! Twenty . . . Twenty-five . . ."

I heard some popping back down the hall and knew that it would be a very dark walk back.

"I'm going to keep things at twenty-five percent power until it stabilizes," she told them. "Please just relax. We don't want to burn out all the power for the entire west bay. Experiment with it. Play with it. See what you can do."

I watched them for a little bit, twisting back and forth, reaching out as if they were somewhere else and doing other things, but it wasn't anything I hadn't seen before deep in the past. It was new to some of these people only because some of them were reincarnates with no past life memories. To them it must have seemed like they'd donned their Superman suits.

What *did* tie these people together? The security aspect was easy, and that I assumed would cover both Al and Lee. Programmers? Well, there had been Brand until the last universe and Ben, Dan/Danielle, Jamie/Jim, and me, all in computer-related fields. In fact, for all that I was peripheral to the project, that was a variation of my direct neural networking helmet they were using. We at least made sense, and if you had to have somebody to handle press and PR, then Rob/Robyn was as good as any, and certainly you'd want a doctor and a couple of high-tech qualified nurses around when you were dealing with this kind of stuff. Then, though, it started to break down. A paleontologist? A couple of sociologists, a preacher, a retail buyer who was also an animal rights activist, and who knows what else? Off-site there was Wilma, who definitely fit in nowhere in this, and Walt, an entrepreneur type with a military background but not in CIA-type stuff or even R&D, Cynthia Matalon from God knew what background, and Rick, who in spite of having the nursing degree and license was still at heart an artist.

And who knew what some of the others were whom I might not have run into, including a few who were here and others who appeared to be in the life-support modules.

The LSMs gave me real pause when I saw how many were activated. *Wilma's in one,* I thought with a chill, *and who-*

ever's trapped in that plastic soulless world, and maybe that other woman we saw that night, and who else?

"Active lines off," Rita Alvarez said with the kind of professionally calm voice you might expect from an airplane pilot going through a checklist. "Increasing to thirty percent."

I could feel the vibration, and the kind of effect it was having on my body was indescribable, turning on every single nerve and pleasure circuit like a great drug embodied in the spirit of a giant lover.

"Forty percent," Rita called out. "Looks good. Forty-five. Stand by! *Mark!* Fifty percent."

This appeared to have some scientific or even mystical meaning, and there were quite a number of ooohs and aaaaahs from the assembled multitude. For me it was as if the whole area were bathed in a tangible dull greenish light, making things not easier to see but more difficult, sickly green on black. There was no mistaking that power, though; I had felt it before.

And then the most unexpected thing of all happened: across the far wall, where the monitors and large screens were, the solid bric-a-brac of the C&C center seemed to dissolve, and the entire far wall became a great, slightly curved screen. No, not a screen—something more.

It's a window! I thought wonderingly.

But a window looking into what?

We seemed to be flying over a vast terrain composed entirely of artificial geometric shapes and structures that bore little resemblance to anything that might make sense, an erector set and Lego nightmare in one. Nor was it a static display; there was raw energy there, energy of the kind we now bathed in, and it was being put to use shooting various patterns from point to point in all directions.

"In all the times we've looked at this," Al said calmly, "we've been able to identify some things that appeared to be very like resistors, capacitors, memory registers, transistors, that kind of thing. Not like anything we know, mind you, but they appear to perform the same logical functions. Who built and designed it we don't know, but it certainly isn't any technology in our records."

"Yes, but just what *is* it that we are seeing?" Dr. Koeder wanted to know. He, like the others, was seeing far more than I could via the VR headsets. I was stuck with the default view.

"The motherboard of the mother of all Brand Boxes," Al told them. "Matt Brand mapped it and spent several lifetimes deciphering just some of its logic. Out of that he managed to build the Brand Boxes themselves. Their motherboards, by comparison, are to this one as an electric watch is to the master computers in the Bureau of Standards. In effect, this isn't a Brand Box—it's the prototype on which Brand Boxes were built. I wish we still had Brand, but he's inaccessible now and much of his data are either gone or so obscure and esoteric that only he could know what they mean. I've been hoping to find someone of that intellect for generations now and have continued to fail."

"Just be the first to the other side after you bump off the god object," Danielle said playfully. "Then you could create a whole *world* of Matt Brands."

"Maybe. Probably wouldn't, though. There's just too much subconscious in the process. You remember that movie: 'Monsters! Monsters from the id'? Same thing. We just don't have the kind of control we need to do it. We've tried getting some of that control by using the Brand Boxes, but it hasn't worked. You can nudge things a hair, but you can't overcome one, let alone many, lifetimes of experience by any kind of conditioning for very long."

"So what are we doing here and now?" somebody asked.

Al sighed. "Experimenting, as usual. We know who the next world will come from: Alice McKee was the first of our happy group to go as far as every tracking system and every piece of data we have. Even our disloyal opposition has been seen since."

"What kind of world would it be, then?" another asked.

He shrugged. "I don't know. We're evaluating everything—psychological profiles, lifestyles, attitudes, all the Brand Box data—but we've been able to do this before with people, and it never predicts the way you think. The human mind is too complex, the sum of biology and experience too diverse. There's always a *'gotcha!'* So what we're trying to do instead is to develop our own complex here, to refine the Brand Boxes, to try to understand the ultimate mystery of what the hell's going on here and see if we can eventually bring those variables into line so that to some extent, not in *this* life and probably not in the next few, but sometime, we can control as many variables as it's possible to control. I also hope at least that Alice has a yen for a higher technological pace than here. The last one was bad enough, but *this* one's the pits. Even so, the past hasn't been wasted. You are already seeing some of what we've accomplished. A kind of real-world view of a kind of science well beyond us but not that far beyond. Just—*different.* The next objective is to gain the ability to alter our environment significantly. If all this is just virtual reality, it should be possible to rewrite snippets of programs, details, on the fly and have the rest conform to it."

"What do you mean by that?"

"At fifty percent power, with proper controls, we can see what otherwise is hidden and can travel and even influence, at least mentally, others connected to the grid if we can find them. At higher levels of power very small dents in what we think of as reality can be made. A blue pen becomes a red pen. Coffee turns to tea. Cheap magic tricks, only done without trickery. We have a long way to go, but eventually there may well be a way to actually take control of our virtual prison. Take what someone hands us and then remake it in our own image as we now do with the limited existences in the Brand Boxes. Once we accomplish that, we'll have control of and access to the core program that is doing this to us. When we have that, we can find out what reality truly is. That's what we're doing here. That's what we've been doing here for thousands of lifetimes."

And will it go beyond becoming God to find reality, Al? I wondered. *Once you have complete control of everything and everybody, will you even* want *to go beyond?*

Alice McKee hadn't trusted Al one bit. She'd gone along but had admitted she would be there only until they had it in their hands and she could take him on. It was a good bet Les and Rita and probably most of the others felt the same. What a crew of gods! As disloyally screwed up as the gods of ancient Olympus!

I realized suddenly why I had clung so hard to traditional values, to Rina and love and home. It didn't last—nothing did—but for a while it was *something*, something to believe in, somebody to trust, a clear sense of right and wrong, good and evil, and what was really important. Maybe I was the real oddball. I didn't want that godlike power; I just wanted *out*. Out, but not on Al's terms or in ignorance of this happy group's attempts to become my overlords.

I leaned back against the corridor wall, letting the energy from who knew what power source beneath us ebb and flow across my body and my mind. For that fleeting moment I touched it without thought and became one with it.

I remembered the sensation as soon as I had it, and I found it easy enough to angle and use. The energy waves were being picked up by every piece of electrical wiring and cabling in the whole complex, and that was what had burned or shorted out most of the conventional stuff. Now I could use that same avenue, at lightspeed minus resistance on the hardwiring, and check out the upper areas while all the important people were still secreted below.

They were working on the electrical system; that I saw. They had the upper control center pretty much up and going with emergency backup power, and I could see the monitors of the occupants of the life-support module below. I hadn't really looked at them before; now I did, if only to see if I could find out who the strange emotionless Spock who'd helped me might be.

One of the two people I didn't know, apparently. I also saw Wilma, out in who knew what limited virtual world, and one other, who seemed to lack focus and detail for some reason. I tried very hard to concentrate, and eventually the physical details resolved, at least for a moment.

If I'd had a mouth, I would have screamed, and I backed up and out of there *fast*. Nothing, not even if it had been Rick in there, would have shocked and disturbed me as much as what, or *who*, was actually in there.

It was me.

Not Rina, not Kori, but Andrew Cornell Maddox. Not dead but held, imprisoned in one sense yet probably less imprisoned than his crippled body had kept him, inside one of the Brand Boxes.

But if Cory was alive and in there, then *who was I*?

"You are incomplete," the plastic creature had said. *"A part of you was taken away from your mind and stored. At the moment there is no way to get to that specific storage medium, but there is a backup that will do. You are linked to the backup but are not in a current position to access it . . ."*

So if *that* was the original, real Cory Maddox, then I was the backup.

My God! Was I real or just part of the program? *Was* I what I thought or the "spook" *they* thought I was?

I forced myself to think clearly, to focus on what was here and now and leave the weighty stuff for later. The fact remained, I was the effective part of Cory Maddox that had some freedom of action and independence of mind. They thought they'd had me sealed away and conveniently out of sight and mind, but they were wrong.

I had all of his memories, two lives worth, until the air crash, plus all of Rina's memories as well. I also had mobility. The

only thing I *didn't* have that I would very much have liked was
the memories locked in that male mind *after* the crash and
coming here and working here.

I could of course follow those connectors down to the Maddox-
variety Brand Box itself just as Rina alone had done with the plastic man to the information. However, that was something that if
I could do it at all, I would prefer to try at a time when most of
the likely suspects, my enemies in the flesh, as it were, weren't all
sitting there ten feet from Cory's body in the LSM, getting
the same kind of energy charge I was and all nicely tied into the
system as I wasn't.

It was preferable by far that they not suspect my existence.
Not now.

I continued looking around and found Angel, awake and
screaming, a nurse trying to calm her when it was clear she
was hungry. Without lights it was evident that there was no
way Angel could get to me below, at least until everything was
corrected and probably a few hundred more light bulbs were
changed as well. I was furious at the nurse for seeming so uncaring. *Use the expressed milk in the refrigerator!* I mentally
screamed at her, knowing that they had "milked" me with a
breast pump for just such emergencies.

The nurse frowned, rocked back and forth a little as if suffering a dizzy spell, then turned, almost automatonlike, and
went out under the emergency lighting and into the medical lab
area, which was lit with its own backup power. She opened the
small refrigerator there and removed one of the prepared bot-
tles. She turned and started back with it, and I lashed out again
with all of me that was there, which is to say my consciousness. *Warm it first, idiot! And test it to make sure it's right before giving it to the baby!*

There was the same sort of reaction on the part of the nurse,
and then she proceeded to do just what I had said.

I hadn't changed my mind about things, but I was beginning
to see a practical side to Al's intention to become a god.

Ten to one this wouldn't work one whit on Al or the others, I thought, although it was tempting to find out for sure. "Modify the program on the fly" had been Al's work, and that was what I was doing.

I didn't want to risk it on any of those below, though. Considering my sudden discovery that I wasn't exactly who and what I thought I was, it was more likely that *I* was vulnerable and *they* weren't.

That was something I didn't want to think much about, at least not yet.

It occurred to me suddenly that my physical body was still in that hallway and that they were bound to end the revival meeting sooner or later. I'd seen to my primary interest; now it was time to go back to playing the dumb broad again.

I got down there in plenty of time; I figured that the assembly would not break up until the power was cut, and it was still on. I got up, checked the area, and then started walking back toward my homely prison room. There wasn't much chance of stumbling in the dark now; I could see perfectly well by the glow of that greenish energy nobody in *front* of me was likely to see.

I suddenly came upon two uniformed workmen fixing overhead corridor lights and adjusting those cute little monitor cameras. There was no way around them, so I concentrated and basically told them, *"You do not see the naked woman walking past you. You will totally ignore her."* And they did!

It was almost as much fun being invisible as it was being God.

It suddenly struck me that I had an opportunity here that might not come again. If all of *them* were below and I had the power to draw on for the others, I could very easily walk out of this place while they were still fixing things up, even with their little cameras whirring and guards all over.

The more I thought about that, the more tempting it became. The only way it could go wrong would be if they turned the power off down there, as they well might. But if they did—well, it was dark in that room, and I was looking for help, right?

Despite feeling that things would suddenly turn off and that I'd fail at any moment, I nonetheless screwed up my courage and headed straight up and across toward the medical unit. They had the lights and cameras back on in much of the area, yet simple will drawing on the energy that was all around me kept anybody from noticing. I even watched myself walk right in front of a big guard at one of the monitors without getting any reaction at all. I wasn't sure my ego liked that, but my security sense sure did.

Angel was awake but mostly just looking around when I got there. I got much of what I needed together and found a cloth first-aid backpack that could serve as a nice diaper bag. I was almost ready to go when it suddenly occurred to me that no matter what else, *I* was still stark naked and that was likely to attract attention on the Stanford campus, let alone beyond it. I couldn't find any shoes that worked, but there were some nurse's white smocks that would do in one of the closets. I wasn't too thrilled at wearing a bright white uniform, but it would have to suffice until I could replace it with something more comfortable and less conspicuous.

The security station was handy for several things. The desk sergeant had money in his wallet that he gave me without a complaint—about forty bucks; not a lot but better than nothing—and some keys as well.

Holding tightly to my baby, I walked out into a cool but not cold Bay Area afternoon; the cement walk felt like ice on my bare feet, but otherwise it was no big deal. The keys proved to be those to an old pickup truck, but it, too, would do for the moment. The first thing I wanted was *out of here* and as far away as I could get before they noticed who was missing.

As I drove away and headed south, it suddenly occurred to me how utterly alone I was and how nearly impossible a get-away would be over the long haul for somebody who looked like me and had a baby with her. As the last vestiges of that powerful energy faded behind me and I was just plain old Kori again, I began to see how hopeless this had to be.

Still, I had to try. I just had to.

When I reached San Jose and there still weren't a lot of flashing red lights behind me, I crossed over and headed back north up the east bay toward Oakland. They would think of it, too, of course, but maybe, just maybe, I could stay one step ahead of them long enough.

VIII

QUEEN BEE

How do you tell a couple of drug-addicted professional call girls that you have just escaped from imprisonment by characters in a superhuman group of immortals who are trying to figure out a way to become gods?

Yeah, me neither. Nobody's *that* smart.

Nor were these the kind of hookers with the hearts of gold you see on TV and in the movies. This pair wasn't very romantic close up when you saw their dreary day-to-day existence and how much they were truly property rather than people to those above them. I had no illusions that I would not be sold out if the price was right. Still, if there was no ax to grind or they felt like it, they could be as friendly and helpful as anyone else; equally important, they lived in the seamy underside of Oakland society where cops and the kinds of feds Al would use weren't all that welcome.

I called them from a pay phone several blocks from the apartment. I knew it was well past time to ditch the pickup, but so far it was all I had.

Marlene was both sad and sympathetic at the basics of the plight I described to her. That is, they'd picked up my husband because they suspected he had violated security, and then they'd kidnapped me and the kid with an eye to making him talk. I'd gotten away during a power failure and had stolen a truck, but I was on the lam with the kid and Rick was probably dead. That at least fit in sufficiently with the facts to be believable. Besides, like everybody else, Marlene and Beth's views of the government were pretty much shaped by television, anyway.

"You stay right where you are, honey," Marlene told me. "We'll be right over!"

I had enough respect for reality not to be exposed when they showed up, just in case, but everything seemed clear.

They were an interesting couple. I never was sure if there was anything sexual between them, but they acted a lot like a couple, even though an odd one. Marlene was tall and leggy, a former exotic dancer, with light brown skin and strikingly exotic west African features mixed with naturally straight but lush black hair. Beth was short, thin, but decently shapely, with explosive red hair, green eyes, and something in her looks and tone that suggested African or perhaps Mexican ancestry, it was hard to tell. Pushing thirty, they were already showing signs of premature aging and burnout, but they still looked good enough to do the job.

They seemed genuinely shocked at my appearance but still were able to coo and make silly faces over Angel, and it was good to see them.

Marlene looked at the truck and then at Beth. "You take the keys and drive it over to San Francisco, maybe, and park it anyplace. Take the BART back and a taxi back home. I'm gonna take her over to Billie's. Ain't great, 'specially for a baby, but it'll do for now."

Beth nodded and was soon off in the truck. I hoped that she would be able to get rid of it before somebody spotted it as a stolen car.

Billie's turned out to be a seedy run-down nightclub in a less than thrilling section of the city. As with many such places, it had "rooms" on upper floors and in the back that allowed for profitable extracurricular activities. It was also entirely black, and I stuck out like a spotlight on a dark night. It was early, though, with very few patrons and not much going on. We were able to pass through pretty well unnoticed except for my own paranoid suspicion that all eyes were following me.

Billie was one of those stereotypical postmenopausal madams who still dressed and made up as if they were twenty and in their prime, even though in her case the makeup was probably put on with a trowel by that point. Still, she knew the routine of keeping somebody out of sight and out of mind of the cops. Unlike Marlene, whose accent was more local, Billie sounded as if she'd started out in someplace like New Orleans long ago.

"Sho'. Ain't no problem. Only trouble we got is lotsa noise once we get goin'—these places ain't quiet no mo'—and keepin' you outa sight of most folks till we can git you someplace bettah." Billie turned to Marlene. "Vernon ain't gonna like it none if he finds out 'bout her, though."

Marlene nodded, and I took Vernon to be either a pimp or possibly the boss who owned this place and probably a lot more.

"I'm gonna try and get her outa here soon as I can," the hooker assured the old madam. "I got to make a few calls. She's gotta git outa the Bay Area completely, and fast. She got the whole damn CIA after her! Still, be kinda fun to see them white bread agents try anything 'round here!"

Marlene gave me a hug. "You just stay put here and trust Billie," she told me. "I know it's swappin' one jail for another right now, but it won't be for long. A day or two at most. I already got some ideas."

I didn't feel at all comfortable being left there, but it sure beat anything else I could think of at the moment, and I was there without guards, anyway.

Billie came over and looked at Angel, and you could see for the briefest of moments in that incredibly tough face and hard

demeanor all the possibilities she might have once had and all
the regret and hurt real life had dealt out. "Been a long, long
time since there be a baby in my place," she sighed, then got
control back. "Okay, you stay heah and you jus' relax. I'll have
Albert whip somethin' up in the grill in back fo' you. Do the
baby need anything? Milk? Formula?"

I shook my head. "No, thanks. I'd love something like a
hamburger or even just cereal and fruit or something, but she's
still eating on me."

Billie chuckled. "We'll see if I kin rustle up somethin' fo'
you to weah a bit bettah than what you got on. We'll covah you
as best we can, but it's moah than a little dang'rous 'round
heah, so keep outa sight and jes' lie low and we'll fix everything up."

I almost believed her.

It was *not* a comfortable evening or the kind of night I'd
have wanted, either. It was noisy enough that at least nobody
noticed the occasional crying, but things went on well into the
night with lots of music, shouting, you name it. Even after the
joint closed down, the upstairs was used for the added and
more profitable activities, which included not only prostitution
but, I suspected, high-level drug binging as well. This was as
low in the underworld as it got, and I got no sleep at all until
nearly dawn.

The next afternoon Marlene brought me some wearable
clothes in my size. That made me feel much better, although
she also came with news that wasn't nearly as good.

"They been around, all right," she told me. "They still got
the whole apartment block staked out, and when I pick up the
phone, there's like two clicks."

I felt some panic. "Maybe they followed you here!"

She smiled. "Gimme more credit than *that*! Besides, them
guys stick out like sore thumbs. Even the black ones look like
they just stepped out of some cop factory. I don't think they
know shit 'bout where you are; they just are coverin' every-
place you *might* be. We'll get you outa heah tonight while all

the shit's goin' full blast downstairs. Friend of mine named Jonny T's gonna take you out the back way and east to Reno. Theah's a coupla clubs theah might need some help in waitin' tables or bussin' or shit, and they got some private child care places so's you can work. Best we can do for now."

I gave her a kiss. "That's more than I had a right to expect. I owe you, Marlene. I owe everybody."

"Just be ready 'bout midnight. Jonny's not a bad guy, either, and he won't make no hit on you or nothin' or ask questions. He's used to gettin' folks outa town what need to git."

I began to feel excited now that things were beginning to move, even sensing that I might make it out of Al's grasp as I had the last time. If I could find the March Hare or anybody who was against the institute, I'd join up, but I wasn't interested in the big fight right then, just in getting me and my kid to relative safety.

That proved a little harder than it looked.

By the time things were jumping downstairs in the club, I was ready. I didn't exactly have a lot of baggage, just the clothes they had brought me and Angel in her blanket and the supplies in the ersatz diaper bag. It was getting close to midnight on the small clock on the shelf in the room when I heard loud voices, the kind of voices that sounded more mean than reassuring, coming toward us down the corridor. I didn't know what was going on, but I was aware that I didn't have much of a backdoor exit here and that this was unlikely to be Jonny T.

I prayed silently that whoever it was would go past, but suddenly the door opened and a very large, rough-looking black man very well dressed in a tailor-made suit and knotted tie walked in. He had the kind of features that appeared to have been chiseled out of stone by somebody who didn't like people very much, and he looked me over the way a critical shopper might look at a piece of meat.

"So you're the bitch the government is looking for," he said after a moment, his voice extremely deep and smooth and, surprisingly for somebody in this sort of dirty business at this level, educated. "One of my people phoned me and said you were here."

He was damned intimidating just standing there, but I figured that only a show of guts, however false, had any chance of registering with him.

"I don't believe we know each other," I came back.

He gave me a bemused grin in response. "My name is Vernon Hitchcock. I own this joint and a few dozen more around the Bay Area just like it. In a sense you are my guest, although not one that I recall inviting. The help is getting very forward these days. I shall have to speak to them about this."

"I was waiting for my ride to leave for good now," I told him.

He shook his head. "It doesn't work that way. I didn't invite you here, so you're here of your own free will, hiding out or not. Anyone who comes into my—domain, as it were—is subject to my wishes and interests."

"Haven't you heard?" I responded, trying not to buckle or tremble. "They abolished slavery in this country."

He gave a low chuckle. "Indeed. At least in the legal sense regarding race, creed, and color. I'm a liberal myself. I believe that anyone can be owned by anybody. Right now it seems that your choice is between the government people and me. Now, what do they want you for?"

I just stared at him.

He suddenly and unexpectedly lashed out and struck me hard on the side of my face. I was knocked backward onto the floor and grabbed at the bed for support, but I didn't get up. It *hurt*!

"I don't like to ask questions more than once," he said ominously.

I shook my head, trying to clear it, and rubbed my jaw. "You wouldn't understand," I told him. "I really don't, either. They *don't* want me. They want my husband for something. I'm just their bait."

He nodded. "I figured it was something like that. Too bad,

though. If you had intrinsic value to them, I might have profited a bit from this." He turned and looked at Angel, who was making random baby noises. He reached down and picked her up, and I managed to get to my feet quickly.

"Let her alone!"

He glowered at me. "Get your things! I'll hold on to your precious package here. It'll be as safe as if it were in your arms so long as you do *exactly* what you are told. No more smart mouth, no more back talk. It makes me lose control."

I understood perfectly well, and there was something in his voice that said that he'd do just about anything he felt like if it advanced his purposes. I'd simply traded masters, after all, and monsters as well.

He led me out and down the back stairs where I had expected to exit with Jonny T and out into the back alley, where a huge man in a black suit and shades waited, smoking a cigarette and leaning on the side of a cream-colored stretch limo. When he saw us, he tossed the cigarette and came around and opened the door. Vernon Hitchcock handed the baby to the very surprised big man and said, "Keep the kid safe and secure up front and drive nice, slow, and easy. Blinders up, do not disturb in back, understand?"

The big man nodded but looked uncertain. "I don't have no car seat or nothin' for the kid."

"Do the best you can and no sudden stops. Go up to the house but make it take a while. You know the routine."

He nodded, and while I was awfully uneasy at this arrangement, I couldn't do much about it.

"Get in the back," Hitchcock ordered, and I took one last look at Angel being placed up front and did as I was told. What choice did I have?

Hitchcock got in and closed the door. It was quite a plush limo with a lot of room, a built-in wet bar, a tiny TV, and plush individual seats flanking a lush, furry carpeted center area.

"Now, bitch, let's get a few ground rules straight," he began. "You don't *ever* smart-mouth me again. You don't *ever* question me or ask me to repeat anything. You do what you're told when you're told. From this moment on I *do* own you, lock, stock, and tits. I can't use you around here—you're too hot—but there's other places. Now, take off your clothes. All of 'em. *Now!*"

I had expected it, but it didn't make it any easier. Even worse, he was dropping his pants, which I'd feared but expected, too.

"Now, I want to see everything you got, your whole arsenal," he told me. "And I want you to absolutely, convincingly, make me believe that you love me and are enjoying every second of it. Any hesitation, any second thoughts, holding back, or making me think maybe you don't *want* this, well, I might get real mad at that little one up front. So, right from this point, you better be good!"

I did all he asked and more, and by the time we reached "the house" I felt battered, bruised, exhausted, and like I'd been rolling in garbage. I was in fact close to being in a state of shock, barely thinking, feeling totally helpless and alone. All those were feelings you kind of knew you'd have in this circumstance, even though nothing could prepare you. But as much as you go over this in your imagination and your nightmares, nothing can prepare you for the real thing and those added details you would never believe of yourself.

Like the fact that I felt almost crushed under a wave of guilt, self-doubt, and complete self-recrimination because I had gotten off. I hadn't enjoyed it; I felt filthy, clammy, all those horrible things, mixed with rage, but even then I felt that I'd betrayed Rick, Angel, and half the human race. He was a true expert at breaking people quickly, and he'd broken me as Al had never been able to do.

Vern Hitchcock hadn't been joking about being an equal opportunity employer. Of the several women who worked or lived or whatever in his very fancy house up in the hills, there were whites, blacks, and Orientals. How he'd missed an Indian I couldn't figure out.

They were all prettier than me, sexier than me, and younger than me, none of which made me feel any better. Even so, you could see in their eyes that they'd been totally broken inside long before I ever knew their boss existed. I knew that look was in my eyes as well.

Having been threatened with but not actually being forced to experience what they'd been through, I could understand it. Hitchcock was a man of great appetites who liked to break in people himself when he had the time. Those who would go on to roles of some sort in his operation, particularly if they were going to be close to him when he was vulnerable, such as in his house, he took around to "men's clubs," safe houses where various men in his organization worked and sometimes lived. Then there was an unceasing set of gang abuses, without letup, without cleanup, until thought, will, and ego were all extinguished. By the time the process was over, there wasn't enough of them left mentally to care if they killed themselves. They just went on . . .

I wasn't as broken as I thought, even though everything I said about how I saw myself was right. I discovered that I still had rage, a consuming, burning hatred for Vern Hitchcock and his cronies that I'd never felt for anyone or anything, not even those at the institute.

If this was all virtual reality, if all these people were simply elaborate programs within a larger programmed context, then whoever or whatever allowed this was worse than sick. It was evil.

Angel had left him enough leverage over me that Hitchcock hadn't bothered with the full treatment, but I was still given a job at the house. I wasn't there as a house sex object; that would have required a new virtual-reality program, particularly considering the other girls there. On the other hand, for a twenty-room house built into the side of a hill with at least a dozen permanent residents and a couple of acres of wooded and fenced ground, a staff of considerable size was needed to keep it cleaned and maintained and keep its occupants provided with their basic needs.

Basically, until the master of the place decided what to do with me, I was just another maid.

Don't let that fool you. In a house that size it was a full-time job, and there were always men on the security staff or sometimes Hitchcock himself coming along and inspecting. If just one thing was missing or out of place, or if there was a scuff mark, drink ring, you name it, it could be both humiliating and painful. They kept the pressure always on, and of course, if any of the guys decided to do anything from cop a feel to find out if maybe you weren't bad in the dark, you had to go along.

One thing being a maid did, however, was give me access to almost the whole house.

The big den with the fireplace and plush carpets and tropical fish and all the rest was the biggest revelation to me and one I found extremely disturbing. Along one wall were all of Vern's certificates of accomplishment in this and that, along with various photos. He'd been a college football player who had just missed the pros because of some lingering injuries, he had a degree from UCLA in political science, of all things, and according to this he'd been a member of the Oakland city council, had spent two terms in the state legislature in Sacramento, and was up to his armpits in big-name political friends and in charitable circles as well. It made you wonder just what could make somebody with all that be so deep-down evil inside. It was almost as if there were two of him.

Unfortunately, we only saw the evil twin, which was how I began to think of him in those moods.

The fact was, though, he wasn't home all that much, so it was more the male staff members throwing their weight around than anything else. Even though there was no doubt that some of those guys were killers and worse, somehow they didn't scare me or the other girls as much as Vern did. Not when all those tough guys were also as scared of Vern as we were.

Make no mistake; my sole reason for staying around and staying alive was to escape for the sake of Angel. Growing up in this atmosphere wasn't going to be a picnic for her, but living the rest of my life here was as good as being dead, too. If it cost me my life, I was going to get her out of their clutches for good. I didn't really want to survive beyond that. Hell, I'd betrayed everybody and everything and I had done no good at all. I didn't want to have to face Rick after this, and if I was going to be reincarnated, I'd rather not remember this life.

After a few months at the house, though, my problems didn't level out, they increased. You see, while I wasn't in such totally lousy mental shape that I forgot why I'd originally pedaled down to Sister Rita to tell her the news, I'd tried hard to put it out of my mind and pretend that it wasn't real.

Now, though, it was becoming impossible to hide the fact that I was pregnant from others or from myself. I pleaded for an abortion even at that stage, as threatening to my life as it would have been; the last thing I could foresee was handling *two* babies in this kind of existence, particularly putting another child in the hands of people like this. Hitchcock, though, was adamantly against it.

I realized that he had the idea that the kid was his.

I knew it was Rick's, and that would become clear in a couple of months when the kid was born, but until then I wasn't going to fight Vernon on this. You didn't argue or fight with Vernon on much of anything. Besides, it gave me a little time with eased pressure and reduced work, and I hoped that at some point during the remaining time something, some way out, would turn up.

Two weeks later a crew of experts from a big corporation arrived and installed a computer-controlled security and communications system for the house and grounds. It was a big, unwieldy affair compared with what I was used to, but it was X

Windows over Berkeley Unix. I knew that system pretty well, and of course nobody at the compound suspected that I might. How could I? Officially I had almost no education, and in any case Unix was the kind of user-hostile environment that gave computers a bad name, even with a moderately pretty X Windows face. Besides, everybody knew girls couldn't program or do math, right?

Like most security systems, it wasn't all that secure deep inside the house and grounds. It wasn't designed for that; it was designed to keep out people who shouldn't be there and to offer both local and remote protection and even some control of basic household functions. It was tied into an elaborate sensor system that Al probably would have loved, and it created an imposing grid through which virtually nothing could get in or out. Anything that transgressed would alert local security and tell them just where somebody sneaking in was and also call for backup. The core of the system was in a minicomputer console in the basement that was supposed to be essentially maintenance-free. Guards looked at grid boards and monitors and terminals, but nobody was baby-sitting the computer itself.

It took me three nights of sneaking in and fiddling around to get the line printer to print out the mechanical operating codes for the entire grid. It took me another day or two of examining the thick printout before I pegged the subtle differences in this System V from the one I'd known so long ago and brought back that knowledge from the distant past into my own brain again.

The fact was, with a vast amount of subjective time since I'd laid hands on a computer or done anything at all with one, even so much as get a directory, it had taken me about a week to decipher enough of the system to feel that I owned it. I felt confident that I could easily come up with subroutines that could be added to the program that would allow somebody who knew them and had something as simple as a watch to literally walk in plain sight from the street right up to and into the front door without that registering on the guards' boards. A routing that avoided the basic black and white cameras was not much more trouble. There was always the chance of bugs and there'd be no way to test it, but my confidence was high.

Of course, this also meant that I could just as easily program a sequence for somebody to *leave* the compound. The real question, the one I hadn't addressed when I had left the institute months earlier, was, What then?

Okay, so if I could carry Angel and she kept reasonably quiet, I could walk or waddle to the street. So then I'd be in a residential area of well-off Oakland, several blocks walk to anywhere in particular. Without money, I couldn't use a bus, taxi, subway, or anything else or get a room. And even if I could find some money, I'd be missed shortly after sunrise, and I sure as hell wouldn't be able to be inconspicuous. It didn't take much imagination to figure out what would happen to me if Hitchcock caught me.

In hindsight, escape from the institute had been pretty dumb and had led to a worse situation. With the station powering up, I'd been able to tap into what they were doing without their knowing, and I'd had a fair amount of power from it. Now— zilch.

The only course of action possible for me was to reverse what I'd done while I still could. Contact the institute some-how and let them know where I was. Even these gangsters wouldn't stand in the way of the kind of force Al could mount, of that I was certain.

The problem was, I couldn't just pick up the phone and call. Not only was that forbidden, it would go through the security shack. In point of fact, the only outlet I could figure that didn't go through that kind of squeeze, or at least wouldn't look obvi-ously wrong to the usual goon on duty, was the modem on the security computer system. The security on it was rudimentary; the programmers who had designed this sucker should have been arrested for fraud. The modem was connected to the line and was randomly monitored to make sure it was fully con-nected and ready. A single random loop subroutine did it; a patch that always gave the right answer to the subroutine was a matter of a few dozen lines of code inputted at the terminal, sent, and saved. The one and only problem would be that the security center would also randomly poll from its remote location, expecting the same answer, and also call in and download the entire system report for each day. The thing was, if they got a busy signal, they'd assume the other routine was working and go on to the next location, calling back the list of decreasingly unsuccessful polls. A second busy signal would alert them to call the guards for a checkup, but it wasn't any big deal.

I couldn't have done it without the pregnancy, though. There wasn't enough time in the day or periods of unsupervised activity long enough to have worked on it. I also probably couldn't have done it if they'd had any sense that I could spell "cat" or knew the world was round, but they pretty much took me for granted as an ignorant little slut of a girl.

It wasn't until I actually made my first attempt that I hit a roadblock. It wasn't something I had planned for or something that had even entered my mind.

I had no idea of any of the phone numbers over there, let alone the modem numbers. Nor were there any phone books for the Stanford area in the house or anywhere else I knew of. The modem was hardwired into the more primitive phone system there and also to the minicomputer, so I couldn't just use the terminal to contact directory assistance. I could dial them, but they would be speaking to a modem tone.

I was crushed. I had come such a long way, and now to be stopped dead because of my lack of access to long-distance information . . .

It took a couple of days to realize that there was in fact one voice phone accessible to me, more or less. Every day, before he left for his "rounds" if he was in at all, Vern had his big stretch limo cleaned and washed and wiped down, vacuumed inside and out, you name it. Two or three of us would do it in about an hour and a half, maybe two—you didn't want to leave *anything* that would make him irritable when you cleaned, as I said—and realistically only one person could do a full cleaning of the interior with the vacuum and the carpet cleaner.

There was a car phone in the limo section. I'd seen it and seen it used and knew it wasn't just an intercom. In fact, there was a mobile antenna on the trunk, and that meant that the call wouldn't go through the master switchboard.

Cleaning the car was one of the jobs I still routinely did, since it wasn't something precluded by my condition.

So it was that while a couple of the other girls, dressed in bikinis, were alternately washing and hand waxing the outside and spraying each other and having what passed for fun among the underclass there, I was inside with a vacuum and a rug-cleaning machine and all the rest.

It was a little nerve-racking. I had three or four false starts before I managed to pick up the phone, call long-distance directory assistance, be heard, and get a few numbers I'd have to memorize quickly over the roar of the cleaning machines, but get them I did. I then spent a good, solid hour and a half getting everything absolutely perfect inside, doing nothing but singing those numbers over and over again in my head to an old tune.

I'd gotten two numbers that were supposedly direct lines to the institute and a third to Stanford's Internet provider. One way or another, I felt I had at least a chance to get a message through.

I wasn't really nervous about this; I was afraid, in spite of my expressed self-confidence, that it wouldn't work. I wasn't that concerned about getting caught. If I'd learned nothing else, I'd learned how stupid evil can be; the scariest thing about it was that it went its way not caring if it blundered. Al had seemed the epitome of evil to me in all my back memories, and who knows, maybe he still was, a giant, immortal, powerful super-Vernon looking to become a god. But Vern was less understandable, more a force beyond all reason.

I had never been scared to die since setting out on this business, but I'd always drawn the line when it came to Angel.

Now I'd come to terms with that, and I hoped I had the nerve to carry it out. Angel deserved to grow up, have a life, find her potential. To Al she was just leverage, a spook kid of a spook, to be discarded the same way you'd throw out obsolete code in a program or clothes you no longer wanted or needed. But the sheer lack of threat gave her, and even me, more of a chance with them than with Vernon.

Angel might as well be dead as grow up knowing only Vernon and his petty empire, sealed off from the world right in the middle of the city. Better that she never know evil firsthand than grow up its property.

So at five in the morning, when the house was pretty well down for the night and all the electronic watchdogs were on, I crept down from the room I shared with three other girls in the west wing and got to the basement. I listened, heard nothing, and went to the always-on terminal attached directly to the minicomputer server.

I brought up my own private encoded files, enabled the safeguard subroutines I'd already checked out one at a time, and took control of the terminal program. For an awful moment I was so nervous that I couldn't remember any of the numbers, but then the song and the mnemonics came back. I tried the first number. Click. Dial tone. Ringing . . .

Abort. Nonworking number . . .

That disturbed me, so I tried the second, hoping I hadn't transposed digits or done all this for nothing.

Same thing.

Well, I *knew* that the Internet line would work. It was the hospital's own home access gateway for its staff as opposed to the dedicated ones in the hospital itself.

Same thing.

What's wrong? Think, Kori, think! What the hell is wrong? Did you screw up the dialing? The numbers themselves? What . . . ?

Why hadn't I just called the fucking voice number from the car phone? *Now you think of it!* Yeah, right . . .

I was in a borderline panic when suddenly the answer hit me in the face. It was as obvious and as dumb an error as using a free phone to get a number but not to make a call.

Stanford was long distance. You had to dial 1 first.

The deflating knowledge that somehow I'd developed mind-dulling stupidity took a lot of the self-confidence out of me, and I decided to take no chances. I dialed the Internet hospital line, got the basic E-mail section, composed much the same message over and over, and sent it to hell and gone to anyone whose address it would take.

How did I know those addresses? They hadn't been in any of the information files . . . I was done, and I logged off, but I sat there for a few minutes, wondering.

I had been too smart on programming skills long disused, knowledgeable about this variant Berkeley System V and the DEC mini. I'd acted almost like two people: one I wanted to be but hardly knew and the other the dumb fat-ass ignorant girl everybody thought of me as.

As I sat there, the modem suddenly came to life. I heard the speaker pop on and watched as a connection was made and matched. Just the download survey, most likely, I told myself, but I watched the screen, anyway. I felt drained, empty, as if something important were over. It was hard to explain. Almost like, well, everything inside me had led up to making those calls, and now that I had, I no longer had a purpose or meaning. Even the programming knowledge seemed distant, even incomprehensible, as it should have from the start. I tried to remember how I'd rigged it up to do what I just had done, and I could no longer follow it. It was fading very fast, and I had no way to hang on to it.

I *had* been two people. At least two. Somehow, somebody, *something*, had programmed me with enough knowledge to do what I had, but I didn't need it anymore. I was slipping fast, becoming more Rina by the moment.

With a start I thought of those sub—sub—whatever they

were called—that I—*me!*—had done to get by all that fancy guard stuff inside the machine. Nobody could know that I would wind up here; nobody coulda known in advance what would happen after I walked outa the institute. But if somebody, somebody *smart*, had figured that I would need to be able to contact them, to maybe use these computers to save myself, and maybe put in other stuff I hadn't needed yet—*that* would make sense.

There was a whole bunch of stuff, numbers and symbols and all sorts of shit that made no sense at all to me now, rolling across the face of the terminal. I peered closely at it, realizing for the first time how nearsighted I was and how close I had to get to something to even try to read it. Not that shit, though. I might have been able to make sense of it only minutes before, but it was Chinese to me now.

Even so, there was a kind of hypnotizing effect to the scroll. Even though it was junk, I couldn't take my eyes off it. My face got closer and closer to the glass until my nose actually touched it.

There was a little crackling sound, the kind you get when you touch a TV that's been on a while, and a little tingle, and then, suddenly, a thin shard of greenish energy no thicker than a piece of yarn leapt out at me. I jumped and actually moved back in my chair, losing my balance and falling to the cold floor. The energy was still there, kinda like a little sickly green lightning storm, kinda like a bunch of skeletonlike fingers playing over the point between me and the screen.

I was suddenly scared that somebody patrolling the house might have heard me cry out or fall, but I didn't hear anything from the direction of the stairs.

And then the green lightning drew something and made it real, the lightninglike "fingers" working in midair, maybe a foot or two above the cement floor, as I watched in a mixture of fear and fascination. It created a—well, a *hat* or something like it. It started in wireframe, a bunch of connected three-dimensional lines that created the outline of the thing, and then it began to fill in. When it was totally solid, it fell to the floor and rattled for a moment.

I just sat there, stunned, for maybe a minute or two, staring at the thing. Then I got up, went over, and picked it up. It looked imposing but was light as a feather. I knew what it was: a variation of the original wireless head-mounted display I'd helped create two lifetimes ago, but a *lot* more refined, more futuristic—and really out of place at that level in this world.

I say "hat," but it was more than that. Light in weight—surprisingly so—it nonetheless was fairly thick, made out of the same kind of plasticlike crap that plastic man had lived in and been made of back at the institute or something very much like it. Inside, the whole thing seemed to be covered with tiny little needles—not sharp but big and flat on the bottom—that came out of the insides maybe a quarter inch when you turned the helmet right side up.

I recognized the pattern. It was a variation, but one hell of an impressive new and improved variation, of "my" own—meaning Cory Maddox, of course—wireless VR head mount.

Well, there wasn't any choice. *Somebody* who knew a hell of a lot more than I did had gone to a lot of trouble to get this thing to me. I put the thing on my head, and the needles came down and fit perfectly on my newly adorned head. Then I pulled the small flaps around to secure it and brought the visor down.

I felt a sudden total disorientation; the world and all in it seemed to vanish, and I fell to the floor. The HMD was active but was causing me extreme disorientation and not giving me pictures or other impressions. I was just being made nauseous and dizzy.

Then it seemed like the whole top of my head exploded. The pain was real, and I'm sure I must have cried out, but it was all-encompassing; I could think of nothing but getting it off me. I reached up and tried to take off the helmet, but it was almost as if there no longer were a helmet there.

I smelled burning hair and felt the green energy flow all around me and then begin what seemed to be a top to bottom scan. At least it no longer hurt, except for a lingering burning on my scalp.

When it was done, sense came back into me, and I managed with some effort to sit up and take a series of deep breaths. The burning on top of my head subsided, and instead it started to feel cold up there. I reached up, if only to see if any damage had been done, and got a really big shock.

My head was totally smooth and hairless. I was as bald as a billiard ball! Eyebrows, yeah, but not a single trace of a hair on the top of my head, not even a feeling of roots and follicles and scratchiness or fuzz. It was as if I'd never had hair at all. And yet—where was the HMD? I looked around. The helmet was nowhere to be seen, yet I still felt the energy connection just as if I were still wearing it. Still, it was the lack of hair that bothered me most.

I knew I was no beauty, but it was more than disturbing to me and would be impossible to explain, too. That I knew. What was this crazy stuff doing to me?

What do I do now? I wondered, and as if in response, there was a sudden tremendous surge in the green power. The ribbon of energy rose up out of the computer and telephone hookup and became direct, flowing both into me via the surface of my newly shorn head and then from me to—where?

Anywhere I want.

"Hey! What you *doin'* down here, girl?" Gasp. "What the hell happened to yo' *hair?*"

I turned, startled, and saw Charlie Mombassa—at least that was how he introduced himself—standing there, gaping at me. He was a big man like all the guards, and he had weapons he wouldn't hesitate to use.

I saw him first as a real man and then in animated wireframe with a long and complex numerical tag along the edge. I had no idea what I was doing, but I acted out of gut will and a little fear, too.

"There's nobody down here, Charlie," I sent to him, watching the incredibly thin tendril of energy deliver the message.

I saw a bunch of numbers and symbols along his wireframe edge roll over like numbers on a gambling wheel and then quickly stop. He frowned, looked straight at me, and said, "Girl, I asked you a question. What in hell you doin' down here, and where's yo' hair?"

Wrong number. *"You really love me, Charlie. You wouldn't betray me or do anything to hurt me. Cover this one up and ask no questions. It's not like it's a threat. Just don't give this another thought. You don't remember that I ever had hair, and you think I'm sexy this way."* Another string went out to him, followed by another slight freeze.

"Please, Charlie! It ain't nothin'. I'm just playin' here. I don't get much time to do that."

He hesitated, then smiled, nodded, and said, "Okay, just this once. But you be careful, now." And he turned as if nothing had happened and went back upstairs and continued on his rounds.

I'd had a brief taste of this in escaping from the institute, but now I realized that I wasn't merely bound to it there but had it, at least through the head unit, right here and now—with limits. Telling Charlie not to see me hadn't worked; I wasn't invisible. Telling Charlie he loved me and should ignore what I was doing *had* worked. So there were limits, but not ones I couldn't figure a way around. I guess you had to be a little smart rather than just wish for things in this business.

Still and all, I had power. Not the kind of total power over everything that Al and Alice and that crew dreamed of but localized power over individuals, that was for sure. Somehow, somebody or something had gotten my message, checked back on the number, and sent me a connection, somebody who could transmit a solid helmet over phone wires and then have that helmet actually *integrate* with my brain and body. *Those* folks had the real power, including probably the power to turn the energy switch on and off, but right now it didn't matter.

In this one change *everything* had gone upside down. Everything. As long as the power held, always an unnerving thing to think about, I was suddenly the mistress of this compound and everybody and everything in it.

Vernon wasn't here now; he hadn't been home for several days while he did some business in Sacramento. He'd be back soon, and even he wouldn't be able to withstand this. The question was, How long would I have this power, and what were its limits? I would still have to sleep and eat. Would it hold up?

Now this—*this*—was worth a bald head and a hell of a lot more. I could always wear wigs later.

Don't get too self-confident or carried away! I warned myself. *Remember who and what you are!*

Well, I wasn't sure anymore who or what I was, but I surely did want to find out the limits to this power and maybe use it for a while before I had to forget having fun and go to work for whoever had sent it.

And whoever that had been had gotten the number via my calls to Stanford, that was sure, but it wasn't Al. I'd seen the HMDs they'd had at the institute. This was something very, very different.

And I was suddenly very, very different, too.

IX

THE MARCH HARE SENDS HELP

The churches and the moral types all say life's about this or that or the other thing, but most of them are folks who never really felt a complete lack of power or absolute power. They can talk without really knowing, the way most people do.

But life's about power, and that's *all* it's about. Who's got it, how much, and who hasn't. Money is power, position is power, brute force against weak, scared little people like me and the other girls there at the compound was power. We had no power, so we had to do whatever the ones with power wanted, no matter what.

Well, now, after not having any power and having to depend on others for it, I had it. Not unlimited, maybe, but more than most folks have. A kind of power I didn't understand but didn't have to. It was magic, maybe, or it was computers, 'cause everything we think we know is wrong. Maybe it was a lot of that shit, since most technology is magic to most people, anyway; they just don't like to admit that they don't have the slightest idea how the hell the lights come on when they flip the switch.

That left me standing there with the question of whether I wanted out or wanted revenge.

Silly question.

Still, what were the limits of this power? If I turned Vern into one of his victims, would he still remember who he'd been and suffer as he should, or would everything adjust so that the chief bad guy here would just be a different scumbag and it would be as if he'd always been that way? The experience with Charlie Mombassa seemed to say that I could change people, certainly minds, maybe a lot more, but that it had to be done in such a way that it seemed normal or logical.

I heard someone upstairs and went toward the sound, eventually bumping into Chalmette on her way back from the john and looking sleepy as all hell. She was wide awake enough to see me coming, stare at the totally bald head, and say, "Rina, what the fuck . . . ?"

Now, Chalmette was a drop-dead gorgeous African-American girl with a figure to die for, but I couldn't help using her as a test subject.

"I've always been bald, and you know it," I both told her and transmitted to her. Then I added, *"You are a natural platinum blond blue-eyed Swedish girl named Inga."* The tendrils shot out and engulfed her, and then there was an amazing top to bottom transformation into just the image I'd had in mind. Now, *that* was impressive! Even more, she didn't seem to notice, and I wondered who else might.

"Oh, okay," she responded in a much higher, breathier kind of voice with the undertones of a Swedish accent. "I guess I yust am still dead to the vorld. Sorry."

"That's okay," I responded. "Um, you have a little smudge on your cheek."

I actually put a slight smudge there with willpower, and she turned and went briefly back into the bathroom and stared at her face in the mirror before running some water and washing off the smudge.

The reflection had been Inga's, not Chalmette's, and she didn't seem to be aware of any change. I had taken one girl and made her entirely different—and she hadn't even noticed!

I wondered if anybody else would. Probably not, which made the kind of revenge I'd have loved to give Vernon null and void.

I walked into the john and looked at myself in the same mirror. She was right about one thing: I sure looked different. Still, the effect wasn't all that bad. I had the head for it, or so it seemed. Even so, I hated to have to reprogram everybody's standard one at a time, including mine.

I'd like my hair back, I ordered, but absolutely nothing happened. I tried asking, pleading, doing just about anything I could think of to talk it into that, but I discovered that not only wouldn't it restore the hair, it wouldn't make *any* change in my body. Wardrobe, jewelry, makeup I could do almost by wishing or imagining, but physical changes—no.

I probably could manage with a wig; I tried some hats, and they stayed. But for now I pretty well said the hell with it.

I sat down on the toilet and tried to figure out what to do next.

This wasn't, after all, the first time I'd been plugged into this kind of energy and been able to use it. I just hadn't been able to use it this well or this precisely before. Now, I had no idea what an Inga should look like except in my mind; the 3-D wireframe showed that something else had done a hell of a piece of programming—probably another computer way beyond what I'd known—and what I was doing was becoming the operator. It was the equivalent of sitting at a keyboard with a view of, say, Chalmette, on a screen in front of me and typing instructions.

If I was a keyboard, the energy linkage was the cord that attached me to the computer that actually did the job. I'd assumed until this moment that it was the one at the institute, but was it? In one way it made sense—if they didn't know where I was, give me the wild card to get out of any nasty situation, after which they could trace me and turn it off. Maybe but maybe not. What if the other group had tapped the phones in and out of the institute and the Stanford Medical Internet connection, hoping they could intercept me? Maybe I was connected to Rick!

How to tell? Once I dealt with my own little battles here, I would have to leave and link up with somebody some-where. I needed information, and I needed it not only on the other end but also on the various capabilities and lim-itations of this thing. I had a sudden thought that seemed so dumb that I almost threw it away in embarrassment, but then I decided that dumb or not, nothing was impossible these days.

"Query help system," I shot out, trying to direct it to the en-ergy flow and out the top of my head.

"?"

I almost stood straight up. That was a response! A prompt?

"What computer am I networked into?"

"Central core."

That wasn't getting me anywhere. *"Whose computer am I linked to? That is, who is the authority that operates it?"*

"Master stabilization program is automatic."

I sighed. Even on this level it was still a damned machine.

"Immediate location of other end of energy link between subject operator and physical computer?"

"Site twenty-seven dash G."

Rats. It was both exciting and frustrating. Somehow I had managed to link up not with one of the computers in this uni-verse but with something *beyond* it! Something *real*. But un-fortunately, getting that far had removed any useful frame of reference.

Maybe I was being too ambitious.

"Name of operator who transmitted device to this operator to link to network?"

"Sysop March Hare Network."

Aha! So it *wasn't* Al! That was exciting.

"Why did I lose my hair when I was connected?"

"Integration of netlinker replaced code."

Okay, that was something. *"Why can't I have the hair back now?"*

"Netlinker includes code which freezes subject code to guarantee solid linkup."

Good lord! *"Do you mean that physically I'm stabilized permanently like this?"* I was pregnant, after all. Did that mean that even *that* was frozen?

"Yes. Even that is frozen," the help system agreed.

"What will unfreeze it?"

"Cessation of netlinker at the source."

So I couldn't even turn it off. The March Hare, whoever *he* was, could, but for now I was playing his game. At least his game wasn't Al's game.

I began to gingerly probe the help system on just what I could and could not do. Like the rest, it took quite a while to get any kind of frame of reference that made sense, but once I got it, there seemed to be some clear-cut rules.

Anything I could see, hear, touch—the things that interacted with me personally—I could alter within a broad range of probabilities. The data link and bandwidth were the most limiting factors, which was why I couldn't turn Oakland into Chicago or give everybody wings or the like. I did, however, work out a system with the query help that proved very handy. I'd think of what I wanted to do, and help would inform me if it was within my limits to do it.

There was also a sort of caution. Every time I used it, there was measurable activity on that energy level that would be detectable by anyone who knew what to look for and had the right equipment and was looking, which meant Al and Les and the gang. Not that I couldn't use it, but if I went nuts over it, I might well be tracked or traced. It was, therefore, best to use it when I had to or on very limited things I'd already worked out.

Fair enough.

Even with the limitations, it's nearly impossible to convey the difference when you go from nearly total powerlessness to this kind of power and confidence. Okay, so I had to waddle around and be bald, but that was a small price to pay for being able to do pretty much what I wanted without fear. Jewelry, clothes, money, even people waiting on me all the time—easy, almost a snap of the fingers.

And I was antsy, uncomfortable, and pissed off. You couldn't even impress anybody. Once you decided that something was so—like everybody loved you—it was like it had *always* been that way, and even you started getting memories of how everything came off to make it different.

That, I realized, was how the damned Brand Boxes worked, how even the big deal worked.

There was one reality, one solid world that was probably not like the two I could remember in detail but pretty comfortable. Now, somebody has some kind of hang-up, and he's the first to get in there or die or whatever, and so that hang-up, no matter how far back in the mind it was, comes out. Some white guy born and raised in a rural southern background might fantasize that the South won the Civil War. Okay, so that becomes truth, and everything is filled in around it, shaped to fit it. What kind of a computer that would require and how much memory I didn't want to think about, but there it was.

That was what happened when I created something, too, whether it was new shoes or a new attitude or changing somebody's race or family background or you name it. Everything adjusted so that it was *always* like that, at least to everybody but me, the operator running the automatic Do It program.

You could materialize ruby slippers right in front of them, and *poof!* Instantly the slippers had a history. *I* knew it because I'd created them, but I also knew the history that had been filled in behind them for everybody else.

If you got into a new universe without dying, you were kind of like the creator. You knew, but nobody else did unless he came in the same way.

Okay, so now I knew the system, but I didn't know what the hell good it was doing me to stick around at that point. I mean, how the hell could you get revenge on somebody who'd never know it, and how much could you do to help people who wouldn't remember they were ever in trouble?

Well, I did one thing for the girls and some of the men as well. I took 'em off drugs. Gave 'em an allergy to them, too, and a little bit of immunity. Some of them just substituted booze for needles or bongs, but so be it.

I wasn't going to make the mistake of going out alone, though. Somebody, maybe a couple of people, would have to be with me, working with and for me, totally dependable. I'd have to be able to trust them with Angel, who was in the early stages of learning to walk but was getting pretty damned heavy to cart around.

I reset "Inga" to Chalmette and added Suzy Nu, whose family was from someplace unpronounceable in southeast Asia, as my associate and guardian. Those choices were easy because Suzy knew all sorts of martial arts for protection and Chalmette was a dead shot and because neither of them had anybody or anyplace to go if they left here and so had nothing to lose.

I didn't debate it or ask for volunteers, though. What the hell; this was the Bay Area, and in my condition, frozen or not, it was hardly a big deal with me. I made 'em heavily, devotedly, beyond any doubt or betrayal of me, completely in love with me. Besides, after what guys had done to them all their lives, they pretty well already swung that way outside of business, anyway. The only really odd thing that came up even though I hadn't wished it, at least consciously, was that neither of them had any hair on her head, either, for all sorts of rationales. I could have fixed that, I guess, but somehow, particularly since they were so great-looking otherwise, I left it in. Besides, it was nearly zero maintenance and we'd be on the road, and with big earrings and care in makeup, it didn't look bad on any of us.

That left Vern, who was due back the next night. I was determined not to leave until I had a firsthand encounter with him or at least could do *something*, and by the afternoon of the day he was due back I had it. After that I didn't even have to see him. We could easily walk or even drive out of there and know that nobody concerned would even remember that we should ever have been there once we left. But Vern, if he set foot back in that mansion, would still be subject to my revenge.

Slowly developing but increasingly painful testicular cancer, both sides. If he saw a doctor in time, he would go under the knife and never again do to any other woman what he had done to me or be able to blame anybody for not being able to do it. If he didn't see it in time, it would be an ugly and painful death.

It was appropriate, and even if he didn't remember or realize that it was me, it didn't matter. He was still the same rotten SOB deep down, and maybe he might reflect on the justice of it all when his disease progressed.

Not as instantly gratifying as, say, turning him into a toad or one of the girls, but *this* wouldn't involve a change in reality. This involved suffering in appropriate amounts by the right guy in the perfect area.

It also didn't take a lot of energy to create the program for it or to leave it in place to be triggered. Instead, it just brought up the one question I'd tried to avoid up to now.

Now what?

Money wasn't a major problem. I gathered that the cash, amounting to several thousand dollars, wasn't from legit sources even when it had its history backfilled by the master program. However, cash didn't leave a lot of traces, and I decided not to press the girls on where it came from even though, in truth, I'd simply wished it into being.

It *was* kind of impressive, I had to admit. I wondered if the backfill was just enough to get by or whether it was so complete that the amount was accounted for all the way back to the mint.

None of us had a driver's license, but I managed to create valid ones for both of the girls, using addresses that had been valid once but not anymore. Then we took a cab over to a place Chalmette knew that rented old but serviceable cars for insurance companies while somebody was fixing your smashed-up one. We managed to rent a small wagon on a monthly basis for a grand down, cash. I doubted if it was worth much more than that, but it didn't seem like it would gas us.

There was no question in my mind where we should head. North. Away from the institute and the damned Boxes but toward an area that seemed to be at least partly controlled by the opposition.

Even without Brand having a history there in this world, I had the eerie feeling that Walt and maybe others would be there, either in and around Yakima and the ranges north of it or at least somewhere between Vancouver, Washington, and Seattle.

It wasn't all intuition, either. If I shifted my vision, I could shift to 3-D wireframe on almost anything and also see the ribbon of energy, like a cable, connecting me to the computer somehow, rising up and vanishing north over the horizon.

We did not, however, hurry. As much as I wanted to find Rick and get all this over with, just leaving the Bay Area and heading toward Oregon seemed to lift an enormous weight from my shoulders and my mind. I was with friends who adored me; we had money and no schedule to speak of and no reason to rush.

It sounds really bizarre, I know, but it was the truth. After all that had happened, all the changes I'd gone through, I was exhausted physically, mentally, and emotionally. I needed a break.

I needed a vacation.

I know it sounds odd, even weird, but the fact was, I deliberately took my time getting anywhere at all except out of the Bay Area. I luxuriated not in snap-your-fingers power but in having people do all the heavy lifting, diaper changing, all that. Meanwhile, I just relaxed and saw the country and stayed at nice motels and took baths when I felt like it and ate nice and drew a line and said, "I'm on a break. Do not disturb."

I could have kept it up for a while, too, in the Oregon mountain resort areas and along the Columbia River. It could have lasted for a nearly indefinite period if it had not been for a couple of things. I'm not sure which disturbed me the most when I finally thought about them.

What disturbed me the least was pursuit. Either they caught me, in which case I was no worse off than I'd been when I had started all this, or they didn't. I was prudent enough to limit what was easiest for them to trace, since I already had things set up for a while, and it hardly entered my mind.

Rick disturbed me or, rather, where Rick was and what shape he was in. I had some mixed opinions on him, too, at that point. Sure, I couldn't blame him for the getaway when he knew they were coming to pick him up, but he'd *stayed* away. Not a word, not an attempt at anything. If things were backward, if it were Rick and Angel in the hands of the enemy or out alone on the streets, I wouldn't back off and turn things over to somebody else. My one and only priority would be to ensure that they were safe and try and figure out how to contact them and eventually spring them.

Nothing. *Nada.* Not a word. If in fact it was Rick who'd sent the amazingly integrable head mount to me, why was there no message, no signature, nothing? Rick wasn't the March Hare, but even Al thought he was in the hands of the network. I admit I had more than a few black thoughts about this and visions, however unreasoning and jealous, of Rick in the arms of Cynthia Matalon vamped up to her finest southern-fried glamour.

The alternatives were almost as bad: he was hurt, or dead, or a prisoner somewhere.

I think, though, that what eventually rubbed me the worst was the way I caught myself thinking about my two companions, Suzy and Chalmette, and, to a lesser extent, about others we met along the way. Not as people, not as fully formed human beings like Rick and me and even Les and Al and Rita but as, well, kind of Disneyland robots, creatures formed by the universe's most awesome CAD program to perform functions for my benefit but, underneath, just—wireframe.

Was that how Al saw most of the rest of humanity? Was that how Walt could blow away a kid without even thinking about it while setting up an attack on the complex in Yakima?

> *You remind me of the man.*
> *What man?*
> *The man with the power . . .*

With just this limited power base and only a brief time with it and free in open country, I'd developed an almost matter-of-fact "us" and "them" mind-set. Hell, even Les had enough of an ethical sense left that he still agonized after all this time and trouble over whether "they" really were any different from us in the end.

Was I so easily corrupted? Was Rick? Might Rick in fact be falling into the same sort of trap concerning me? I wasn't obviously an "us" but was much more clearly a "them" to everybody else. That was the way the institute, Al, and all the others had seen me. Al even claimed he'd created me for his own purposes.

Well, I needed "them," at least these two women, at least for now. But I had no right to use them beyond my need or manipulate them the same way we drove a car or used any other tool. They weren't devices or shouldn't be thought of as devices, anyway. They should be treated with some respect, as people.

If the March Hare and his people thought that way, I wasn't sure I liked them any better than I liked Al and his crew, but at least now, for the first time, I could understand them. How many lifetimes had Al claimed he went back? Eight? Nine? Something like that. I couldn't help wondering about Walt's memories as well. Augmented with their own Brand Box recordings of the past, how many lives, how much experience *could* people like that muster? And if this little bit of power had done this to me in a week, what must that enormous gulf of time do to them?

I wanted Al to lose, but did I want Walt and his people to win? How could I know?

It was time to go find the March Hare and see.

The United States had been more impoverished, more devastated, and slower to develop the technology of World War II here than in the first universe I could remember. There were only signs of the potential interstate and defense highway system that was so taken for granted and overused in my first lifetime that it had already been falling apart. Here it was barely begun, but that meant that the other roads were still busy routes and that their own services hadn't died out yet.

In that previous life Yakima had had a period when it had acquired and restored a couple of old streetcars and run them along the industrial apple railroad tracks when they weren't being used by commercial trains as a kind of tourist attraction. *This* Yakima was different; here they still ran trolley cars as public transportation even though Yakima was a bit smaller and less developed than I remembered it.

I almost despaired upon seeing it, even though it was also prettier and much more appealing than the town I remembered from a previous existence. This was a place built upon the almighty Washington State apple and, to a much lesser extent, tourism heading toward Mount Rainier from the east. The only high tech in this town was the canning factory, and the fruit company inventories and accounts were being handled by room-sized mainframes at best.

Silicon Valley had started to develop in the Bay Area, it was true, only twenty-five years or so late, drawn by the same factors as before, including climate and ready money. But the concurrent Washington State industry that would become its match simply did not exist, at least not yet, not now, and maybe not ever.

And yet this was where the filtered vision of the energy thread connecting my smooth dome to the March Hare Network led. Somebody or something was up here, and it was up to me to find it.

I remembered a time that seemed so very, very long ago when we'd chased Cynthia and Walt up through the badland center of the state to that air force firing range and watched—what?

Well, it was worth a try, anyway, if in fact there was anything like a decent road up through there. The last time, in another world, there had been an interstate, but the only thing like that in this Washington was the part of what would become I-5 to the west of the mountains. The road atlas showed a small road in its worst pale red code snaking up there. Not even U.S. 97, the old reliable that the interstate had replaced in that other region. Nope, a squiggly red line said State 821 from Yakima, following the course of its namesake river. Not many folks wanted to go there, at least not yet, I thought. U.S. 12 northwest toward Rainier and Tacoma or southeast toward Richland—that was it. And that didn't go where I wanted to look.

But Yakima Ridge was there, and the Saddle Mountains, and between was something that simply said U.S. MILITARY RES. RESTRICTED.

Okay, Walt, let's see if you're hiding up there . . .

It was amazing how quickly the landscape changed once you started north. Beyond the river, which continued to feed lush trees and bushes, there was only painted desert landscape, a kind of desolate region that looked out of place anywhere else in the state or even in the northwest and was more like Arizona or Utah or New Mexico. Formed in the rain shadow of the Cascades and the giant volcanoes within them, it was an eerie little patch of nothing in the middle of an otherwise wet and green state.

We followed the road north slowly and comfortably, and I couldn't help thinking that at least it was next to impossible for anybody to follow us very closely without being obvious. Not that it was worth doing, anyway; I mean, if this was the main road, we didn't really want to see the side streets.

"Need gas," Chalmette commented. She'd been driving much of the stretch and seemed undisturbed by its twists and turns.

"Stop at the next place with a pump," I told her. "I need to ask a few questions of the natives."

"Natives" was the right word. The area was essentially all in the Yakima Indian Reservation, with the military reservation starting maybe a quarter mile to the east and paralleling the road. The place was a small stone building with a faded Coke sign that probably had been there for forty years on top of the door and a single weathered old-fashioned pump outside. A beat-up pickup was parked on one side, and an even more aged and worn Chevy was being worked on by a fellow in jeans and T-shirt on the far side of the pump.

I debated going for the wigs for my companions, but since I wanted to talk to somebody myself and couldn't wear one, I figured, what the hell, I'll take the funny looks.

It wasn't that I couldn't put on a wig or a hat, but doing so appeared to do something to the energy connection. It didn't break it, but the energy got erratic or beyond use, and it was the only power and insurance I had. I might use it for very short stretches, such as from the car to a motel room or something. Certainly, if somebody who could also see that energy thread was following us, I could make it hard to pinpoint myself that way, but otherwise I didn't like it at all. I'd come to terms with this and accepted it for the time being.

On the other hand, the sight of three bald women wearing sunglasses and large jewelry and pronounced makeup was pretty eerie to somebody who hadn't seen anything like it before. Sort of like a car with cult members or something, I figured. That was why I wasn't at all surprised when the old Indian station hand looked nervous and startled when he saw us or when the younger fellow working on the car looked up and had a minor dropping of the jaw and some staring.

"Fill it," I told him as Suzy helped me out of the backseat. "You got a ladies' room here?"

"Not fancy," he responded, sounding nervous. "Out back yonder."

He wasn't kidding. It was a wooden stall complete with a half-moon on the door and a pit going down to the true home of every fly in Washington State.

Well, at least he didn't have to worry about folks lingering in his rest rooms. If the flies and such didn't chase you away, the smell would.

I walked back around and saw that the old man was still filling us up. Gas at least wasn't expensive even in this day and age, certainly not compared to what I remembered back in the old world. You actually got pumped and had your windows washed and your oil checked even in places like this.

"You get many strangers coming in here?" I asked him, trying to sound casual and friendly.

He looked briefly at me, then turned away and gave his attention to the pump. "Not many," he commented.

I caught something in his face and tone, though. I hadn't noticed it before, but it sure leapt out at me now.

The old Indian was afraid.

Of what? Of us? We looked a little otherworldly, I guess, but I couldn't believe that even such an odd trio would cause that kind of reaction in a man like that. Disapproval, even disgust, maybe, but *fear*?

"We've been looking for a couple of people we know are up this way," I told him, a bit puzzled by this palpable reaction on his part. "One would be a thin, attractive woman with a thick southern accent. She'd be with a guy who probably looks like a shoe salesman, probably named Walt or Walter. You seen either of them?"

"I don't pay attention," he replied curtly. The pump clicked off, and he pulled the nozzle out, hung it back on the pump, and screwed on the cap.

"I mean folks who live around here or at least come here often," I pressed. "Think."

"No. Not many white folks live around here. They keep down in Yakima or up in Ellensburg. You ask there. This is tribal country."

"What about the military? Don't they work on that place over to the east?"

He sighed. "Ma'am, they don't come out this way. Sorry. That'll be eight fifty, please."

I told Suzy to pay him and got back in the car, as did the other two, this time with Suzy at the wheel. We slowly pulled out of the station and started north on the road.

"Something was funny back there," I commented. "He was hiding something. I wonder what."

"I think that cute young guy workin' on the Chevy was some kinda cop," Chalmette replied. "I can smell 'em, I think."

"You sure? I know that these reservations have their own cops, but he just looked like the old guy's son or grandson to me."

"He was definitely more'n that," Suzy said, agreeing with Chalmette. "I smelled him, too. Hard to say if he was official or just there workin' on his car, but he was definitely the man 'round these sticks."

I thought for a moment. "Can you find a place where the trees are thick near the river and do a nice, slow turnoff so we can't be seen from the road and there aren't any big tire marks?" I asked her. "Maybe we should find out if we need to worry."

It wasn't that hard to do, although I have to say that if Indians were the kind of trackers that they might have been in the old days or at least are in the movies, we'd have been dead meat. As it was, we sat there well concealed, and eventually we saw the old Chevy come into view and pass us heading north, nice and slow and steady.

"Let him get a little ahead and then let's follow *him* for a change," I suggested.

Suzy nodded. I couldn't help but notice that neither of them had asked a single question about why we were up here, why we might be chasing or avoiding cops, or anything. The mere fact that this was what I wanted to do was enough for them. I mentally promised myself that if we all came out of this okay, I'd make it worth their while to have been along.

We pulled out and drove even slower than the Indian cop had been going. Then Suzy slowly sped up to where we'd maybe come briefly into view behind him if he was looking in his rearview mirror. She was doing it like a real pro; the street smarts of the past helped, of course, but again it struck me that she hadn't known how to drive until I'd bestowed that on her and that she was now doing it like a natural.

We came around a bend and could see a whole stretch of road ahead. Suzy suddenly braked. "This ain't right!" she exclaimed, suspicious and irritated at the same time.

"Huh? What's the matter?"

"I think he pulled it back on us! *Got* to be behind us! No way he coulda cleared that whole stretch we can see ahead before we got here. Uh uh. You want to double back on him?"

"Forget the cat and mouse," I told her. "Let's find him."

We turned around and headed back south again, but only for a mile or so.

"I see him!" Chalmette called. "Look! He turned off over there, and he's headin' off on that dirt road!"

He sure was, at least from the tiny speck and the large cloud of dust we could see.

"Maybe he was just a reservation cop," Suzy said hopefully.

I shook my head. "Uh uh. That's not the reservation he's heading into over there. That's the federal military reservation."

She thought a moment. "Hmph! Gonna make it rough to follow him, I guess. Unless we *really* hold back. Even then, if there's somebody watchin' the gates, with that kind of dust it's gonna be impossible to get in there without everybody knowin'."

"Maybe," I responded. "Maybe not. This is pretty close to where I was once before, when I saw stuff that scared the living shit out of me. Now, what I saw and who I saw is just who and what I *want* to see. Let's get back to where we can hide out for a little while." I looked at the car clock, which sort of kept decent time. "We got maybe two, three hours to sunset. You think you could follow that road after dark?"

"I dunno. It gets blacker'n pitch out here ten minutes after sundown."

"Not tonight. There's a nearly full moon. I noticed it last night. No clouds to speak of, should be fairly bright. You game?"

"Sure. Why not? What else I got to do?"

But being game wasn't the same as facing unpleasant truths. Throughout this whole thing I'd come to junctions, one after the other. Some had worked out, others had not, but all of them had affected only me. That made it easier to take risks. The one that hadn't, getting out of the institute with Angel, was still as much in Angel's interest as in mine and came under the "protecting the kid" flag.

Not this. What I decided at this point affected at least three others: Angel, of course, and Chalmette and Suzy. I was tempted to drive back to Yakima or north to that town at the other end, find a motel, and leave one of the women there with Angel, but what would that do? If I couldn't get back, what would I have done to them? And if there were spies even in little gas stations, how long would either Suzy or Chalmette remain free once we left them there?

I could ignore this and run. Assuming I could elude any chasers—not a sure thing but possible—what would happen then? My physical body was frozen in a kind of joke. Bald, frozen at a high level of pregnancy, but not high enough to solve the problem. I probably wasn't aging physically, either, so if I just turned my back on things this time, I would be like this indefinitely. That was not a choice.

Or I could charge in and risk my young child and the only two adults in the world I could trust.

These were choices?

"Query help system."

"?"

"Are choices of future direction as stated?"

"Substantially correct. There are many millions of fine permutations."

"And if I did walk away from it, just remain as I am, get away? Would things continue as they are?"

"Too many variables. However, energy link will be broken when central core moves to next creation plane. At that point programs would become permanent and dynamic."

"How can something become both permanent and dynamic? Seems like those are opposites."

"Not at all. Change is a constant. Loss of connection would leave you without any power to alter programs but as you are. Fetus could be delivered by C-section and would then develop normally."

This was something new. Not the C-section business but the idea that things would still be around, would still exist, if the core, if the master computer and master Brand Boxes, went on to another virtual universe.

"You mean prior universes are not destroyed once they've been created?"

"Not unless specifically terminated by instruction, no. Never if any core subjects remain within."

So there was a sort of future here if we walked, although God knew if it would be much of a life. It wasn't enough to just live; there had to be some reason to keep living.

"Percentage that going into the reservation this time will gain me anything except maybe an arrest?"

"Incalculable but probably even. This was the site of a number of previous major core installations and thus is a weak point. There is a power nexus at this point."

"What's that mean?"

"Master program can be suspended locally, patched, or bypassed within limits at a nexus if proper knowledge and access are present."

There wasn't much choice in this. I didn't see any future in dropping out this time, nor would there be much of a future for my kids. No, it was better in this case to be in than out.

Darkness proved more of an asset than a liability, something I hadn't expected. By shifting to wireframe mode and looking out across that bleak landscape, I was able to see the entire region not as an eerie land of shadows and shapes but as an almost equally eerie rendering of topographically outlined contours. And beyond the shielding low range in the distance, from about where Rick, as Riki, and I had once stood and watched Walt and Cynthia and others off-load from a rabbit hole, I could see the weakness in the overall structural integrity there and at that point a liquidlike pool, mostly calm at the moment, of that dull green energy that gave the real power. It was energy that flowed out and through the wireframes, creating and maintaining them.

More startling, I could feel it tugging on me, or at least on my skull. Not pain, not a headache, not a pounding, just a gentle tug that made me suddenly aware of the artificial head mount integrated with my skull up there and its connection to all this.

The source of my own energy thread had not been this pool, although that was what I'd thought until I saw it. But this close, with this sort of proximity to that much raw power, even if it

was currently dormant in this spot like one of those big volcanoes in the distance, the pull, the attraction was so great that I
felt things switch. I could feel that energy thread break and
swing out, freed from its prior source, and curve instead into
this shimmering lake of pale green energy.

For a moment the power had left me and things had blanked
out, but now that the other end was clearly inserted into and
drawing from this pool, the power surged through it and into
me, stronger than before. This diversion had created something
new, something those who'd sent the head mount and its
strange integration program hadn't figured on.

As a part of the March Hare Network I'd been connected to
the equivalent of a server, but I'd been a workstation, under the
server's limits and subject to its call. Not now. Although not
the central computer, source of all the Brand Boxes and of all
reality, this energy permeated the world, perhaps the universe,
and kept the program stable. This weak point, perhaps one of
many around the world, was sort of a bug in the system, a hidden connector to the same power source that was in the core. I
now had power equal to that of Al or Walt or anybody else;
what I did not have that they had was a connection to the
knowledge base, the network server and its files. I was like a
savage standing in front of the world's most powerful main-
frame, knowing its vast power but, staring at the keyboard,
wishing I knew how to type.

"Query help system."

Silence.

"Query help system!"

There was nothing. I was no longer connected in any way. I
was strictly on my own.

"Let me drive," I told the women.

"But you don't know *how!*" Chalmette protested.

I gave a soft smile. "I know how to drive a car. Don't
worry."

The very limited use of nearly absolute power was the easiest. I could fry somebody or do other simple, visceral things as

they came up. Approaching the fence and gate, I simply ignored them and the protests from my passengers.

The car passed through the gate. It didn't open it or clear it, nor did the gate and fence cease to exist. We just went through it like ghosts.

We didn't, however, find ourselves immune from the bumps in the far less than perfect dirt road. I found the bumps irritating and uncomfortable and got angry at their presence; the road suddenly smoothed out, a small but now paved ribbon.

We climbed the ridge on that impossibly steep switchbacked single-lane road and finally reached the point where you could see the other side and maybe fifty miles beyond. Down on the valley floor was the energy lake I'd been incapable of seeing the last time I'd been up there.

That had been the source of Walt's rabbit hole. He'd created it, drawn it from this lake of power somehow.

I turned off the headlights and started down. The others were even more nervous at this, since they couldn't see things the way I could, but nobody made a sound or objected to what I was doing. It wouldn't have made any difference.

Aware that I was the only one who could see it among my party, I drove right down to the edge of the lake, stopped the car, and got out. Down here, so close, the pulsating power was almost overwhelming, but I forced myself to get very close, ignoring the fear that it might burn or consume me. I needed to know how to use it, how to control it beyond this gut level and these limits. I needed to connect to a knowledge base in some fashion, no matter what the source.

I had resolved to go for broke. Did I have the nerve to do it?

I took a deep breath, hesitated a moment, and then walked directly into the lake of bubbling green energy.

I felt sudden dizziness and total disorientation, then "saw," in a way I never remembered seeing before, my whole self, my *real* self, the wireframe and internal flowing equations that made me who I was. I felt sudden pain and discomfort in several areas and realized that this was the head mount and other patched programs I hadn't even been aware I carried being burned off, consumed by the fire.

The child in my belly, a boy, rotated, turned, and seemed to grow and flow up and into me. I was a woman, I was a man, I was an adult, a child, old, ancient, and a baby all at once. Tendrils of energy went down into the lake and then out in all directions at the speed of light, seeking, searching, and finding data.

There seemed to be others as well around me. Strange creatures, more than one race, including those small aliens we'd been told were the Roswell bunch and were later seen actively helping Walt Slidecker. Others were of different shapes and consistencies, gargoyles and angels all at once, shifting in form and nature all the time, the royal court of the dominion of chaos bowing and asking, *"How can we serve my lady?"*

"Information!" I told them. "I need a data link!"

"We can't, my lady! Not directly. We are so sorry, most noble one! We grovel and humble ourselves in our failure!"

"Why not? Why can't you hook me up from here?"

"Because, my lady, you are only in the matrix for this creation set! You are not part of the divine matrix! You are not in the master program. Please forgive us, o magnificent one! We do what we can . . ."

What did they mean? Not part of the divine matrix? Not in the master program? Then that must mean . . .

I stepped out of the lake of energy and back on solid ground once again. Chalmette and Suzy both stood there; Angel was sleeping in the back of the car. They seemed oddly frozen, a tableau in lifelike wax, unmoving, not even breathing.

And not alone.

It sat there on a big Harley Davidson motorcycle looking at me with a bemused expression on its stupid-looking buck-toothed face. A giant white rabbit in waistcoat and breeches, sitting there on that huge bike and not at all frozen.

"Hello, luvah!" it said in a familiar voice from long ago. "My, oh my! Have you evah changed."

"Hello, Cynthia," I responded. "I kind of expected you to show up sooner or later, but not looking like that."

She chuckled. "One of deah depahted Matthew's bits o' humah, ah'm told. We—each of us—got assigned some charactah from *Alice in Wondahland* to be the basic ID. No mattah who or what this wild system makes me, ah'm always the White Rabbit undahneath. You see me on that level, you know who ah am. Yo'ah too close to the flames, so to speak. Yoah Miss Injun Squaw's the Red Queen, foah example. Al, he's the Walrus, and Doctah Cohen's the Cahpentah. They like to lie to all the oystahs befoah they eat 'em, y' see. Rick, now, is the King of Hearts, but don't let that trouble you none. Nothin' goin' on 'tween him and the Red Queen. Nevah was. Deah Walt's the Cheshire Cat. You see the system?"

I nodded. The system was pretty basic and obvious, and for a mad genius with a passion for Wonderland it was also a direct system. Brand gave the character name IDs to each and every one of us, based on his own sense of humor rather than on any priorities or associations. Those IDs stood in the master program as our basic file names, our basic identities. Anything and everything that happened to us, no matter what these incarnations and reincarnations did, was overlaid on the base file, which didn't change. The Brand Boxes were personalized, or at least most were, probably by the same codes.

It didn't matter if you became male or female, grew fangs, had wings, or suddenly herded yaks outside Ulan Bator. Scrape it all away and you were still the Red King or the Walrus.

"And what am I, Cynthia?"

The rabbit looked a bit uncomfortable. "Cory Maddox? Cory Maddox is Alice. Kinda looks like that theah l'il guhl in the old drawin's, if you know what I mean. Don't get no big head on it, though. Ev'body says it wasn't 'cause Cory was the stah of the show or nothin' like that. In fact, it's supposta be a kinda dig, a soaht of mild insult, 'cause heah was tiny Alice exploahin' a whole new crazy univehse and all she kept doin' was whinin' and complainin' and wantin' t' go home, y' see."

I wasn't all that thrilled with the description, but I was more interested in the shift in her tense as she said that. "Why do you say Cory, Cynthia? Aren't *I* Cory?"

"You'll do," she responded enigmatically.

"I want to know the truth! Am I Cory Maddox or not? Yes or no?"

"It ain't that simple, dahlin'," she replied. "It ain't that simple at all."

X

THE QUEEN OF BROKEN HEARTS

"What do you mean, it isn't that simple?" I asked her nervously. "Damn it, something either *is* or it *isn't*. Even here."

"Uh uh, dahlin'. That ain't necessarahly so." She kick started the Harley, and it roared into life. "C'mon," she called over the noise. "Hop on back and we'll go wheah the ansahs lie!"

"I can't! The girls and Angel—I can't leave them!"

"They'll be jes' fine! They been put on hold, won't know nothin' when they come outa it. C'mon! We'll be back foah 'em, I sweah! Now c'mon, sugah! Weah late as it is! They tell me that's why Ah got stuck with this one. Always late foah jes' 'bout any old thing."

I walked over to the Harley and hesitantly climbed on. It was really weird; I knew it was Cynthia Matalon there, but I could even feel the rabbit hair as I grabbed on to her. She put the big bike into gear, and we were off at a fast clip.

A swirling mass of energy opened up right ahead of us on the road, not from the lake but spontaneously, as if arising out of thin air. It had the same power and properties as the rest but seemed a more golden color, and it was spinning around and making alternate dark-light swirls so that it seemed at once a tunnel and some kind of spinning cornucopia. The White Rabbit didn't hesitate; she aimed right for it, and the big hog seemed to go up a slight ramp and straight into it.

I'd been in a rabbit hole once before, but this was different in its look, feel, and properties. I suspected that no two holes were ever really the same and might even partly reflect their creators or at least those who summoned them. Still, this was a new wrinkle all around and certainly the first time Alice had ever ridden to Wonderland on a Harley.

We came out in a desolate place with water all around and a huge, eerie rock rising up from the depths, surrounded by a thin but serviceable yellow sand beach. The sky was as dark as when we'd left and seemed unnatural in its total lack of light or anything, more like a roof or a painted ceiling. In some ways it was the same effect as the shaman's land I'd used to such good effect so far.

There was a fire on one end of the beach and a bunch of, well, *creatures* gathered around that fire. The Harley leapt out of the rabbit hole and onto the sand, spraying it all over, and Cynthia braked, turned, and used the sand to stop.

"All out, sugah. Go on ovah and Ah'll join y'all in a minute."

The March Hare was there, but I'd expected him. Here, too, was a dodo quite similar to the hologram I'd seen when navigating through the previous hole, and here, too, was a grotesque woman all in white cuddling what at first seemed to be a baby in her oversized arms but at second glance turned out to be a piglet in a baby's nightclothes. To one side a mock turtle was lighting a griffin's huge cigar from the flame of its own stogie.

They turned and stopped their conversation when I approached, and the March Hare said, "Well, well! Welcome to our little group! You'll excuse the John Tenniel look, but there's a bit of a security matter here, you see, and the less you know right now on some scores, the better."

"John who?" I managed. At least the voice of the March

Hare was the same as the not terribly familiar voice I'd heard from the same creature in my bedroom back at the home. It meant that I probably was dealing with the people I thought I was dealing with, for all the good that did.

"Tenniel. The first guy who illustrated the *Alice* books, or so I'm told. That's the look we got here rather than, say, Disney, for which I'm eternally grateful. Matt Brand liked the Disney model, but I doubt if he ever read the books. Come! Sit! We have various drinks and goodies here, even, um, tea, if you dare around me. Also good wine, beer and ale, fresh lemonade, Ovaltine . . . Whatever you want, you get. It's easy when it's all made up anyway, right?"

"I don't think I better take anything alcoholic for the sake of—" I began, then I suddenly realized something: I wasn't pregnant. I was absolutely positively day to day and feeling quite normal. I wondered for a moment if I now bore the appearance and attributes of this artist's Alice, but my shadow on the rock indicated otherwise, as did the fact that I put my hand to my head and discovered that there still wasn't any hair there.

No, I was more like I'd been the first time I remembered waking up in the project apartment, minus the hair. It was weird.

"Maybe I will have a white wine," I told the March Hare. "It's been a very long time since I took anything in that area."

He reached down and with a flip of his big brown hand came up with a perfect wineglass. He then picked up an old-fashioned flagon, poured white wine into it, and handed it to me.

"Hey! Got any Chardonnay?" the Mock Turtle asked, flicking his cigar ash.

"Certainly," the March Hare responded, adroitly materializing another glass and pouring a reddish wine *from the same flagon.* He handed it to the Mock Turtle, who nodded.

There were also some pastries and cookies of a sort, sugary things and chocolaty ones. I found myself munching, and the others did likewise.

"Now," the March Hare sighed, settling back with a glass of

what appeared to be champagne, "I guess we better get to business here, huh?"

"The White Rabbit told me who a couple of you might be," I commented. "The rest of you—well, I have no idea who you are, but hello."

"Oh, I think you might remember me even if you didn't know that I was also, um, involved," the Mock Turtle said, his slightly accented voice very familiar-sounding indeed.

"Father Pete?" I was astonished.

"A priest is a priest, but a good cigar is a smoke," Father Pierre Lebeck responded, nodding his reptilian head toward me. "I must say you look as startlingly different now to me as I must to you, and you are not, shall we say, disguised."

I looked around the bizarre assemblage and felt some disappointment. "No King of Hearts, huh?"

"He's with us," Father Pete responded softly. "It was my suggestion that he not be present right at this moment. He wanted to be, believe me. We didn't keep him away for your sake so much as for his. He wanted to come, but I think you need to hear everything out first."

I didn't like the sound of that at all. "What do you mean?"

The March Hare sighed. "Kori, I, um . . ."

"I'll do it," the Mock Turtle said. "This sort of thing is what I do for a living, at least in this life. Cory, I want you to look around this assemblage here and tell me which creature here is not like the others."

"That's easy," I replied. "Me. You're all out of *Alice in Wonderland*, and me, I'm out of Oakland."

"That's pretty much it. I'm sure that by now you have it fairly well figured out, at least in the basics. You know *why* you aren't like us, don't you?"

I nodded, feeling sick. "Because I'm not. When Al claimed that he invented me, he wasn't bragging, was he? He was telling the truth."

"In a sense he was, yes. In another, no. If you look around, you'll see that there are far fewer of us here than there were people at the institute who'd have similar *Alice in Wonderland* personae here. And while there are a few of us missing, there aren't *that* many. So long as we can keep control of some of the Brand Boxes and at least one of us who knows how things work, we can generally manage to keep an opposition going time after time. Keep it going, but—well, you can see who's ahead. As far as we can tell, they've *always* been ahead. We have a few routine devices hidden away, a few methods for accessing the basics, but we're at a distinct disadvantage. Al and his crew control the main computer. They control Matthew Brand's control center. They don't understand it any more than we do, but they know how to run it. We have only two things we can do. We can try to attack it and get as much out by hook or crook as we can, and we can infiltrate and hope we don't get caught before we get something of value. It can hurt them, but it can't *harm* them. Not really. Temporary pain is satisfying, but it's not a permanent injury to anything except Al's ego. And of course we *die*. We die and lose much of our experience. *They* have active Brand Boxes down there in that center that record every single thought and experience of each of the people for whom they have a Box. Each of them has a continuous two-way networked thread like the one you have, feeding every experience, every thought, of a lifetime. Even if they die, they can get much of it back."

"Or they get back as much as Al and Les think they should, anyway," the griffin commented.

"We can *sort* of do that," the March Hare put in. "However, we don't have all that equipment, that software. Just some backup stuff we were able to get to long ago, before the others remembered it was there. We have to hook up directly and let it record our experiences. Anything that happens between sessions we don't have until they come in, so we never have the last bit of business, only the data, the life experiences, since the last physical backup. We have some control from the experience and equipment we do have, thanks to the weak points like that lake on the firing range back in Washington, but there are limits for us even in that. We're different from the people born and raised here. We have something that travels between, that continues after death and into the next existence. As long as we're different, we're linked to that monster machine and we're vulnerable. In point of fact, until the Maddox wireless head mount interface, we were fighting shadows."

"Huh? My gadget?"

"Cory's gadget, which you remember since you have Cory Maddox's memories. We gave them to you. Al kind of danced around things and tried to create the bare minimum, but we gave the rest to you. The price was pretty high. They got Wilma, and that was something unexpected and not something we think they'd ever managed before, at least not in any of the records we have."

"You're making me feel guilty now."

"I don't mean to. She knew the risks. We all do. You see, we took Cory Maddox's complete and up-to-date records when you were at the home in Vancouver. That was simple, and you—*Cory*—sure weren't going anywhere. The thing was, we needed to put Cory Maddox in play. We needed to get somebody into the institute who wouldn't record directly into the Brand Box. McKee had already taken and matched you up to your Box, so as soon as you got down to the institute, they'd hook you up and maybe say it was just another fun exercise in some virtual world like before; when you came out, you'd be on continuous record. We had to prevent that, and that meant securing and altering the Brand Box she was using. That and, of course, ensuring that she didn't report how far along she'd taken the process."

"So you brought down the plane, killed her, and—what? I know Cory Maddox is currently in one of the life-support modules there and hooked to a Box in some virtual state. I *saw* him. And before that I saw him actually operating stuff in the upper control center, stuff I couldn't follow."

"The method isn't worth going into at this point, nor would I

like to describe it if for some reason Starkey learns of this, but
suffice it to say that we were able to patch in another program
to Cory Maddox, one that his own Brand Box would not pick
up. It enabled him at the first opportunity to do something he
otherwise would never have had the nerve to do—sorry—let
alone the skill level in that area. We're patched into them. For
the first time everyone who puts on the Maddox head mount
sends in two channels, not just one. The problem is, we can't
get our own line, as it were, connected up to do the readouts,
get the output. They could detect our presence on any virtual
I/O system we might use."

I sat there a moment, letting dead silence drop in the gathering, the only sounds those of the fire and the rippling waves.
Finally I said, "I don't understand one damned word of what
you just said."

Suddenly the Duchess's pig started to squeal, and she
rudely shoved an apple in its mouth to silence it. It did the
trick.

"Bottom lime, dahlin'," the White Rabbit said after a moment. "I don't follow this shit, neithah, so don't be so upset.
Thing is, we got a way to get into and out of that theah institute
without them knowin'. A way that'll work even if we move on.
The jacks we got installed, but we can't get the phone man to
connect us up without them knowin'."

"Who the hell *am* I?" I demanded to know.

"We have no idea what your original name was. Al picked
you, and Al used one of the programmable Brand Boxes and
reinvented you in there. You've seen what can be done with
the kind of power we're dealing with. You've used it. You
have all the stuff Al gave you, all that Al created for you, and
you also have a dump of Cory Maddox's Brand Box recordings up to the moment of the air crash. Your—programming—
takes precedence over the memories, which is why you feel
more Rina than Cory and why you can't do some of the things
Cory can with some of the technical stuff. You are Korinna

Ajani Wilisczik, wife of Richard Wilisczik, mother of Angel
Wilisczik. With our aid, you've been able to tap and use some
of the same sort of power that we can use, and in some ways
power we cannot use, but you are *not* Cory Maddox and you
are *not* one of us. Cory Maddox, whose own memories extend
in a different path after the accident, is now a prisoner inside a
life-support module while they decide whether to let him live
or die for the next cycle. Wilma is there, too, in the same
shape. If we can have your help, we have a chance of freeing
them and perhaps making that phone connection that will be
the first true blow to them we've ever been able to strike."

That I could follow, even though I felt sick to my stomach
by all the confirmations I was receiving. Damn it, what can you
think when you're told that you're a combination of two
frauds?

*What does it feel like to be told by a group of immortals that
you have no soul?*

I felt I should be in tears, but the tears wouldn't come. I was
too angry to be anything else.

"So what?" I asked them. "Why the hell should I give a
damn about you and your bizarre war? I'm not real, you know.
I'm a spook. You know that, and so do I. Expendable, a creation, like a character in some video game. I've been programmed, manipulated, kicked, and stretched, but now it's
down to winding up the program and seeing if it really does the
job, isn't it? And *this* program doesn't do that sort of thing."

There was some more silence, and then the March Hare said,
"Cory, I—"

"Can it. No speeches about God and country, huh? Spare me
at least from that. Walt, you gave me Cory Maddox's memories, all two lifetimes worth. Maybe not all his skills, but all
those memories are as clear to me as they would be to him.
That means that not many things stand out, but the things that
do are doozies. Like the one in some other universe, a universe
which I was never in, Walt, but which wasn't all that different

from this one. A universe in which you were mounting some sort of crazy attack with some creature allies against Al and Les and that crew and some migrant farm workers got in your way. I watched you blow 'em away, Walt, without blinking an eye. *I watched you coolly blow away a kid, Walt! A kid!* And not think twice about it because they weren't 'real.' They were just spooks, right? No different from taking up the joystick in a video game and blasting away at the creatures you can see. Nothing harmed. It's not *real*. Well, I'm maybe the most artificial person ever put together, and *I'm real*, Walt. Us spooks are sick and tired of doin' what you bastard programmers command and getting no respect! No, sir! In one fell swoop you took away who I am and everything I care for and every hope and dream I might have for the future both for myself and for my kid. And I can't even turn to God, can I, Father Pete? Spooks have programmers for their gods, not the real things."

The Mock Turtle looked sheepish and a little bit taken aback but said nothing. The March Hare had even less to say.

Not even the pig had a comment.

Finally the March Hare looked at me and asked softly, "What can we do?"

I looked at each of them in turn. "What? No arguments? No pep talks? No lies or threats? How about 'Do this or we'll toss your kid in the shredder'? Al kind of likes variations on that, and there ain't a dime's worth of difference between Al and you in the end, not really. Nobody ever sees himself as the bad guy. It's always for somebody or everybody's good. Al lies, cheats, steals, and brainwashes. You assassinate your own kind if they're in the wrong place, and you don't think twice about blowin' away us spooks for even less. What can you offer me, guys? I don't even know what you want me to do, but whatever it is, I don't see any reason to do it."

"Rina . . ." Cynthia Matalon began, but she didn't know where the hell to go from there, and neither did I.

"Why don't you just kill me, Walt, like you did that kid?" I nearly taunted him. "It's not like we're *people*. You smart bastards did too good a job, didn't you? Frankenstein's monster. The nerd's revenge. Hey, don't look so down. There hasn't been any software in many lifetimes without bugs, right? This one just happened to bite *you*."

"Stop it," Walt responded.

"Why? Damn it, Walt, what the hell did you expect me to do? I mean, I've kinda known this for some time. They practically drew pictures for me. I didn't want to think about it, though. Who would?" I turned to the White Rabbit. "Fire up that Harley and let's get out of here," I told her. "Or you can just blow me away or erase me or whatever right here."

"I asked you what you wanted," Walt said. "If that's it, then so be it. If there's more, then let's talk."

I stared at the creature. "What the hell can you offer me, Walt? Goddess of my own universe until you all leave it for the next one and this one gets overwritten or turned off? I have no identity, no future, and no way to tell your side from the other one except that you're on the losing end at the moment. I—"

Suddenly I stopped my tirade as a newcomer walked from the shadows and up toward the fire. He was quite short, probably no more than three feet high, and chunky, with a squared-off beard and twirling mustache. He looked like he'd just walked out of a deck of cards someplace, and his suit was hearts.

"Hello, Rini," he said.

"Hello, Rick. So you're the trump card, huh? You're supposed to get me to do it for love and 'cause you're the father of my kid and all that, right?"

"It wasn't supposed to be like this, Rini," he said in an almost pleading tone. "It wasn't supposed to be like this at all. *I didn't know!* You have to believe that! I had no idea you were part of somebody's crazy plot, let alone *both* sides in this. I didn't even know we were in any way different until much later."

I stared at him. "I want to believe you, Rick. In fact, I want to believe you so much after all we did together that I *will* believe you. Don't change much, though, does it? How's it feel to have a spook daughter? She's walking now, sort of, you know. You missed that. You mighta had a spook son, too, but I dunno what happened to him."

"He's still there, or potentially there," said the griffin. "What was factored out can be factored back in. You haven't lost anything physical, anything tangible that you had before."

"Rini," Rick tried, sounding very sad and hesitant, "I don't know if these people are any better or any worse than the institute. I'm not sure I like either one. But I do know that some very good people are stuck inside that building at the mercy of Starkey, Cohen, and Sister Rita. We wanted to get to you, but there was no way we could get into the institute without all sorts of problems once the guard went up, and Al's intelligence buddies have an APB out on me, so I couldn't show up anywhere in the area. Once you got out on your own, using the kind of stuff you can do and we can't, we didn't know where you'd gone. We couldn't know you were gonna escape until you did, and then you vanished. We tapped every line in and around Stanford Medical and the institute until we got your information, and we blocked it from them and sent you the means to get out. I don't understand it. I'm not a programmer, as you know, and I particularly don't understand all *this* stuff. I *do* know that we got to you as soon as we could. They kept me from jumping any guns. I was ready to charge in there and probably woulda just blown everything. You know me well enough to tell if I'm being honest with you."

He was right, or at least I thought he was, anyway. "Does it matter, Rick? I'm not the girl you married anymore. Not since they fed all that Cory Maddox stuff into me. Instant education. It's something else. Put Angel in one of those head units and she can skip her whole education and still be a genius, at least until the world shuts down."

"We don't know what happens to these universes after we all leave," Father Pete noted. "That's a fact. You can't go back.

You're somebody else. But is that any different from facing death deep down? Who knows for certain that everything ceases or that one goes to heaven or hell or purgatory? Aren't we *all* just programs? Genetic codes or lines of code—what is the difference? None of us are any more or less real than you are. You're no different than you were before you knew about any of this. You're no different than Cory Maddox was before he learned about all this. What's real and what's not? Are we simply turning on universes like sets in a stage play, or are we creating new realities as we go? We can't know. I am not even certain that we would know the answers to that if we knew who we all really were and where we came from and what this is all about."

I knew that Rick had been reincarnated, not incarnated like Cory. Rick really hadn't known, and that was something, anyway. Something, but not enough.

"I'll always be grateful for you, Rick, but what's that now? You *know*. How can you just forget?"

The Red King nodded. "Yeah, I *do* know, but I also love you, Rini. And that's *our* daughter you're talking about. Nobody here has kids or can have them. You know that? They don't mate outside their group, and they can't reproduce their own kind—*our* own kind, I guess I should say." He looked over at the Duchess with her pig. "They'd love some permanence. They'd love a kid and not a pet. They can't. I couldn't, but somehow circumstances made it possible. Rini, unless you throw me out, I'm not gonna desert you or Angel. I'm not going to leave you all. Till death, Rini."

I sighed and really did feel tears coming. Still, I responded. "Words, Rick. Take a look. Chubby, bald, not real attractive, and too smart to just be good old Rini and not smart enough to actually use any of that shit. You really want to spend the rest of your life, *this* life, anyway, with somebody like me?"

He paused and thought for a moment. "No. Not like you are now. The looks I don't care about at all. Big deal. I think they'll bother you a lot more than me. But I didn't marry some-body this bitter or this cynical. I married somebody who saw the beauty in sunsets and liked playing in the fog at sunup. You say you're alive, a real individual human being just like we are. Prove it. *Live!*"

"You'd come with me? Stay with me? Even if I didn't help these people?"

"Honey, I don't care if you help *these* people at all. I do care that you can help the other people, the ones trapped down there. The ones we know about, including the real Cory and Wilma, and the ones you or we maybe don't. Even so, if you think it's of no value or that the risk is too great, we'll leave them to fate, too. Just go away, the two of us. Raise kids, forget this, watch sunsets and sunrises and dance and sing and maybe just live lives. Nothing's gonna shut down until the last one of us goes, so you're safe until I die and maybe beyond. You'll sure know if that's so. And if you go first, how's that different than if this was all there was? You pick it, doll. But if you want to go back and turn your back on me, you'll have to tell me flat out and do it to my face right here and now."

He knew I couldn't do that. I couldn't do it even if I *didn't* believe him, and I couldn't do it even though a lot more stuff that wasn't jargon and nerd babble was coming together.

This is what it's all been for, I realized. I *was* a tool, maybe a minor one in Al's case, but with the potential to be a big one in the case of Walt and the March Hare Network. They'd trained me, honed me, fooled me, befriended me, done all that just so I'd get to this moment. You could almost say they'd designed me for it. The only thing they couldn't do was take me seri-ously as a real, live person. They—maybe not Rick, but most of them—always thought of me as nothing more than a tool, a program, that was all. And they hadn't been prepared for a pro-gram to balk, argue, and make them seem small.

I was entirely of this world, and because I was, when I delved into the power, the energy, the structure of it, I appeared to all monitors and all observations just like any other native benign data stream. Because Al and Rita and the rest didn't take spooks seriously as real people, either.

I might well be able to get those people out of the institute or at least show them a way to get out. It was an ability these people might not have without being flagged, and it was at the risk of one little spook who didn't matter, anyway.

I didn't like being used at all, particularly like this, but what the hell was I going to do? I didn't want to spend a lifetime as I had, living a lie with my two companions, who were in effect being treated by me just as callously as I was being treated by these people. In a sense, just having them and doing to them what I had done made my decision for me, no matter what other factors were involved.

I'd had the power, and I'd treated those people just the same as these people had treated me. Not out of a love of power or meanness or anything like that but because I needed them.

And these people needed me.

Not for themselves, not for their own service directly, but to spring their companions from whatever prisons Al had created for them, prisons within the mind. I could never forgive or forget the vision of Walt shooting that boy, nor could I ever embrace them for creating me and forcing me to this point. What I was going to do wasn't for Rick, it wasn't for Walt, and it wasn't even for the prisoners of the institute. It was for me.

It was a chance to save my soul even if I didn't really have one. It was a chance to show that on a single moral plane this crude and ignorant program was morally superior to the lot of them.

"What could you offer me beyond Rick's presence to make me assume this kind of risk for people like you?" I asked them.

"Name it," Walt replied. "Anything within our power. We can't take you with us; we have no idea how to reincarnate somebody. On the other hand, we recorded you when you were within our own data stream, and we will continue to update. If life is re-

ally the sum total of all our experiences, you, too, are immortal
even now, at least in the way that a reincarnate who gets back his
or her past through the Brand recordings is. Beyond that ...
Money? Beauty? Youth? You name it. Whatever we have."

"Words, just words. Easy to say, easy to promise," I told
him, then took a breath. "Okay, I'll do it for nothing. No
promises, no fidelity, no nothing. After it is over, if it works
out, if we're all able to stand and speak like this, then choices
and truths will be discussed. Not now. I'm not going to do this
for you. I'm not going to do this for Rick, or for the folks in the
Brand Boxes, or to get even with Al and the rest, or to secure
life and liberty for my kid. I'm going to do it because it's the
right thing to do. That alone should illustrate that some of us
spooks are more human now than some of you cartoon-type
animals."

"Al has to know about this place," I commented, looking
around at the underground bunkers and fully concealed complex beneath the Washington State minidesert test range.
"How have you avoided detection?"

"Sometimes the best way to hide something is right in plain
sight and under your enemy's nose," Walt replied. He looked
his old self now that we were back in what was, at least for me,
the real world. He claimed that his eye color was different and
that he was an inch taller, but why would I notice that? I couldn't
remember, using Cory Maddox's old memories, what his original eye color was in the first place.

I looked around at the spare, austere unit that could only be
called early bomb shelter period decor and shivered. It wasn't
cold outside, but there was something chill-inducing about
such a place.

"We're so close to the weak point here that it makes direct
detection impossible," he explained. "By the same token, it isn't
a great place to do exacting business for us, either. It's a great

hideout, but the same thing that masks us screws us. We use this for what we can, but not as a base."

I couldn't help feeling a vibration running through the whole complex, making things resonate somehow. "What's that deep-to-the-bone sound?"

"A marked forty-cycle hum. It can drive you nuts after a while, which is why we insulate the key rooms so well. Our own subwoofer, as it were, but it comes from that weak point and from the resonating energy. Some folks think that this whole universe is just a bunch of us inside a big Brand Box. Crack one of the smaller ones open and you'll find the same kind of plasma energy field, the same regulated deep bass frequency, a lot more. That's the ironic thing, you see. We might be just like you— constructs inside a Brand Box or moving from Box to Box. And inside our Box we have smaller Boxes. You see what I mean."

I nodded. Walt might still consider me some kind of construct, but I knew better. Maybe I had been the virtual-reality equivalent of a robot once, an android, programmed to think I was somebody else and act just so and have certain abilities, but I'd had my own lifetime now as well as those fed into me, and I knew a lot more about the world. I could never be sure, but I had the very definite feeling that I was just exactly as human inside as Walt or Rick or any of the rest.

I looked around and frowned. "If this is all so close to the raw stuff that it scrambles even your equipment, what makes you think it won't scramble *me*?"

"We can isolate and insulate you, I think, and with a linkage directly back to the lake going through a series of regulators we think you'll be able to draw on whatever power you need. Come on, let's go to the control center."

I had deliberately asked Rick not to be there, and in fact he was well away, I hoped, with Angel and her two godmothers. I wasn't concerned about him and the godmothers; they weren't much interested in men anymore no matter what temptation he might feel, and it wasn't in him to be pushy.

Father Pete was there in the control center, checking the

readings. Compared with the stuff at the institute, this looked like a low-budget movie set, but I figured it worked or they wouldn't have gone to all this trouble. There were two and only two life-support modules of roughly the same make and model as the many more in the institute over against a far wall, and there was a large rectangular console in which a series of Brand Boxes had been inserted. It could hold two dozen at least, but there were only nine Boxes.

Unlike the institute, which had to draw power in through some sort of high-tech method that was unclear to me, we were practically awash in the stuff.

"Gives you a real feeling of being Superman or something, doesn't it?" Father Pete commented, seeing my reaction. "It's all over, as it is, but in *here* it's tremendous."

We went past and into another small room, and it was as if someone had flipped the "off" switch. It was as dead a room as I have ever been in anywhere, and it left me feeling creepily isolated and alone.

In the center was a VR gyro. They put me in a kind of rub-berized suit with all sorts of sensors, thousands of them, all over the inside, then snapped down a full-surround head mount and attached it with clasps and Velcro-type strips. Since it wasn't hooked up, I couldn't see or hear much of anything, but I felt Walt and Father Pete take me and guide me into the gyro and clamp me in. Although I of course had never done this myself, memories of Cory's past life in Seattle and his experiences with this made it seem almost familiar.

Now there was only the sound of my breathing and the sound of my pounding pulse and a tiny hiss of air from the breathing unit to sustain me. I was completely locked into the gyro, and any movement, no matter how small, was exe-cuted with incredible smoothness. I could move in any direc-tion, up, down, around, reach out, kick, you name it.

I didn't feel I needed any of this, particularly not after we made contact, but I figured I'd let them do what they thought they needed to do just in case they were right.

"Testing comm link," I heard Walt's voice, kind of far-off-sounding, in one ear. "One, two, three, four, five."

"I can hear you, Walt. Let's get this show on the road."

He hesitated a moment. "You remember, now—once you're inside, fuse the linkup and then try to interface with the various people in the Brand Boxes. Your only job is to show them the way out. If they won't take the invitation, then don't linger. At any moment something could trap you in one of the Boxes with them, and that would sever everything here, not to mention probably killing you. If you feel that there's any detection of your presence by any of the operators there or that anything, *anything*, smells wrong, you get out and back here and hang it up. Understand?"

"Don't worry, Walt. I'm just a spook, remember?"

He didn't respond to that one. "All right, Pete's giving you juice now. We'll bring you up very, very slowly since even you have never experienced the kind of jolt this can deliver."

"Just shut up and start it," I told him. "And make sure that when you get my signal, you dial the right damned number!"

I had no idea what to expect, but I sure as hell was nervous. I knew damned well that I was expendable in spades no matter what they said or how much guilt I heaped on them.

I felt the power flow into the suit. The head mount flickered and came on, and I immediately grabbed it; as soon as the power was sufficient, I integrated the entire assemblage into myself. The power continued to flow in and continued to build, and at each incremental increase I used more and more of it to control, fashion, and re-form myself. It wasn't programming; it was more like sculpting.

Monsters! Monsters from the id!

Only this time it was the monster on the side of the good guys.

I couldn't help wondering what I looked like at that point with all that perfectly regulated energy plasma at my command. They didn't have a way of seeing unless one of them dared to enter the chamber; most of the conventional cameras would burn out with this much power fed in.

Everything was fading, becoming less solid. All was now wireframe, easy to see and see through, as malleable as modeling clay, as easy to alter or manipulate as a drawing on a chalkboard.

"Dial it!" I sent to them.

On the board I watched a stick-figure human being reach over and punch in a number which was linked to the secondary feed on my apparatus. I saw the signal go out, and I followed it, not waiting for it to answer. It went along, bounced from packet switch to packet switch, exchange to exchange, all at the speed of light, all rather circuitous even if it was a long-distance call hundreds of miles long.

By the time we reached the special government security exchange at Stanford, I had completely taken over the regulation and control of the energy flow. As soon as the switchboard operator at the institute's front desk picked up the telephone, I was through, into the central pbx and then from there into the electrical and computer net of the entire place. By the time the receptionist, getting only static, finally gave up and hung up the telephone, I no longer needed that connection.

Until then I had been fighting to be considered human; now I was not, nor did I wish to be. I was on a different plane, a plane of energy and mind where things were very different.

I had the master console in sight in nothing flat; indeed, I was working entirely at the speed of light and with almost no lag time except that going through the wires in the building caused some drag.

None of this was anything like the virtual-reality stuff you see in movies or video games and basic computer graphics. About the only thing that was really the same was that the visuals were somewhat bizarre and presented themselves in shapes and colors beyond belief. It is difficult to go further with this; how do you explain to anybody seeing all sides of objects at once, *including the inside*? I can bring up a mental picture of what I experienced, but I can't convey it to anybody else.

Cory had done his work well, or whoever had programmed

him to input the various patches and enhancements into the
system where they could not be noticed or used by others had.
To me they stood out like lighthouses on a dark shore; connecting them up to the system and to me was no more difficult than
connecting the dots in a puzzle.

Once it was done, I spread out, flowed myself into every
single channel, and allowed myself to fill all gaps and outline
all forms. Just as the head device had integrated with my skull
back at Vern's, now I was taking that same talent and integrat-
ing the entire structure that I could perceive into myself, or
myself into it. I was no longer merely inhabiting the circuitry, I
was the circuitry, and it was me, at least on the level of reality
for this world. There were areas below that were still beyond
me, if only because they drew their energy from different
sources that were not connected to the main building. I had no
direct access; they were as isolated as I'd been back in the
chamber.

And far below there was still the place I did not dare to look
at, that sensation of power beyond imagining, power in something or somethings that were somehow *alive* deep below . . .

I began to run tracers from the upper console to the Brand
Boxes and life-support units below. There was no clear way to
correlate who was in them with the Brand Boxes they were
connected to; too much back-and-forth was going on, and there
was also considerable isolation in the Brand Boxes.

There were currently six occupants of the Brand Boxes; I
could guess a bit, based on the wireframe information, about
ones I might know, but otherwise it was a crapshoot. It was
ironic that I could analyze things to an incredible degree but
couldn't read a printed label on the side of a Brand Box. It
didn't really matter; the trick was to open communication as I
had when I'd been here before without getting irreparably
sucked into the thing.

Well, there was one I could recognize, but it was the most
dangerous of them. Cory's body was all too comfortably familiar in that box but all too close to my own imposed patterns as

well. He would have to wait a bit; I didn't want to risk having whatever was holding him grab and imprison me as well.

There was nothing to do but pick one, attempt to select an exit point with a timed out, and then go inside. If the interruption I'd programmed into it didn't kick in, wasn't long enough, or didn't do the job, I'd be stuck inside no matter what. If it worked, I would be able to pull out not only myself but possibly other material as well.

The first one was definitely a woman. It was worth a try, and I set it up as best I could and then flowed my consciousness down into the life-support module, through the connections, and into another virtual world.

XI

STALKING THE BOXES

I was used to Brand Box transitions by then, what with the eerie shaman's world Wilma used and the island with the Wonderland characters. Still, this was a shock, and coming from the domain of the energy plane, it was more dramatic than I had figured.

I wasn't myself, but from an ego standpoint, even if the face was ugly, which I didn't think it was, it was an improvement. I had hair again—man! Did I have hair! Long, straight, black, but lush, way down below my ass. I was stark naked, and the only thing that seemed unnatural about me was that there were some exotic colored designs on my skin that had the look of tattoos but not the same feeling of permanence. I suspected that they were stained in somehow, but a couple of older ones showed that the designs faded with age and exposure. My skin was a deep rich brown, the kind one gets from daily exposure to the sun in tropical climates.

And this *was* tropical; no doubt about that. Lush jungle growth spread out in all directions below me, while above loomed a mist-shrouded valley flanked on either side by tall, imposing volcanoes reaching up into the clouds.

Okay, I told myself. *What's a nice girl like you doing out naked and alone on a rocky ridge?*

Water certainly wasn't a problem. There were countless small waterfalls all over the place running down from the high mountains to the sea below. Food *shouldn't* be a problem in a place like this, although it might be; there certainly was nothing obvious and close.

I hadn't given myself a lot of time here, but that was *real* time; subjectively I could be here for quite some time, and that meant finding out more about this place and then finding where the hell the people were. There had to be at least one here.

If there were a lot of folks, finding and figuring out which was the one I wanted and which were just parts of the programmer's cast of characters might be tough.

I certainly didn't have any immediate complaints about this place. It was warm, lush, comfortable, a really nice getaway spot. On the other hand, if this was Polynesia or Melanesia in preexplorer times, it wasn't exactly the best culture even of a very bad lot in which to be a woman.

But what exactly was the culture here, if there was one? These were local Brand Box miniuniverses; they had limits, and they were mostly thought up and fine-tuned by programmers at the institute who knew how to use Brand's interfacing tools. I don't think anybody really understood how it worked, but they knew how to operate the controls and make things happen. Cory's experience and the anecdotal experience of others indicated that these were used as much for a kind of brainwashing by Al and his crew as for the research into mind and culture they were probably intended for.

I stretched and was very aware of the high level of muscle development in my legs. Running, perhaps even climbing, would be no problem and might well be necessary in a place like this with the kind of rough and undeveloped landscape that I could see all around me. What I could not see was any sign of human habitation. No sign even of well-worn paths or trails close by or in the distance, no sign of human structures of any sort, no smoke or other indicators that I wasn't completely alone.

But I was not alone. I'd followed this line in via an active female life-support hookup, and there had been a warm body there. The fact that I hadn't been able to make any kind of mental contact, though, was worrisome.

It was a hot sun, and I decided to move toward the shade and perhaps get a drink of water from a nearby small waterfall. I walked over to where the stream tumbled down the rocks, perhaps a yard wide but steady, cupped my hands, and put them out to catch a drink.

The water shied away from my hands.

It was a startling thing to have happen, and I almost lost my balance. It was as if my hands were a positive magnet and the water was also a positively charged magnetic substance. You couldn't touch it. It ran away from you. Stepping under it simply made it divide and fall on both sides of my body, but try as I might, I could not take a drink.

This was a wrinkle I hadn't considered.

I gave up on that waterfall and went to another, which exhibited the same behavior. I finally decided that there wasn't any point fighting with a bunch of flowing streams on the ledge and moved off and into the lush green beyond.

I had hoped to find some kind of fruit or other edible growth common to such areas, but the only ones that seemed to be around were very high in the trees. The lack of any on the ground was curious, but there were clearly bunches of coconuts in large numbers in the trees and bunches of large fruits that seemed to be related to bananas up there as well. However, the trees were smooth and very tall, and there was no easy way to climb up and get any.

I kept on, becoming increasingly hungry and thirsty as I did, sweat beginning to pour out of me in the tropical heat and lack of wind.

Still, it was a lot worse by the time I actually came upon other people.

I didn't make myself known right away, even though I really needed some company and some advice by that point. I wanted to see what sort of people were here and how they coped with these, well, situations.

It was a man and two women, all Polynesian-looking, all sun-weathered and dark bronze, and all with varying painted-on symbols covering their bodies. The women, neither of whom looked older than their early teens but both of whom seemed to be perhaps halfway through pregnancy, had even dyed their hair—one a kind of steely blue, the other a forest green—while the man had his tied in two pigtails that dangled down his back. They looked kind of childlike in the way they were walking and reacting with each other, with odd eyes and strange half smiles. They stopped before the start of a grove of coconut trees, looked up, and then went down on their knees. Then the two women began to bow toward the trees, torsos and hands going out and back in supplication, while between them the man was completely prostrate, groveling in the dirt before those trees.

"Almighty goddess of the earth, almighty spirits of the trees that give life, hear our prayers," they chanted together in a rhythmic style. "Command us as thou will and reward us to the measure of our obedience."

There was an eerie silence, and then sounds, words, whispered through the grove, as if every tree had a soft voice or perhaps the wind could speak.

"Sing! Dance!" they commanded.

The women began to chant and use the flats of their hands like drumsticks on their own bodies, and to the chant and slapping beat the man rose and danced a strange, whirling dance that seemed to go on and on. After a while one of the women rose and joined the man, and they began an erotic pair routine that was insane, illogical, and much too much work in this heat. Suddenly the eerie voice said *"Enough!"* and they stopped and dropped, eyes closed, heads bowed.

There was a slight crackling sound from high above them,

and three coconuts dropped from on high and struck the ground, none breaking, all coming to rest very close to the trio.

"All praise be to the almighty goddess of the earth, and to her servants the spirits of the trees that give life," they responded together. Only then did the women gather the coconuts and bring them to the kneeling man, who took the first coconut and brought it down on a rock protruding from the ground with an expert motion. The coconut cracked, and he used powerful hands to twist it open. The milk sloshed out, and he lost a little, but he gave half to one of the women; the other half, to my surprise, he poured out in front of him on the ground.

This ceremony was repeated with the other two until each of them had half a coconut and about half the milk and the rest had been returned to the ground as some sort of sacrifice, I guessed.

After a while they got up, and so help me, the three of them went to the bathroom right then and there in the middle of the grove; that, too, seemed to be some kind of offering. Then they wandered off, chanting some reverential prayer.

We weren't alone, then, in this place. Some sort of supernatural entities had been postulated and had actually been formed here and had the power. Apparently people were at the bottom of this authority chain; you prayed and danced and sang and did whatever was commanded, and if you pleased the gods, they let you eat or drink or whatever, always demanding a part of that back.

I could see at once how nasty this was. No clothes, no tools, no nothing. You didn't own anything, and you didn't produce anything except maybe diversion for the higher beings. Everything you needed to survive—food and water, primarily—was provided if you prayed, begged, and obeyed. This was serious for several reasons. For one thing, it might be a little late to find and get through to whoever was stuck in here. For another, it might be a *very* long time, subjectively, before I could eat or drink.

I decided to follow the threesome and see if they'd lead me to others. They weren't hard to find; subtlety in Eden was limited to snakes.

There appeared to be little in the way of group or tribal cohesion, but there were people all over the livable areas of the island, as it turned out. There appeared to be more women than men, and there were a lot of kids as well, but the population wasn't huge and certainly wasn't in any immediate danger of outgrowing the place. Of course, since this was all a virtual-reality world, it was pretty easy to maintain whatever numbers the programmers desired and to expand or contract the size and resources as needed.

I was struck by the fact that they mostly played childish games, chasing after one another, some surf splashing, tag, lying around, and, if they felt like it, some purely physical sexual activity that might or might not go anywhere as the mood struck them. There was no violence and no sense of anyone, male, female, old, young, whatever, being above anybody else.

There also was very little talk. Lots of giggling, laughing, chanting, that sort of thing, but words were used very sparingly, as if they were sacred and limited and very costly to speak; these people spoke only if they had to.

I exposed myself without having much concern at that stage about how they would react to me. The fact was, they didn't much. I was pretty well ignored, or somebody tried to get me into some play activity or whatever, but if I didn't immediately go along, they dropped it. As I said, no pressure on anybody to do anything.

The problem was, I was getting thirstier and thirstier and wasn't seeing anyone who looked the least bit familiar. If the local gods would let me out, I began to wonder if I'd find anybody before my timer instruction pulled me from there and back into the energy plasma state outside this place.

Frankly, this part of the job had sounded a lot easier than it now seemed to be.

I was beginning to wonder when I would have to start

performing for the gods to get a drink when I saw her. She was barely recognizable, thinner, more toward the Pacific Oriental than the North American one, better built, younger, and painted with all sorts of designs like a tattooed lady. Still, it was clearly Wilma.

She was with a guy—*two* guys, in fact—and took no notice of me. That wasn't so unusual, considering that I probably neither looked nor acted like anybody she'd known.

Without jealousy, possessiveness, or anything else like that, it was easy to join her little group of playmates. For all her physical attributes, she didn't look good. There was a dullness in her eyes, the same kind of mindless, childlike innocence and vacancy I could see in the others, and I got the strong impression that if much of Wilma was left, it was very well suppressed. Hell, how long had she been here? *Months?* And if this was lasting even a day subjectively for me, it might seem far longer to her than that, and that was bad enough.

I stuck close to her and her companions, hoping that there would be some way I could get in, break through. No wonder I'd been unable to make mental contact! There had to be something *there* for that.

When the group got hungry, we all went up to a grove of fruit trees and did almost word for word what the previous group had done.

This time, however, the demands were for even more nonsensical things. Do somersaults, hop on first one leg, and then the other, silly stuff, but it had to be done and it had to be done as quickly as the commands to do it arrived or the spirits weren't happy. And if the spirits weren't happy, as they were not with me, you not only didn't get a fruit cup, you got severe cramps or what I can only describe as full-body charley horses—painful stuff. And each time you were punished, the others had to watch as you were ordered to do a series of rapid-fire senseless things until you pleased those spirits. Finally we got our bananas and what appeared to be grapefruit-sized oranges as well.

I couldn't help but be impressed by the system even as it exhausted and humiliated me. What was something like this doing to the real Wilma, stuck there in the LSU in the lab? What would it do to me in just a few subjective days? You survived here by praying aloud with all your might for the supernatural to give you basic needs; then it was *command* → *obey* → *inadequate* → *pain* → *command* → *obey* → *very good* → *reward.* I hadn't seen any glassy-eyed slaves around the complex, but maybe it wasn't that obvious. Maybe when they brought you back, you naturally obeyed authority figures, those above you. Maybe you just became passive and dependent and didn't notice it or think about it.

I felt that I just had to get through somehow to Wilma if there was any of her left and do so before my timer pulled me out or I succumbed to this system and threw out my own reason. I had already managed, after a lot of grief, to pass muster with some of the others by religiously observing them and doing just what the other women did and acting as quickly and as unthinkingly as they did. I wasn't sure I was proud of it, but I'd finally gotten something to eat and drink.

Pretty tough nut to crack when the spirits were watching everything and, beyond prayers, conversation was basically monosyllabic. I finally decided to try when the two of us were effectively isolated, sitting on a rock looking out at the ocean just after we'd prayed to the sun god at sunset but before his bride the moon goddess appeared.

Interpersonal relationships here were brief, touchy-feely affairs, and you never actually talked to somebody else. In the evenings and often at midday, they would sit around pools and groom each other or decorate each other with the dyelike colors that bubbled up in the mud pots all around. I knew what it all reminded me of: zoo apes. Perform for the public, get a banana.

As I unknotted and tried to straighten and finger comb Wilma's long hair, I got close to her ear and whispered, "Monkeys."

There was no reaction, and I was afraid to push things too far. I waited a bit and then, in a natural motion, going to the other ear, whispered, *"Wilma."*

I could sense a tensing in her for a moment, not so much from fear as from puzzlement, as she tried to decide if what she was hearing was anything that made sense.

"Wilma Gorilla," I whispered when my natural movement again brought me close.

This time she turned and looked at me, and I could see that way in the back of her mind there was a mixture of suspicion and fear. Parts of her brain were waking up in ways she'd rather they not do.

"Cory," I whispered, since that was the name she knew. *"Out."* Then, later, *"Stay close."*

I saw some real hope light up, even if it was still behind glassy eyes, and I felt my hand being gripped and squeezed even as she looked away not at me but at the rising half-moon.

We slept together on the beach and the next day stayed together, attempting to maintain some kind of physical linkup. I had set my timer for eight hours inside, but that was real time. How long it would take for those eight hours to pass in this subjective and created miniuniverse was impossible to say. In the one Cory had previous experience with, Dan Tanaka's slave girl–run castle island, a full day in real terms had lasted over a week subjectively. I hoped that it wouldn't be the same here; I wasn't sure I could take even three days here without my mind turning into ape mush, and certainly the longer Wilma waited, the more tenuous her hold on reason and hope would be. I could already see it fading, and I began to wonder just how much longer I could keep my own sanity.

It was this first real taste of the powers of this "ultimate virtual reality" that brought home to me just why it was so dangerous. In its own way, it was another atomic bomb, or biological weapon, or chemical warfare device. In the right hands it could be a wonderful tool for learning, but these things always had a tendency to wind up eventually in the wrong hands, like this. To turn normal, modern, intelligent people into little better than apes so easily was scary.

I instantly appreciated with this first foray just why the March Hare people hadn't done this themselves and just why they'd prepared me for it. I was as smart and as vulnerable as they were, but unlike them, I was expendable.

I had already lost track of time and was beginning to succumb to the program when the timer suddenly kicked in. It was sheer luck that I'd stuck with Wilma for some reason, and at the first shock I reacted by grabbing her and holding her as tightly as I could to me.

The island vanished, light vanished, and we were speeding along this dark tunnel. Suddenly there was feeling again, and I knew that somehow I'd brought Wilma out. I had no corporeal body at this site, but I was still wired into her console and had a fair amount of time at the speed at which I could operate before the operators at the controls could react, get here, and see what was wrong, and try to correct it.

I used direct input into the LSU and straight into Wilma's cognitive center.

"Wilma! Listen carefully and snap out of it! Just listen to me!"

Damn it! She was too confused, too far gone, in there for much too long to get it back to a reasonable degree at this speed. I thought furiously, then sent, *"Wilma! Obey me! Send your thoughts to the connection I will show you!"*

She was conditioned to obey but didn't know *who* to obey. I managed to switch one of my patches into her box interconnection. For the first time I realized what the Maddox wireless head mount could do beyond the obvious. Since it was wireless, over even a very short distance it had a very tiny broadcast and receive capability that was pretty much within the limits of the life-support unit. One connection was being maintained by the LSU itself; I now established a second.

There was no hope of getting Wilma physically out of there, and even I was physically someplace far to the north, let's face it. What we could do, though, if somebody was wearing a Maddox head mount, as were all the LSU folks, was tie into the net. Cory had developed the thing for Walt's company; Walt had every single spec. The fact that it was then adopted by Al was a godsend and provided access Al and his folks had never dreamed of because they felt that their internal network was impregnable.

I had to hand it to Walt, though. Not only had he had Cory build a great mousetrap, he'd even built, or at least extensively modified, the exterminator.

Me.

The March Hare Network was also plugged into Wilma's Brand Box even here. If they could not rescue Wilma, they could give support if they had to and get a complete recording for restoration.

It was done. Now I had to lay low for a bit while the technicians and experienced crew of this bizarre institute worked to find out what had gone wrong and repair it.

If I could have figured out a way to electrocute the bastards as they worked, I would have, but the fact was that I didn't dare. It wouldn't do them any harm but might cause a whole shutdown and overhaul of the system. If they so much as suspected that I or anyone else was present, let alone that the Box was now connected to a source outside the institute, things might get very ugly.

Lee Henreid was on the local head mount checking things out, and Ben Sloan was looking at the computer readouts, the mechanic under the hood, as it were. I really wanted to drop down and push Henreid into the world that Wilma would soon be forced back into, but I didn't dare. There were others there as well.

"Could she have somehow willed herself out?" Henreid was asking worriedly.

"Impossible. Never has happened," Sloan replied. "The indications here are that there was some kind of power fluctuation in the connection or maybe within the networking.

Remember, we're dealing with newer hardware, and software that's constantly under revision. Bound to be an occasional problem."

"Yeah, and that girl a few months ago just walked out and took her baby and was never seen again, right through all our guards and monitors and locks and security. Don't forget that!"

"Oh, we've been through that over and over. Starkey brought the power up too fast and blew the hell out of all the in-plane gadgetry, power, you name it. The girl just saw her chance and lucked out. Hell, it was dark as pitch up there, and we all were down here. She's a damned *spook*, remember. Not a real person! Ain't no way it coulda happened any other way!"

"Yeah, well, could be, but I'm reporting this to Al, anyway. Things are getting too bizarre and uncertain these days. I'll tell you, I'd feel better if we just said the hell with it and moved to the next plane, whatever that will be. This one's been too damned flaky and unpredictable!"

"Yeah, like you got some assurance the next one won't be worse?" Sloan retorted. "I liked the *last* one better'n this, and look at what *that* got us. I tell you, what we need is consistency, work in a single plane with a single set of rules and experienced personnel over a period of many years. That's what we got the possibility of here. The reason we're havin' all these problems and glitches is that we haven't had that in too long a time. You just looked in there. Anything unusual?"

"Looks normal, including her," Henreid admitted. "On the other hand, it's not exactly a place where you're going to stand out for long. What about you?"

"Hard to say. There's only one subject in there, and the record seems to indicate a momentary loss of connection due to surge protection in the net. Power's down a bit from nominal, but that's to be expected. You're too paranoid, Lee. What the hell could anybody do in here, anyway?"

Henreid sighed. "I dunno. Maybe you're right. Still, I'm going to discuss this with Al when he gets back. And I want a full watch on all the subjects, particularly her. Anything, and I mean *anything*, unexpected happens again any time soon and we're calling a council meeting."

They packed up and went away, with Ben leaving some sort of diagnostic software monitor attached to Wilma's LSU. That no longer bothered me. I was beginning to get enough of my wits back to think about trying for new game.

The trouble was, I didn't know if I was lucky or skilled at getting away with this. What were those other programs like? Which one was the one with my mental number on it?

There was no question that I wouldn't have a second opportunity to get in there unless Walt suddenly figured out how to be so much of a god that he could overrule the institute's own computers and those beyond. This was, therefore, the only shot these people had. I owed it to them to do what I could.

I was, however, disturbed at the exchange between Lee and Ben. The chances were at least even that I'd trip something again, and there were six people here. It put me in a horrible position. I was happy that I'd lucked into Wilma, but if I could save only one of the remaining five and I couldn't know who they were until I "met" them, then who did I dare choose?

There was one obvious choice where I could use the LSU data to isolate from the rest. Since there were three women and I knew the identity and location of one of them, they could be excluded. Of the three men, only one LSU unit needed additional software and additional motorized stimulation units to compensate for motor dysfunction.

This was going to be tough, but in a sense it was what I had to do and might be the most liberating thing yet.

No matter what little horror he was encased in, I needed to come face to face with Cory Maddox.

I approached the network connection gingerly, tentatively, and did a great many tests and made several false moves. I'm not sure even now if that was because I wanted to make very sure that Ben had left no traps there to snare the unwary or because

I was very hesitant to move toward meeting what was in many ways my psychic twin and the person I had believed myself to be.

Finally, though, I tapped into the connection and felt a sense of awareness but not the eager embrace. I took that to mean that Cory had not been left to rot as Wilma had but had frequent visitors from the institute via the standard VR monitor head mount. You didn't become anything when you used that; you just manipulated yourself in a virtual environment pretty much like a video game.

There was nothing to do but transmit *"Friend. Rescue!"* and hope he'd bite, but he didn't. He was too paranoid or too far gone by then to do simple back-and-forth conversation. Like Wilma, I was going to have to go inside, and I wasn't thrilled by that at all. In one sense Cory was far more of a threat to the institute and its people than Wilma was, and I wasn't looking forward to seeing what they'd cooked up for him.

Still, it had to be done. I found the connection, entered, and proceeded down this long, dark, dull greenish tunnel, suddenly exploding into a very real-seeming place.

My first reaction was that it was some sort of humongous mall with a vast enclosed dome looking out on a night sky and a whole center city spread out below in all directions. There were plenty of flowers, trees, and bushes and large areas of green fields, but they were surrounded by pedestrian streets that went by well-lit establishments. There were walkways above that and farther up, all interconnected by a series of ramps, escalators, stairs, elevators, you name it. That's why I say it reminded me of a vast mall, even though it wasn't clear that some places might be stores and restaurants.

It was hard to see anything outside the dome in the darkness, but it looked pretty bleak. The only lights that could be seen were reflections on the dark-coated interior dome.

What was most startling was the look of the people. They had the same density you'd expect in an enclosed place like this, but they all were dressed alike in form-fitting black body stockings and rubber-soled black boots. And all were as bald as I had been made by the March Hare's head mount.

They were also all not only absolutely identical, right down to height, weight, and even the way they moved, but familiar.

Although thinner and nearly perfectly built, every single person in there I could see not only dressed alike, walked alike, and probably talked alike—they were all *me*.

I looked down in some wonder at this assemblage of people, all of whom seemed to know what they were doing or where they were going, and couldn't help wondering if somehow the program reacted to whoever was injected into it and that they had all suddenly become me on my arrival. Somehow I doubted it; whoever had designed this thing would have had used first person in as the template, and that had been a male Cory Maddox. The whole thing from the start had been that I was said to look like Cory's female persona when that was the case from plane to plane; if that was so, somebody wanted him to be that other self in here.

I was up on a high level in the place, and I decided it was time to walk down to the bottom and see what all this was about. It had already occurred to me that it was going to be pretty damned hard to find one Cory Maddox among anywhere from hundreds to thousands of identical-looking people.

I knew, of course, not just from self-examination but from reflections that I now looked and was dressed just like everybody else. It was a vast sea of conformity, and I didn't feel at all out of place.

There wasn't a lot of conversation, and what did occur was of the routine kind—"Excuse us," "Pardon us," and the like— or specific to their jobs—"We have to begin the level five survey of burned out lights and organize a replacement group." This made such a crowd a bit quieter than usual, although sound and conversation were magnified and there was always an ambient roar that you quickly tuned out.

As noticeable as the sameness to everyone was the use, when anyone *did* speak, of group pronouns. I didn't hear "I" or "me" or anything like them at any time; it was always "we" and "us" and so forth. Occasionally individuals would be picked out for a job, and only then would I hear "You two start cleaning over there." That was about as individualistic as it got.

There was no way to tell who had what job or who assigned things; everybody just seemed to know. That made things a bit awkward for me, and I tried to walk steadily but slowly and take in everything I could and try to determine how this thing worked.

What had appeared to be stores now seemed more like supply areas. There were laundry-type establishments where people essentially went in with bedding and/or clothing and handed it in and got a new batch—easy to do when everybody was exactly the same size!—and places that dispensed paint and plaster and tools and equipment. There were medical units where I couldn't tell the medics from the patients, nurseries and lighting supply places, and you name it. Things were well computerized; there was a terminal at each place, and every transaction—no money; you just went in and asked—was duly recorded by passing something across a scanner. Nothing was typed in.

There were also collection points for used material, from burned-out bulbs to worn-out gears, all sorted and placed in bins which had pictographs showing what each one should contain.

It struck me that there was no writing of any kind. Everybody had a function and knew just how to do it, and writing simply wasn't necessary even on the functional level.

Equally striking was the fact that there were no men, no children, and no old people and that everybody looked to be maybe eighteen to twenty years old. I certainly *felt* great, young, no aches or pains, good shape overall, and with well-developed muscles even in the upper arms.

They all, as I said, knew their functions. They cut grass, trimmed or cared for the plants, changed the lights, and cleaned everything constantly—the shiny marble floors all looked like you could safely eat off them. Even the more technical skills, such as electrician and painter and inventory controller, were taken care of. You sure knew your place here.

Human beings as insects, I thought as I continued my tour. Absolutely nobody noticed me; I doubted if any of them could conceive of anyone without a job to do. *The drones are here maintaining the hive, all female, all strong, all probably sterile, too.*

I couldn't help but wonder where the queen was.

Someone had left a fingerprint on a shiny part of a refuse bin, I noticed, and I went over to it. There was enough surface that I could easily make my own print by placing my right middle finger next to it. There wasn't time to study things, but they sure looked absolutely identical.

Okay, so which one of you is Cory Maddox? I wondered.

I wasn't at all sure that I wasn't in as much danger from this place as from Wilma's human ape colony, but at least there I could pick her out eventually. After months and months in this environment, where conformity would be necessary just to get along without problems, how could anybody be told apart from the rest?

Just as lacking for a newcomer on a practical level were "you are here" signs. This was a very large place, and it wasn't at all clear what was where. I'd already gone through corridors that weren't obvious and wound up in whole new sections of the place, but I had no idea where I was going or how to get back.

There were restaurants, if you want to call them that, on every corridor, every level. It seemed that if you were hungry, you just went into one and stated whether it was the "first meal" or "light meal" or "main meal." Then you were handed a tray with indefinable stuff on it that didn't have much in the way of color but varied in texture. Oddly, though, the stuff tasted good, almost like some of my favorite foods. The drinks changed from restaurant to restaurant—heaven forbid that there be a choice at any one!—but all were more than acceptable, and the portions were perfect.

If your clothes or you got sweaty or dirty, you just found a laundry, walked in, removed everything and handed it in, went in back and showered in a large communal shower that left no doubt about everyone's being absolutely the same, and then got a clean outfit on the way out, shoes and all.

Even the toilets were, while wide-open communal barracks-type affairs, clean and maintained at all times. You couldn't keep them sweet-smelling, of course, but they worked at it.

And when you were tired, you went to a laundry, removed and handed in your clothes, and received some bedding. You then went, naked, and found a dorm—they were all over the place—and went in and climbed a ladder until you found one among the tiers of sleeper compartments that wasn't occupied. Then you crawled in, made up the bed, got in, and went to sleep. An automatic timer logged when you entered and later woke you up. I wasn't sure how long it allowed, but it wasn't eight hours. It was, however, *enough*. Again, when you have one physical standard, it becomes fairly easy to do these things. Even the size of each cubicle was just right, with absolutely no wasted space but also no point at which more was required.

I was standing there, figuring out and partly admiring this system, which, if not exactly the kind of life I'd want to live, was at least totally peaceful and nonthreatening and had its points, when someone came up to me.

"Pardon us," I heard my own voice saying, "but may we be of assistance? Are we lost, disoriented, ill?"

"No, thanks," I managed. "I—we are fine."

That was a tip-off, of course. "What is our function, please?" the other asked.

I thought fast. "Quality assurance and inspection," I told her. "We walk through it all and see what needs to be done."

It didn't wash. "Please come with us," she said as nicely as before, but there really wasn't much choice. There were a lot of drones around, and besides, where was I going to run?

I doubted that they needed police or security, and I was

right. Instead, they brought me to a medical station. "We believe this is a new arrival requiring adaptation," the other me said to yet another me.

The medical unit came over and looked me over, including pulling out one of those eye and ear viewers and the like and taking a good hard physical look. Finally she said, "So. New arrival, eh? Please lie down on the examining table there. Yes, thank you. Like that. Do not worry."

When people like that tell you not to worry, you start to worry, but again, there wasn't much I could do about it.

I felt something being placed on my head and started to reach up, but she said, "Please just relax and do not interfere. This will not take long. We must see where we fit in the cosmos." I heard her pushing a few buttons and throwing a few switches, and then things got dizzy and disoriented. I just lay there without pain or any other sensations to speak of, but it seemed like I was blacking out and coming back. That is, I'd lie there, and suddenly people walking in front of me and within my sight would be shifted somewhat or would jerk forward. It was an eerie sensation, but it didn't last long.

"What—" I tried, but the doctor unit simply responded, "Don't speak. Almost done."

There was a sudden sense of dizziness and disorientation, and I literally seemed to freeze up, and the world with me, as if suspended in time and space. Then, just as suddenly, it was over. No pain, no problems; as far as I could tell, I was still me.

She lifted the cold thing off my head and said, "Now, sit up. How do we feel?"

"We feel simply *wonderful*!" I responded.

"Excellent. Go and serve."

I nodded and without another thought walked out into the "cosmos" once again. I felt totally comfortable now, totally at ease with the society. I headed for a supply center and then drew a bucket, mop, and cleaning solution. I filled the bucket, mixed the solution, carried it up to the second-level causeway, and began to mop. It felt *good* to do this; it would have felt unnatural to do anything else. It wasn't a question of "want" or "not want." This felt *right*, almost *natural*. It was *what we did to contribute*.

My old memories and identity hadn't been erased; I suspect that the system that ran this place simply considered all that irrelevant. What happened, though, was that I was programmed in as a part of this place and couldn't do anything about it, nor did I have the desire to do so. I still wanted to find Cory in this mass, but it had to be in the context of the community.

Some maintenance people did the same job over and over; it seemed that there were always lights burned out somewhere, for example, and painting and such never stopped. However, most jobs needed to be done only once during a day period and did not take very long, so once I finished mopping the area, I cleaned up, returned all the materials, turned in my clothes and showered, got new ones, and then went to a maintenance cubicle and placed a small head mount on my dome and pushed a single green button. This apparently reported to central that my first function was accomplished and then surveyed other needs within my talents and capabilities and assigned me a new one, this time washing glass surfaces along the same corridor. As before, it simply felt right and natural to do it; there was no desire or thought of fighting it.

This went on for some time, with breaks for meals and a break any old time for the bathroom. Finally I was given no new assignment but immediately felt tired and headed for the laundry for bedding and then to the nearest dorm for sleep.

The funny thing was, I still knew who I was and still wanted to find Cory Maddox. I knew that if I didn't within a time limit, I was going to be yanked out of there, but no matter what, I was going to continue working just as I was. It was unthinkable to do otherwise.

It was the damnedest system I'd ever seen, in any event. I mean, totalitarian? Sure. But oppressive? No. Cold? Not really— people went out of their way to help you, to be nice, to make everybody feel wanted and needed and appreciated. It was like a good family. And since everybody looked the same, sounded the same, dressed the same, there wasn't any sense of somebody being prettier or whatever or having more than anybody else. You even got a variety of things to do, since you could be reprogrammed for any skills as quickly as they were needed, and you always knew that whatever you were doing was something that needed doing. You'd think that it would be a way to go crazy, but somehow it wasn't. I'm not sure I'd recommend it on a permanent basis or even that I think it's possible except in that virtual world, but while I was there, it wasn't bad at all. It wasn't even the kind of "do it or else!" feeling; you *wanted* to work, to help out, and there was nobody screaming at you or recriminations for making human mistakes or taking occasional breaks or whatever. The potential to goof off was omnipresent, but neither I nor anybody else around me took it.

So long as you didn't have an outside agenda, of course.

As I lay down in the comfortable bunk, I found that there was another small, light head mount there on a coiled cord. I pulled it out of the wall, put it on, and settled back to relax.

I was immediately asleep, and on the level of physical necessity it was nearly perfect sleep. Yet while I was out, I was being taken on a pleasant and beautiful dream trip in my subconscious so I'd wake up not only refreshed but come out of a beautiful experience. On a third level, I knew that there were subliminals that were helping ease me even more into my role here. I had no idea what they were saying, but I suspected that they continued in the ambient background of the city. I know that when I awoke, I felt happy, totally refreshed, wide awake, and eager to go to work.

It was pretty clear, though, that finding Cory Maddox wasn't going to be possible. I frankly was finding things so pleasant here that I didn't even think of it much the next day.

Fortunately not for me but for him, Cory Maddox found me.

Not that I would have known it, of course. At various tasks I was often joined by one or more others, particularly on larger maintenance jobs. Since everybody was essentially alike, I didn't pay much attention to the crew the second morning, but one came over as we prepared to do a total window cleaning of the entire second level.

"We have something in common," she commented, probably the most outrageous and hilarious statement I'd ever heard in that context. Hell, *everybody* had almost *everything* in common! When I laughed, she saw the humor.

"Neither of us is originally from the cosmos," she added, and that got my attention.

I nodded, overjoyed at this seeming break. "We were once a Cory Maddox?"

She nodded. "Deep down still are, we suppose. It seems like we've been here forever now. Harder and harder to remember any other way. If Al didn't come by once in a while, we would probably be lost in the masses."

I was suddenly alarmed. "*Al* comes *here*?"

"Al would look like any of us in here but would not actually be one of us. The external head mount is enough. We thought you were Al, and only when we saw you stay and join the community did we realize you weren't."

"But—don't we serve where we are needed? How is it that we are here together?"

Cory gave a slight smile. "When we're here a while and there are computers involved, there are ways to do what we wish without betraying the cosmos. Took us both days to get down to this level. It is partly a matter of where we go for assignments. We will teach you. Plenty of time. We are both stuck here."

"No! Not so!"

Her head came up. "No?"

"We two have a way out. There is a trickle charge timer. When it expires, *this* body," I said, pointing to myself, "will cease to exist and this mind will be pulled back out. When that happens, *that* mental connection—" I pointed to Cory's head. "—can be drawn with it, hooked up to a backup Box, and continuously read out. We understand?"

She nodded. "When? And how?"

"How? We were designed for this, it seems. When? When the charge wears down. Depends on real versus subjective time. If we remain together and close, it will happen."

She nodded. "We hope it won't be during a sleep period. No double bunks. But we aren't imprisoned? We were *sent*?"

I nodded. "The March Hare sent us. We have many of Cory Maddox's memories in our head. We are even closer than we are to any others here in that way."

Maddox was thoughtful but impressed. "Twin sisters, huh?"

I nodded. "Sort of. But why are we female in here at all? And why this form?"

Maddox sighed. "We think it has to do with some time long ago that is beyond our memory but not beyond Al's. One time, lifetimes ago, we—he and a female Cory—were lovers of some kind. Something happened. Al got to acting the way we know him as acting, and Cory left him for Rick. Al has never quite gotten over it. This is an Albert Starkey creation. A whole world of the woman he loved who walked out on him."

"Al does not like hair?"

Cory chuckled. "Al described the system as much as possible. The computers then fill in the rest, and if something flows logically, no matter how bizarre, it just *is*. We doubt if Al really cares, or minds, either way."

Over the next few hours I got a lot more details and in some cases suppositions as we continued to work and during eating breaks.

What exactly had downed the airplane Cory didn't know, but it was large and solid, and he had the distinct impression that it glowed. The plane was held, the top almost torn off, and then there was no memory until he awoke at the crash site with a monstrous headache and two mysterious small spots, each the size of a quarter, shaved out of his hair just above and slightly in back of each ear.

It wasn't until he got to the institute, though, and settled down that he began to suspect that something was wrong beyond his paralysis. There would be periods when he would black out and others when he'd be put to sleep by a nurse in the infirmary room they'd made into a regular care room for him. He then would wake up elsewhere in the complex in his wheelchair, sometimes partly dressed.

I told him what I had seen that time, the massive equations inputted into the upper-level computer console, and he was truly amazed. I assured him that once we had his readouts, they would be merged with mine on that, so that he might well recover those equations and perhaps also some of the knowledge I was getting via the energy form.

He was also more than fascinated by the fact that I had truly believed that I was he and, in at least one measure, was and would be. "Our memories shall mix if we can pull this off," I was reminded. "What are we if not that? The bodies are not the same; only the mind and the memories matter."

Like me, Cory found this strange, somewhat hivelike virtual world of identical selves agreeable. I wasn't sure if this was because, deep down, we were really both the same person, but I think the twins analogy was better. It didn't bother me at all that I liked it; it *did* bother Cory.

It was so very strange and yet so very nice to have this kind of relationship, too. In spite of the limitations placed on us by Al's strange system, we thought alike and shared many of the same memories and virtually all of the same viewpoints. Cory was fascinated by the energy state I had attained and some of the things I'd seen while in it, not just by the big details such as the March Hare and Father Pete's involvement and all the rest but also by the smaller, more personal things, too. Rick and Angel, too. There was almost a longing there, and I had the bizarre feeling that on at least one level, Cory envied *me*, something I found hard to handle. One thing did differentiate us and was painfully clear, though, even in memories: he understood the technical jargon and much of the virtualized systems and might be able to figure out what he'd inputted into the institute while under someone else's control; I never could. It wasn't brain structure or sex or anything like that; it was just that deep down I could be given all the facts but never had the aptitude.

Which was why I was cleaning windows and scrubbing floors by the choice of the system, while Cory was doing it because of the need to contact and stay close to me. But one thing above all still puzzled me. How in the world did he/she learn that I was here and just where I was?

"Gossip," Cory responded. "Just what we are doing now. So little out of the ordinary happens here that when something does, it goes from low to high and through every level at perhaps not the speed of light but certainly the speed of talk."

I had been terribly nervous, even afraid to face Cory Maddox, but now I didn't want to leave. It wasn't just Cosmos City, it was Cory. Damn it, we might make a real team! It was a shame that after finally meeting in equal circumstances on what was basically neutral ground, we would not have long together.

But before the timer ran out we had one other thing to face, one other threat that was totally unexpected.

She looked just like Cory or me or anyone else in Cosmos City. Same pullover clothing, same face, same walk, everything, but she wasn't the same. In fact, that was how I noticed her, one level below and coming toward us up the escalator.

Somebody had failed to get out of the way, and this one unit had simply ignored the other and walked straight through her with no harm to either one.

When I saw it, I froze and my blood ran cold. Cory hadn't been looking that way, but I reached out, took her arm, and whispered, "Al."

"Pay no attention and do not react to anything," Cory whispered back. "Just keep on working."

But Al seemed slightly confused when he approached us where we worked. I could feel his gaze on first Cory and then me and then Cory again.

He knows! I thought with some panic, but I fought it down. He didn't know. He might *suspect*, but he did not know.

"Cory?" Al called.

"We are here, as always," she responded. "Where else would we be?"

Al looked around. "Slumming?"

"As the creator of Cosmos City, you know that we serve wherever there is need and do so with joy and without complaint. In this case there was a need, and we needed to get out a bit as well. This is not easy. Were it not for your visits, we would have long ago totally integrated into this society, which is not at all displeasing to us."

Al sighed. "Sometimes it seems like there's more Cory than Al in this setup. It could be changed, you know."

"Not without a lot of trouble. *That* we know. And why? What is all this for, anyway, Al? You have never said."

"Funny stuff started happening after you arrived," Starkey told her. "All sorts of stuff nobody ever saw before. Weird stuff. Unexplainable stuff."

"We've been down this path before. We were never good enough to do any of the sorts of things that worry the institute."

"That's right. You weren't. But too much stuff is going funny here. Even now, here, I'm having problems with the VR interface. Blurring, double vision. Not at all normal. And we just had a surge and short in another unit for no reason and with no trace."

Oh, please! If there is a God anywhere, don't let us get yanked out while Al's on the VR monitor! I prayed.

"Nine lives, Al," Cory responded. "Nine lifetimes, and what do you have to show for it? Do you, we, anybody know more, really, about what this all is truly about? Have you more friends and more colleagues who respect you or fewer? The more everything is set up to go Al Starkey's way, the more muddled and mixed up and messy it all gets. Al, we don't know what this is about ourselves, but you are more problem than solution."

Al shook his virtual head, which of course looked just like ours. But this was clearly an emphatic no.

"I need a team, Cory. I need a symbiotic assemblage of people who can solve this thing. We were part of a team once. We should be again."

Cory sighed. "We have this same talk over and over. We are female here, but here there is nothing but the female Cory. Outside, though, we're not the same Cory that was once a team with you."

"You can be. And probably will be in the next cycle," Starkey said ominously. "I think we will ratchet up the programming here. I don't think I'll be coming again."

Cory was unfazed by the threatening tone. "We don't really care, Al. If you don't come again, we will not mind and eventually not care. Only one thing would we love to know, and that is denied us. We'd love to know what you were like nine lifetimes ago that we could have seen so much to like in you."

"*Damn you, Cory!* Maybe I should teach you a little more about obedience and respect. The Box with the previous problem is a real beauty for that!" The tone was fiery, and the threat unquestionably genuine and full of the hate of someone scorned. In fact, he was so upset that the image, the very real form of one of us that represented him in this world, actually broke up in spots as he ranted.

Suddenly I felt a budding surge of energy. *Oh, no! Not now!*

But it *was* now, and I turned and moved close to Cory and gave her a hug. Al stared, then said, "What—? Who . . . ? *You!* That little spook bitch who walked out on me! How did you . . . ?"

We exploded and dissolved into energy and flowed back up into the LSU, where Cory's body suddenly was more or less inhabited again. I took off after hooking him first into the March Hare Network so that no matter what Al did, it wouldn't matter in the end, and then right into the console.

There he was, the bastard, just backing up in shock at seeing *both* of us dissolve. He was moving in the slowest of slow motion, being pinned down now to real time while I still had near lightspeed and sent the inevitable power surge from the exit straight into the VR head mount Al was wearing.

He screamed, and I could see real electrical energy and hear pain in his screaming; smoke rose from the console at the connector jack. Al pulled off the visor and threw it away from himself. His handsome face showed severe burns, and some of his hair had burned off in front, along with all of his eyebrows.

"Help! Emergency!" he screamed to anybody and everybody who might hear him. "God damn it all, that bitch blinded me!"

XII

THE MARCH HARE'S SAUCER

They came out of the woodwork as Al continued to bellow in pain, and alarms started going off all over the place. Since nobody but Al knew what was going on, though, what resulted was mostly pandemonium.

Ben Sloan ran in and immediately saw that the panel was smoking and that Al was hurting and holding his face, and he took charge. "Call the doc down here immediately! We've got a burn!" he yelled to somebody. "And get a fire extinguisher on that panel!"

I don't know where Les Cohen was in the building, but he seemed to appear in nearly record time. I hoped that subjectively it was an eternity for Al, but that didn't matter. I couldn't do much but mark time in energy mode and get my views from intercepted video cameras, though; going into any of the remaining four LSUs was out of the question for a while. I did have some hope that maybe I'd killed him, but I knew from the start that it was no such luck.

Still, he was pretty badly injured and definitely in pain. Les had him down on the floor with Ben and another big guy holding him down while the doctor gave him a shot, which took maybe a minute to have a real effect. Then the doctor looked around. "How'd this happen?"

"I dunno. One minute he was on the VR monitor; the next thing I know it's *this*," Sloan told him. "He was yelling about his usual paranoid shit—you know, the spook bitch was out to get him, was some kind of ghost in the computer, stuff like that. Didn't make any sense. I'm beginning to worry about him."

The doctor sighed. "Not half as much as I am." He examined Al's face, then said, "Get some people down here with a stretcher. I want him up in the infirmary as fast as possible. These burns look pretty bad, and I want to treat them as soon as possible. He may have scorched corneas, too." He got up, went over, and examined the small standard head mount. "Jesus! Looks like the damned goggles *melted*! How could this happen?"

"I don't know that, either," Sloan admitted. "We had a surge and an emergency disconnect on the Indian woman's LSU. I checked it over, couldn't find anything wrong, and reconnected her, but Doc Lee insisted on notifying Al, anyway. He came down about ten minutes ago and, after checking things over, decided to take a look inside and see if anything seemed wrong. You know how he was. Always going into Maddox's box. He's always had a real vengeful streak; you know that."

"Yes, yes. Go on," Les prompted, looking worried. "Where's that damned stretcher team?"

"Well, he was in there a while. I was monitoring the energy regulators to see if I could isolate the short, and *bam!*"

"Was he talking to Cory when it happened? That is, was he observing or did he virtualize in there?"

"He was talkin', yeah. So what? He always did that."

"I don't like it. One of these I can see, but two shorts, two isolated Box connections, and this kind of feedback directly into a simple virtualizer head mount—no, I don't like it at all."

At that point a team arrived and quickly transferred Al's unconscious body to the stretcher and started off. Les barked orders and told them he was coming straight away, but he turned and looked at Ben first.

"Isolate the two with problems from each other and from any junction points on the main system," he told Sloan. "Use the hard system and forget the broadcast stuff. If anything prevents it or if there's a short in either one again, kill 'em. Understand?"

"Yeah, okay."

"Do it for Cholder and Prine, too. And get Tanaka out of that damned pleasure unit and Alvarez out of training and brief them. It may just be a fluke or old hardware or something, but it might be the start of an attack as well. *Move!*"

Okay, so now I knew the other four, and it seemed that luck was with me. Not everybody was a prisoner, it appeared. I couldn't imagine what Jamie and Sally had done to deserve what they were getting, but Tanaka and dear Sister Rita were using the system for other purposes. I would have liked to have gone in with either or both of them knowingly, though. In general, the brain and the Box were so integrated when everything was right that if you died in there, you died, period. The brain couldn't tell the difference between a virtual heart stoppage and the real thing.

I would have loved to have stopped Ben from his work, too, but Les had been pretty cold-blooded about the consequences. There was no way I could act without it looking like a surge to the equipment there, and to do much of anything more to friends or foes would have the effect of executing them.

Unless, of course, I could do a little something with Ben Sloan.

Ben was officially a programmer but was really a technician and a damned good one. He was one of the few people who could keep this all up and running and fix it or kludge it when he had to, and as such, he was considered damned near essential. If I could just get to him, do something to him that wouldn't appear to be related to this work, I might be able to stop him from doing any real harm.

I broke from the analog monitors and examined the whole area in my energy state, which placed everything in three-dimensional wireframe view. Everything was now abstract, a combination of lines, curves, corners, tiny sets of numbers and labels, and X-Y coordinates.

Even Ben Sloan.

They'd called me a name, "spook," meaning that I wasn't real, wasn't alive. I was just a program running its semirandom course within the greater program that was my world. Now I was a *real* one, a kind of poltergeist in their machine, in their domain, reduced to the pure program level but also able to see and interact with everything else on that level.

Everything else . . .

"Who cares for you?" said Alice. "You're nothing but a pack of cards!"

It was suddenly so obvious, so self-evident, that I was pissed at myself for not realizing it and looking at it this way before.

This wasn't magic; it was technology. The fact that I didn't understand it and thought of it as magic didn't make what was real and what was not any different, except from my viewpoint.

Boxes within Boxes within Boxes . . . How many levels deep was it?

So there they were, in their Brand Box miniuniverses, sent into virtual reality by this machine and the programmers and operators who ran and maintained it. Inside, it was real while I was there, and it was real to them, but it was in actuality only an illusion. Everything was really taking place not in Cosmos City or the human ape island but inside their minds.

But all this—the institute, me, these people, this whole damned world—was no different from the Brand Box worlds. It was just bigger and more elaborate. That was how I could be there at all. That was how I was riding the wireframe mode along lines of energy and force and interacting with them.

This was real to me, but it was in a sense no more real than Cosmos City. We were all inside a bigger Brand Box or whatever did the same thing, only bigger and better, and I was a valid subroutine here. But on this level and in this virtual cosmos I wasn't a spook; *I was as real as they were*. They might be able to leave, to pick up their program and go to another giant Box where I couldn't follow, but while they were here, they were in the same condition I was. Just as the Cosmos City folks could lay hands on me and speak to me and interact with me, so could I with anybody here.

This was crazy. I was beginning to have ideas that mere little programs shouldn't think about. Sure, I'd done this with my own kind, with Vern and the girls, but it had never occurred to me that in this context somebody like Ben Sloan was no different from them. If Ben and Al could lock Cory and Wilma away in these things, then why wouldn't he or anybody else also be subject to the rules of this universe?

Ben was standing over Cory's LSU, checking connections and feeds and the like. I moved to that point and examined him. Except for the tagging and that inner glow bar square within the wireframe, he didn't seem different from any of the others. Just an animated wireframe and strings and strings of numbers. Similarly, Cory Maddox gave off the same information. The only thing was, most of the brain activity was inside the Brand Box it was connected to; the glowing bar with the tag was kind of halfway in and halfway out of the Box; this was, I suspected, all part of how my own brain could interpret the unimaginable. But that didn't matter. So long as Cory was connected to the Box, the entire pattern of brain activity, a dynamic and pulsing unit that changed colors and shapes and all that as I watched, was concentrated inside the Box, while Ben's Box was entirely inside his head and a little of his neck.

Ben was actually clamping down a cable or something onto the LSU. He had hold of it, and in wireframe mode that connected him to it. I waited and timed it. When he plugged the other end into the box, I executed a simple instruction.

Everything happened so damned fast that I could hardly believe it or even feel fear or exultation or anything like that until it was over. And when I *did* look, I was absolutely astonished at what I had done.

I had completely inverted the circuitry. Ben Sloan had gone from the LSU interface into Cory's Brand Box; Cory had been extracted and now was where Ben had been, looking very, very confused.

Only Cory was also still in the LSU!

Now, wait a minute . . .

But this wasn't the Cory who was in the LSU; it was the Cory I'd met in Cosmos City! It had Cory Maddox's bright internal bar and label, but it wasn't his body. It was the one that looked like an idealized version of me, pullover clothes and all!

Both the new Cory and I seemed to realize what had happened if not how or why and immediately checked the life-support unit.

The paralyzed Cory Maddox body maintained inside had no activity at all. It was kept alive by the unit's own monitoring, but brain function was nil. The new Cory barely hesitated; she went over to the unit and shut it off.

The body registered sudden distress; then the whirling numbers and coordinates inside seemed to slow and stop. I could see the end of the file marker; Cory Maddox was dead.

Only Cory Maddox was also standing there.

I went to a speaker and hoped I could reach her. "Cory?"

"Rini? How'd you *do* that? And where are you?"

"I—I didn't know I *could* do that," I admitted. "I'm not anywhere, really. I'm sort of riding along in the wiring for the room. They kind of squirted me here by telephone or something. It was beyond me."

Cory frowned. "Intelligence and power by modem. Scary. They haven't even wired for fiber optics or ISDN here yet! *Modem!* Wow. We're glad it's you and not Al with this kind of power." She looked around. "How'd we wind up taking this body out with us, though?"

"I—I don't know. Ben was going to lock you in or something,

so I tried to stop him. He went in and you came out, completely bypassing your original body." I paused. "Cory? Are you *real* in that, or did I invent somebody like me?"

"We think we're real, but this is not a question we tend to think much about since it's guaranteed to drive us all nuts. Hmmm . . . And Ben Sloan is now inside Cosmos City?"

"I guess. His code went in, and where else *could* he have gone? Even his body's not here!"

"Well, if you could get the Brand Box code out, you could feed Ben's code to the Box, we suppose. We have to work fast, though. Somebody's sure to come down here any time."

"Not Al and probably not Les," I told her. "Seems Al's head mount exploded while he was wearing it."

"Dead?" Cory asked hopefully.

"No, not dead but badly burned, maybe blinded."

"Then we have to work doubly fast. Ah! Here's Wilma or whatever her name is. We could bring her out, but she'd be unconscious for hours and not much good for a day or so. Too bad we can't bypass this physical body like we did ours and create one that's independent. Or can you?"

"I probably can. I have her hooked up to the outside line now, so I can tap in and pull her out, and I don't have to worry about a Ben Sloan. But if I *can* do it, she's bound to be in awful shape. Primitive, passive, more ape than human. It would almost be a mercy to kill her and let her come back normal."

"That will happen anyway. She never had a Brand Box here that we know of, and she doesn't now that we can see. All right, bring her out as she is, then reverse the connection. They have to have a backup Brand Box for her up at Walt's. Give it a try. What have we got to lose, all things considered, and since there's a ton of folks all out to kill us all between us and any exit?"

It was a good point. This was sheer godlike magic to me even though I was the god, and I had no idea how far it would take me. On the other hand, I had very few illusions that bullets would terminate Cory and anybody else down here and that somebody, maybe several of the smartest folks here, might well be able to screw up somebody flowing and existing in the wiring, too.

Still, this wasn't the same as what I'd done with Cory. In that case I'd switched a whole unit for a whole unit; in this case I was trying to isolate part of the unit from the body into which it was still integrated and bring it out with the coding from the Brand Box. That wasn't something for me to do; it was something for a superbrain with a supercomputer to do. Still, Cory was right—there wasn't a hell of a lot to lose here either way.

Still, I wasn't all that confident. I kept trying to isolate all of her and nothing else and getting frustrated.

"I can't risk it! I just don't know enough!"

"You knew enough to make *me*," Cory responded. "You're trying too hard. Forget math. Think *shapes* and *forms*. Don't calculate, *visualize!*"

For a moment I wasn't sure what she meant, and then, trying to clear everything out of my mind, I suddenly saw it. Shapes ... solid geometry ... That part of Cory's knowledge combined with my gut instincts, and I just, well, *saw* it.

Cory gasped as the very air and space beside Wilma's LSU seemed to shimmer, glisten like little green fireflies in fast agitation, and then begin to rapidly draw the wireframe and fill it. When the fill was complete, the resultant figure was that of a naked human female of Polynesian origin, about five-seven, with long black hair down to the ankles and a tanned, weathered, but superbly lean and muscled body painted with colorful designs in well-worn dyes. She was also speechless and looked terrified as hell, and she started to drop to the floor and pray.

"Stand!" I ordered. "Obey the woman you see. She is your only friend. All others for now are out to get you and send you back to the island. Understand?"

I wasn't sure that she did, but slowly she did stand and begin looking around.

"Wilma! Look at me! You're Wilma, also known as Sasucha! I am Cory. Say it!"

She looked uncertain. "W-wil-wilma? Sa-su-cha? Co-ree?"

"Good enough! It'll start to come back to you. Look, those who captured us and sent you to the island are coming soon to get us. We must not let them send us back. Understand?"

She nodded uncertainly.

Cory went over to the other LSUs. "Damn! Wish we knew what these folks were living in!"

"I'd love to get the physical code for Danielle, myself," I responded. "I'm the one who's gonna have to stay here when you all leave, remember." I paused. "Uh oh! They must have Al treated and security up. There's a repair team headed down here, I suspect to help Ben out."

Wilma didn't blink an eye at this voice coming from thin air. She was used to being commanded by unseen gods.

"Who? How many?"

"The only ID tag I can get is Lee Henreid; the others seem to be, um, locals. I'm not going to use the word 'spooks.' Three in all, all men."

"Can you do anything with or about them?"

I thought furiously, but the only thing that kept coming back was *"You're nothing but a pack of cards . . . pack of cards . . . pack of cards."*

Cory looked at Wilma and said, "Hide over there behind that thing and don't do or say anything until I tell you, understand?"

She nodded, quickly went over to the VR console that still had scorch marks on it, and crouched down behind it. Not a great hiding place, but it was enough if they weren't expecting anybody to be hiding there.

"Let them lay hands on you," I instructed Cory. "I think I have an idea."

There was no time to explain it, though, since the trio of men came out of the corridor and into the control room almost at that very moment.

Lee was dressed in a casual sweater and jeans and looked every bit the Scandinavian superman he had always been. The other two, the spooks, were big, burly men, one in navy whites and the other in marine khaki, the kind of young military types who guarded and took care of the routine running of the place upstairs. None of them were armed, and all stopped dead at the sight of Cory standing there with that bald head and form-fitting knit bodysuit.

Lee frowned. "Cory?" he managed, then looked over at the LSU. He saw that a body was in there but that the emergency lights were flashing. Still, the Cory he'd put in there wasn't the one in front of him now.

"You—you're Rick's wife? The one who walked out of here?"

Cory smiled. "No, Lee. Cory. Cory as Al recreated her in that damned Box. Since our old body wasn't all that useful or mobile, we kept this one."

He tensed. "Where's Ben?"

Cory gestured toward the Brand Boxes in the wall. "I don't think Dorothy is going to like him much anymore."

"Grab her!" Lee ordered the two servicemen. "We'll take her up to Les and soon see what all this nonsense is about!"

That was what I had been waiting for. The men walked up, not sensing any danger from this small woman, and each took an arm in a casual yet professional way that made it unlikely she could escape their grasp.

Nothing but a pack of cards . . .

I centered on the geometry of Cory Maddox and made it pre-eminent; then I allowed it to flow into and replace the codes of the spooks on either side. They were barely aware of it, and it was so fast that it was probably just a full-body tingle or per-haps a single swipe of static going from head to toe.

Lee cried out and stepped back at one and the same time, and the two former macho men, now identical to Cory right down to the form-fitting bodysuit, sensed the wrongness, let go of her, and stared at one another, jaws dropping and eyes popping.

Cory saw it immediately. "They won't be able to see any

difference in us," she warned, "so you better change sides fast or they're going to blow all three of us away. Understand?"

They did, and I'd made certain that just like the two women I'd taken with me from Vern's, these two now thought along Cosmos City lines even though they'd never been there.

Lee was backing up, and I knew he was heading for an alarm. I gave him a jolt through the floor wiring, and he staggered and dropped unconscious to the floor.

"We can't keep doing this," I told Cory. "The power's not that controllable, and we're playing hell with everything upstairs. We'd better start on a new plan real quick."

Cory looked at the unconscious Lee Henreid. "Did you kill him?"

"I don't think so," I replied. "Truth is, I'm not sure I have it in me. We'll see."

"You two keep watch," Cory instructed her new look-alikes. "We will have to stick together on this." She then headed over to the controls at the main console.

"Okay," she said, as much to herself as to any of us, "we don't know everything about how this works, but we *do* know a few things about hooking up, detaching, and altering that we learned in our two separate times here. Let's see . . . Why don't we switch Dannie from whatever perverted sex world she's created for herself and stick her in Cosmos City with Ben. She'll *love* that. Rita . . . Instead of a week's experience hunting and capturing fugitives for fun and profit, let's let the good sister enjoy Dannie's pleasures. It'll give her moral fits, but we always did believe in making love, not war." She began tapping codes into the console and then got a graphics screen with Brand Box IDs as squares on the top half and subject LSUs on the bottom. After that, it was simply drag and drop to switch what was connected to what.

"Now, we can't be sure what Sally and Jamie are going through except that it's a good bet they have things as crazy as we've seen elsewhere. Jamie could probably use some training, so we'll connect that LSU to Rita's old place, and Sally—

oh, heck, she might as well go to Cosmos City, too. She isn't the security type, and we wouldn't wish whatever world did that to Wilma on anybody except maybe Al. Now, we'll relabel a few obvious things here so that what we did is by no means obvious. There! Done!"

"What about Ben?" I asked her. "I mean, he's not in the LSU; his whole self went in!"

"And was digitized and remade into the same form we now occupy. Yes, that's sort of what they say happened to Matt Brand. Well, he won't reincarnate or incarnate when this moves; he'll stay in the Box, that's all, and you've seen what Cosmos City can do to make you a happy and productive member. If we pull him at some time, he'll look and probably act and think pretty much like us. Yes, we think that's fitting considering he was going to seal Wilma into that place, among other things."

She thought a moment. "You say Al was very badly burned?"

"Yes. Head and eyes."

"Hmmm . . . One last thing." A little bit of retagging, and that was that.

"What did you do?" I asked her.

"Just switched labels. Sometimes, when they are badly injured, the procedure here is to wrap them in healing suits, stick them in an LSU, and let them enjoy a pleasant time while their bodies heal themselves. If Les does that to Al, I've ensured that no matter what they pick, Al will go directly for the one Wilma came from."

"*That* would kill him if nothing else did." I giggled. "So now what? I can get out of here, but you?"

Cory looked around. "Wilma? Uh—Sasucha?"

Wilma got up from behind the console. There did seem to be a little more deliberateness inside her as she moved, a bit less hesitancy. But it sure wasn't the old Wilma and probably wouldn't be for a very long time, and maybe then only with therapy.

"I am here," Wilma told Cory.

"Okay. Stick with us. Rini? Can you hook the Cosmos City Brand Box program into the main network wiring here going upstairs? We mean, take the basics of the thing and use it without letting anybody in there out?"

I took a look. "I don't know how, but I *think* so. At least I can take the program output and feed it through your LSU back into the console, if that's what you mean. I don't think anybody inside could use that as a way out unless they were in your LSU."

"Good girl! That's what we figured. Now, take it in, feed it, and let it run through this whole complex."

"But that might turn the whole institute into a little Cosmos City!" I noted.

"It could, but it probably won't. There are sure to be protective mechanisms we can't even dream of that will prevent it from going out of control, not to mention the fact that the power required would be enormous. Even so, we're going to crank up the power here if the control isn't burned out and give ourselves a steady half power. You feed into the net when that starts. What it *should* do, however, is produce enough imitations of us that nobody will be able to tell the good guys from the bad guys. You do it, then cover us as we go out. Sasucha, you will stay with us and do as we say. Understand?"

"Yes, Priestess."

"Good enough. And Rini, once we are clear, *get out*! Get back home! If they get desperate, they'll go to full power as soon as they can and move to the next plane. You in particular do not want to be in here or in the line at all when that happens. If you do, you die. Understand?"

"Yes. Let's do it!"

"Okay. It's on a steady ten percent; that's standby. Here goes. It's going to go up fast, so be prepared to suddenly feel like you can conquer Mars. Here goes. Twenty . . . thirty . . . forty . . . fifty! Wow! What a kick!"

I brought the program out and tapped into the console, then

fused it in line. It went out almost as a broadcast through the network lines. Down here it didn't seem to do much, not even to the still-unconscious Lee Henreid, but upstairs, where it was more of this plane than of the permanent installation, things were clearly happening.

Cory, Wilma, and the two clones I'd created moved forward and down the corridor. It didn't take long, just a matter of going up the small stairs at the other end, to find more Cory clones all looking and acting very much the same and seeming totally confused. These were not part of the immortal pack, but clearly anyone of this plane, what Al called "spooks," who touched anything connected to the net got reprogrammed on the fly.

The result was pandemonium, mass confusion beyond our wildest hopes. Wilma normally would have stood out, but there was so much confusion over this sudden changeover of staff into female bald Cory look-alikes wearing gray knit form-fitting bodysuits that nobody was paying much attention to anybody. The fact that all the lights had blown again, along with much of the rest of the upstairs electrical equipment, leaving only eerie emergency lighting going, didn't help them at all.

A good-looking marine lieutenant who clearly wasn't close to a terminal or net port was so startled and confused that he'd drawn his pistol. Cory saw him in the green energy glow even though the officer, oblivious to this energy, could barely see a thing and was mostly scared to death, and headed for him. She reached out and touched him, taking the pistol with one hand and then surging the program through a nearby conduit from her into him.

He became another confused and frightened clone, and Cory held a pistol.

I released any control over the original two I'd made down below. They were more trouble than they were worth to keep with us, anyway, and up here they were just two more.

We were past the upper control room now, its monitors dark,

and could almost see the way out when I suddenly felt a tremendous disorienting sensation, almost as if I'd been struck a physical blow. Then, suddenly, I was falling, *falling out of the electrical system and to the floor,* where I coalesced as a wireframe and then a solid individual. The program followed me down, and I realized that I'd become real, solid, another clone of Cory's, and also at that point powerless. I spotted Cory with the pistol in one hand and Wilma behind and yelled, "Wait! It's Rini! We—we got disconnected!"

I broke for the two of them, and Cory turned and frowned. "Damn! The thing must've broken all the lines, even the direct ones in. Okay, we're on our own, and we can already sense a power-down."

I could, too. Somebody was regaining control and also shutting down the net feeds. Regardless of who or what, we were no longer doing any harm to anybody. On the other hand, the harm we'd already done with our trick was still causing chaos, and that was all that mattered.

The main entrance was ahead, but it was now blocked by two armed people, one male and the other female, both of whom were unfazed by the programs and whatever else had happened and were in front of the doors. I could tell that Cory was wondering if she could knock those two off with the pistol, but she might not be able to, and then there would be hell to pay. We ducked back into the dispensary, heading for the usually unguarded emergency ambulance dock. It was unguarded because it was built like a bank vault door and could be opened only from the inside.

Fortunately, we were inside.

We reached the door and started throwing the electronic seals that would allow the mechanical bars to come back, when I noticed some movement out of the corner of my eye and just in back of me. I turned and screamed. *"Cory!"*

Al was standing there. He looked like hell, the bandages covering his eyes, which were also shut with padlike compresses. The hair on his head had been shaved back at least halfway, and there was a shimmering gel over the burned area below the eyes and around to the ears.

"By God! I can't believe it!" he swore just as if he were looking straight at us. With a start, I realized that he *was* seeing us, possibly on the same level as I'd seen him down below. "How the hell did you get *out*, Cory? And the Indian, too. No, wait a minute. It is and it isn't. What the hell did you do? And *how*?"

I felt suddenly powerless, but Cory just sighed. "Al, you can't be serious here. Why stop us? You're wrecked, and the institute is a mess you'll have a terrible time sorting out. Why not just let this one go for now?"

"No more. Last time you came right in here trying to challenge me, and you remember what happened."

"Sure. You came close to stopping us, but we got away. So this is even easier. We're not going into any rabbit hole, at least not now. Let's just call it a draw."

"*Never!* You've discovered things we must know, and you'll not get them to those traitorous bastards up north! You're still an amateur at this, Cory! You're *all* amateurs. Nothing in these damned planes is irreversible if you have enough power and know what you're doing!"

He reached up and began to remove the bandages from his eyes. They looked awful when the stuff came off and dropped to the floor, but then there was a crackling and shimmering to Al's face, and like some movie trickery, the face began to reshape itself into its old form once more. There was no question that the eyes could see and that even the burned hair was sprouting back at the pace of those stop-action pictures of flowers growing.

"Oh, Al!" Cory sighed, and shot him through the lower forehead, right between the eyes.

Al's head snapped back, and he lurched back a few steps, a look of almost indescribable surprise on his face. There was a flash and more of this morphinglike effect on the head, and for a moment I thought the bastard was going to reassemble himself once more. Instead, blood came from his nostrils and from the corner of his mouth, and he suddenly collapsed like an empty sack on the floor.

"Get this door open!" Cory snapped. "We'll watch our backs here. We doubt if Al's going to rise again, but who knows? If a shovel to the head diverted him last time, we figured a bullet in the brain would probably do him in just like it would any of us. Now, move!"

We got it open, and it swung in and revealed the concrete platform and dock and the road beyond. It also happened to be midday, broad daylight, and raining. With an amazing sense of déjà vu I looked on the wall for the keys to something official, didn't find any this time, moved forward, and started looking through the desk. There were some car keys there, and I figured we'd just have to hope we could figure out which car they went with. Hell, there couldn't be that many BMWs in the parking lot.

"Let's move!" I snapped, holding up the keys.

Cory looked at Wilma. "What about *her*? As conspicuous as *we* are, she's a real standout in broad daylight."

"We'll just have to trust to shock value or something," I responded. "Damn it, they'll think of something soon, and if *Al* had that kind of power, well . . ."

She didn't need any further argument. We went out into the wet, and all three of us managed to slam the door shut behind us.

The rain was steady but not terribly heavy; it was, however, probably enough to keep pedestrians down, and I suspected that much of the interior of the institute was sealed off at that point. The mere fact that nobody would expect to see a fairly tall Polynesian Amazon with no clothes and lots of hair and body designs was in our favor; hell, I'm not sure *I'd* believe it, either. We were safe as long as the local Stanford cops didn't cruise by.

There were a lot of cars in the lot, as usual, and for a moment I panicked when I couldn't find any BMWs, then almost freaked again when the first one I found, a sports coupé, wasn't the right one. Cory called to me, though, and I ran over. We found a convertible with two seats in front and a kind of jump seat that was more for parcel storage than intended for human beings behind, but it was the one the key opened. Cory jumped in the rear, while Wilma got in on the passenger side and I got in on the driver's side and started the car.

"This thing stands out like a sore thumb," I noted, "but it'll get us out of here."

We pulled out, and Cory yelled, "Go south, then east through San Jose and beyond. We figure that'll buy us a little time. How's the gas?"

Whoops! The route Cory suggested was almost precisely what I was thinking of—still twins in a closer than normal sense—but I hadn't thought of that! "Not bad," I reported with some relief. "Three-quarters of a tank."

"Well, it's enough to get us away from here. We'll have to figure out what to do next once we get clear and the gas is down a bit, but we'd have to dump this car, anyway. Stands out like a sore thumb, and they'll have an all points bulletin on it. Best to figure out where to hide out until dark, anyway, if you see anyplace along the way. We're not exactly gonna be tough to spot. Two identical bald girls in tight gray and a naked savage. Worse, we've lost our power and have no money for food, gas, lodging, you name it."

"I thought of that. We'll have to just make do on the food and other necessities until we can figure out some kind of move." I paused for a moment, more concerned right now with something else than with what the future might hold.

"You know," I finally added, "I think I know you. At one time I thought I *was* you, and I still have a lot of those memories. That and this program and I just about know what you're thinking before you can say a word. But I can't believe you really killed Al. I just can't believe it!"

"No choice. We weren't strong enough to knock him sense-less, and there wasn't much around in the way of help. Besides, he tried to kill us and worse more than once, and we *know* he killed Rick at least twice. Not three times, we hope."

"No, not yet, anyway. Rick's fine. He's with our daughter up north."

"Daughter . . . Yeah, we forgot that. Umph! That's one thing we were always denied. We don't regret doing that to Al, though. If they'd left the power up where we set it, it's doubtful even the head shot would have done any good in there. Fortunately, Lee revived or somebody else got down there and turned it down to normal standby. Enough power to do some self-repair, not enough to take a bullet to a vital area, thank heaven. He had it coming after nine successes—or is it ten, counting this one? All that. Well, he'll stay in storage now until everyone moves to the new plane at whatever point that is, and then he'll reincarnate as a woman. We can never imagine Al as a woman, but that's the system. Twice now we started off a man and wound up a woman, but that's no big deal to us anymore. The pattern, though—if we can stay alive a while longer and cross, we might wind up a man yet again the next time. And with Al a woman, considering the societies so far, we might even wind up with Al a lot weaker and ignorant."

I thought about it. "I don't understand why you all don't wind up shooting each other and doing all sorts of other nasty things to one another. God knows you build up grudges."

"You can't learn anything from a dead man. It's always best to capture, interrogate, turn, or store. But this was a case where there was precious little choice. Still, it makes us even more of a hot potato if Lee and Les want to stick on the wanted list that we're a murderer."

"Tough to nail you specifically," I noted. "We not only look alike, we have the same fingerprints. And so do maybe two, three dozen of us still back there miserable and confused."

"Well, we won't be executed, just given life as accessories, then." Cory sighed. "Whose car is this, anyway? Maybe it's one of the ones we converted back there."

I reached up and took a look at the registration certificate.

"No such luck. It's Les's car. It would be. BMW sports convertible. That's a doctor's car if there ever was one."

I felt almost like I was doing the same thing twice, only this time the car was easier to trace. I had no power, no money, and nobody I could trust; I was going to be much easier to find. The clock was really running now.

I swung west as the rain grew harder. I hadn't expected it, but this time of year anything was possible. I was a little worried at the chill and dampness and the effect it might have on Wilma, but she just stared stoically ahead and neither complained nor injected herself into the conversation, lost in her own not very pleasant mental realm.

I sighed. "Wilma, Wilma . . . I sure wish we could drop into that shaman land now. If only we could get through to you, at least we could eat and drink and relax until we got some way to be picked up."

Cory shifted uncomfortably in the back. "Yeah, we agree with *that*. At least it's starting to get dark. Maybe we can make a pit stop of some kind. We might not be able to afford to drink anything but rain, but the good news is we got plenty of rain."

"I'll look for something inconspicuous. How long do you think it's gonna take you before you stop speaking in the plural?"

"Probably to the next lifetime. Too much habit and conditioning, and it doesn't really matter enough to concentrate on losing it. On the other hand, it's probably gonna be the only way somebody's gonna tell which one of us is Cory and which is Rini once we find some friends."

I thought about that. "Might still be handy *not* to have them figure it out, even if I have to start doing the plurals."

"Eh?"

"This started off with somebody wanting to convince somebody else that I was you. Might be safer even now if they didn't know which one of us was which."

I found a small picnic grove and rest area off the state route we were using to head east, and there didn't seem to be anybody else around. Cory was first, and then I went into the little ladies' room there, sort of a modern version of an outhouse with commercials for the state and county parks system all over it. We were both soaked and it was muddy as hell, but it had to be done. Wilma, too, took advantage of it, but she didn't seem aware of the use of a john. She just went in back of the place and did it in the rain and let that rain and some runoff from the public rest room roofs wash her clean.

We had the minds still working in our heads, and Wilma had all the hair. It wasn't fair. We ought to have been able to trade a little of each, I thought sourly.

The car clock said it was almost seven. I was starved and knew they were, too, but there wasn't any way to get anything to eat right now; the car, after a lot of searching, contained about two bucks in change for tolls and a single candy bar. Splitting it in three helped a little but not much.

I looked over at the trio of phone booths next to the rest rooms. "I wonder if you need money to make a collect call," I mused aloud.

"Huh? Hey! Yeah! You know the number to call up there?"

"I know *a* number to call that should get through." I opened the door. "I'm soaked, anyway. May as well see. Besides, so what if it requires some money? We got the toll coins here." I scooped them up and opened the car door, then got out and walked to the booth.

The first one was out of order, the second leaked like a sieve, but the third, while showing some wear and tear, was serviceable. Deposit twenty-five cents and dial O.

There's some frustration when you make a collect call from a lot of places, since you can hear what's going on but can't participate.

Two rings . . . three . . . four. Where were they? Then, suddenly, a pickup.

"Hello?"

"I have a collect call for anyone from a Rini Wilisczik. Will you accept the charges?"

I felt a definite chill. *God, Rick! Say yes! What the hell you got to lose?* I could hear Angel crying her self-centered demanding cry in the background.

"Sir? Will you accept the charges?"

"Um. Hmmmm . . . Might as well."

"Rick, you asshole! I need rescuing down here! Don't hang up on me!"

"Rini? That's really you?"

"You bet your sweet ass it is! Look, I got Cory out in pretty good shape and got Wilma out, but she's in awful shape. We're on the lam in Les's stolen car, and we're in the dark and rain and middle of nowhere and need help *bad*. No food, no money, no nothin'."

"Where—? What? I mean, can you tell me where you're at?"

"State parks rest stop about two-thirds of the way to Yosemite on California 49. Last town we went through was Coulterville, maybe two, three miles back."

"Rini, what's the number there?"

"Pay phone. I dunno if you can call or not. Still, it's worth giving." I told him the number and area code and all that.

He took it down and repeated it back. "Okay, you stay there. Any chance you might get nabbed, like cops checking on the rest stops or something?"

"Anything's possible, but who knows? If we got real problems, we got plenty of cover in the mud, rain, and trees, I guess. It's really miserable. Why were you so hesitant to take the call, though?"

"Um, well, I got a call a few hours ago from you know who, and he said you got severed and were lying in a coma or something. I mean, you aren't supposed to have really *gone* there!"

"Oh, great! Now I got an extra body, too! Yeah, well, not much I can do to explain this now. Tell 'em to send help and fast, huh? We're cold, wet, miserable, and starving, and I got none of the powers I used to."

"Do you—what do you look like?"

"The same, only thinner and in better shape. Cory looks the

same. Look, we'll explain it when we get help. *Please!* Get 'em to get somebody here, huh?"

He thought for a moment. "Okay, I'll call 'em right away. But just in case, was there anyplace in that town you mentioned where you might be able to pick up money if I wired it to you?"

I hadn't thought of that. "Well, there was a drugstore there that might still be open, I guess. Dunno if it has the service, but maybe."

"Well, look, stay by the phone, gimme an hour. If you don't hear from me or somebody by then, go back up to the town and if they got a Western Union place, go there. If they don't, come back to where you are and call collect to this number again. Understand?"

"Yeah, I got it. They ain't gonna believe that I'm here as well as there, but they *got* to, Rick! Cory shot Al. Shot Al dead. And Cory right now looks just like me."

"Al? Starkey? Dead?"

"As a doornail. Until reincarnation, anyway. You tell 'em that, too."

"Yeah, I sure will . . ."

I felt the hesitation. "What's wrong, Rick? I can feel something wrong."

"Are—are you sure it's really you? I mean, how the hell can you be in two places at the same time?"

"Ask Walt." I decided it wasn't worth explaining that I might well be in more than two places, depending on how you looked at it. "But get somebody here *fast!*"

I went back to the car and got in, wishing I at least had a towel. The simple outfit I had on was cold and soaked through, and it was also coming apart. "Cheap suit," I commented, noting a hole on the shoulder and a long unraveling thread.

"Hey, they were disposable and for indoor use, right?" Cory responded. "Now, clue us in on this."

I did. Cory wasn't sure she liked the idea of picking up money at a local store even if it might help us get some food. "We stand out in a crowd," she reminded me, "and in a small town it's a million times worse. Let's give them a little time. We got some heat, and the reserve light hasn't come on yet, so let's relax. Try to catnap. We'll take the watch. We're not gonna get much of a nap ourselves in this crawl space back here."

But even with the heat on and the air aimed at me, I was too wet and miserable to get any rest. Wilma, after trying a few prayers for food and getting nothing, had zonked off on her own, and for that I envied her.

During the next hour the rain slacked off, anyway, but the reserve light came on. Reluctantly I switched off the ignition to save the little fuel we had left, and the silence was deafening.

"Uh oh," I heard Cory mutter in the back.

"What?"

"We're not sure, but it might be trouble. We just saw what looked like a police car or something heading slowly past here. It definitely had a bank of lights on top. If they come back, we could have problems. Not only our looks and Wilma's nakedness, but we don't have much in the way of ID or drivers' licenses, either, and we sure don't look like Doctor Lester Cohen."

"What do you think? If they *do* check us out, we're dead ducks. Should I move or what?"

"To where? Besides, this is where Walt's crew will look for us, and we don't have enough gas to get far, anyway. Wake up Sleeping Beauty there and let's ease out and off into the woods. Let 'em have the car. We need the location and the phone booth."

I nodded and turned out the overhead light so it wouldn't go on when the door opened, and we woke up Wilma and told her to follow us and obey orders. Then I got out, Cory got out by crawling over into my seat and then sliding out, and Wilma exited from the other door, shut it, and, as told, started toward the rest rooms. I closed the door and locked the car, and we all headed back beyond the booths and rest rooms to the mud-drenched picnic grounds and trees beyond. There were no dry spots, but at least it was only a light rain now.

We had no sooner cleared the lighted area than the cop car returned and pulled slowly, leisurely into the parking lot. A spotlight went on, illuminating the car's interior, the license plate, and such, and I knew we'd gotten out of there in the nick of time.

"We think we'd have had it if the weather had been better," Cory whispered. "You notice they didn't make any rounds until the rain let up?"

The cop car stopped, and a man got out on the passenger side. He was dressed in uniform and wearing a yellow raincoat over it.

"They called in the stolen car but not the murder," I noted. "He knows it's on his list, but he isn't approaching with drawn pistol."

Drawn flashlight was more like it. He approached carefully, and I was sure that he had a partner whom we couldn't make out in the darkness but who was covering him from the car. He shined the light in the driver's window, looked for a long time, then tried the door and failed. Then he walked around and did the same on the other side, with the same result.

"Nobody inside!" he called. "Want to call Bert and have him pick the lock?"

"We could just bust it in," another voice said. "Oh, hell, that's a BMW sportster. Anybody who can afford one of those can make a stink. I'll call in and we'll get it towed."

The other man nodded and kept trying to make out what he could inside. He stopped, then walked back over to his partner, who was still in the car. We couldn't make it out completely at that distance, but I clearly picked out a couple of words.

"He's seen the mud all over the seats," I told Cory. "He knows somebody was there recently. See? They're shining the spot over the area. Down flat! Wilma! You, too! Flat on the ground!"

We dropped just as the light passed over us, but it was so

dark and damp and misty that it was unlikely that they could have made us out at that distance. Still, best not to chance it. The result was, though, to further cake us with mud from top to bottom. I pitied poor Wilma for what that mass of hair would weigh or feel like if and when we dried out and that mud solidified. It had to be a pain in the head now.

A tow truck showed up from the direction of town and pulled in, yellow lights flashing. They met it and said something to the driver, and the driver cop pulled the car back and parked it, lights flashing as well. He then got out, and the three conferred. There were nods all around, and then the two cops started walking up the path toward the phone booths and rest rooms.

It occurred to me that they could probably trace a collect assisted call made from the pay phone. I could only hope that that wouldn't occur to them for a while.

They did the usual with the rest rooms, both of them, with one staying outside with a drawn pistol and the other shouting a warning and then going in first the men's side and then the women's. They finally gave up, relaxed, and started back toward the tow truck, seeming relieved and chuckling a little. Things looked just right, and then, damn it, when they were maybe ten paces beyond the phone booths, the third phone in the set rang.

Only a pack of cards, I thought, but right then I wasn't much more than a two of clubs or, considering the mud, maybe spades, one of two such in my deck. *Sheesh!* This was so damned complicated even when it wasn't crazy! *From goddess to mud-drenched fugitive in one day,* I thought ruefully.

"He's actually gonna answer it!" Cory breathed, amazed, and I saw just what she was talking about.

The cops stopped, turned almost as one, looked at each other, and then walked up to the ringing phone. One of them picked it up.

"Hello?"

Pause.

"Well, who is *this*?"

Pause.

"Hello? Hello?" *Click, click.* "Operator? This is Deputy Sheriff Mantz. Can you tell me where the call placed to this booth came from?" Pause. "No, huh. Too bad." Light bulb on. "Have any long-distance calls been placed from this number this evening? Yes, I'll hold on." He leaned out of the booth and called to his buddy.

"Hey, Harry! Get some county deputies down here, maybe with a couple from town. I think we spooked 'em into the woods here, and ten to one they're right around here, maybe watching us right now. I bet that was a call for them to get picked up. They knew we spotted the car as stolen and called for a pickup."

"Sounds reasonable. You want to search tonight?"

"Naw. Lousy weather. Rain could start back up any time, and there's that slide over on 108 to take care of. We'll stick here so they can't use the phones or get picked up, and we'll wait. Only maybe three, four hours to dawn. I'd much rather *they* be sloshing around in rain and mud and crap than us."

"He's right on, too," Cory noted sourly. "Damn! You did the impossible, girl! You got two of us *out of a Brand Box prison*, and then we got completely out of the institute and away! Absolutely impossible. Couldn't be done. And yet, now we get stuck and caught by two hick sheriffs in the middle of nowhere. *Damn!*"

I sighed. "It's been going like this since I started. I know, I know. But I can't believe that with all their powers, they can't find us and get us out. I just *can't.*"

For about twenty minutes or so it went the cops' way, and we started talking about dreaming up some kind of story or maybe hiking into town and stealing a car or something. But it seemed so ridiculous even on our own, and with Wilma . . . Well . . .

Then, from above and in back of us, we heard what sounded like thunder.

"Great," I grumped, sitting in the mud and splashing it idly.

"Now we're gonna get lightning and a thunderstorm. Just what we need."

Cory nodded morosely, then looked up at the sky and frowned. "Man! That's the weirdest thing we can *ever* remember seeing! Looks like something out of a Spielberg movie!"

"Huh?" I turned, looked, and saw what she meant. Behind the clouds the lightning seemed to be concentrated in one spot, going off and lighting up the cloud layer, which was seething like something alive.

"Yeah," I commented. "If I didn't know better, I'd swear that was some kind of spaceship or something behind that." I chuckled. "That's all we need in this crap! A flying saucer!"

Sharp beams of light shone down from the seething mass of apparent fire in and above the clouds and played over the ground. Out in the parking lot the sheriff's car's engine died, and then its lights as well. We heard the two cops swearing, but even their flashlights appeared not to work. The streetlights illuminating the stop and the power in the rest rooms died, too. It was pitch dark all of a sudden, and I do mean *pitch*, except for . . .

The playing lights passed over us and went straight to the phone booths, which were suddenly bathed in a somewhat familiar greenish light.

"The phone booths!" I hissed. "Come on! Both of you! Follow me!"

"But the cops'll see us!"

"We have to take a chance. Come on! Wilma, get into the first phone booth and close the door. Cory, take the second, and I'll take the third. *Move!*"

As we made for the phone booths, all three phones, even the out-of-order one, started ringing and the booths began shaking.

I made my booth, saw Wilma get in the first, and saw Cory get in the second, looking very worried.

I looked out and saw, in the glow, the figures of the two cops, guns drawn, jaws dropping, staring at us from only a few feet away.

"Come out of there with your hands up! Jesus, Harry! That

one's *naked*!" the first one shouted over the noise of the phones and the thunder.

"Drugs for sure!" Harry screamed back. "Keep the gun on 'em! *Out!*"

And then, as I had almost known would happen, all three phone booths, with us inside, rose up into the air bathed in the greenish light and kept going slowly up, up into the clouds. I could hear wiring snap as we rose several feet, and up we still went.

One of the cops was shouting, and I think he actually tried to fire his pistol at us, but it didn't seem to work. In a minute more we were enshrouded in clouds.

I couldn't get a view of the whole thing even from below, considering the clouds and the rest. But we passed through some kind of hatch in tractor beams, and it closed below us the way a camera lens closed, leaving no sign that it was there. We were in a small, featureless chamber glowing with that familiar shade of green, and I had very little doubt that we were rising into the air and heading off somewhere.

And all I could mutter was, "*Now* what?"

XIII

DECISIONS AT
SADDLE MOUNTAIN

I opened the phone booth door carefully. At least the phones had stopped ringing when the aperture below had closed, but my ears were still vibrating.

I was relieved to discover that the doors weren't jammed. I stepped out onto the surface, not at all certain I wasn't on some sort of virtualized craft that might be far less solid than it appeared. However, it seemed solid enough, so solid that I slipped and damn near fell from the mud that was still on my boots.

I called to the other two, who also emerged, looking uncertain. Finally Cory said, almost in a tone of wonder, "Rini, you have most of our memories. Have we seen this movie before?"

I nodded. "Sort of. But the greenish glow is even more familiar, and I ain't at all sure that this thing isn't somehow connected."

Cory sighed. "Well, long ago, when Al got us down to the old Brand labs in Yakima a lifetime ago, we remember they gave us the cover story that the first Brand Boxes were taken from some flying saucer crash half a century or more ago down in the Southwest and were used by little green men or something to pilot and navigate the thing. At least we figured it was a cover story after we found out what they were really up to, and we sure didn't hear anything about them *this* trip, even though we met some little creatures last time. We got a real strong impression, though, that Al was as surprised to see them as we were."

A section of wall seemed to vanish, and several of those little creatures dressed in dull silver-gray uniforms walked right into the chamber. They weren't human—that was for sure—and they hadn't been born or raised anywhere on my planet.

I raised a hand and said, "Greetings! Take us to your leader."

The nearest alien creature, barely a meter tall, turned and looked at me with heart-shaped shiny eyes and an expression and body gesture that was the universal symbol for "Oy vey!" and went on.

"Sweet Jesus! They really *are* aliens!" Cory managed. "As far back as we can remember, we dreamed of this, of just this, even growing up. Another race, a spaceship . . . Somehow it was different, though. Somehow there was awe and even a little fear associated with it."

Two of the creatures were examining the phone booths as if they were cans of months-old garbage and shaking their heads. They didn't make a sound, but it was clear that they could hear and understand us and that they were definitely communicating with one another.

"Virtualizers," I muttered.

Cory seemed surprised I even knew the term. "Huh? What?"

"The last time I was trapped after getting away from the institute, they sent me a head-mounted unit right over the network lines. Like we saw—you know, broadcast, wireframe draw, fill, and presto! Solid. When I put it on, it took off my hair and integrated with my skull. I was networked, but it became part of me. I bet these guys or whatever they are do it the same way! It's integrated with them in their shiny big heads. They're *networked*!"

"Hmmm . . . we could make some jokes here, but we'll pass. Looks like they want us to exit."

I nodded. "I think they're gonna dump those booths. Well, let's go, girls. Follow the leader!"

We went through the door, and I began to look at the ship the way Cory might analyze it, using the part of the program that had been transferred to me and putting it together with what I'd known and what I'd done up to then.

If they all had all the control-mechanisms they needed integrated into their heads, maybe their brains and nervous systems, then this whole ship was being run by mental powers, just as Al had intimated with the crash. Might it be more? If I could change people's looks and attitudes and do all sorts of stuff, why couldn't a civilization that had mastered it do the same or more?

Even the inside of the ship, to a degree. Need a door? One appears, and then it vanishes when you don't need it anymore. An infinitely malleable, morphable ship's interior with a collective mind as its demigod. A power source from somewhere—who knew where or how?—and a kind of Brand Box as its engine. Wow. No wonder they could never track these suckers!

"We think you're right," Cory commented.

"Huh? Sorry, was I thinking aloud?"

She looked a bit puzzled as we climbed a circular ramp. "Come to think of it, I'm not too sure."

I knew what she meant all of a sudden. I was getting double vision, both seeing Cory and Wilma from behind and looking ahead with Wilma and Cory behind. No, that couldn't be right . . .

It was being inside a Brand Box and encased in the power source. I could swear we were merging, becoming one individual even more than we had been.

We are, I told myself. *And we're gonna have to concentrate on being two instead of one and not doing and saying everything together.*

We emerged into a central console that contained a master captain's chair on a raised dais in the center of the saucer around which was a circular battery of instruments that the chair could swirl around and examine. Along the wall small saucer people sat or stood, apparently doing nothing, but it was clear that they were running the show. But if it was all done mentally, who was in the command chair? And what was that god-awful *smell*?

It swiveled around at just that moment, and there was Cynthia Matalon in one of her spray-on tight leather biker outfits, complete with shades, looking right at us and puffing on a big cigar.

"Hi, y'all! Mah, mah, mah! How y'all *do* seem to multiply! Goodness! And who's the volcano goddess?"

Concentrate. "*You* run this saucer?" I managed, only both Cory and I said it at the same time in spite of my efforts.

"Don't all just speak at the same tiame, now, huh? Kinda cute, though."

Concentrate! "The power in here has matched up our minds, looks like," I managed, with the other only mouthing some of the words.

"Thanks to what happened, we already had identical bodies," the other me said, with the first me getting a little more control. "And they put the Cory Maddox Brand Box backup into Rini, so she was all of Cory and Rini, too. Now this place has synced us up the last little bit, so data are treating both as one and Cory now has all of Rini's memories just as Rini has all of Cory's. Identical minds plus identical data equals identical people."

She laughed. "Well, I declaiah! Mah goodness! Poah Rick's gonna have a real problem, isn't he?"

We nodded. "Considering there's another Rini lying in an LSU at Saddle Mountain."

She sighed. "Well, we'll be theah in just a couple moah minutes. We got to fly a soaht of pattahn to keep the air fohce off oah tails. Othawise, we'da been theah by the time y'all got heah."

In point of fact, we felt a slight thump, and there was a feeling of powering down and even the sound of compressed air or something like it being let out; even the very slight vibration that had been present all along stopped. We'd landed.

A section of wall between two consoles dissolved into a doorway, and we headed for it, Cynthia bounding up and leading the way, looking very pleased with herself. We—Cory and Rini—suspected that a lot of the stuff with the special effects and blowing the cops' minds had been Cynthia having fun. It *would* be interesting to know just what those two guys put in their report and whether they ever brought this up again.

We walked into a vast hanger complex that I didn't remember seeing before. It looked reinforced and underground, but the saucer, only the bottom part of which was visible even now, appeared to fill it.

As we walked out, we felt a lessening of the power, and the double vision as such stopped as soon as we cleared the ship. I no longer felt like I was in two bodies and neither did Cory, but the fact was that we retained the information and synchronicity we'd established.

Walt came out along with Father Peter, and they both seemed astonished to see us. Cynthia went up to Walt and planted a sexy one on him, then turned and watched as they continued up to us.

"I don't believe it!" Walt exclaimed, looking at both of us. "And who's *this*?"

"Wilma, or Sasucha," we both said at once, then chuckled together in perfect synchronicity as well. "Sorry. Right one, take over!"

I managed to keep my mouth shut even though I knew precisely what Cory was going to say as she said it. It wasn't telepathy; there was no need for telepathy. We were two copies of the same person but in two bodies, and we'd picked "right" at random as the spokesman this time.

"Sorry, Walt, Father," Cory apologized. "We'll try to give you a full and complete report. Since getting all of Rini's memories we haven't had a chance to assimilate them and try to figure out how anything was done. The bottom line, though, is that we were pulled out of institute Brand Box universes— this was Al's for Cory and a really insidious one for Wilma— and this is what we were like *in there*. The Cory body is dead, we think, or at best a vegetable, with only automatic functions. We disconnected the LSU. In Wilma's case there wasn't time to do any more than what we did. But—Walt, what the *hell* is this flying saucer? And who are these little aliens?"

Walt chuckled. "Before your time, Cory. Um, you *are* Cory, right? And that's Rini?"

"Why not?" she responded. "At this point it makes no difference at all." She stopped. "Poor Rick!"

Walt sighed. "Yeah, well, we'll get to that. And Father Pete can have a fun time figuring out the theology of *that* marriage. However, for now let's just say that the boys are from a prior existence that some of us know and some others of us don't remember."

"And they *reincarnated*?"

"No, not exactly. That ship moves right along with everything else, plane to plane. I'm not even positive it's a spaceship. It might be designed to do what it does."

Both of us gave a gasp at that and said as one, "Then they *know* what this is all about!"

Walt shook his head. "Sorry, no, they don't. They're as stuck as we are. Worse, because their records were in a part of the ship that was damaged and wiped. Their own records don't go back any further than Al's, if that far."

"Left," we decided. "Al's records don't go back far at all anymore, Walt. We killed him. Shot him right between the eyes. Forgive us, Father, but it was necessary."

Father Pete shrugged, giving the definite impression that if he thought it was a sin at all, it was on a par with jaywalking. He made a perfunctory sign of the cross.

Walt suddenly looked worried. "Then we better start moving fast on this," he said at last. "They might panic and move any time they feel they can. If we're not ready, the backwash of them taking the whole damned control center through might well short us out or wipe our memories and our Boxes. Father, you want to see to that?"

"I'll get on it," the priest responded. "We're pretty well set up now, though. Won't take an awful long time."

"I need a debriefing, and fast," Walt told us. "Cynthia, take charge of Wilma and see what you can do about her."

"We could all use something to eat and drink," we suggested.

"Okay, then, come on. We'll rustle up something here for you all, and then we'll have to make some decisions. Cynthia, tell the padre we need Rick and the baby here quickly, huh?"

"Will do, Yoah Majesty!" she responded mockingly, curtsying. Until that very moment we'd never once imagined how you could make a curtsy look sexy and obscene, but she managed with very little effort. It was damned impressive.

"What's the matter, Walt?" we asked.

"It's suddenly very dangerous for us, and I think more than a few choices will have to be made, including ones by Rick and by you, Rini."

"If the control center moves, will you have any warning?"

"A little. Hours only, though. They'll need time to make sure they're okay and that all their principals are in place and to come to full power. At full it's dangerous even for them, so that's done for a very short length of time and just when they move. We'll need to be in LSUs here. Even being in the saucer will kill us or maybe worse. I have a feeling that at least a couple of those creatures were once people we knew who got caught in the wrong place at the wrong time and wound up part of their race for good. I don't want that."

"Will being in the LSUs at full power preserve you as you are?" we asked, genuinely curious.

"No. But we'll translate without dying, and that's vital. And we'll translate with the Boxes here, so no matter what happens, we'll keep having a backup."

* * *

In point of fact, it wasn't nearly the emergency Walt feared, and there wasn't even a sense or feel that the power was being raised until weeks later. By that time Walt had gotten information from down south that was at once fascinating and bizarre but at least put things in perspective.

Someone, somebody in security, had been given the ugly job of clone disposal. I didn't want to think about that, since I'd been responsible for it as a diversion, but like Walt some of the time in the past, they didn't think of folks on this plane as real people.

They figured out the trick of switching around the IDs and the Brand Boxes, of course, but by that point they had all been in there a while and they never did figure out which was Ben Sloan.

And in a bizarre development they'd just gotten back to normal and were discussing a possible raid on the Saddle Mountain complex, when Les Cohen, in a perfectly ordinary drive under reasonable conditions, had spun out in his newly returned BMW and gone into a bridge abutment. He had died instantly.

This was still a slightly more primitive world. They hadn't mandated air bags and had only basic seat belts which nobody wore.

So the two big shots at the complex had both met their ends. Al was gone, and now Les was gone, and with them Ben Sloan. Lee had survived, but while he was a capable administrator, he was no Al Starkey and he knew it. Worse, Rita had come out of that sex world we'd sent her to a real psychiatric case and, like Wilma, would need death or another incarnation to have a hope of straightening out.

I got the impression that it wasn't much fun for Lee now, and even Walt couldn't figure out why he was hesitating. What could he accomplish now, risking his own life in some random thing like the thing that got Les or risking his own team more and more? He'd be better off taking the folks who were still with him and on his side and moving to the next plane down, even if that meant waiting until everybody joined him. There was no subjective passage of time in that, so there would be no harm done.

The only thing we could come up with was that there was no guarantee of what the next plane would be like. Alice had been the first to go, so she'd be the first injected into what was theorized to be a massive void waiting to form into a universe based on her perceptions of that universe and then backfilled from the previous one.

"Sister Alice wasn't a lesbian, although many thought she was," Father Pete told us. "I was never her confessor, but I got the impression that she simply didn't care for the society she felt men had built and dominated, even the Church. I wouldn't expect a unisex world or anything like that, but I suspect, and the computers agree, that it will probably be one where women have a much stronger role in society, perhaps even over men. I'm not sure how that will work out, considering the childbearing function, but this system is rather adept at solving those sorts of problems."

"Women on top, huh?" Cynthia Matalon commented. "Sounds fine to me! 'Bout time!"

"Well, perhaps," Father Pete said, seeming uncomfortable. We got the distinct impression that unlike Alice and Rita, he'd been a priest for more than one lifetime. "Still, there would be a few problems even if the society seemed just."

"Huh? Like what?" Cynthia asked belligerently.

"I can think of a few wrinkles if the women are the authority figures," Walt put in, rescuing Pete. "For one thing, Al finally died this time, and so did Doc Cohen. That means that under the rules, they're going to come back as women the next go-round. Think about *that*. And they have enough friends that they might well get some of their old memories restored."

"A female Al Starkey. Scary," I commented.

"You can see where it leaves Lee Henreid, too," Walt noted.

"For the first time he's in charge. Whether the job fits or not, he's got to like it. He incarnates, he'll still be the same old Lee, more or less, and male. It could be more of a demotion than he wants to think about. I'm sure there's been a lot of soul-searching and breast-beating there, but they're going to have to do it. They can't afford any more losses. The number of committed people is down. If they can't get them back, they may wind up ceding control to us. I think they'll move rather than do that."

But since they weren't in any immediate danger of going, neither were we, and things pretty well settled in for another couple of months. This allowed for some adjustments to my own life as well.

Frankly, I would have preferred to keep the Cosmos City version of myself if I had had that kind of vote. It was in super shape, seemed to stay that way no matter what I did or didn't do or eat or whatever, and it felt comfortable. It unfortunately had a drawback in the physical department, though, that made it a real problem for any long-term use.

It was a platonic, neuter-type body.

That is, it was a woman's body, all right, but it didn't have the interior plumbing or the capacity for orgasm. You couldn't even turn on, and frankly, you didn't want to. Now, that doesn't mean that I didn't still love Rick or feel like Angie's mommie; it was just that I had no desire to do anything physical with Rick, and that wasn't fair to him.

My old body still lived, maintained in a kind of coma, with all the vital stuff going on and supported by an LSU for automatic exercising, intravenous feeding, waste collection, and the like, but there was no "there" inside that head. More, it had been maintained in that static, unchanging field I'd created for it when I had escaped from Vern's place. To remove that without somebody being "home" would be to kill it, but that body had all the plumbing, including a nearly eight-month-old fetus that had been caught up in that maintenance field as well.

They trotted out Father Pete to discuss things. He was pretty blunt for a priest, but he was also dealing with something those seminary lessons and little books don't prepare you for. "They tell me that they can't maintain the body. If the institute decides to move, we'll need that LSU. We should disconnect and flush now. We can't get the baby out unless there's consciousness there, since the moment we counter that static program loop, the body will quickly deteriorate. The odds of it lasting long enough or being strong enough on its own to survive even an immediate cesarean are just about nil."

"I wouldn't want to do that. You know how I have to go on this, Father. What do you want me to do? Or what would you advise?"

He sighed. "It's not that easy, Rini. You're almost a mental duplicate of Cory; you know the score. We don't know how to do any body switching or stuff like that. What we do is copy programs, alter programs, and transfer information. I can't put you back in that body. Frankly, neither I nor anybody else in this universe understands how you got out of it in the first place. Oh, I can follow it mathematically, but I still can hardly believe it. What we can do is take that Brand Box there and copy everything that's you mentally into it, then copy that back into that body. Period. She'll wake up, we'll be able to neutralize the stasis loop, the body and the kid will start normal development again, and that'll be that. She should be normal and go home to Rick."

I swallowed hard. "I see. And when Lee orders the move, everybody else here goes, too, including Cory. And I'm stuck here with no life, no future, no nothing."

"You could be a sister," he suggested. "Baby-sit, keep in touch with the kids, and you've got a level of sophisticated knowledge that is still ahead of this world."

I shook my head. "You and I know that knowledge won't do squat. I don't have a real past, I don't have any education on the record, and there's no reason why anybody should hire me."

"You remember the medical director at Stanford who was so impressed with the network design when you were crippled?

Cory wasn't any better off in those areas than you are. There's an established California ID for you, and it was sufficient to qualify you for some state assistance, so between those two things I would think there are wedges in for a smart person, and you're a smart person. The personality, the soul that you more or less share, was down and defeated by a crippled body but managed to pull itself up and out. You're disgustingly healthy. We had the doctor examine both Cory and you— absolutely identical, by the way, including DNA, fingerprints, retinal patterns, the works—and it's quite likely you have incredible healing and an immune system that's beyond belief."

"I'm not sure I want to go anywhere near Stanford or maybe even California again," I told him. "Too many memories, too much paranoia, and probably an outstanding stolen car warrant, too, at the least."

"Pick a state, a country, an institution. I think we can arrange something for you. You have full Catholic training in the faith. Consider one of the orders, perhaps. Your lack of sexual drive would probably be an advantage there. It's up to you, but we must know."

I thought a bit. Maybe he was right. "Well, why not leave me some of the money you can't take with you and I'll see a little of the world first, maybe find some kind of education. I'm willing to try. Who knows? When the last of your folks dies here, it's possible that all this, everything, will cease to exist. Until then, maybe I will see what I can see."

"Very well. Rick has definitely decided to remain behind, then?"

I nodded. "For the kids, really. I mean, he's never had them. He and the real Rini might well have a hell of a nice, long life here, maybe even see grandkids. All the time you'll be sleeping and sliding on that crazy circuit board roller coaster, going around and around until he comes out there."

I knew Father Pete understood the hurt and the sense of aloneness I was already feeling, apart and always doomed to be apart, but he didn't let on about it. It would be a strange life, but who knew?

In the meantime I'd also be part of that circuit board roller coaster set marking time, since everything I had, both as Rini and as Cory, up to when we diverged after arriving here would be there as well.

"God bless you, Rini. God be with you always," Father Pete intoned, and made the sign of the cross.

By my own choice I was far away when they reactivated her, but I kept in touch with Cory and Father Pete by phone and knew that all went well. The child, which they worried about until they saw it, was a seven-pound, six-ounce baby boy, and mother and baby were doing fine, although there didn't appear to be any way known to get hair to grow on that head again.

Well, mine, neither, but I had some fairly comfortable short-hair wigs and was sure she did, too, so it wasn't any big deal.

Cory was certain that Walt and the others knew a lot more about those tiny aliens and their fantastic craft than they wanted to admit and that the aliens knew more than *they* were supposed to as well, but nobody wanted to tell her anything about it. Maybe now that she was with the opposition, though, it might be different.

Three months later, on a bright, sunny afternoon, as I was sailing off Molokai, I felt a sudden, unnatural chill come over me that was inexplicable in terms of the weather. I feared that for the first time I was coming down with something, but I knew what had really happened. There was a certain hollow-ness, a certain total sense of isolation, of aloneness, that is impossible to describe present within me, and it still hasn't gone completely away.

I never tried calling back there again, not even out of curiosity, to Rick and Rini, the former now a doctor with a pediatric practice. I won't call, either. You see, if I don't, then there's still the feeling that somehow they're all still there, still going, looking just like they did the last time I saw them. They aren't gone until I *know* they are gone, and so long as I don't, I can beat off the cold darkness inside and feel that nothing's really changed and I'm not truly alone.

I've still got almost 2 million bucks fully certified as an after-tax inheritance, and I have invested some of it in growing technology stocks and lived off the interest in style for some time. I have a number of social friends and throw some nice parties, and I'm something of an arts patron and even have done some charity work. However, other than investments, I've not gone near computers again.

I do admit to wondering about the lot of them now and then. I still have no more idea than they do about what lies behind all this; I admit to having dabbled in Buddhism and a few other Oriental faiths with themes of a search for meaning and continual reincarnation, but I've found no answers there.

I wonder if they ever will find out, but I think of it less and less these days. It seems so bizarre, so long ago, so far away. Still, I can't help wondering what Al would be like as a woman, and I keep thinking about what the psychological profile of Alice McKee suggested they were going to wake up to one of these days. If women were really on top, then Al and Les would be back where they usually were in the power game, but what about the March Hare Network? There were far more men than women in that. Cory, hopefully, but who could say? The last time she'd gone through as a woman and had come out a man, and that may not change. If so, would that leave Cynthia Matalon as the boss of the opposition?

Rick and Rini got the best of the deal, but maybe, just maybe, I didn't get the worst of it myself . . .

The Wonderland Gambit
will continue with
The Hot-Wired Dodo

ABOUT THE AUTHOR

Jack L. Chalker was born in Baltimore, Maryland, on December 17, 1944. He began reading at an early age and naturally gravitated to what are still his twin loves: science fiction and history. While still in high school, Chalker began writing for the amateur science-fiction press and in 1960 launched the Hugo-nominated amateur magazine *Mirage*. A year later he founded The Mirage Press, which grew into a major specialty publishing company for nonfiction and reference books about science fiction and fantasy. During this time, he developed correspondence and friendships with many leading SF and fantasy authors and editors, many of whom wrote for his magazine and his press. He is an internationally recognized expert on H. P. Lovecraft and on the specialty press in SF and fantasy.

After graduating with twin majors in history and English from Towson State College in 1966, Chalker taught high school history and geography in the Baltimore city public schools with time out to serve with the 135th Air Commando Group, Maryland Air National Guard, during the Vietnam era and, as a sideline, sound engineered some of the period's outdoor rock concerts. He received a graduate degree in the esoteric field of the History of Ideas from Johns Hopkins University in 1969.

His first novel, *A Jungle of Stars*, was published in 1976, and two years later, with the major popular success of his novel *Midnight at the Well of Souls*, he quit teaching to become a full-time professional novelist. That same year, he married Eva C. Whitley on a ferryboat in the middle of the Susquehanna River and moved to rural western Maryland. Their first son, David, was born in 1981.

Chalker is an active conversationalist, a traveler who has been through all fifty states and in dozens of foreign countries, and a member of numerous local and national organizations ranging from the Sierra Club to The American Film Institute, the Maryland Academy of Sciences, and the Washington Science Fiction Association, to name a few. He retains his interest in consumer electronics, has his own satellite dish, and frequently reviews computer hardware and software for national magazines. For five years, until the magazine's demise, he had a regular column on science fantasy publishing in *Fantasy Review* and continues to write a column on computers for *S-100 Journal*. He is a three-term past treasurer of the Science Fiction and Fantasy Writers of America, a noted speaker on science fiction at numerous colleges and universities as well as a past lecturer at the Smithsonian and the National Institutes of Health, and a well-known auctioneer of science fiction and fantasy art, having sold over five million dollars' worth to date.

Chalker has received many writing awards, including the Hamilton-Brackett Memorial Award for his "Well World" books, the Gold Medal of the prestigious *West Coast Review of Books for Spirits of Flux and Anchor*, the Dedalus Award, and the E. E. Smith Skylark Award for his career writings. He is also a passionate lover of steamboats and particularly ferryboats and has ridden over three hundred ferries in the United States and elsewhere.

He lives with his wife, Eva, sons David and Steven, a Pekingese named Marva Chang, and Stonewall J. Pussycat, the world's dumbest cat, in the Catoctin Mountain region of western Maryland, near Camp David. A short story collection with autobiographical commentary, *Dance Band on the Titanic*, was published by Del Rey Books in 1988.